FORGOTTEN REALMS

MIDNIGHT'S MASK

Book III

†

THE EREVIS CALE TRILOGY

PAUL S. KEMP

Wizards
OF THE COAST

THE EREVIS CALE TRILOGY, BOOK III
MIDNIGHT'S MASK

©2005 Wizards of the Coast, Inc.

Distributed in the United States by Holtzbrinck Publishing. Distributed in Canada by Fenn Ltd.

Distributed to the hobby, toy, and comic trade in the United States and Canada by regional distributors.

Distributed worldwide by Wizards of the Coast, Inc. and regional distributors.

Cover art by Ron Spears
Map by Nick Bartoletti
First Printing: November 2005
Library of Congress Catalog Card Number: 2004116912

9 8 7 6 5 4 3 2 1

US ISBN: 0-7869-3643-6
ISBN-13: 978-0-7869-3643-4
620-17727740-001-EN

U.S., CANADA,
ASIA, PACIFIC, & LATIN AMERICA
Wizards of the Coast, Inc.
P.O. Box 707
Renton, WA 98057-0707
+1-800-324-6496

EUROPEAN HEADQUARTERS
Hasbro UK Ltd
Caswell Way
Newport, Gwent NP9 0YH
GREAT BRITAIN
Save this address for your records.

Visit our web site at www.wizards.com

The Crown of Flame

Vhostym was young when he and his father first had walked in the shadow of the Crown of Flame. He still remembered the smell of the wind off the water, the feel of the air on his skin, the sounds of the surface heard through his own ears. The light burned his skin but he had endured; his father had made him endure. Father had intended to harden Vhostym to pain, and to excite his ambition by showing him the possibility of a life on the surface, a life under the sun.

The Weave Tap

The Weave Tap stood in the center of the room, its golden leaves charged with the stored power of two Netherese mantles, possibly more magical power than ever had been assembled in a single place.

It would be enough, he thought. He would poke a hole in the sun and take a day, a single day, and make it his.

Towers of the Eternal Eclipse

Vhostym's hands shook, glowed white with the power they channeled. The tower trembled, flared brightly, then disappeared.

He allowed a smile to split his thin lips. He was close. Very close. Only a jagged hole in the soil indicated that the western Tower of the Eternal Eclipse had ever stood in the vale. Vhostym had effaced it.

Potato Soup

"That's my mother's potato soup!" he said.

"It is, Jak. She's waiting for you. She and your father. Even your younger brother Cob. Do you remember him?"

"Remember him? Of course!" Jak could hardly believe his ears. He had not seen any of those people for years, not since they all had—

Not since they all had died.

BOOK II

THE
EREVIS CALE
TRILOGY

For Jen, Roarke, and Riordan

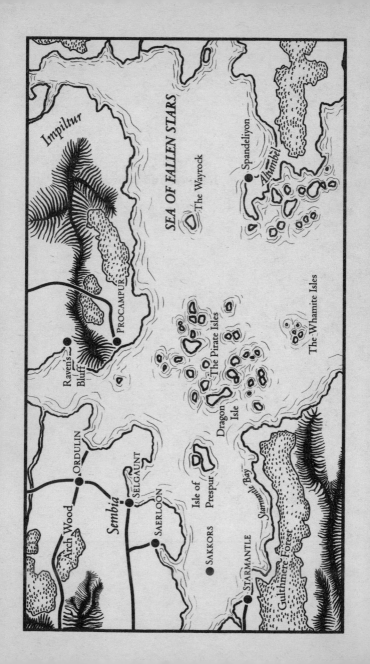

There's a divinity that shapes our ends,
rough hew them how we will.

—the Bard, from *Hamlet*

SSESSIMYTH

The darkness of the deep enshrouded Ssessimyth. Ponderous currents caressed his body, flowed over and past his bloated, pained bulk. In a lazy, distant way, he remembered long ago swimming those currents, hunting in them. Then, fear at his approach had emptied the sea before him for a league. But no longer. He had not left the bottom in centuries; he had hardly stirred at all since he had found the Source.

Centuries ago the Source's plaintive cries had welled up from the depths and filled Ssessimyth's mind, drawn him to the ruins piled on the sea floor at the base of an underwater cliff. Even that slight initial touch—a mental brushing, little more—had stimulated his brain and sent pulses of pleasure through his limbs. He had been addicted from the first. He had swum down into the dark, torn feverishly at the cast-offs of the ruined city, dislodging stones, pillars, buildings, and mud, until. . . .

He had found it buried beneath the sediment-covered ruins of the ancient city in which it had been born, partially embedded in the rock of the sea bed. Its sparkling facets had hypnotized him. Their soft orange light was the sole illumination in the depths, and the Source's soft, hypnotic voice was the sole illumination in his soul.

He had extended two tentacles to touch it and the contact changed him forever. Almost instantly, the outside world became vague and unimportant, while the world of his mind, and the mind of the Source, *their* mind became his universe.

Ever since, he lay in the mud and drank, contented.

Over time, the Source had ceased calling to the outside. Ssessimyth swallowed its cries until it had surrendered to a hopeless, dozy slumber. Now it spoke only to him. He had its universe to himself.

The real world intruded upon his perception only distantly. He felt upon his body the pressure of the ruined temples, shops, academies, columns, and broken statues that lay in a towering heap around and atop him. He had burrowed into the ruins over the years, to get nearer the Source. He lay at the root of a desolate city. The humans who had built the city were dead, destroyed by the foolishness of one of their greatest. When the Source had called for them there had been no one to hear, no one but Ssessimyth. Their city had become their graveyard, his paradise.

Ssessimyth lay unmoving in the ruin's embrace, at the center of creation. Silence reigned; darkness ruled. He and the Source were one. Nothing need ever change.

He lay in the mud and drank, contented.

In the tunnels around him he sensed the movement of his minions. They had found him a few centuries after he had bonded with the Source. Thinking him a god, they worshiped him. He sometimes thrilled them by using the

Source to communicate with the minds of their priests. The tribe made him offerings, bringing meat for his beak and cleaning the open wound in his head.

The wound and the chronic pain were Ssessimyth's offering to the Source, his self-mortification. In return, he received a universe.

Over the centuries, he had driven the soft flesh of his head against the Source until his brain had touched it. That physical contact, coupled with the mental oneness, had expanded his consciousness and transformed him into something more than mortal, though perhaps less than divine.

He did not open his eyes to see his minions, though he knew the priests were about to perform some ritual near his body. In truth, he had not opened his eyes in decades. Everything he wanted to see he saw in his mind, in the dreaming mind of the Source. He felt his minions' thoughts around him only as distant echoes.

He lived through past ages in his mind. He felt the elated, terrifying moment when the Source was born, felt it rise from nothingness to sentience on the strength of an arcanist's spell; he saw a city built on a mountaintop that floated through the sky; he saw the arts and sciences of surface-dwellers rise to glorified heights. He lived and died the lives of thousands, alternating experiences as his whim took him.

He saw, too, the death of the city. The magic holding it aloft had failed—for a time, *all* magic had failed—and the city had plummeted into the sea, leaving the Source as its only survivor, alone in the dark. That part he had relived only once, and never again.

He squirmed his enormous bulk harder against the Source and it sank a miniscule degree deeper into his brain. Pain knifed through his head, but ecstasy too. His tentacles spasmed slightly. The ruins shifted with a grating sound, and he knew his movement had cast up a cloud of mud and sediment.

Ssessimyth sensed the alarm and delight among his minions. They considered any movement of his body to be a propitious sign. No doubt they considered his movement a response to their ritual. Likely the priests would organize a hunt that night and bring him what they slew as an offering.

The acute pain in his head passed, leaving only an ache, ecstasy, and wonder. He let his tentacles fall once more into their places on the sea floor as another mental vista opened before him. He was an arcanist, plumbing the subtleties and mysteries of the Weave; he was a courtesan serving the peculiar tastes of the highborn; he was a priest of Kozah the Thunderer whose sermons sent thousands into battle.

He drank the Source's dreams eagerly—living and dying a hundred times in an hour, eating, drinking, copulating, vomiting, loving, laughing, hating, crying, killing, all within a mental universe in which only he and the Source existed.

Meanwhile, his great body lay quiescent in the cold dark.

He was content. Things need never change.

CHAPTER 1

The Best Laid Plans

Plummeting from the tower, Cale perceived the moment stretching. Air roared past his ears. Shadows poured from his flesh, no doubt trailing after his fall like the tail of a comet.

Above him sounded the despondent, furious wail of the Skulls and the crack of breaking stone. The cavern was falling to pieces, smashing the ruined Netherese city on the cavern floor. Lightning and a baleful green beam split the air beside him—ill-aimed spells from the Skulls.

Beside him, Magadon and Jak shouted as they fell. He clutched each of their cloaks in one of his hands. They clutched at him, whatever they could grab. The shadows leaking from his flesh coalesced, enshrouded them.

The floor of the collapsing cavern rushed up to

meet them. The moment was stretched to its limit; it was ending. Cale had to act or die alongside his friends.

Cale felt the darkness around him the same way he felt the air—a tangible sensation on his skin. Its touch was as light and seductive as that of a lover. He always felt the darkness now.

Opening his mind, he attuned himself to the correspondence between the Prime Plane and the Plane of Shadow, the link that lived in every shadow. He reached for it, took it in his mental grasp and willed them all to move from one plane to the other. At the same time, he consciously dispelled the inertia of their fall.

Sound fell away. Darkness swallowed them. In the span of a heartbeat they moved between worlds.

They found themselves lying face down on the cold, damp stone of the Plane of Shadow. The Skulls were gone; the ruins were gone. They were alone in the dark, but alive.

The breath of his friends came in ragged gasps. The slow drip of water sounded from somewhere. The air smelled dank, pungent with some vague foulness.

Cale remained still for a moment as stabs of pain shot through his body—the regenerative properties of his shade flesh closing the wounds Riven had inflicted on him.

Riven.

Cale sat up, and as he did he remembered it all, or thought he did. Riven's betrayal had been *planned*, or at least Cale thought it had. Unless he had dreamed it. . . .

Beside him, Magadon rolled over with a groan, still breathing hard.

"Demon's teeth," the guide swore, and his voice echoed loudly, jarring in the silence.

Beside Magadon, Jak sat up with a groan of his own. He looked around blindly, eyes wide. "I can't see a thing. Cale?"

Cale had become so accustomed to his ability to see

perfectly in darkness that he forgot that others could not. The chamber was as dark as a devil's heart, thick with the black air of the Plane of Shadow.

"Here, little man," he answered, and reached out a hand to touch Jak's shoulder. The halfling clutched his hand and gave it a brief squeeze.

"I will get a light," Magadon said. He unstrapped his pack and searched for a sunrod. Cale remembered that Magadon's fiendish heritage allowed him to see in the darkness, probably not as well as a shade, but well enough.

Cale stood, wincing as the last of his wounds closed.

"Can the Skulls track us?" Magadon asked as he searched his pack.

Cale had not considered that. "I don't see how," he said after a moment's thought. As far as he knew, his ability to walk the shadows between worlds left no footprints.

The guide nodded, found the sunrod he sought within his pack. He struck it on the chamber floor and the alchemical substance on its tip flared to life. He held it aloft and lit the cavern—dimly. The darkness gave ground only grudgingly.

Jak and Magadon blinked in the sudden illumination, but Cale felt a part of him boil away in the sunrod's light. He refused to cover his eyes despite the sting. His shadow hand, he was pleased to see, had not disappeared. Perhaps only real sunlight could cause that.

"The Plane of Shadow," Jak observed, eyeing their surroundings. "But where this time? This is not where we were before."

A large natural cavern opened around them. Loose stone and stalagmites covered the uneven floor. Irregularly shaped holes in the walls opened onto tunnels that led into darkness. An oily black substance clung in patches to the stone. It shimmered in the sunrod's light like polished basalt. Water dripped from the stalactite-dotted ceiling to fall into a dark pool in the center of the chamber. The pool was as black as jet. The air felt heavy and still, threatening.

"Something akin to the Underdark but on the Plane of Shadow, I would guess," Magadon offered as he stood. "Do not use the water to fill your skins and do not touch the walls. That's some kind of lichen, but I've never seen its like before."

Jak nodded, his eyes thoughtful. He looked up at Cale.

"Are you are all right? The wounds, they're healed?"

When Cale regarded him to answer, Jak recoiled slightly but masked it quickly.

"Dark, but I cannot get used to the way your eyes look here," the little man said.

Cale felt himself flush.

"I'm all right," he said. He extended a hand and pulled Jak to his feet. Cale put his fingers through the hole Riven had made in the front of his cloak and armor. He had similar holes in the back. The holes in his flesh were closed. "What about you two?"

Both Jak and Magadon were pale, exhausted, and obviously wounded. Claw rakes had opened cloaks, rent armor, and torn flesh.

"I'm well enough," Magadon said, and moved to the edge of the pool. The guide knelt and stared at the water. He dipped his fingers, smelled them, and wiped them clean on his breeches.

Jak said, "I am all right, too. We killed one of the slaadi, Cale. The small one. The other one. . . ."

Magadon stood and finished for Jak. "In our hurry to get to you, we left the other alive but enspelled. He may have died in the cavern's collapse."

Cale doubted it, but kept his thought to himself.

"We should have killed him," Jak said, and reached into his belt pouch for his pipe. "Just to be sure." He came out with a wooden pipe, the one he had given to Riven, the one Riven had thrown back at him atop the tower. He must have picked it up before they fled. He eyed it for a moment, then threw it past Magadon and into the pool, where it vanished. He withdrew his other pipe—the ivory bowled affair—and popped it into his mouth. He chewed its end in agitation, but did not light up. Around the pipe stem he said, "I'm personally going to drive an armspan of steel into Drasek Riven's gut for what he did." For Magadon's benefit, Jak added, "I've done it before, you know. Treacherous Zhent bastard."

Cale thought the little man's anger might be misplaced. To Magadon, Cale asked tentatively, "Do you . . . remember what happened between you, me, and Riven, last time we were on the Plane of Shadow?"

Jak looked up, a furrow in his brow.

Magadon started to speak, stopped, finally nodded. "Erevis, I thought I had dreamed it all, or conceived it in a meditation. Sometimes my mind manifests wishes as reali—" He stopped and smiled. "Never mind all that. I do remember. It started to come back to me shortly after I saw him atop the tower with the slaad."

"What came back to you?" Jak asked.

Cale nodded, pleased to have his own hazy memory confirmed. Magadon had set Riven's betrayal—itself the product of a latent psionic compulsion—as the trigger that would allow the guide and Cale to remember the stratagem they had developed.

"So what next, then?" Magadon asked.

Jak took his pipe from his mouth and regarded them with narrowed eyes.

"What are you two talking about?"

Magadon's question sent Cale's mind racing. He thought first of Riven and of Varra. He made up his mind.

"A return to Skullport," he announced. "Just me. For only a moment or two."

He wanted to determine if the city still stood. He needed to see if Varra was all right.

"Skullport?" Jak asked. "Why would we return there? Again, what in the Seven Heavens are you two—"

Magadon stared into Cale's face and shook his head. "We cannot go back to Skullport, Erevis. Not right now. Riven is relying on us."

"Riven!" Jak exclaimed.

"Because of what we did, the cavern could be collapsing," Cale said. "We've only been gone moments. I am going back, Mags. I can get her out."

Magadon did not ask who Cale meant by *her*. Instead, he shook his head and said, "I understand what you want to do, Erevis. But if it was going to collapse, then it already has. She's either alive or . . . not, and you won't be able to affect which it is. But wherever Riven is right now, he will soon remember what happened, too. That makes him vulnerable. The slaadi have displayed telepathy, and we think they can read minds."

Cale hesitated. Magadon must have seen it. The guide added, "He trusted you when he agreed to do this. We've got to back him up. We can return to Skullport afterward. I'll go with you. Jak will go with you."

"I will?" Jak asked, confused. "Wait a—"

"But not right now," Magadon said. "Right now, we do what we intended to do."

"And what in the Hells is that?" Jak exclaimed.

Cale stared at Magadon, not in anger, but in frustration. He knew Magadon was speaking sense but he felt as though he were abandoning Varra. He made one last play. "You're sure you have Riven?"

If Magadon did not have a sensory link on Riven, they would have no way to locate him. Cale did not know how he wanted Magadon to answer.

Magadon nodded and replied, "Since the moment I stepped into the cupola atop the tower. Erevis, if he makes a play for the Sojourner because he expects our help. . . ."

Cale sighed and nodded. The guide spoke the truth. Riven *had* trusted him. Cale silently prayed to Mask to protect Varra until he could return to Skullport.

If there still was a Skullport.

Fed up, Jak stepped between Magadon and Cale. He pointed his pipe at Cale, glared, and said, "I'll ask again. What in the Hells are you two talking about?"

Cale smiled and said, "Sorry, little man." He quickly explained to Jak the plan they had developed on the Plane of Shadow: Magadon had implanted a latent mental urging in Riven's mind to betray them at an opportune moment and ally himself with the slaadi. They had hoped that Riven would thereby get close to the Sojourner, where he would serve as a beacon for the rest of them. To avoid discovery by the slaadi, who likely could read minds, Magadon had wiped the scheme from their memories until the triggering event occurred—Riven's putative betrayal. Riven's trigger was different. He would not remember the plan until he saw the Sojourner.

Jak absorbed the story in wide-eyed silence. Finally, he said, "He's a plant? Burn me! Every time I think I have that blackheart figured. . . ."

"You are not alone in that," Magadon said.

Jak popped his pipe in his mouth and looked up at Cale, his expression mildly hurt. "You could have trusted me with it."

"I know that, little man," Cale answered. "It wasn't trust. I figured the fewer who knew, the better. And I wanted at least one of us to be outside of it, in case something went wrong. If we all started to go mad, I wanted someone who could figure things out and fix it."

Jak seemed to accept that. He chewed his pipe, thoughtful, and said, "You three were talking a long while to come up with this little scheme. And you said something in a foreign language, Cale. What about that?"

"We did?" Cale asked.

"You did," Jak answered.

Cale had no idea what Jak was talking about. He looked to Magadon, whose face showed similar confusion.

"Something else?" Cale asked Magadon. "Another contingency?"

Magadon shook his head. "Perhaps. We won't know until we know."

"Trickster's hairy toes," Jak softly said.

Cale agreed. The idea that something else might have been placed in his mind but he was ignorant of it. . . .

From far down one of the tunnels, whispers sounded, hisses. They trailed back to silence. Still, whatever lived in the Underdark of the Plane of Shadow must have heard their voices or perhaps seen their light.

All three had blades in hand before they drew their next breath. Jak pocketed his pipe and licked his lips.

"We should not stay here overlong," the little man said.

Weaveshear leaked shadows; so too did Cale's flesh.

"We aren't," Cale said. "Mags, show me what Riven sees. We go on my word. We wait for the Sojourner to show, find out what we can, then hit him with everything we have."

Magadon nodded, closed his eyes, and concentrated. A violet halo surrounded his head and he held up his free hand. Cale took it.

And saw.

For the hundredth time, Riven rebuked himself for leaving Cale bleeding but alive. He still did not understand why he had done it. He *never* left opponents alive. A simple flick of his blade would have opened Cale's throat and put an end to the First of the Shadowlord. Cale's shade flesh could not have regenerated the damage that Riven could have done.

He could not explain his behavior. When he looked back, it was as though someone else had been controlling him. The events atop the tower were a blur in his memory.

He pushed the recriminations out of his mind as unproductive nonsense. He needed to focus on the present. He stood on a sword's edge and he knew it. He had taken a gamble allying with the slaadi. The creatures were unreliable; they might turn on him at any time.

He did not know where the slaadi had brought him. From the crumbling cavern near Skullport, they had teleported to the surface, mentally communicated with their master, the Sojourner, and from there teleported to. . . .

Here, Riven thought.

The foppish slaad Azriim, in his preferred half-drow form, stood to one side of him, and the dull slaad, Dolgan, stood to the other. Both seemed to have already recovered from the wounds inflicted on them at the Skulls' tower.

"Where are we?" Riven asked.

"Home," Azriim answered.

They were in the center of a smooth-walled, hemispherical chamber. There were no windows and the stone, while smooth, was not masonry, so Riven assumed they were underground. The dry air smelled faintly of medicines or perhaps alchemical preparations. The smell made his nose tingle.

A thick carpet covered the floor, and a single, dim green glowglobe on the far side of the chamber provided the only light. The globe cast only enough illumination to raise shadows in the room. Riven could see little. Irregularly-shaped mounds dotted the floor and it took Riven a moment's study to recognize them as cushions and furniture. In better light, the place must have looked like a Calishite Caliph's harem room.

Riven saw no means of egress, no doors or archways of any kind. That made him uncomfortable, and he let his hands fall to the hilts of his sabers. It would have been ridiculous for the slaadi to have brought him all the way here only to ambush him, but. . . .

They are unpredictable, he thought. And it's better to be cautious than dead.

He decided to take steps to ensure a means of escape, should he need it.

"Home is dark," he said. "How about a light? I can't see past my hands."

He deliberately stepped on a cushion at his feet and feigned a stumble into Dolgan. Cursing, he intentionally entangled himself in the slaad's cloak and limbs—the slaad's form looked fat but his body was as solid as a tree—and used the short-lived tussle to lift the teleportation rod from the slaad's cloak pocket.

"Watch where you step, human," the big slaad said, dislodging Riven and shoving him away.

"I can't watch anything, oaf," Riven answered. "I said I cannot see." He feigned a second stumble on another cushion and used the movement to secrete the rod in his cloak. "There are cushions all over the floor and walking on this ridiculous carpet is like moving through mud."

"I selected these carpets myself," Azriim said, his tone mildly hurt.

"I'm not surprised," Riven answered, putting a sneer in his voice.

Dolgan said to Azriim, "Why can't I just kill him?"

"I am tempted," Azriim said lightly, "given his view of my carpets."

Riven stared into Dolgan's face, the features indistinguishable in the darkness. "His permission to try won't make it so, slaad. I'd put you down in less than a tencount, darkness or no."

Riven kicked away the cushions near him, to clear any trip hazards. Both hands went to saber hilts and he balanced on the balls of his feet. Dolgan took a step forward but Azriim stopped him with an arm across his chest.

"Enough," Azriim commanded, smiling indulgently. "You're adding to his tension."

Riven kept his gaze on Dolgan but said to Azriim, "You haven't yet seen me tense, slaad."

"I can smell your sweat at ten paces," Azriim said.

Dolgan glared at Riven and said, "I do not understand

why we have not killed him. His brood killed Serrin, wounded you, wounded me."

"Brood?" Riven asked derisively. "I'm a man, oaf. I don't have a brood. And you're fortunate that it wasn't me who gave you the wound. If it had, you wouldn't be standing here to annoy me."

Azriim ignored Riven and said to Dolgan, "You enjoy being wounded, Dolgan, so no harm done. And besides, I like him." He looked at Riven and smiled broadly. "Even though he has poor taste in clothes, friends . . . and carpets."

Dolgan started to speak but Azriim cut him off, saying, "Silence, now. The Sojourner comes."

Riven felt something . . . a presence . . . join them, fill the space. He could find no other way to characterize it.

The slaadi looked past him, their eyes wide.

Riven could not help himself, though it meant turning his back to the slaadi. He turned around to see a circular hole in the wall where none had been before. Floating a hand's-breadth off the floor before it was a humanoid creature that could only be the Sojourner. The instant Riven laid eyes on the creature, memories from the Plane of Shadow flooded him.

"Father," said Dolgan, awe in his tone, and Riven heard the big slaad abase himself.

Azriim stepped forward and put a hand on Riven's shoulder. The sudden contact gave Riven a start but he managed not to gut the slaad.

Azriim said, "Sojourner, I've brought you a present."

    ❀ ❀ ❀ ❀ ❀

"What in all the Hells is that?" Cale breathed. Wisps of shadow snaked from his flesh.

"The Sojourner," Magadon answered softly. "It must be."

"Dark," Cale swore. He knew that at that moment Riven's memory was filling in.

Beside them, Jak asked, "What does he look like? What is he?"

Cale only shook his head. "I don't know, Jak." He had never seen a creature like the Sojourner.

The Sojourner was neither slaad nor human, though he was humanoid in shape. With his pale flesh and skeletal frame, Cale might have thought him undead had it not been for the thready black veins pulsing beneath his skin. He bore a staff, and several magical gemstones orbited his head.

Magadon said, "Gods. I can detect his mental energies even through the link with Riven. He has a *presence*, Erevis. Do you feel it? I think he's not only a wizard but also a mindmage."

"A mindmage? Like you?" Cale asked.

"Not like me," Magadon corrected. "More powerful, Erevis. Much more. Riven is in very real danger."

Cale nodded. To Jak, he said, "Little man, cast every defensive spell on us that you can. Hurry. Do whatever you can to shield us from spells and mental attacks."

"Done," Jak said. He pulled out his holy symbol, a jeweled pendant, and recited the words to a spell, then another.

Still watching through Riven's eyes, Cale said, "Speed and surprise are all we have. When we get there, we concentrate everything on the Sojourner. He's the target. The slaadi are incidental. Mags, can you tell Riven that we're coming?"

"Not without risk of detection by the Sojourner," Magadon answered. "He will be sensitive to mental emanations. I'm surprised he hasn't yet detected the visual leech."

"Then we'll surprise Riven, too," Cale said. "Get ready. We go when I say."

Cale held off because he wanted to give Riven a moment to gather himself. The rush of memories was intense. Besides, he also wanted to learn as much as he could before attacking. He could not hear through the mind leech but he could see enough to read the Sojourner's thin lips.

Meanwhile, Jak continued to cast.

In a rush, Riven remembered why he had betrayed Cale, why he had left the First of the Shadowlord bleeding but not dead. The torrent of memories made his temples burn.

He was a plant.

Only long practice allowed him to keep his face expressionless. He suddenly became painfully conscious that a mind-reading slaad stood beside him and another behind him, and that the Sojourner—a creature of obvious but unknown power—hovered across the chamber.

Riven, Magadon, and Cale had devised a plot back on the Plane of Shadow to get Riven close to the Sojourner. Riven's betrayal of Cale was designed to gain the slaadi's trust, which it had. Magadon and Cale would then use Riven as a beacon to bring them to the Sojourner.

Snippets of the exchange played in his mind.

Why me? Riven had asked, when Cale had related his idea.

You already know why, Cale had answered, and Riven *had* known why: because a betrayal by a former Zhent and assassin was believable; because the Second of the Shadowlord would surely covet the position of the First; because Riven was a better killer than Cale.

It was believable enough that it was almost true. Hells, perhaps it *was* true.

Riven's mind raced; he pored through his memories. What had he really intended? He could not remember many of the details. But he did remember that he'd wanted to keep other options available. And at that moment other options were looking more and more appealing.

When Riven had told Azriim in Skullport that he

always sided with the winner, he had meant it. And while he deplored being second to Cale in Mask's eyes, he also had thought back then that they would succeed. Mask was blessing him with more powers every tenday. He'd had no intention of remaining the Shadowlord's Second forever.

But he could see now that his calculus had been off. He had stood face to face with high-ranking members of the Zhentarim, powerful priests, skilled warriors, all of them powerful men and women, but he had never before stood in the presence of anything like the Sojourner. The creature's thin body fairly sparked with pent-up power; his presence implied might. There would be no defeating him.

If Riven wanted to side with the winner, he had to side with the Sojourner and the slaadi.

He reconsidered the plan, reconsidered everything. He may or may not have planned a betrayal of the betrayal back on the Plane of Shadow, but now. . . .

Don't come, he thought to Cale and Magadon, in case Magadon was somehow connected to him. *Don't bother*.

The Sojourner looked past Riven and Azriim to Dolgan and said, "Stand, Dolgan." His soft voice leaked so much power that it seemed to squeeze everything else out of the room.

Over his shoulder, Riven watched the big slaad lurch to his feet, as obedient as a well-trained dog. Dolgan was gnawing excitedly at his lower lip, so hard it was bleeding. Riven wanted to sneer at the oaf's obsequiousness but could not quite manage it. Obsequiousness seemed appropriate, somehow.

Dolgan caught his gaze, made a bloody grin, and said, "Maybe you're tense now, eh?"

Riven resisted the urge to slit the bastard's throat and turned back to face the Sojourner.

The creature held a smooth duskwood staff in his pale, long-fingered hands. A tracery of gold or electrum spiraled around the shaft from base to top. He inclined the staff slightly and the hole in the wall behind him vanished, replaced again by smooth stone.

No wonder Riven had seen no exits. The Sojourner created them as needed. Riven was doubly pleased that he had lifted Dolgan's teleportation rod. He would need to figure out its operation quickly, should an emergency arise.

Riven considered the Sojourner. He looked vaguely human, but unlike any race of humans with which the assassin was familiar. Standing a head taller than even Cale, the Sojourner's thin body looked as though it had been stretched overlong by pulling him at the ankles and head. Sunken black eyes in cavernous sockets stared out of a similarly elongated face. His nose was little more than a bump with two vertical slits, his lips as thin as blades. The points of his backswept ears reached nearly to the top of his bald, spotted pate. A handful of magical gemstones whirred around his head in different orbits. Seeing them, Riven was reminded somehow of Cale's celestial sphere, the magical artifact that had started everything.

"A present, Azriim?" the Sojourner asked, letting his gaze fall on Riven as he floated forward across the room. Outside the light of the glow globe, the Sojourner was reduced to a shadow in Riven's sight.

With great effort, Riven kept his face a mask—no fear, no wonder, no dread—even while his mind moved through possibilities.

Azriim said, "Yes, Sojourner. This human was . . . helpful in our successful use of the Weave Tap. His clothes are unfortunate, I acknowledge. And his taste is poor in general. But neither of those are fatal flaws."

Riven did not bother to correct Azriim, though he had been more than merely helpful with planting the Weave Tap seed—he had been instrumental. Without Riven's intervention, Cale would have killed Azriim.

But instead of speaking, Riven made a stiff bow. The gesture did not come easily to him.

"Sojourner," Riven said.

The creature did not acknowledge him, and Riven dared take no offense. The Sojourner stopped in the air two paces from Riven. Up close, his power was even more palpable. Fear threatened, but Riven managed to hold his ground and his expressionless mask. Riven's eyesight adjusted somewhat to the darkness and he could again mark the Sojourner's features.

Though he was not a slaad, the nose slits, spotted skin, and the shape of his eyes reminded Riven of something slaadlike, or at least reptilian. He wore a short-sleeved robe of red silk, trimmed in gold, over which hung an ermine-trimmed black cape clasped at his throat with a silver pin. His thin body swam in the clothing, and both robe and cape hung off his frame as though he were made of sticks.

The Sojourner fixed Riven with a stare, started to say something, but stopped, blinked, and inhaled sharply.

At first Riven did not know what had happened, then it hit him. The Sojourner had felt a stab of pain.

"Father?" Dolgan asked.

Beside him, Azriim wore a sneer nearly the match of Riven's.

The Sojourner had to be sick or injured, Riven reasoned, which explained why the creature had moved his body hardly at all since entering the room. Perhaps even small movements pained him.

Riven tried to figure how that fit into his calculations, if at all.

The Sojourner's spasm passed as quickly as it had appeared.

"I am well, Dolgan," he said, and eyed Riven. "You were a companion of the priest of Mask?"

Riven nodded tightly. The mention of Cale as a *priest* irritated him.

"You betrayed your friend to join my sons?"

"I don't have friends," Riven answered, and kept his

voice steady. "I have allies and enemies. Allies I use. Enemies I kill."

The Sojourner smiled, a barely perceptible rise in the corners of his mouth. "Which are we, then?"

Behind Riven, Dolgan chortled. The big slaad shifted on his feet.

"Allies," Riven said, but could not prevent himself from adding over his shoulder, "For now."

Dolgan growled, moved a step closer.

Riven tensed, readied himself. Azriim dispelled the tension. "You see?" the foppish slaad said, grinning and thumping Riven on the shoulder. "I like him. So does Dolgan."

Dolgan scoffed and spat on the carpet.

Azriim frowned at that and said, "Mind the carpet, fool."

The Sojourner remained expressionless, motionless, and considered. Riven knew his life sat on a blade's edge. The moments seemed hours. Finally, the Sojourner said to Azriim, "The timing is poor, Azriim. Things are nearing completion and you have introduced a . . . random element into my plans."

"I enjoy random elements," Azriim answered, a challenge in his tone.

Anger flashed in the Sojourner's eyes. He raised his staff slightly and Dolgan fell to the floor. Azriim bowed his head and took his hand from Riven.

Riven considered using the teleportation rod to get the Nine Hells clear of there, but his pride refused to let him run. He would make his play and see it through.

"Time is short," the Sojourner said to the room, and Riven wondered at his meaning. "I am disinclined to indulge you. You will take another seed by sea to the Eldritch Temple of Mystryl. Your human is an unnecessary risk. Accordingly—"

"I can be an asset," Riven interrupted, even as he put one hand to the teleportation rod. "I know Cale well."

Azriim nodded and said, "He was his companion."

"He was, Azriim, and that is why I wonder why he aided you." The Sojourner turned his gaze to Riven. "That is the question."

"Why do we aid *you*?" Azriim asked. "That, too, is a question."

Behind Riven, Dolgan whined in dismay.

Riven turned one of the dials on the rod with his thumb. He was not certain he could operate it. He certainly could not dictate a location. But if things went poorly, anywhere would be better than where he stood.

The Sojourner's eyes bored into Azriim. "You aid me because I give you no choice. But also because I offer something you crave. And because you fear me." He said the last in a soft, tight tone that caused Azriim to take a half-step backward, leaving Riven alone and exposed.

"And appropriately so," the Sojourner added. He nodded at Riven. "This one does not fear you. That is evident. So what do you offer him?"

Azriim made no answer.

Riven gave his own: "Cale—the priest of Mask—I want him dead."

The Sojourner stared at him, baring his soul. "Why?"

Riven gritted his teeth and looked away. He would not admit, even to the Sojourner, that being the *Second* of Mask galled him. Instead, he said simply, "I have my reasons. It's enough that I'm here of my own choice, and for my own benefit."

"I will decide if it is enough," the Sojourner said softly.

To that, Riven said nothing. His thumb hovered over the rod's dials, gave another half turn.

The only sound in the room was the Sojourner's wheeze.

Riven decided to make one last play.

"Make the decision," he said softly. "I'm either with you or I'm not. And if not, then we are no longer allies."

Dolgan lurched to his feet with a growl. Riven put a hand to a saber hilt.

A look from the Sojourner froze the big slaad. The mysterious creature eyed Riven with something akin to appreciation.

"You remind me of Azriim," he said.

Riven did not consider that a compliment but kept his feelings to himself.

Perhaps sensing a change in the Sojourner's sentiments, Azriim again took station beside Riven. "He can accompany Dolgan and me, Sojourner, to the Eldritch Temple. He has already proven his usefulness. I believe his words—he wants the priest dead."

"No," Dolgan said. "Kill him."

Riven wanted nothing so much as to turn around and slit Dolgan's throat.

The Sojourner smiled distantly. To Riven, he said, "You are here of your own choice? For your own benefit?"

"Those are my words," Riven answered.

"They are," the Sojourner acknowledged. "Now let us see if they are true."

The Sojourner never moved, gave no warning, but agony wracked Riven's head.

He screamed, clutched his skull in his palms, and fell to his knees. He felt as if five long fingers had burrowed knuckle-deep into his brain. There, they began to sift through what they found. Riven had never before felt more violated. He resisted the intrusion and fought— futile. The Sojourner's will was inexorable, the pain unbearable. Riven's eye felt as though it would pop out of his skull. He forced his blurry gaze upward and stared into the Sojourner's eyes, fell into them. His body shook, convulsed, but he held the Sojourner's gaze. He bit open his tongue. Screams, spit, and blood poured from his mouth. He felt his consciousness being cracked open like a nut. He could not move; his body would not answer his commands. He could do nothing but suffer and scream.

He forced himself to stay conscious.

Mental fingers peeled away the layers of his brain, baring memories, hopes, fears, ambitions. He screamed again, again.

The Sojourner's expression did not change.

Distantly, he heard Dolgan laughing and Azriim shouting.

He, too, is a servant of Mask the Shadowlord, the Sojourner mentally projected, sorting Riven's life and laying it out for the slaadi. *A mistreated boy who became an assassin. He hates his life up to now. Religion has given him purpose. . . .*

"Get out," Riven tried to mutter, but the syllables emerged only as an indecipherable mumble.

Ah, the Sojourner projected, and nodded. *He is much like you two in that he also desires a transformation, not to gray, but from Second to First. He hates the priest for being First.*

Riven tried again to speak, failed. His heart hammered in his chest. He tried to dismiss from his mind the events that had occurred in the Plane of Shadow, tried to tuck them into some distant corner of his consciousness, but the Sojourner burrowed like a gnome through the dirt of his life.

The Sojourner reached the memory. Riven screamed again. Blood leaked from his nose. Surely his skull must explode. Surely.

And here is this, the Sojourner said, his mental voice hard. *He came to kill me, to draw others here to kill me. The betrayal of the priest of Mask was a fraud, a ploy. You have brought a would-be murderer into my presence, Azriim.*

The full force of the Sojourner's mind and will assaulted Riven's mind, pinioning him, burying him under its weight. He fell flat on the floor. His vision went dark; something warm dripped from his ears. He was falling, falling.

Riven tried to mouth the words, "No. It is real. I want him dead." His lips would not form the words so he thought them instead: *I want him dead! I want him dead!*

A booted foot slammed into Riven's ribs—Dolgan. Riven's leather armor kept the bones intact but his breath went out in a whoosh.

"Kill him," Dolgan said.

He was going to die prone on the floor, helpless as a babe. Distantly, he wondered if Cale and Magadon were watching, laughing.

They must have a practitioner of the Invisible Art among their number, the Sojourner observed, surprise in his mental voice. *He has moderate skill.*

The pain in Riven's mind intensified. He was too far gone to scream anymore. He dug his fingers into the carpet so hard that he tore three fingernails from their beds. He felt a peculiar sensation through the pain. A tickle in his consciousness. Something scurried around the edges of his sentience, trying to avoid the Sojourner's mental perception. To no avail. Nothing could avoid the Sojourner.

The Sojourner said, *We have a mindmage in our midst.* To someone Riven could not see, the Sojourner projected, *I see you.*

It must have been Magadon. They had been watching the whole time.

With the Sojourner's attention temporarily diverted, Riven managed to claw his way back to coherence.

"Get . . . out . . . of my head!" he shouted, and pulled himself up to all fours.

❧ ❧ ❧ ❧ ❧

Magadon lurched back, clutching his temples and groaning with pain. Jak stopped whatever spell he had been casting and leaped to the guide's aid.

"He sensed me," Magadon managed, leaning on Jak. "Such a mind. . . ."

Cale knew. He had felt the Sojourner make contact through Magadon, had felt the residuum of power that had accompanied the contact. Cale had let the mental scrying go on far too long. Riven had suffered unnecessarily. He had hoped to learn the Sojourner's full plans for the Weave Tap, but he had learned only snippets.

He started to draw the darkness around them. The light from Magadon's sunrod dimmed. Shadows intensified.

"Mags?" Cale asked while he summoned shadows.

"I'm all right," the guide said. He took his hand off Jak's shoulder and massaged his brow. He unslung his bow and nocked an arrow, though he did not draw. "I'm ready."

The air around Cale's body crackled with magical energy; the hairs on his arms stood up—the result of Jak's various protective spells. Cale hoped the magic would be enough.

"I did what I could," Jak said by way of explanation, and gripped his holy symbol, shortsword, and dagger.

Magadon concentrated, and a handful of coin-sized spheres of light formed around his head and quickly faded.

"I cannot mindlink us," he said. "Jak's spell is blocking *my* abilities, at least. Let us hope it does the same to the Sojourner."

Cale nodded and quickly donned his mask. To Jak, he said, "It's a dark cavern, little man. Cluttered with cushions and furniture. The two slaadi—one in human form, one as a half-drow—and the Sojourner. Riven is on the floor. "

He hefted Weaveshear, looked each of his comrades in the eye.

Both nodded.

"We go," he said.

Cale let himself sink into the darkness around them, let it seep into him. He understood that the shadows anywhere were the shadows everywhere. He pictured the

Sojourner's cavern in his mind, the shadows that filled its corners.

Pulling his comrades into his personal night, he moved them through the black, from a cavern on the Plane of Shadow to a distant cavern elsewhere.

CHAPTER 2

SHIFTING ALLIANCES

The instant they materialized, Magadon's sunrod went dark, probably extinguished by some ambient magic in the cavern. Only the dim glowglobe provided illumination in the chamber. It was enough for Cale. He hoped it was enough for Jak and Magadon.

They stood on soft carpet on one side of the cavern, perhaps fifteen paces from the slaadi and the Sojourner. On the floor between the slaadi, Riven struggled feebly to draw his weapons.

Azriim and Dolgan went wide-eyed at the sudden appearance of the three comrades.

"Cale," Azriim hissed, and fumbled at his blade hilt.

Dolgan growled and unslung his axe.

The three comrades went straight after the Sojourner.

Jak held his holy symbol before him and shouted the words to a spell. Beams of white fire shot from his hand at the Sojourner. They never reached their target. Instead, one of the gems circling the Sojourner's head attracted and absorbed the beams as if they had never been.

Magadon's bow sang and an arrow flew, its tip glowing red with mental energy. The arrow slammed against some invisible shield before the Sojourner, stopped in mid-flight, and fell to the ground, inert.

Cale felt a twinge behind his eyes and feared a mental attack, but the sensation never grew beyond the initial sensation. Perhaps Jak's spell had shielded him from the Sojourner's attack.

Jak's and Magadon's failed attacks confirmed what Cale had already suspected: A formidable array of defensive spells and wards protected the Sojourner. Cale had to bring them down or weaken them.

Hurriedly, he recited a prayer that pitted the power of his magic against that of the Sojourner. When the spell took effect, the contest proved short-lived and one-sided. The Sojourner's power overwhelmed Cale's spell, which dissipated without effect.

Cale saw then that magic would be of little use against the superior spellcraft of the Sojourner.

"Use steel," he called, and charged, leaping over a couch as he went.

Jak and Magadon brandished their blades and joined his rush.

Before they had taken five strides, the Sojourner responded. Unlike most wizards Cale had encountered, the Sojourner did not speak a complex phrase or manipulate some esoteric ingredient. Instead, he simply raised his left hand—wincing with pain as he did so—and spoke a single word.

An expanding wedge-shaped spray of variously colored

beams shot outward from his fingertips. The three companions had no time to dodge.

A yellow beam struck Magadon in the chest and blew him from his feet. Lightning played over his body, leaving him smoking and sparking on the floor.

An orange beam struck Jak in the left leg as he jumped the couch. His trousers, boots, and flesh blackened, bubbled, started to melt. The little man screamed in agony, collapsed to the couch, and rolled onto the floor, clutching his melting thigh and writhing. The stink of burning flesh filled the chamber.

The green and blue beams intended for Cale diverted into Weaveshear. The blade drank them greedily, though the magical impact staggered Cale and stopped his charge. Weaveshear shook in his hands, bleeding shadows. He clutched it in both hands to keep his grip.

The Sojourner eyed the sword with raised eyebrows—as though surprised that it had been able to absorb his spell—and spoke another word of power, this time without a gesture of any kind.

A sphere of lightning took shape around the creature, surrounding him at arm's length. It sizzled and spun, charging the air in the chamber with energy. Bolts arced out to touch the metal of the slaadi's weapons, to burn the cushions and furniture at the Sojourner's feet. Even at a distance, the hairs on Cale's arms rose.

Cale knew that he could not allow the Sojourner the freedom to continue casting, but the slaadi were in his way.

Azriim and Dolgan, seeing Cale alone, seized weapons in their hands and advanced. Dolgan held his huge axe in his ham hands; Azriim held his blade in one hand and one of his many wands in the other.

Cale pointed Weaveshear at them and released the pent up magical energy he had stolen from the Sojourner. The unsuspecting slaadi had no time to avoid the attack, and the green and blue beams intended for Cale struck Azriim and Dolgan.

The blue beam hit Azriim squarely in the chest. His mouth opened to exclaim in surprise, but before a sound could emerge, his body went rigid. In the span of a single heartbeat, starting at his chest but spreading rapidly to the rest of his body, the magic transformed his flesh, clothing, and weapons into gray stone. In an instant, he was no more than a statue.

Dolgan took the green beam in his right arm. The impact spun him around and he groaned, wobbled, and fell over, only a few paces from Riven. Cale did not know what the spell had done to him but the slaad was down, and that was enough.

It was only he and the Sojourner now.

Cale spared a glance at his friends. Jak's face was twisted with pain but he had his holy symbol in hand and already was casting a healing spell on his wounded leg. Magadon, still smoking, was climbing clumsily to his feet, his expression dazed.

The Sojourner started to cast again, this time using gestures and words. His casting with a mere word must be limited, Cale reasoned. That pleased Cale. It made the Sojourner more ordinary.

Before the creature could complete his spell, Cale stepped into the shadowy space that existed in reality's interstices. He moved from one side of the chamber to the other in a single stride. He materialized behind the Sojourner, a little to the right, near Riven and the slaadi.

The Sojourner's sheath of energy spat arcs of lightning that burned Cale's skin. The resistance to magic granted by the shadowstuff in his being was no match for the Sojourner's power. Cale gritted his teeth, endured the pain, and stabbed Weaveshear's point at the Sojourner's spine and kidneys, a killing blow.

The blade cut only empty air.

The Sojourner winked out and reappeared ten paces away.

Some kind of contingency, Cale presumed.

Three bolts of lightning discharged at Cale from the ring of energy around the Sojourner. Weaveshear absorbed two but the third slammed into him. The bolt lifted him from his feet and blew him bodily across the chamber until he slammed into the far wall. His breath left him. His skin smoked and burned. He sagged to the carpeted floor amidst several cushions, gasping, shot through with pain. His shade flesh began to regenerate the injuries.

The Sojourner began to cast another spell, again using elaborate phrasing and gestures.

Cale found his breath and clambered to his feet. He pulled the shadows to him and formed them into five images of himself. They flitted around him, exact duplicates that mirrored his movements. Hopefully they would confuse the Sojourner.

To the left of the creature, Cale saw that Riven had drawn his blades and at last found his feet. The assassin stood on wobbly legs not far from the slaadi, one petrified, the other prone and vulnerable. Riven looked down at Dolgan, back at Magadon and Jak, over at the Sojourner, at Cale.

What in the Nine Hells was he waiting for?

"Do it," Cale shouted, meaning that Riven should kill Dolgan.

Riven's eye narrowed but instead of executing the prone slaad, he stared at Cale and offered his signature sneer. Turning toward Magadon and Jak, Riven shouted a series of words in the foul tongue Mask had taught him in his dreams. The words rang off Cale's ears, sent vomit up his throat. Even Dolgan writhed on the ground. Magadon staggered, fell. Jak vomited, covered his ears.

Cale cursed Riven, cursed Mask, cursed everything. Riven turned back to grin at him. Cale stared hatefully in answer, leveled Weaveshear at him, and discharged the two stored lightning bolts. They ripped the air between Cale and the assassin but Riven anticipated the move and dived aside in an awkward roll. The bolts slammed into the far wall, blackening stone, setting a divan afire, and narrowly missing Jak.

Riven regained his feet, wobbled, stayed upright.

"I told you what I wanted, Sojourner," Riven called. With that, he turned and advanced unsteadily toward Jak and Magadon, sabers bare.

If the Sojourner heard Riven, he showed no sign. He spoke the final word to his spell and a globe of nothingness as big as an ogre's head formed in the air near Cale. Its edge brushed a stuffed chair and the piece of furniture was reduced to dust instantly. It touched one of Cale's shadow images and annihilated it, too. Cale dived aside, his images trailing him, mirroring his movements. The sphere followed, ponderously but inexorably, and what it touched, it destroyed.

For a moment, Cale thought of testing Weaveshear against the annihilating sphere but decided against it. He did not know if the blade could survive it.

The Sojourner spoke another word, a single word, and Cale's magical images and all of Jak's protective spells were annihilated. He was exposed, vulnerable.

Cale felt the Sojourner's mental fingers reaching for his mind. He knew what the creature had done to Riven, what he would do to Cale.

Meanwhile, Riven was three strides away from the little man and Magadon, neither of whom would be able to defend themselves. Still prone, Jak watched Riven approach, a snarl on his face, blades in his hands.

The Sojourner's fingers found purchase in Cale's mind, started to burrow in. He felt as though needles skewered his eyes.

Cale gritted his teeth against the intrusion and made his decision: the fight was lost. He had to get his friends out of there.

He shot a final glare at the Sojourner, and thought: *This is not over.*

The Sojourner answered, *No, but nearly so.*

Cale did not bother pondering the response as he slid between the shadows. He stepped to Jak's side, grabbed him by the shirt, and stepped in another stride to Magadon.

At Cale's appearance, Riven aborted his advance.

Cale wanted to give Riven an arm's length of sharp steel but had time only to give him a glare. He pulled the darkness around him.

"Faithless bastard," Jak said to Riven. The little man's leg looked raw and chewed. Puke stained the front of his shirt.

"There will be another time, Zhent," Cale promised, as the shadows closed around him.

"I'm relying on it," Riven said. "We're on other sides in this from now on, Cale. Do you remember what I once told you on the street in Selgaunt after I put down that Cyricist?" He paused before saying, "I meant it."

Cale was glad that his mask hid the confusion he knew his face must have shown.

Behind Riven, the Sojourner spoke another word and pointed a long finger at Cale. A black bolt of energy flew from the Sojourner's finger but Cale already had found the correspondence between the chamber and the first safe place he could think of—the Plane of Shadow.

Strange, Cale thought to himself as the darkness moved him and his friends between worlds, that he would consider the Plane of Shadow a safe place.

❧ ❧ ❧ ❧ ❧

Cale, Jak, and Magadon vanished, swallowed by shadows. The black beam from the Sojourner's spell struck the stone where Cale had crouched with his two comrades, and dissolved a wagonload of floor into nothingness.

Riven still felt a bit muzzy-headed from the Sojourner's mental attack, but he knew he had done the right thing.

He ignored the hollow feeling in his gut. It would pass. It always did.

He took a deep breath and turned to look on the Sojourner. He had thrown the dice by betraying Cale. Now he would see if they came up asp eyes or full pips.

The Sojourner gestured with his staff and the circle of lightning sizzling around him dissipated. Despite the frenetic combat, the mage's wheezing breath came steady and slow. His eyes, as dark as the magical sphere that floated in the air beside him, bored like awls into Riven.

Riven sheathed his blades and held his ground.

Not far from him, the big slaad, still groaning with pain from whatever the magical beam had done to him, managed to turn around and sit up.

"Poison," Dolgan said, as much to himself as anyone else. He grinned stupidly. "Stole my strength. Makes me want to. . . ."

A retch swallowed the big slaad's next words and he sprayed vomit onto the floor and down his shirt. Riven wrinkled his nose at the smell. He did not look closely at the contents of the slaad's stomach; he did not want to know what they might contain.

Dolgan laughed as though the retching amused him. The laughter triggered another round of vomiting.

Riven eyed the Sojourner and said, "I told you that I want Cale dead. I've just proven it." He indicated Dolgan.

"I could have killed him. Him too," he said, indicating Azriim. "I could have knocked him over and broken off his head. Did you see all that?"

"I saw," the Sojourner said, his voice soft. "But even had you killed them, that still would have left me."

Riven kept his face expressionless, though the Sojourner's words hit near to his thinking. Too near.

"Yes," he said, and left unspoken the acknowledgment that he could not have killed the Sojourner. "But I could have fled after putting them down."

He pulled Dolgan's teleportation rod from his cloak and showed it to the Sojourner.

Dolgan got control of his retching and laughing, and patted at his cloak.

The Sojourner gave a soft smile.

"That is mine!" Dolgan said, and climbed to his feet. He wobbled, but managed not to fall.

Riven did not bother to respond. He kept his gaze on the Sojourner.

"I would have found you," the Sojourner said.

Riven shrugged a "maybe."

"Why did you not run?" the Sojourner asked. The black globe—the void—still hovered beside him. Riven understood the implicit threat it represented

"I just told you why," Riven answered, and was reminded by those words of Cale's response to him back on the Plane of Shadow, when they first had put together the plan to get Riven close to the Sojourner.

"You chafe at being Second," said the Sojourner, and floated nearer to him, nearer. The void orb and the stink of medicines drifted at his side.

Riven's jaw tightened. He said nothing but gave a brusque nod.

Holding his axe in both hands, Dolgan advanced and stood beside the Sojourner. Vomit stained the front of his cloak. The stink was abominable. He looked like the idiot he was.

"Kill him, father," the big slaad said to the Sojourner. "Or let me kill him."

Riven put a hand to a saber hilt. "*He* could do it," he said, pointing his chin at the Sojourner. "You would not have a chance."

Dolgan snarled at him, ran his finger along his axe blade until it bled, but did not advance.

Riven looked to the Sojourner.

"Enemy or ally?" he asked.

"Kill him," Dolgan said again, his voice hard. He

sliced open his entire palm on the axe blade.

Riven felt the Sojourner touch his mind. Riven did not resist, even though he did not like the intrusion. There was only mild pain this time. The ordeal ended quickly.

"You believe me now?" Riven asked.

"I do not have to believe," the Sojourner said. "I know."

Riven nodded. "Then that's the last time anyone gets into my head. Agreed?"

The Sojourner answered by letting the void orb wink out.

Dolgan deflated visibly.

The Sojourner eyed him sidelong and said, "Do not let embarrassment color your judgment, Dolgan. As I said before, this one wants transformation as much as you and Azriim. He wishes to be First in the eyes of the Shadowlord. And he cannot be First so long as he is the ally of Erevis Cale. Is that not correct, Drasek Riven?"

Riven acknowledged the point with a tilt of his head. He decided to take the final step—he tossed the teleportation rod back to Dolgan. He now had no way out.

The big slaad caught the rod, looked at it suspiciously, sniffed it, and shoved it back into his vomit-stained cloak.

"Done, then," Riven said.

The Sojourner turned away from him and floated back to Azriim. He touched the slaad with his staff. Magical energy flashed and Azriim reverted at once back to flesh.

The slaad gasped, stumbled, looked around. When he saw Riven, his eyes narrowed and his face burned with embarrassment and anger.

"You," he said, his voice a hiss. He leveled the wand he still held.

Riven held up his hands. "I didn't remember," he explained. "There was no way either of us could have known."

"Do not fret, Azriim," said the Sojourner. "He has won a place here. He is much like you, and is a worthy replacement for Serrin."

Azriim's expression showed confusion, but he did not appear displeased. He sheathed his wand with the others he carried in a thigh case.

"He wants to be transformed," Dolgan said, mimicking the Sojourner's words.

Riven explained, "I want Cale dead. I should be the First of Mask."

Azriim grinned a mouthful of perfect teeth. He clapped his hands together and said, "Well, aren't we all just a joyous family, then?" He turned, noticed Dolgan's vomit-stained cloak, and asked, "What happened to your clothes? You're more disgusting than usual."

"Puke," the big slaad said, and pulled his cloak up to his nose to sniff it. He licked at the cloth.

Azriim wrinkled his nose and shook his head. "Yes, well . . . change it, won't you? You stink like a sty." He turned to face the Sojourner. "Meanwhile . . . Father, we have spoken of Riven's transformation but not ours. What of that?"

Dolgan quit licking his cloak and looked expectantly at the Sojourner.

"My sons wish to be made new as grays," the Sojourner explained to Riven, though the explanation meant nothing. The Sojourner looked upon his slaadi with a benevolent smile.

"I promised you transformation when our work was done. There are tasks yet unfinished."

Azriim and Dolgan sagged.

"Still," the Sojourner said. "You did accomplish much in Skullport. And for that you deserve something."

Both slaadi looked up.

"A partial transformation to gray," the Sojourner said. "A taste of what is to come."

Without further preamble, he held forth his hand

and two small black spheres appeared in his palm. To Riven, they looked like peach pits, except that both glowed with energy and spun in mid-air, each on an invisible axis.

"Assume your natural forms," the Sojourner said. "And eat."

Eagerly, the slaadi began to change. Azriim and Dolgan grunted as their bodies twisted and cracked. The half-drow and human forms stretched, grew, gained bulk. In their eagerness, both had forgotten to remove or loosen their garb. Clothes ripped.

Skin tore and gave way to leathery green hides. Faces and skulls distended to accommodate cavernous mouths filled with fangs. Claws poked from the ends of fingers and toes. In less than a tencount, the slaadi had taken their natural form, that of hulking reptilian bipeds, both as tall as Cale. Dolgan's shoulders were nearly as broad as he was tall.

Riven reminded himself to never forget what they really were, allies or not.

The Sojourner flicked his fingers and one of the magical seeds floated toward each of the slaadi. Both snatched them out of the air and gobbled them greedily.

Instantly a silvery glow suffused them both, leaked from their ears, their eyes.

"It tingles," Dolgan said, and his voice was deeper.

Azriim grinned maniacally. He held his arms out before him and studied his hands as they began to change.

The silver glow intensified, flashed, and the slaadi began again to change. Their hulking green forms diminished. Muscles became leaner, bordered with visible sinew and lined with veins. Heads became sleeker, more angled. Eyes narrowed; eye ridges became more pronounced. Mouths shrank and fangs thinned, lengthened, visibly sharpened. Green leathery hides faded to slate gray.

Then it was over.

Both slaadi were smaller but the strength implied by their former bulk had been replaced by something that suggested . . . predation. They looked sleeker, faster, more efficient. It was as though they had changed from bears to hunting cats. Dolgan, of course, remained the larger of the two.

Both slaadi smiled a mouthful of new fangs, though Azriim frowned when he realized that he had rent his shirt and breeches. Dolgan smiled at his brother's displeasure.

Azriim disappeared from sight, but his disembodied voice said, "Excellent."

He reappeared. Dolgan grinned and also disappeared and reappeared, disappeared and reappeared, like a child delighted with a new toy.

Riven now knew that the transformation had changed not only the slaadi's bodies, but their magical abilities. At the very least, they could turn themselves invisible merely by willing it. Riven wondered what other new abilities the slaadi could manifest.

"Enough of this," the Sojourner said, and Dolgan's grin vanished. "Time is short. Sakkors awaits."

"Sakkors?" Dolgan asked, stumbling over the word with his new lips and teeth.

"A onetime Netherese city," the Sojourner answered. "Now in ruins."

"Unfortunate," said Azriim, and grinned. "I like to leave cities in ruins, not find them so."

Dolgan guffawed.

Riven kept his disdain from his face. He thought the slaadi unprofessional fools. They were as undisciplined as children.

The Sojourner said, "Sakkors was destroyed and lost long ago, when the ambition of the greatest of human mages exceeded his reach. But the city's mantle remains intact."

"We can teleport there," Dolgan said. He held up his teleportation rod, shot Riven a glare, and tucked it back in his pocket. "Then we tap the mantle with another seed and complete our transformation."

"You are not listening, Dolgan," Azriim said, and tsked. "The Sojourner said Sakkors was lost. That means he does not know where it is."

Dolgan stared at Azriim, confusion in his dull eyes and slack mouth. He asked, "How can we go there if he does not know where it is?"

"I am certain he will inform us," Azriim said, and made a flourish at the Sojourner.

The Sojourner frowned at Azriim's flamboyance but said only, "I have been unable to locate Sakkors's *exact* location, but my research and divinations have revealed its general vicinity."

"You see?" Azriim said to Dolgan.

"Scry it," Riven said, thinking of how Cale used Magadon to see a location before teleporting there. "Then teleport in."

"It resists remote scrying," said the Sojourner. "Even mine. Instead, you will find its exact location with this." The Sojourner tapped his staff on the floor and a device appeared out of the air—in form, it reminded Riven of a ship's compass. A thin needle with a golden point hung suspended in a clear liquid within a transparent sphere chased in gold. The whole rested in a tripod gimbal.

"It looks like a compass," Riven observed. He had seen sailors use such devices for navigation. He understood their use, though he could not use one himself.

The Sojourner smiled at Riven. "That is not far from the truth. But this compass is attuned to the emanations of Sakkors's mantle, rather than to the magnetic sheath that surrounds your world."

"So we need only get in the area of the ruins," Azriim said. "And the compass will guide us to it exactly?"

"Yes," the Sojourner said. "I have determined that Sakkors lies somewhere beneath the waters of the Inner Sea—"

"Underwater?" Riven asked.

"Not to worry," Azriim said, but offered no further explanation.

"Yes," the Sojourner said. "Underwater. Not far off the coast of the realm of Sembia, near the city of Selgaunt."

"Your old haunts," Azriim said, slapping Riven on the shoulder and grinning. "I almost killed you there, not long ago."

"I haven't forgotten," Riven said in a low tone. He let the slaad make of that what he would.

The Sojourner continued. "You will take a ship to sea and the compass will guide you to the ruins. Once there, you will tap Sakkors's mantle, exactly as you did in Skullport."

"And after that?" Azriim asked.

"After that, the Crown of Flame," said the Sojourner, his voice almost wistful.

"I meant for us," Azriim said.

"Of course you did," the Sojourner answered. "For you, completion of your transformation to gray, freedom from service to me, and something else. . . ."

"What else?" Azriim asked.

The Sojourner shook his head and admonished, "Patience, Azriim."

Riven had never before heard them mention the Crown of Flame. He dared ask, "The Crown of Flame?"

The Sojourner waved a hand casually, though the movement caused him obvious pain. "Something I saw once in my youth, and would see again in my dotage."

"Saw?" Dolgan asked. "I thought you wore it."

"In a manner of speaking, Dolgan," the Sojourner replied. "Now, let me see to our new . . . broodmate, and you three can be about your tasks, while I am about mine."

Azriim cocked his head. "You have a task?"

"I do," the Sojourner said. "And after I've completed it and you have tapped the mantle in Sakkors, you will not be returning to this plane. Say your farewells."

Azriim's tone was wary. "Where then?"

"I will advise you," the Sojourner said, and offered nothing more.

While Azriim pondered, the Sojourner used another minor summoning spell to provide Riven with his own teleportation rod, similar to that of the slaadi, and instructed him in its use. Then he cast several spells on Riven, ostensibly to ward him from detection by Magadon or Cale. Riven was in no position to protest, though the spells could have been anything.

Afterward, the Sojourner provided Azriim with a silvery seed pod threaded with black veins—a Weave Tap seed—exactly like the one the slaad had used back in Skullport.

After changing back to his preferred half-drow form—now with a prominent gray streak through his otherwise pale hair—Azriim touched the compass and seed with a magical glove he wore and both disappeared, safely stored in some extradimensional space accessible only through the magic of the glove. Finally, Azriim opened a hole in the wall with a command word and disappeared for a time. He returned with new clothes for him, Dolgan, and Riven.

Riven managed not to laugh in Azriim's face. He said, "I'll manage my own wardrobe, slaad."

Azriim looked disappointed but shrugged it off. "If you must," he said, and donned his own finery—a silk shirt, high boots, tailored trousers, and a lace-trimmed cloak. He strapped on his quiver of wands and his weapon belt.

"Now I feel ready," he announced.

Dolgan fumbled into his new clothes—ripping them in the process, of course—and all was prepared.

Without further ado, Riven and the slaadi activated their rods and teleported back to the city where everything had begun—Selgaunt.

CHAPTER 3

RETURNING TO THE SHADOWS

Cale materialized with his friends in the same cavern in the Plane of Shadow from which they had staged their attack. All three sagged to the ground, breathing heavily. No hisses or whispers issued from the nearby tunnels, and the darkness of the plane filled Cale, comforted him. He removed his mask but kept it in his hand.

Magadon shrugged off his pack and struck another of his seemingly endless supply of sunrods. The three companions stared at one another in its dim light. Cale saw the pain in the eyes of Jak and Magadon, in their wan complexions. Cale whispered prayers of healing and touched each of his friends in turn, healing fully the black holes in Magadon's skin and the terrible burns in Jak's legs. The little man bit back a scream as the dead flesh fell from his leg, replaced by new. Both smiled their gratitude. Cale's regenerative flesh was already healing his own wounds so he did not expend a spell.

For a time, the three sat in silence under the roof of stone, an island of dim light in an ocean of pitch. The sunrod's light flickered over their faces. No one seemed willing to say what Cale was thinking, what all of them must have been thinking.

Finally, Jak gave it voice. "I've never even heard of anyone that powerful. Elminster of Shadowdale, maybe. A user of both the Art *and* the Invisible Art?" He paused, looked at Magadon, looked at Cale, and said softly, "I don't know if we can defeat him. Maybe we need to get help. Harpers or . . . someone."

The statement hung in the air between them, heavier than the darkness.

"No," Cale said. "This is our affair." He absently twisted shadows around his fingers. "Maybe we can't defeat him, but that means nothing. We try. And try again. And again." He released the shadows from his fingertips and they dissipated into the air. "There's something large at stake here. I can't see it but I can feel it. Can't you, Mags? Jak? You saw him, his power. He would not bother himself with something small."

"Agreed," Jak said, looking at Cale quizzically. "And I'm pleased to hear you thinking that way."

Cale nodded. He was mildly pleased to hear himself thinking that way too.

The little man dug for his pipe, found it, and said, "Things might have gone differently anyway, if not for that thrice-damned Zhent traitor."

Cale thought back to Riven's last words to him. He weighed them, then finally said, "I am not certain that he betrayed us."

Jak looked up, holding a burning tindertwig in the air before his pipe.

"Not again. What do you mean?"

Magadon leaned forward, pale eyes intense. "Yes, what do you mean, Erevis?"

Jak's tindertwig burned down almost to his thumb while Cale tried to frame an answer. The little man cursed softly but managed to light his pipe with the stub before tossing it away. The shadows snuffed the flame as efficiently as a bucket of water.

Cale said, "You heard what he said to me just as we got out of there?"

Magadon nodded. "That you're on opposite sides."

"Opposite sides," Jak said, nodding. "How is that not a betrayal?"

"He also said something about a Cyricist priest," Magadon added.

"Yes," Cale agreed. "He said that he meant what he once told me back in Selgaunt, after we'd put down a Cyricist priest together."

Magadon asked, "What did he say to you, then?"

Jak blew out a cloud of smoke.

Cale hesitated, searching his memory for something else Riven might have said. Finding nothing, he answered, "He said, 'we work well together'."

Magadon blew out a breath, leaned back, and looked off into the darkness.

Jak took his pipe from his mouth and swore.

Cale understood their mood.

"What kind of game is he playing?" Magadon asked, as much of himself as Cale and Jak.

"The same kind he always plays," Jak said, taking a draw on his pipe. "He is an actor, an assassin. He has been playing us all along. And now he's playing us again. For his own ends. Don't believe him, Cale."

Cale was not so sure. Riven had always been a difficult read, true, and the assassin's unhappiness at being Second to Cale made him more difficult still. They shared a faith, a past occupation, but little else. Still, Cale had felt something almost like camaraderie developing between Riven and the rest of them. Was that an act? Cale did not know. The assassin could have been telling Cale that he remained an ally, or he could simply have been hedging his wager by playing both sides.

"We'll know when we see him next," Cale said.

Jak harrumphed, stood, and tested his leg. It appeared fine, though his breeches were melted.

"I still don't trust him," the little man said.

Cale said, "Neither do I."

Not fully, at least. He could not afford to.

"So then," Magadon said, pulling some hardtack from his pack and passing it around. "What now? How do we find him after he leaves the Sojourner's lair?"

"I'm working on that," Cale said. He had been able to scry the slaadi in Skullport, but assumed that the Sojourner would better mask his servants this time, including Riven.

"We learned a few things from your visual leech," Cale continued. "The Sojourner said something about a journey to the Eldritch Temple of Mystryl. Perhaps we can use that."

Magadon looked at him curiously. "How do you know what he said? We could not hear through the mental contact."

"He read his lips," Jak said.

Magadon raised his eyebrows and nodded appreciatively.

The little man said, "I've never heard of Mystryl, nor any Eldritch Temple. On an island somewhere, maybe?"

Cale shrugged. "I have never heard the name before either. But we'll find someone who has. Let me think on it."

Jak snuffed his pipe, tapped out the ashes, and said, "Meanwhile, let's get the Nine Hells out of here, eh? Can you . . . move us back to Faerûn again?"

Cale assumed so. He had not yet noticed any limits on his ability to transport himself and his comrades through the shadows, though Jak's comment caused him to wonder. If he had no limits, he thought it must have less to do with his transformation into a shade and more to do with his position as the First of Mask.

"I can," he said. "I'll take you two to Selgaunt. Then I need to return to Skullport."

Jak and Magadon shared a look.

"We'll accompany you to Skullport," Magadon said. He stood and shouldered on the straps of his pack.

Cale shook his head. "No, Mags. Transporting into the Underdark is dangerous. The journey can go wrong. Besides, Skullport may be in ruins. We could materialize in a rock."

"We know the risks," Magadon answered.

"The Skulls may be looking for us . . . ," Cale said.

"*We know the risks*," Jak repeated. "And we're still coming."

Cale looked each of them in the eyes, saw the resolve there, and admitted there was no point in arguing further.

"Well enough. We go, then."

His friends readied themselves.

In his mind Cale pictured the dim streets of Skullport, the catwalks and rope bridges of the Hemp Highway, the palpable despair. He let himself feel the connection between the shadows of the Plane of Shadow and the darkness of the Port of Shadow. The connection came easy. The two locations were linked by more than their lack of illumination.

The darkness around them intensified, snuffed Magadon's sunrod.

With an effort of will, Cale moved them between planes. They materialized in the darkness of a narrow alley, off a quiet street.

The smells hit Cale first. He had forgotten how foul was the air in Skullport—dank water, dead fish, urine, unwashed bodies, uncollected rot. He gave the smell a name: hopelessness.

"Still standing," Jak said in a soft tone, peeking out of the alley and onto the street.

He did not have to add the "unfortunately." Cale heard it in his voice.

"But barely," Magadon added, for the destruction was evident even from the alley.

They stepped out onto the street.

Dust filled the air like fog, so thick Cale had to pull his cloak up over his mouth to act as a filter. Jak and Magadon did the same. Buildings from higher in the cavern had fallen to the floor, crushing people and structures below and leaving huge, shapeless piles of stone and wood sprayed across the cavern's bottom. Limbs jutted from some of the piles. Many of the buildings still standing at ground level leaned so far to one side that collapse was imminent. Jagged orange lines of arcane energy flashed at random through the air near the cavern's ceiling, like tiny bolts of lightning.

Some side effect of the mantle being tapped, Cale assumed. But at least the magic had remained intact enough to hold up the cavern.

Heaps of debris littered the street: piles of broken wood, shattered pottery, chunks of finished stone, and pieces of stalactites. Tangled piles of the Hemp Highway lay twisted among the wreckage, the whole a mess of rope and ruin.

"Stay sharp," Cale said softly, as they started to walk. "And stay close to me. We leave instantly if any Skulls show."

His comrades nodded, looking around wide-eyed.

The destruction was barely an hour old but already skulkers worked to brace the remaining structures with stray timbers. Others picked among the heaps, probably looters looking for valuables or food. Orcs, humans, half-breeds, illithids, and drow moved quietly among the wreckage in the streets, their eyes more furtive than usual, their weapons and wands more in evidence. Stray animals wandered throughout, dogs among them. Cale thought of Riven.

"Gods," Magadon oathed as they navigated the destruction.

Cale could only nod. While the slaadi had been responsible for the destruction, Cale still felt soiled by his participation in the events that had led up to it. Skullport was a pit, true, but nothing and no one deserved what he was seeing.

They continued on, the tension as thick as the dust. Thankfully, they saw no sign of the Skulls.

They did see slaves. Plenty of them. Coffles of humans, elves, dwarves, and less common races walked the streets, chained together and clinking. Bugbear overseers with morningstars growled commands. Not even the partial collapse of the city could halt the slave trade.

Cale tried to find something familiar that would give him his bearings. At last he did—the Rusty Anchor. It still stood, seemingly untouched by the destruction. He thought of checking for Varra there, but decided against it. She would not be at the inn. She would be home or . . . not. He knew they were not far from her row house. He remembered walking her home from the inn. He ignored the hole in his stomach that formed around his fear that she might be harmed . . . or worse.

Cale picked up the pace. The comrades took care to not draw attention to themselves, and Cale kept the shadows knit tightly about them.

"Someday," Jak whispered, as they passed a half-orc leading three male human slaves in neck chains.

"Someday," Cale echoed, and meant it.

As they walked, he saw that the destruction was worse in some places, not as bad in others. He estimated that perhaps three-quarters of the buildings at ground level had survived. No doubt the upper levels had suffered more. Still, he could see that many of those had actually survived too.

And everywhere the life of the city continued, albeit in a more subdued manner. The inns they passed were less raucous, the hawking of the flesh vendors less vigorous, the expressions of the slaves more despondent.

The city had survived and would rebuild, Cale figured. He was not sure whether that was a good or bad thing.

"I hate this place," Jak said softly.

Cale nodded. He did, too.

He changed the subject, saying, "No sign of the Skulls, at least."

He wondered if Skullport's rulers had survived the tapping of the mantle. He knew several had been destroyed in the battle the slaadi had engineered between the slavers' factions. But that left several unaccounted for.

Sidestepping piles of debris, they picked their way through the city until they reached its northern edge. Cale's throat tightened as they neared Varra's row house.

When he saw that it was still standing, he blew out a relieved breath. For a moment, he debated with himself about whether he should approach her home. It seemed somehow . . . presumptuous.

But he made up his mind quickly. He had to confirm that she was all right. And he wanted her to know that he cared whether she was all right.

"Stay here," he said to Jak and Magadon.

"Here?" Jak asked.

"I won't be long," Cale answered. "Keep your eyes open."

As he approached Varra's home his feet felt suddenly heavy. From behind, he caught the whiff of Jak's tobacco. The little man had lit up.

He saw no movement behind the papered windows of the row house. The roof sagged and one wall bowed, but he thought the structure might have looked like that even before the cavern had partially collapsed.

He walked to the door, a weather-beaten cabin door

probably taken from a wrecked ship long ago. It occurred to him only then that he had no idea what he would say to her. Too late.

He stood before the door for a moment, undecided. Finally he rapped on it, gingerly at first, then harder.

Muffled voices from within, at least two women.

"Who is there?" asked a female voice from behind the closed door. "There's no food here. And I am armed."

For a moment, he could not find his voice. Finally he managed, "I'm looking for Varra. Is she here?"

The door flew open so fast that Cale barely avoided it.

Varra stood in the doorway, dressed in the same homespun dress in which Cale had last seen her. When she saw him, she put her hand to her mouth and her eyes welled. The rusty dagger she held in her other hand fell to the ground.

"You," she said at last.

"I told you I would come back," he said.

She nodded, stared at him. Her mouth opened, closed, and finally she said, "Where were you? Were you hurt in all this?" Her gesture took in the destruction.

"I was . . . nearby," he said. "I was not hurt. I was worried that you were."

"I kept hoping. . . ." she said. She looked away from him and took a deep breath. "I'm glad you are here."

"I am too," he said.

She looked into his eyes and smiled.

He wanted to touch her, to hold her, but did not feel that he was entitled. He wanted her to fly into his arms but she did not. He wanted to smile but it wouldn't come. They looked past and around each other for a few uncomfortable breaths.

From within the row house, a woman's voice called, "Who is it, Varra?"

"It's none of your affair," Varra snapped over her shoulder.

Grumbles answered her but quickly faded.

She turned and looked Cale in the face. Before she could speak, Cale plunged into deep water. "I am here for you," he said.

At that, her eyes flashed. She leaned toward him, perhaps unconsciously.

"I am leaving and I want to take you out of here," he continued. "It's not safe anymore, if it ever was."

She looked alternately surprised, grateful, and afraid. "When?" she said.

"Right now," Cale said. "I can take you to Selgaunt. A city on the surface. In a breath you can be gone from here."

He reached out and took her hand, held it lightly. Her skin was so soft, so warm.

"Now . . ." she said, as though trying out the word. "But. . . ."

"Now," he said. "You can start anew there."

At his words, she looked at him sharply and he wondered what he had said. He saw the struggle on her face but he did not understand it. After a moment, the struggle ended. She took his hand between hers.

"Do you feel something between us? Something . . . special?"

Cale hesitated. He had known her for only hours. Still, he could not deny the . . . connection. Her touch set him aflame. He nodded, and Varra exhaled.

"I do too," she said. "That's why I want *us* to start anew, not just me. Why not, '*We* can start anew there?' "

Cale understood it then. He struggled for an answer, at last decided that he would not lie to her.

"I'm involved in something. Something big. Bigger than even this, I think." He indicated the destruction of Skullport. "I won't be able to be with you, not for a while . . . maybe not ever. My life is . . . moving in unexpected directions."

She stared into his eyes, sadness in the set of her mouth. But resolve, too.

"Then come back when it's over," she said. "Come back when fate permits a 'we.'"

Cale looked at her sorrowful face and could not stop himself. He pulled her close—she did not resist—and softly kissed her lips.

"I will," he said.

With that, he turned and walked away, not knowing if he would ever see her again.

He met up with Jak and Magadon. Both looked questions at him but had the sense not to ask anything. In silence, he drew the darkness around them and pictured in his mind's eye an alley in Selgaunt that he knew well.

His last sight before the darkness moved them across Faerûn was of Varra standing in the crooked doorway of her dilapidated row house.

CHAPTER 4

OLD HAUNTS

Cale, Magadon, and Jak materialized on a deserted side street in Selgaunt's Foreign District. The bustle of a thriving city hit their ears. Cale pulled up his hood and the three companions walked out of the alley to find themselves on Rauncel's Ride, one of the main thoroughfares of Selgaunt.

Selgaunt's plenty contrasted starkly with the ruin and deprivation of Skullport.

Shop after shop lined the broad, paved avenue, their doors thrown open, their proprietors offering seller's smiles at the passersby. The typical mix of travelers, traders, merchants, mercenaries, adventurers, pickpockets, laborers, and beggars populated the walkways. Horse-drawn carts, noble coaches, and humble farmers' wagons loaded with grain and other foodstuffs rolled along the cobblestone streets. Livestock lowed and grunted from roadside pens. A squad of Scepters, Selgaunt's city watchmen, walked amongst the milling crowd, eyes alert for thieves. Each wore black leather armor and a silver-hilted blade, with a green weather-cloak thrown over the whole. Out of habit, Cale avoided eye contact.

Children darted between the pedestrians. The call of street vendors filled the air, rising above the general rush of the crowd to hawk everything from dried flowers to three-day-old bread.

The afternoon sunshine did not quite offset the coolness of the brisk autumn wind. The air carried the faint tang of Inner Sea salt, horse manure, and the aroma of cooking meat.Everything looked, sounded, and smelled exactly as it always had, but Cale could not quite shake the feeling that Selgaunt was different.

Walking beside Cale, Jak said, "Not a slave in sight. Nice to be home, eh?"

It struck Cale then.

Selgaunt was not different; *Cale* was different. Worse, he was not sure the city was his home anymore.

"Cale?" Jak prodded.

Cale kept his brooding to himself and said to Jak only, "It is good to be back, little man."

Though he knew it would sting his skin, he decided to pull back his hood and endure the sunlight. He could not spend the rest of his life hiding from the sun or he would end up like the majority of Skullport's skulkers—pale shadows slinking furtively through the darkness. He wondered how Varra had maintained her dignity while living in such a sunless pit; he wondered, too, what she would think of Selgaunt, gleaming in the sunshine. Thinking of her reminded him of their kiss. He could still taste her lips. It took real effort to put thoughts of her out of his mind. He tucked the stump of his wrist into his cloak pocket and walked along.

"This is a different city than Starmantle," Magadon observed, eyeing the people, high fashions, and elaborately architectured buildings of Selgaunt. "Quite different."

Cale nodded.

In Starmantle, still more or less a frontier town, buildings and fashion were designed to be functional. In Selgaunt, one of the most sophisticated cities in the Heartlands, buildings and fashion were styled to be stunning. Wooden buildings with simple architecture predominated in Starmantle, while in Selgaunt, fully half the buildings were made of stone or brick, and almost all of them had one kind of architectural flourish or another. In fact, an architecturally ordinary home or shop in Selgaunt was a sign of tastelessness at best, financial distress at worst.

"Bit different from Skullport, too," Jak said, and there was no mirth in his voice.

"Truth," Magadon said somberly.

Cale said nothing, merely looked out on the sea of pale faces around him. He had little in common with them anymore, if he ever had. They were human; he was a shade. He wondered if he would happen upon anyone from the Uskevren household: Tamlin, Shamur, or . . . Tazi. The thought summoned a pit in his stomach. He could imagine how they would look upon him now that he was . . . transformed. Nine Hells, even Jak sometimes looked at him with fear in his eyes. Only Varra and Magadon looked at him like he was still a man, and Cale suspected that was because both of them knew darkness almost as well as Cale.

He pushed the maudlin thoughts from his mind and distracted himself by focusing on the passersby, noting weapons, movements, glances. He had not lost his trained eyes, and he picked out the professionals with satisfying ease. The thieves were apparent enough to him that they might as well have been wearing a uniform.

And something else was apparent to him, too—shadows. He was as conscious of the location of shadows as he was of his own hand—those cast by people, by buildings, by carts. They were his tools now; he was connected intuitively to the dark places around him. The realization both comforted and disquieted him.

"I think I'll purchase a new hat," Jak said, eyeing with admiration the wide-brimmed wool cap perched atop the head of a fat merchant with a ratty moustache. The little man doffed his filthy and torn hat and slapped it against his thigh, then replaced it on his head. "Mine is a little road worn. Some new clothes, too, maybe." He eyed his burned pants with dismay.

"We should re-equip entirely while we're here," Magadon said. "Rations. Field gear. Arrows for me. I'll handle that. I assume we won't remain long, Erevis?"

Cale did not know, so he shook his head. "We will see, Mags. It depends on what we can learn."

They had very little to go on. The Sojourner had mentioned the Eldritch Temple of Mystryl but the reference meant nothing to Cale. He thought he knew someone who might be able to help—Elaena, the High Priest of Deneir in Selgaunt. She had healed Jak once, when he had been wounded by a demon, and she, along with all priests of Deneir, valued lore and lost knowledge. She might have heard of the Eldritch Temple. Cale hoped she would remember them and agree to assist.

"Surely we'll be here at least long enough to clean up?" Jak asked. "I mean, look at you two. You look like you've been swimming in a sewer."

Magadon smiled. "We *have* been swimming in a sewer. And you look little better, Jak Fleet."

Jak grinned, doffed his cap, and bowed.

Cale agreed with Magadon's assessment. Skullport *was* a sewer, and its stink still clung tenaciously to his clothes, to his skin, to his soul.

"We ought to fill our bellies, too," Jak said, warming to his subject. "Roadtack and conjured food can sustain a halfling only so long."

Magadon nodded at Jak and smiled. "Especially this halfling."

"That's truth," Jak said, and patted his stomach. "Venison, I say. Or pork."

"Hot beef stew," Magadon said.

Cale forced a smile and nodded agreement. He knew that recent events had left a mark on his friends. Over the last few hours—*hours*, he thought, marveling that so much could have occurred in so short a time—they had fought the Skulls of Skullport, barely escaped a collapsing cavern in the Underdark, journeyed to and from the Plane of Shadow twice, and fought the most powerful spellcaster and mindmage that any of them had ever encountered. Jak and Magadon looked drawn, wrung out. Their banter told Cale that they needed to engage in something ordinary to remind them that all was not slaves, shadows, spells, darkness, and danger. Walking under the sun on the streets of Selgaunt, they looked as relaxed as Cale had seen them in a tenday. They needed human activity. Strange that Cale did not feel the same need.

"Let's take a meal now," Cale said to accommodate his friends. "And gear up. Afterward, we will call on Deneir's temple."

"Elaena," Jak said, nodding. "A good thought. Worth a die cast. But as you said, food first. So follow me. I know a place."

The halfling turned off Rauncel's Ride and led them a few blocks to a clapboard-sided tavern and eatery called The Workbench, frequented by watermen and laborers. Oars, a rusty anchor, and various old tools hung from the walls. The thin tapmaster took in their appearance, wiped his hands on his apron, and frowned. When Cale flashed platinum the man grew immediately solicitous.

Sembia remained Sembia, Cale thought, as he handed over a pair of platinum suns.

Few other patrons sat at The Workbench's sturdy tables, and those who did minded their own affairs.

Cale, Magadon, and Jak enjoyed a hearty meal of day-old chicken stew, stale bread, and an entire wheel of soft, sharp goat cheese. Cale surprised himself by savoring every bite. He could not remember anything ever tasting so good. Perhaps he needed ordinary activity after all.

Afterward, the trio spent an hour in one of Selgaunt's many shopblocks. There, they replaced travel-tattered cloaks, tunics, breeches, and boots, and Magadon re-equipped them with field gear and more hardtack. Cale enjoyed watching Jak haggle with the merchants. The little man was as professional and skillful a haggler as he was a gambler and pickpocket.

By the time they were done, the bell tower of the Temple of Song and the hour-callers on the street announced the fifth hour after noon. They'd enjoyed nearly two hours of peace. It had done them all good.

"Back to it," Cale said, and the three headed toward Temple Avenue.

They walked east along Tormyn's Way, leaving behind the shops and inns of the northwest corner of town. Soon they were moving through narrow avenues lined with residences. The homes, though small, were built of sturdy wood or brick, and even the most modest had a tiled roof—a long distance from the ramshackle squalor of Skullport.

As they moved east, the small structures gave way to grander homes built of quarried and magically-sculpted stone. Squads of Scepters grew more commonplace, as did the presence of carriages.

In the distance ahead, overlooking the city from its perch atop a high rise, stood the crenellated towers and high walls of the ridiculous Hunting Garden of the Hulorn. The thick, gaudy towers of the Hulorn's palace stood behind the garden and just poked their tops over the garden's walls, as though peeking out in embarrassment.

Not far from there, Cale knew, stood the sprawling grounds and manses of Selgaunt's Old Chauncel, including the squat, walled towers of Stormweather. He grew wistful, thinking of his old life.

He had been away from the city only a few tendays, but felt as though he had been gone a lifetime. His stomach clenched when he thought about what he had left behind. Jak must have seen it in his expression.

"You all right?" Jak asked him, looking up with concern.

"Yes," Cale lied. "The light is bothering me some, that's all."

"Of course," Jak said. The little man's gaze looked off toward the Hulorn's palace, toward the abodes of the Old Chauncel. He knew the city as well as Cale.

Jak said, "I left Mistledale after I'd seen twenty winters. I went back once and only once, a few years after leaving. Did I ever tell you about that?"

Cale shook his head.

"I wanted to see the lake where I'd fished as a boy with my father and uncle, to see some of my childhood friends, the hillside home I grew up in. That sort of thing, you know?"

Cale nodded.

"And while I was there I realized that my memory of things had more shine than the things themselves. I realized, too, that sometimes leaving a place changes you, and when you go back, you realize it isn't really your home anymore. That's how it was for me in Mistledale. By the time I came back, I'd changed, grown beyond it. It's sad in a way. Old friends drift away, sometimes even family. But growth is part of life."

"It is, eh?" Cale asked.

"It is," Jak affirmed, and popped his pipe into his mouth. "I think you understand that as well as any."

Cale did not answer, so Jak lit with a tindertwig, took a draw, and blew it out. Eyeing Cale sidelong, he said, "For some people, a place is home. But for men like us, people have to be home. And not just any people. Friends. The friends who live through the changes with us, who grow with us."

"Truly said," Magadon offered.

Cale took Jak's meaning, and it helped him get perspective. He had changed, perhaps grown beyond the Uskevrens. Perhaps he was nostalgic for Stormweather and his old family because they represented the simpler life he'd once known, the smaller stakes. It had not always seemed so then, but he had been an ordinary man when he had served Thamalon the Elder– not a shade, not the First of Five—and events had not felt quite so big as now.

"I hear your words," he said to his friends. "And thank you."

His friends said nothing, merely walked beside him in silence.

Cale knew that he had to adjust—to what he had become and to the scale of events in which he was participating. His days as an ordinary man were long over. He had only a short time to ponder the realization. They rounded a corner and walked through the large granite arch that signified the western end of Temple Avenue.

The wide street stretched before them, teeming as always. Pilgrims, petitioners, and priests crowded the stone-flagged avenue, praying, preaching, and proselytizing. Chants and songs filled the air, with the ring of gongs and chimes. The multitudinous colors and styles of robes, vestments, and cloaks created a swirling sea of colors that ran the length of the street.

The brisk wind and nearness of the bay did not efface the aroma of incense, perfume, and unwashed bodies. The air was syrupy with the smell. Cale inhaled deeply, cleansing his nostrils of the last of Skullport's fetor.

Five temples dominated Temple Avenue—fanes dedicated to Milil, Sune, Deneir, Oghma, and Lliira—though another dozen or so shrines stood in their shadows. Midway down the avenue, the construction on a new temple to Siamorphe, the goddess of hereditary nobility, was progressing apace. Cale knew that the cornerstone had been hallowed and the foundation laid three months earlier. In another month or three, the structure would be complete. The Talendar family, a rival to the Uskevren, was financing the construction. The second son of the Talendar, Vees, had returned from Waterdeep as a priest and vocal advocate of Siamorphe. By financing the building of the Noble Lady's temple, the Talendars hoped to curry favor with the church hierarchy, expand the worship of Siamorphe to the most cosmopolitan city in the Heart lands, and ensconce their son as a high-ranking priest.

Cale smiled. As always, rank was not necessarily earned in Selgaunt. Sometimes it was bought. But from what little Cale knew of Siamorphe's faith, he imagined that things might not go as the Talendar hoped. Bloodline meant everything to the faithful of Siamorphe, but Selgauntans little understood that. Wealth mattered in Selgaunt, not lineage.

Sitting areas for public contemplation dotted the street—stone and wood benches situated under the red and yellow autumn canopies of dwarf maples. Each bench generally shared the shade with one or two monstrous sculptures, the legacy of the late Hulorn's fetish for peculiar statuary. All of the works depicted this or that hybrid monster: manticores, chimerae, owlbears, and the like. Starlings perched in the nooks of the statues and their droppings painted the stone and marble with splashes of white.

Cale, Magadon, and Jak weaved their way into the crowd and moved toward the Hallowed House of Higher Achievement, Deneir's temple, which stood near the eastern end of the avenue, where the street curled back into the city proper.

As they walked through the throng, they saw a gray-robed trio of Ilmatari priests sprinkling flower petals into a fountain and praying to their god for an end to a pox afflicting an outlying village. Dancers in red gossamer and adorned with finger gongs swayed through the crowd, lay worshipers of Sune who promised with the swing of their hips the pleasures of the Firehair's worship. The tallest of the dancers ran her fingertips over Cale's shoulder as she passed. When her painted fingernails came away trailing shadows, her eyes went wide.

As they passed the small but popular shrine to Tymora, the Lady of Luck, Jak and Magadon both walked over and flipped a copper piece into the public offering plate set outside the doors.

"A copper to the Lady returns tenfold in gold," Jak said, uttering a traditional Tymoran prayer of offering. Other passersby did the same, offering the same prayer or a slightly modified version. The priestess standing near the offering plate, garbed in a blue robe chased in silver piping, thanked them all and offered the Lady's benediction.

"Dare much," she said. "And the Lady keep you."

Cale kept his coppers in his pocket. He did not think that the Lady of Luck would appreciate the coins of a servant of the Shadowlord.

Groups of faithful walked past them in close-knit groups, talking amongst themselves, eyeing the wonders of the street. All looked suspiciously at Cale, Jak, and Magadon. Cale knew that he and his companions looked less like worshipers and more like predators. Other than Cale, Jak, and Magadon, and a few pairs of whistle-carrying Scepters on patrol, almost no one else on the avenue bore weapons openly.

Cranks and aberrant philosophers held court on the avenue's walkways, or under the eaves of a maple, shouting sermons and nonsense at anyone with whom they made eye contact. They reminded Cale of the madman who had accosted him back in Skullport. Cale could not remember what the man had said to him but for some reason he thought it important. It escaped him and he put it out of his mind.

A few noble coaches rolled slowly down the center of the road, the occupants looking out from their lacquered havens with looks of benign disdain. Cale knew that worship on Temple Avenue by the nobility was more about status than piety. All noble households had at least a shrine to the family's patron deity within their manse. The rich worshiped in the public temples to see and be seen, mingle with the other rich, flaunt their baubles, make and break alliances, and gossip.

Cale remembered Thamalon once telling him that more deals were done in the churches and festhalls of the city than ever were done across a desk or in a parlor. Cale knew it to be true, and thinking of the Old Owl and his practical wisdom turned Cale sentimental.

To his left, the whitewashed bell tower of the Temple of Song jutted into the sky like the finger of a titan. A quartet of songhornists, accompanied by a shawm player, stood on the temple's portico and softly played. A crowd stood around them, smiling and clapping.

Farther up the avenue stood the sprawling Palace of Holy Festivals, Lliira's temple. Colorful pennons atop its roof flapped in the breeze. Music and laughter leaked from the doors, audible even from a distance.

Across the street from Lliira's temple stood the elegant, soaring spires of Firehair's House, the temple of Sune. The architecture of Sune's temple sported many suggestive protuberances, shafts, openings, and curves. Two flaming braziers shaped like salamanders flanked the tiered stairway that led to the temple's double doors. The priestesses never let the flames in the braziers go out, even in thunderstorms. Beauty was everlasting—that was the message of the ever-burning flames. Sune's temple served not only hedonists, artists, and aesthetes, but also Selgaunt's prostitutes by providing temporary shelter and minor healing magic to those in need. Many such women subsequently converted to the worship of Sune and thereby turned the practice of their livelihood into a kind of worship. Cale remembered that a jest among the men of the Old Chauncel was that the temple's presence had resulted in Selgaunt having some of the most attractive and disease-free working women in the Heartlands.

Jak elbowed Cale in the thigh. "Strange that I do not see a worship hall for Mask. Do you, Magadon?" Jak shaded his eyes with his palm and made a show of looking about.

Magadon chuckled.

Cale smiled and said, "Brandobaris seems to be similarly absent, little man."

Jak laughed and shook his head. "Ah, but that is where you're wrong, my friend."

With the ease of the practiced expert, Jak casually lifted the coin purse from a passing pilgrim, a thin, middle-aged man with a scar running down one cheek. Jak's skill impressed even Cale, who had seen seasoned Night Mask lifters operate.

Jak held up the purse for Cale to see as the pilgrim went on his way.

Jak said, "The Trickster's temples are where I find them. Turns out, that's mostly in the pockets of others." He grinned at Magadon, who wore an appalled expression. "Never fear, Mags. I'm not in the mood to worship today. And I only take the Trickster's Tithe from those who deserve their pockets emptied."

Jak turned and called to the pilgrim, "Goodsir! Goodsir! You dropped this."

The pilgrim turned, saw his purse in Jak's hand, and patted at his empty vest pocket. He seemed too shocked to speak.

Jak jogged up to him and pressed the purse into his hand.

"My mother always said to keep your coin purse in your underlinens. Along with the rest of your jewels. That's sound advice."

Leaving a speechless pilgrim in his wake, Jak sauntered

back to rejoin Cale and Magadon, neither of whom could help but smile.

"Now that, my friends—"

Jak looked past them and froze in mid stride.

Alarmed, Cale whirled, but he saw nothing other than the sea of faces and heads. He started to turn back to Jak, but then saw what Jak had seen.

"Dark and empty," he swore. He could not believe his eyes.

"It cannot be," Jak said behind him.

Sephris Dwendon, Chosen of Oghma and likely madman, walked slowly through the crowd toward the low, stalwart walls of the Sanctum of the Scroll, Oghma's temple. A group of somber priests surrounded him, forming a protective circle and keeping passersby from getting too close. All of the Oghmanyte bodyguards wore white shirts, white trousers, and black vests adorned with embroidered characters from a variety of alphabets—the typical outerwear of priests of Oghma. Each also wore a crimson harlequin mask over their eyes and an iron mace at their belts. They eyed the crowd warily but did not seem to notice Cale's and Jak's stares.

Sephris wore a simple red robe and worn shoes. He carried a book in the crook of his elbow. The loremaster's distant gaze carried sadness, and he did not seem to see those around him.

Cale did not remember Sephris being so tall. The loremaster stood half-a-head taller than any of the bodyguards, almost as tall as Cale.

"What is it?" Magadon asked, stepping beside him.

"That man should be dead," Cale said, and nodded at Sephris.

"Which? The tall one with the Oghmanytes?"

Cale nodded.

Jak stepped beside them and added, "The slaadi killed him, gutted him. We saw his body."

"Then he could be a slaad," Magadon said, eyeing

Sephris coldly. "Shapechanged to resemble your man. Remember Nestor?"

Cale remembered. Nestor had been a comrade of Magadon's. One of the slaadi had killed him and taken his form.

"I remember," Cale said. "But we just saw both slaadi hours ago. You two killed the third. This . . . this would have required several tendays to put in place."

"They can teleport from place to place quickly, Erevis," Magadon said. "They could have been moving between Skullport, the Sojourner's lair, and here. Or there could be another slaad that we haven't yet seen. We should be certain."

Cale nodded. Magadon was right.

"If he is a slaad," Cale said. "Then we kill him on the street. We'll deal with the Scepters afterward."

To his surprise, Magadon and Jak both nodded, faces grim.

Cale put his hand to the velvet mask in his pocket and whispered the words to a spell that allowed him to see dweomers.

Once cast, the spell was indiscriminate in its application. Many trinkets, weapons, rings, and robes of passersby lit up as they walked through Cale's field of vision. He ignored them and picked his way through the press toward Sephris, with Magadon and Jak beside him. The three circled wide and fell in beside and slightly behind the loremaster and his bodyguard priests.

The maces of the bodyguards all shone a soft red, and two wore magical belts that glowed, but Sephris's body did not show an aura in Cale's sight, as it would if he were a shapechanged slaad. Only a single ring on his right hand radiated an aura.

"He's no slaad," Cale said.

Jak blew out a soft whistle. "Then they must have brought him back. He was dead and they brought him back. Dark."

Cale said nothing but his skin went gooseflesh. Not because Sephris had been returned from the dead, but because too many things seemed to be happening at just the right time, in just the right place. Had they not stopped to take a meal and re-equip, they would not have seen Sephris at all. Cale found it increasingly difficult to deny the presence of Fate in events. He felt as though he were being propelled toward something, something important, something he might not like.

"Perhaps I should have thrown a copper into Tymora's plate, after all," he muttered.

"What did you say?" Jak asked.

"Nothing. Speaking to myself."

Like Sephris sometimes did, he thought, and he did not like where those thoughts started to lead.

Any idea of asking Elaena and the temple of Denier for assistance vanished. If Fate had determined that Cale would happen upon Sephris, then Cale would consult him.

Riven despised Selgaunt's Dock District, always had. The alleys all stank of fish, puke, and urine, and with rare exceptions, the food served in the ramshackle inns along the waterfront smelled only mildly better. The whores were all too cheap and the sailors all too drunk. The place was a cesspit of human weakness.

Beside him, Azriim, still in the flesh of a half-drow, walked along as though he might step in something unpleasant at any moment. Despite the slaad's efforts, his otherwise shiny black boots had picked up a coat of road muck. Riven took satisfaction in the slaad's unhappiness about that.

Dolgan, once more in his guise as a bald, muscular, Cormyrean axman, stumped along beside Azriim. Unlike Azriim, with the prominent gray streak that cut through his hair, Dolgan's new form showed no telltale sign that he had been partially transformed into a gray slaad.

"We should not be walking the docks undisguised," Riven said. "Cale may have returned to the city."

Cale had magically transported himself somewhere with Fleet and Magadon. Selgaunt seemed as probable a destination as any.

"Why would he?" Dolgan said. "This place is a hole."

Riven thought the dolt's words ironic, considering he had worn vomit on his clothes as though it were a badge of honor. But he kept his thoughts to himself and said, "He would return because he's got nowhere else to go."

"Let's count on him being here, then, shall we?" said Azriim as he surveyed the piers. "If he shows, grand. And if not, then not."

Riven grunted noncommittally. He still had not made up his own mind what he would do when the *First* of the Shadowlord showed. He had laid the groundwork to make Cale think him a possible ally. Riven was not yet certain that was his best play.

"What type of ship are we seeking?" he asked, eyeing the wharfs.

Ships thronged the bay and a forest of masts dotted the sky—schooners, carracks, longships, barges, frigates, caravels—and most of them flew a pennon denoting their country or city of origin. Dock hands shouted, cursed, and sang as they furled and unfurled sails, loaded and unloaded crates of cargo. The fat harbormaster and his agents prowled the piers, assessing cargo taxes, recording the names of berthed ships and their captains. Gulls squawked in the air above. Deckhands on a nearby caravel took shots at the birds with a sling. They missed every time.

"Something in particular," Azriim answered.

Riven spit and said, "You won't find one with silk sheets and a feather bed."

Azriim missed his sarcasm, or chose to ignore it. "I

know. Isn't that unfortunate? Sailors." He tsked. "Oh. Here's the very thing, now."

They stopped before a twin-masted, square-sailed cog. The blazing red and gold pennon dangling from the midmast declared its port of origin to be Bezantur, a city in Thay. Several other flags and pennons adorned the masts. Riven had no idea of their meanings. A stylized demonic face decorated the prow, mouth open, fangs bare. Riven could not read the writing on the hull and would be damned to admit as much to the slaadi.

"Demon Binder," Azriim said aloud. "What a quaint name."

Deckhands climbed the ship's rigging, swabbed the decks, and formed a human chain to load barrels and crates from the pier into the hold. The ship would be setting to soon enough.

Riven knew enough about the Thayans to think it likely that the ship carried more than barrels in its hold. Thayans were notorious slavers. Slavery and trafficking in slaves were technically illegal in Sembia, but the right coins in the right palms made enforcement lax, particularly when the ship carrying the human cargo was merely stopping in Sembian ports for a refit.

"Thayan," Dolgan observed, unnecessarily.

"See the captain there, on the sterncastle?" Azriim asked. "My, he *is* a nice dresser. And that thin fellow beside him, with the earring, beard, and long hair, leaning on the rail? That must be the first mate."

Riven saw the two men to whom Azriim referred. The captain wore a fitted jacket with shiny buttons, black pantaloons, high boots, and a tailored, high-collared red shirt and vest. A cutlass hung from his belt. The first mate wore similar clothes, but without the jacket and cutlass. Instead, he wore a long fighting knife on his hip.

Riven understood immediately what the slaadi proposed to do.

"We could just purchase passage," he said, not because

he cared about the slavers, but because he was not sure how they could easily dispose of bodies. Besides, if the ship boasted one of the notorious and powerful Thayan Red Wizards as a passenger, things could get ugly very fast.

Dolgan chuckled.

Azriim grinned. "Now where is the enjoyment in merely buying passage?"

Riven looked into the slaad's mismatched eyes. "I did not realize that enjoyment was the object. Efficiency and effectiveness are the only things I'm interested in."

"Enjoyment is the only goal worth pursuing," Azriim said, still smiling.

Frustrated with the slaad's unprofessionalism, Riven could not hold his tongue. "You and your boy here are sloppy. You'll leave a trail."

"Boy?" Dolgan growled.

Azriim's grin widened. "Indeed we will. And that's the very point. Now, I'm sure there's something you can do in this city to occupy yourself for a time. At the very least, get some better attire. Really. I'm embarrassed to be seen with you. Return here tonight, say, around the tenth hour. You are to be a wealthy merchant with a secret destination. Dolgan and I will . . . relieve the captain and first mate of their duties and prepare the crew for your arrival."

Riven saw no point in arguing further. He shook his head in disgust, spun on his heel, and walked off. As he headed away from the slaadi and the docks, still stewing, he saw a trio of stray dogs slink down an alley. He thought of his girls and the anger went out of him.

He would have gone to his old garret already to check on them but he had not had a moment away from the slaadi, and he had not wanted the creatures to know of his girls. He knew well that affection for anything was a weakness others could exploit.

He wandered for a time, circling back a few blocks to ensure that neither of the slaadi was following him.

Neither was.

Relieved, he turned a corner and headed south and west, toward the Warehouse District. He would take a moment to check in on the girls.

After the assassin walked away, Dolgan said, "I think we should kill him. Father is wrong about him."

"You have made your views clear," Azriim replied, looking up and down the wharfs.

Azriim needed to procure the services of a second ship. He agreed with Riven that the priest of Mask would not easily give up his pursuit, so he was planning a misdirection.

"I just made them clear again," Dolgan said, and spat a glob of saliva onto the street. "He called me 'boy'."

"He certainly did," Azriim said, and grinned.

Azriim was fond of Riven. He regarded the human as a fosterling, not unlike the way in which the Sojourner regarded Azriim and Dolgan. It amused and pleased him to have a ward of his own. He turned and faced his broodmate.

"He *is* an ally, Dolgan. He hates this priest of Mask, is that not clear? The Sojourner read his mind, is that not enough?"

"But . . ."

"Dolgan, of the two of us that are standing here now, one of us is stupid." He let the meaning sink in; as he expected, it took a moment. "Let us leave the decisions to the other one, eh?"

Dolgan's brow furrowed and he showed his teeth in a snarl. "One of us standing here is the stronger, too."

"True," Azriim acknowledged. "Which is why I leave the axe work to you. Now leave the thinking to me. Done?"

Dolgan shrugged noncommittally and chewed his lip. Azriim decided to take that as acquiescence.

"Come," he said, and started walking the wharf. He did

not seem able to keep mud from his boots, so he resigned himself to a layer of filth.

"Where?" Dolgan asked.

"You will see."

Azriim found what he wanted within an hour—a large, three-masted open sea caravel sporting the scarlet and green flag of Urlamspyr. He knew the Sembian caravel would be faster than the Thayan cog.

An open-mouthed wooden porpoise adorned the caravel's prow; it held in its jaws a representation of a coffer filled with gold coins. Azriim smiled. Everything in Sembia related back to coin in one way or another. He saw only a few crewmen on deck, tying off lines or climbing in the rigging. Most of the hands must have been on shore leave.

"Remain here," Azriim said. "I will return apace."

"Another ship?" Dolgan asked. "Why?"

"Because I have learned to respect the doggedness of our priest of Mask."

"Huh?" Dolgan asked. "Doggedness?"

Azriim patted his broodmate on his muscular shoulder. "Remember, Dolgan—I do the thinking. Remain here."

Though it galled him a bit, Azriim changed his facial structure to eliminate the half-drow features. As he walked, he lightened his skin, rounded his eyes and ears, and softened his cheekbones. Then, donning a business-like smile, he walked down the pier toward the gangplank. He hailed the first sailor who made eye contact, a thin youth who had seen fewer than twenty winters.

"Is the captain aboard?" he called up.

The sailor rested his hands on the rail and squinted. "Who wants to know?" The human had a hole where one of his front teeth should have been.

"I do," Azriim answered, and flicked a fivestar up to the sailor.

The youth caught it and the coin vanished into his sash belt.

"He is," said the youth, and he vanished from the side. From above, Azriim heard the sailor calling, "Lubber to see the Captain!"

Azriim walked to the edge of the wooden gangplank and waited. He knew it would be rude to go aboard without an invitation. The other crewmen aboard the ship eyed him as they worked, laughing and making the occasional snide comment at Azriim's expense. Azriim ignored them. He had business to do. And besides, they dressed like buffoons.

With his left hand, he drew one of his wands—a finger-long shaft of ash capped with gold—and palmed it.

After a time, Azriim heard the call, "Captain on deck," as it passed from sailor to sailor. Hearing this, Azriim deemed at least some of the crew, and probably the captain, to be ex-navy. He rebuked himself for not anticipating that. He could have adopted the form of a scarred veteran. Still, coin spoke with a loud enough voice to a Sembian crew.

The captain appeared at the top of the gangplank. Black hair worn in a short helmcut topped a clean-shaven, pockmarked face. Bags hung under his piggish eyes. He wore fitted wool breeches, high boots, a broad belt with a silver buckle, and a stiff-collared blue shirt. A broadsword and dagger hung from his hip. He did not advance down the gangplank to offer Azriim his hand.

"I am captain of *Dolphin's Coffer*," he said, his voice loud and resonant. "Captain Sertan."

Azriim made a bow and wasted no time. "Well met, Captain. I need your services and that of your ship."

The captain frowned. "You want a berth on my ship? You know where we're headed, do you?"

Azriim reached into his shirt pocket with his right hand and withdrew three rubies, each as big around as a fivestar. Several sailors in the rigging caught their sparkle and whistled.

With onlookers focused on his extended right hand,

Azriim used his body to shield his left hand. He surreptitiously pointed the tip of the wand at the captain and mentally activated its magic, which made the target open to suggestion. Azriim contained a smile when the captain's expression slackened—a telltale sign that the magic had worked.

Azriim said, "No. I want to reserve your entire ship into my service, and I want you to head where I request. No questions asked. This is half of what I'm willing to pay."

Captain Sertan eyed the gems and licked his lips. He might have agreed to Azriim's request even without the aid of the wand. There was no cargo he could carry that would profit him more than what Azriim offered.

"That sounds quite reasonable, friend," said the captain, and he walked down the gangplank. His voice had the lazy lilt of the enspelled. "Tell me more."

Azriim smiled in a comradely fashion. "I want you to set to tonight and sail for Traitor's Isle. Anchor there and wait for up to a tenday. I and my two companions will meet you there, probably within only a few days."

"Meet us? You won't be aboard?"

"Not at first. But we will show eventually." He pressed the rubies into the captain's hands. "And if we do not, keep what I have paid you and be about your own affairs."

"Very well," the captain said. "I will recall the crew."

Azriim smiled. "Excellent! But first show me your ship." Azriim needed to memorize the appearance of the vessel, to make teleporting there easier.

They turned and walked up the gangplank. Azriim knew that the wand's effect would last only a few days, but he figured that would be long enough. Cale would either show within that time or he would not. And if Azriim had need, he could always renew the effect of the wand once he came aboard near Traitor's Isle.

He looked the captain up and down and said, "I admire your garb, by the way."

CHAPTER 5

ANGRY GHOSTS

Cale, Jak, and Magadon followed Sephris and the Oghmanytes as they walked toward the Sanctum of the Scroll.

"He must have moved into the temple," Jak said. "Or they forced him to move there."

"So it appears," Cale said.

When they first had met Sephris, the Chosen of Oghma had lived with a caretaker in a small residence near Temple Avenue. Sephris had covered the walls of his home with erudite mathematical scribblings. That was where Jak and Cale later had found his corpse, gutted by the slaadi. The creatures had murdered the loremaster for helping Cale and Jak. Cale guessed that the Oghmanyte high priest had moved Sephris into the temple for his own security.

"Do you think he will be . . . upset when he sees us?" Jak asked. He twirled his pipe in his fingers, a nervous habit.

"We'll soon know," Cale answered.

"Who is he talking to?" Magadon asked, indicating Sephris.

From their position behind and slightly oblique to Sephris and the Oghmanytes, they could see the lore-master in profile. His lips moved continuously, though he appeared to be talking to no one in particular. Cale was too far away to read them, but he knew well enough what the words were.

"He is talking to himself," Cale said. "Calculating."

"Calculating?" Magadon asked.

Jak said, "He does mathematics, the kind no one understands but him. That's how he knows things. He's always doing it."

Magadon's eyes narrowed. "What do you mean, 'knows things'? Is he a prophet?"

"Of sorts," Cale said. "Wait, and watch."

The priests neared the tiered steps that led up to the double doors of Oghma's temple.

Still muttering as he walked, Sephris pulled a stylus—the kind with a sharpened tip that was used to write in wet clay—from an inner pocket of his robes and pushed up his sleeve. He pressed the stylus's tip into his forearm and began to write on his flesh. His expression never changed, even when he started to bleed.

"Gods," Magadon oathed, aghast. "Is he mad?"

"Maybe," Jak said. "But I've never before seen him do anything self-destructive. What's wrong with him?"

Cale shook his head.

At first the priests accompanying Sephris did not notice his wounds. When they did, one of them shouted and the whole group stopped. Another of the Oghmanytes, a young, brown-haired woman, gently pried the stylus from Sephris's fingers, all while speaking what Cale took to be gentle reassurance. The loremaster calculated throughout, offering the woman only token resistance. Another of the priests, a middle-aged man with wavy blond hair, stepped forward, took Sephris's bleeding forearm in his hands, and whispered what Cale assumed to be a healing spell. The wounds in Sephris's arm closed.

"This may not be a good idea, after all," Jak offered.

Cale agreed. It appeared that Sephris may have truly gone mad.

"Agreed," he said. "Let's see where his sums take him. If he wants to see us, he will let us know. Otherwise, we go to Elaena."

The priests escorting Sephris closed their circle more tightly around the loremaster and hustled him forward. He moved with them, as stiff as an automaton, still calculating. The group reached the stairs and started up.

Sephris put three stairs under him and stopped, head cocked to the side. The priests tried to pull him along but he resisted.

"Here we go," Cale said.

The three of them continued their slow walk forward, eyeing Sephris.

One of the priests asked Sephris a question and the whole group tried to move him forward, but the loremaster held his ground. He irritably pushed away the hands that tried to force him up the stairs. He turned around, numbers and formulae still tumbling from his lips. He dropped the book under his arm and scanned the crowd as he calculated. The gazes of his escorts followed his.

Sephris's eyes found Cale and Cale read his lips: " . . . two and two are four," the loremaster said.

Korvikoum, thought Cale.

They stared at one another over the crowd of passersby. Sephris looked to Magadon, to Jak, and Cale did not see pleasure in the loremaster's expression. More like . . . resignation.

The little man waved tentatively.

Sephris did not wave back. The priests escorting him saw Jak's wave, Sephris's stare, and frowned. Brows furrowed; hands went to maces. Quiet words passed between them. Two spoke aloud the words to spells that Cale guessed to be divinations. They were examining the trio. They reported whatever they learned to the tallest priest in the group, who nodded. The two others tried to turn Sephris around and guide him up the steps.

"What do we do?" Jak asked softly.

Before Cale could answer, Sephris pushed away the two priests near him—demonstrating surprising strength—and started down the stairs toward Cale. The two priests caught him quickly and stopped him cold. Sephris struggled, began to shout numbers, formulae. The loremaster's words made no sense to Cale. He sounded like the madmen elsewhere on the street. Passersby watched with wide eyes.

"What in the Hells are they doing to him?" Jak said.

"Come on," Cale said, and hurried forward.

The two priests forcibly turned Sephris around and bodily carried him up the stairs. He continued to shout over his shoulder, kicking and flailing. The rest of the priests moved to the base of the stairs to intercept Cale. There, they formed up and waited, their expressions hard, their hands on mace hafts.

Cale did not slow until he stood face to face with the tallest of the four.

"We are here to see Sephris Dwendon," Cale said, and started to push past the priest. The man put a hand to Cale's chest and halted his advance. With effort, Cale resisted the urge to punch him in the face.

"He is not seeing anyone at this time," the priest said. He stood a head shorter than Cale, but looked to be built as solid as a tree.

"That's a horse's pile," Jak said.

On the stairs above, Sephris struggled furiously in the grasp of his fellow priests.

"The three are come," the loremaster called. "Let me go. Let them come. I need to hear their words to finish the equation."

Jak tried to dart past the priests, but they stepped before him and blocked his way. They started to draw their maces and Jak backed off, palms raised.

Cale stared into the eyes of the priest. He could not control the shadows that sweated from his pores.

The priest's eyes widened behind his scarlet mask but to his credit, he did not back down.

"He needs our words," Cale said, his voice low. "You heard him."

"You heard him," Jak echoed, nodding.

"What did they just say?" Sephris shouted from above. "What did they just say? I know their sums. Let them come, now! It is important."

The priests trying to manhandle Sephris up the stairs had not managed to get the loremaster very far along. Both of their masks sat askew on their faces. Both were huffing.

A crowd started to gather at the base of the stairway, looking on. Cale could feel dozens of eyes on his back.

The priests looked twitchy but did not stand aside.

"I will summon the Scepters," the priest said.

"He wants to see us," Cale answered, and nodded up at Sephris.

"That is not his decision," the priest said, his mouth a hard line. The other three priests shifted their stances nervously.

"Not his decision?" Jak exclaimed. "We are his friends. He's not your slave."

Before the priest could reply, another priest appeared at the top of the stairs, above Sephris and the priests wrestling with him. He wore an elaborate black vest embroidered with gold thread. A neatly trimmed dark beard housed a severe mouth. He called to the priests below.

"Enough! Veen, let them come up! Now. Enough, loremaster," he said to Sephris. "They are allowed to pass."

Veen, the priest in front of Cale, looked relieved. He and his fellows stepped out of the way and the three companions hurried up the steps, two at a time. Behind them, Veen ordered the crowd to move along and the four Oghmanytes fell in behind Cale and his comrades.

The two priests who had tried to restrain Sephris released him. The loremaster stood between the sweating priests, gasping and still calculating as he waited for Cale, Jak, and Magadon to approach. He appeared to be counting their steps as they climbed. When they stood before him, he said, "Three of you, on the ninth day of the ninth month during the fifth hour after noon." His gaze looked not at Cale but through him. To Cale's surprise, Sephris's voice lacked its typical mania-fed intensity. "The variables are . . . complex."

"Loremaster," Cale said. "We are surprised to see you."

"I am not surprised to see you," Sephris said, and gave a mirthless smile. Cale saw an unexpected hardness in the loremaster's expression. He remembered Sephris's words to them when they had called to his spirit after his death—*Release me, Erevis Cale. My time on Toril is complete. It has not summed to zero.* The loremaster had seemed at peace then, for the first and only time since Cale had made his acquaintance.

"What have they done to you?" Jak softly asked, and stared accusingly at the two priests to either side of Sephris. They did not meet the little man's gaze.

Sephris ignored the question, looked Cale up and down, and said, "The darkness has found you, First of Five. Soaked you. And you think it is done. But it has only begun. There is more, much more, yet to come. To all of us. Did you know that? Did you know what you were doing? What you were causing?"

Cale felt Jak's and Magadon's eyes on him. The priests, too, stared holes into him.

He swallowed and managed to say, "I've done what I've had to. I can't always see the consequences."

"Come inside, Sephris," called the bearded priest at the top of the stairs. "You can speak with them inside. Come."

"You do not see them because you do not want to see them, First of Five," Sephris said. He spun and stalked up the stairs.

The six Ogmanytes fell in behind him, along with Jak, Cale, and Magadon. Cale's legs felt heavier with each step.

❧ ❧ ❧ ❧ ❧

Riven sat for more than an hour in the late afternoon shadows across the street from the scribe's shop. His old garret, adjacent to the shop, stood dark and closed.

At last he saw what he had come to see and his brewing anger dissipated. A butcher's boy hurried through the street traffic with a package of wet cloth in his hand. He carried it to the door of the scribe's store, knocked, and waited, shifting anxiously from foot to foot. When no one responded to his knock, he opened the door and took a step inside.

The fat scribe appeared in the doorway, irritated, and hustled him out.

"I told you not to bring that into my shop," the scribe said.

"Then answer my knock, goodsir," the boy said, and pushed the package into the scribe's hands.

The scribe fumbled with a retort, managed nothing, pushed a few coins into the boy's hand, and hurried him off. The boy ran past Riven, never noticing him.

The scribe—Riven could not remember his name—unwrapped the cloth to reveal a pile of boiled meat scraps. Seemingly satisfied, he retrieved two shallow buckets he kept near his stoop and put equal portions of the scraps in each.

Whistling a tune and nodding at a passerby, he carried the buckets to the doorway of Riven's garret. He used a key to open the door and entered. Some bustling sounds issued from just within. After a moment, he exited with another bucket and put both down on the ground.

"Come, girls!" he called, and gave a whistle so loud and piercing that Riven figured the sailors back in the Dock District had covered their ears. "Here, dogs!"

The few passersby on the street eyed the scribe curiously but otherwise paid him no heed.

Riven waited, watching, expectant, hopeful. To his surprise, his heart was racing.

"Come on, girls!" the scribe called again. "Are you out there? Here!"

The scribe put his fingers to his mouth and was about to unleash another whistle on the world when two small, four legged figures padded out of an alley to Riven's left and started across the street.

Riven could not contain a grin when he saw his girls.

"There you are," said the scribe. He nudged the bucket of scraps with his toe. "Come now. Mealtime. It's boiled organ meat. Very good. And water I drew this morning."

The dogs pelted across the street, tails wagging, but skidded to a stop halfway. They stood in the street, noses in the air, sniffing. Both of their tails went stiff, then began to wag. The older bitch turned an excited circle, chuffing. Her whelp fairly jumped on her back in excitement.

Riven's grin broadened.

The girls looked in Riven's direction and bounded toward his hiding place, tongues lolling. That they had recognized his scent gave Riven more pleasure than anything had in a long while.

"Dogs!" the scribe called, and stomped his foot. "No! Come, here! Here! Beware the wagons!"

The dogs darted out of the way of two vegetable carts

pulled by mules and crossed the street.

Riven rose from the shadows.

The scribe saw him and his expression fell. He reached for a post to help him keep his feet.

The girls swarmed Riven, jumping up on his legs, yipping. He held a hand down and they licked his fingers. He scratched their ears, petted their flanks, each in turn. They looked exactly as they had when he had left them. Both were well fed. The scribe had kept his word.

"You," called the scribe across the street, a nervous tremor in his voice. "You've returned."

Despite his delight at seeing the girls, Riven put on his professional sneer before walking across the street. The girls trailed him, circled him, tails wagging. He found it difficult to look intimidating with two small dogs jumping about his legs and yapping.

The scribe watched him approach, mouth open, as though he wanted to speak, but said nothing.

"I told you I would check on you from time to time," Riven said, and kept his voice hard.

The scribe nodded rapidly enough to shake his paunch. "Yes. I've done as you asked. You see?" He pointed at the buckets of scraps, the other bucket of water.

"I don't recall *asking*," Riven said.

For a moment, the scribe lost his tongue. "Yes. Well, they're good dogs. Very good. They come every day." He kneeled and patted their flanks with genuine affection. They licked his hand but quickly returned to circle excitedly around Riven. "Look how happy they are to see you," the scribe said, standing. "They've even forgotten their food."

Riven had trouble keeping his expression hostile.

"You've done well," Riven said, and it was the best show of appreciation he could manage. He left unstated the fact that he would have killed the scribe without hesitation had he done any less. "I will be leaving again soon. But I will be back for them. Until I am, keep doing as you have. You have enough coin?"

"Of course," the scribe said.

Riven had paid him enough previously to care for the dogs for a year or more.

"Good. Go, now." Riven waved him back to his shop. "Be about your business. I want to check on my garret in privacy."

The scribe looked to Riven, to the dogs, and almost smiled. He was wise enough to keep a straight face, however, and melted back into his shop.

Riven watched him go, then gathered the three buckets and entered the garret with the girls.

The moment he shut the door behind him, he sank to the floor and put the buckets before him.

"Eat, girls," he said.

They seemed more interested in him than the food, so he accommodated them with stomach rubs and head scratching. Finally, he coaxed them into eating. As always, they shared space around the bucket rather than squabbling for position as most dogs would.

"No rivalry for First and Second, eh?" he said. The older bitch turned to regard him with a question in her brown eyes and scraps dangling from her jaws. He only smiled and she returned to her meal.

Afterward he spent a few hours with his girls, doing nothing more than playing or petting them. He wondered what they did all day, and the wondering made him worry. They could run afoul of a wagon cart, a horse, or some petty bastards like the pirates Riven had left dead on the streets of Skullport.

His girls were gentle creatures—he had no idea why—but he did know that gentleness was not rewarded on the street. He had learned that lesson often in his youth. But somehow his girls had managed to survive without becoming vicious.

He watched as they ran circles around the room,

barking, nipping playfully at each other, licking him, tackling each other. They were friends, inasmuch as dogs could be friends.

"Friends," he said softly, and pondered.

The bearded priest who had called down from the top of the stairs awaited them just outside the temple's double doors.

"Welcome to the Sanctum," he said to Cale, Magadon, and Jak, though the hardness of his voice belied his words.

Engraved characters from a dozen or more Faerûnian alphabets covered the verdigris-stained copper double doors of the Sanctum of the Scroll. Cut into the smooth stone lintel above the doors was a phrase in the common tongue that captured the pith of Oghma's doctrine: *Strength can move only mountains. Ideas can shake worlds.*

Magadon nudged Cale, nodded at the inscription, and said, "Can you mark that?"

Cale nodded, read it for the guide.

"True, that," Magadon said, as they entered the temple.

The double doors opened directly onto a small foyer beyond which stood the worship hall itself. Cale welcomed the shelter from the late afternoon sun. Once within the foyer, the priests uttered a short invocation and removed the masks they wore.

Within the worship hall, small wooden desks stood in a circle around a lectern on a raised dais. Acolytes in unadorned black vests sat at a third or so of the desks, copying manuscripts, scrolls, even entire books. They did not look up from their work. Wooden shelves taller than Cale and stuffed with sheaves of parchment and scrolls covered much of the walls. A small dome composed entirely of glass capped the ceiling. Sunlight poured in through it. Several doors led out of the worship hall.

Cale knew the services in Oghma's temple were often as much a classroom lesson as a sermon. The priesthood frequently offered lectures on subjects as broad as the history of the Creator Races and planar mechanics, and as narrow as brick making, leather working, and literacy. Oghmanytes served Oghma the Binder by encouraging creative thought and disseminating knowledge and ideas. Cale wondered if they maintained a lending library, like the Temple of Deneir.

"I will inform High Loremaster Yannathar of our visitors," the middle-aged priest with the beard said to Sephris.

"Of course you will, Hrin," Sephris said dismissively. "Tell him also what you suspect, for it is truth—these *are* the men who were indirectly responsible for my death. Tell the High Loremaster that they, like Undryl Yannathar himself, questioned my spirit after my body's death. But unlike him, they at least had the good grace to let me sleep again after they'd had their answers."

Hrin flushed at that. Sephris continued. "Tell him, too, that I am in no danger from them, or at least no more than the entirety of this realm is in danger from them."

Cale flushed at that. Sephris went on. "And tell him finally that I am tired but that I serve the Binder and this temple still. Do you understand all that I just said?"

Hrin nodded curtly. He and his fellow priests stood around for a moment, embarrassed.

"His heart will fail him in five hundred thirty-two days," Sephris muttered as he watched Hrin walk away. He came back to himself and said to Cale and his comrades, "Follow me."

The loremaster led them away from the priests, into the worship hall, and through one of several doors that lined the walls. He did not speak as they went. They walked dim, windowless corridors lined with framed maps until they came to a small conference room. A large slate hung from one of the walls and five chairs sat around a rectangular table set before it. A shelf against one wall held sheaves of papers and bound scrolls. Sunlight leaked through a small window to provide light. Cale avoided the beams.

"Sit," Sephris ordered, and they did. The loremaster did not sit; instead, he went to the slate on the wall, took a piece of chalk in his hand, looked at it, and . . . closed his fist over it without writing anything. He turned to the table and looked at Jak, at Magadon, at Cale. His eyes were not friendly.

"Darkness follows you three with the certainty that night follows day. A storm dogs you all. Do you sense it?"

"You do not even know me, priest," Magadon said.

Sephris laughed, a barking, derisive sound. "No. But I know of you."

"You are mistaken," Magadon said.

Sephris grinned evilly and said, "Would you like a number, Magadon devilspawn? There are Nine Hells. Your father rules—"

"You close your mouth," Magadon said, flushing red. He rose from his chair, his pale eyes ablaze. The guide's hands were fists.

Cale put a hand on Magadon's arm to calm him.

"Who is he, to speak of me?" Magadon said angrily to Cale, but sat back down at Cale's and Jak's urging.

"I am a dutiful servant of my god, devilspawn," Sephris said, his tone bitter. "Nothing more. But nothing less. You have come, so you must listen."

"What have they done to you, Sephris?" asked Jak. "You are . . . bitter."

"They've done naught but what you did, Jak Fleet," Sephris answered. "Use me for your own ends, as you hope to now."

Cale understood it then, and the words came out before he could stop them.

"You did not want to come back."

Sephris stared at Cale for a moment, then slammed the chalk against the slate so hard it splintered in his grasp.

"Of course I did not want to come back! Bitter?" He glared at the little man. "I have every right to be bitter, Jak Fleet. What once was a gift is now a curse. My mind is filled with numbers and formulae, whether I am awake or asleep. The seven words you just spoke, the number of buttons on your tunic, the number of steps it takes me to reach the market, the number of worshipers in the hall, the number of priests in this . . . *prison*." He looked at the three companions. "Numbers haunt me. Answers torment me. Do you see, mindmage?" he spat at Magadon. "*That* is who I am and why I speak to you of your lineage. I *know*. There is no rest for me except in death, and even that is denied me."

Sephris stopped, took a deep breath, and gathered himself.

Jak and Magadon stared at him, too dumbfounded to speak.

"But my wants in this matter are secondary, First of Five," Sephris said softly to Cale. "And two and two are and always shall be four. What is, is."

Cale could think of nothing to say. Sephris had allowed himself to return from the dead when his high priest had called because he had thought it his duty as a priest, as a Chosen. The latter realization made Cale squirm in his chair. But he reminded himself that he had made no promises to the Shadowlord.

Sephris smiled at him, then asked in a conspiratorial tone, "You see it, don't you?" The smile was not friendly. "It is an ugly truth, what we bear. What you will bear is uglier than most. Prepare yourself."

Cale decided to let the reference to "we" pass. Instead, he said, "You know why we've come, Sephris. Tell us what we want to know and we will leave you be."

Sephris replied, "Of course I know why you've come. Do you?"

Cale shook his head. "I do not understand."

"You are a variable in a larger equation. I am looking through you, through all of you, trying to solve for the darkness behind you." After a pause, he added, "In all permutations one thing always occurs: Many will die because of you, First of Five."

Cale's skin went gooseflesh. He could not look at Magadon or Jak, not then.

"You do not know that," he said to Sephris, and his words sounded empty even to him.

"Do I not?" asked the loremaster.

"Then help us," Jak said to Sephris. "We don't want that to happen."

"Wants are secondary," Sephris said with a nasty smirk.

Cale could take no more of Sephris's self-pity and deliberate obfuscation. He stared daggers at the loremaster.

"Help me stop it, old fool. If knowledge is your curse, then tell me what you know. If there are permutations, then we can control outcomes. Stop the cryptic clues and tell me what I need to know."

"Being cryptic is my lot," Sephris answered in an infuriatingly calm tone. "Have you not noticed? And control is an illusion. Is that how you sleep, First?"

Cale ground his teeth and barely contained an expletive. Shadows poured from his flesh. The room dimmed.

"And so it begins," Sephris said softly.

The door to the conference chamber flew open and Veen appeared, backed by three more priests. The Oghmanytes must have been scrying the chamber or watching through a peephole.

"Is all well, Chosen One?" Veen asked.

Sephris chuckled, waved a hand, and said, "As well as it gets, Veen. Begone."

Veen eyed each of the three comrades.

"Do not tax the loremaster with your questions. We will be nearby." He closed the door.

Cale's anger went out the door with Veen. He just felt . . . tired. He sensed a doom overtaking him and he was too fatigued to outrun it.

"Let's leave here," Magadon said to him. "This is futile. And he is mad."

"You won't help us, Sephris?" Jak said, obviously hurt.

Sephris glared at Jak. "Jak Fleet. My *friend*. A seventeen going on a two. Of course I will help you." He looked up to the ceiling and said in a loud voice, "For I am a dutiful servant of the Binder!"

"We don't need your help," Cale said, and stood. "And I don't want it."

Sephris chuckled. "As I said: Wants are secondary."

Cale moved for the door, shepherding Magadon and Jak along. He'd had enough.

Behind them, Sephris spoke in a low tone without inflection. "More than two thousand years ago, the cities of Netheril floated through the sky on flattened mountaintops. You three seek one of those—Sakkors, on which sat the Eldritch Temple of Mystryl."

Cale froze but did not turn. Sephris continued. "Exactly one thousand, seven hundred twelve years ago magic failed, and Sakkors fell from the sky. The waves swallowed it and there it lies still, buried under the Inner Sea, sixty leagues from Selgaunt Bay. The fourth of your number, the Second of Mask, will take a ship to find it. And when he finds it, and you find him, you will summon the thunderhead. The storm will follow."

Cale struggled with the notion of asking Sephris for more information but decided against it.

"Goodbye, loremaster," he said over his shoulder, and opened the door.

"Sakkors is only the beginning," Sephris said as Cale and his comrades walked out and pulled closed the door.

Sephris shouted from behind it. "Sacrifices must sometimes be made, First of Five! Remember that, when the darkness comes and all of this is gone!"

Cale stood in the hall for a moment, leaning on the door, dizzy. He gathered himself and shared a look with Jak. The little man looked like he wanted to say something but held his tongue. They walked the maze of corridors in silence until they reached the worship hall.

Hrin waited for them there. Jak saw the bearded priest and his expression hardened.

"Give me a moment," the little man said and stalked up to the priest. Cale and Magadon followed a few paces behind.

Jak poked a finger into Hrin's stomach and said, "You are a wretched bunch of prigs. Look at what you've done to him. He was at peace, finally. And now. . . ."

Acolytes looked up from their desks with alarmed gazes. Doors opened and several more mace-armed priests entered the worship hall.

Hrin gave no ground. His eyes went past Jak, to Cale, to the corridor out of which they had just exited, back to Jak.

"The Chosen One is an asset of the church, halfling. His death was premature, thanks to you. Only the willing can return. He could have refused the call."

"That's a dungpile," Jak spat, eliciting raised eyebrows and shocked looks from the acolytes at the desks. "He came back because he felt it was his duty. And you all knew he would. If you really had regarded him as highly as you say, you never would have asked."

Hrin's brow furrowed with anger and his lips formed a tight line behind his beard. "Get out. Or I'll have you escorted out forcibly."

Cale stepped forward and said, "I doubt that very much."

The priest regarded Cale coolly. "Do you, servant of Mask?"

Several underpriests stood at a distance, hands on mace hafts, angry scowls on their faces. Jak, too, looked ready to do battle on the spot.

Cale's sword hand twitched. The light in the worship hall dimmed.

"Let's move on, Jak," Magadon said, pulling Jak and Cale away. "Erevis, come on."

Jak allowed himself to be led away. Cale shook off Magadon's hand and followed, eyeing Hrin all the while.

"It stinks in here anyway," Jak said over his shoulder.

"Do not return here," called Hrin. "Not ever."

None of the three companions replied. They pushed their way through a group of priests near the door and exited the temple.

When they descended the stairs and reached the street, Jak continued to fume.

"Can you believe they did that to him? *Organized* religion." He turned and spat on the church stairs and several passersby went wide-eyed.

"Would you want that?" the little man asked, turning to Cale. "I wouldn't. When I am dead, I want to stay that way."

"I hear you, little man," Cale said. Cale had put Hrin out of his mind and was parsing Sephris's words and the dire predictions the loremaster had made. Thousands would die, he had said.

Because of Cale.

For a time, the three wandered in silence. No one seemed to know what to say. Finally, Magadon asked, "Do you believe what he said?"

Cale did not lie. "Yes. You heard him, Mags. He knows things. He was angry, embittered, but I think he spoke truth."

Magadon nodded, considered. "But do you believe *all* of what he said?"

Jak asked, "You mean the darkness, the storm, and such?"

Magadon nodded.

Cale could only nod. "He has never been wrong. But that was vague enough that it could mean anything. It does not change what we are going to do."

"It doesn't?" Magadon asked.

"It doesn't," Cale affirmed. "It can't, Mags. It's madness to walk that path."

Magadon stared at him for a time, nodded, then said, "Well enough. So what now? We know where the slaadi are going and we know it's somewhere off the coast of Selgaunt, apparently at the bottom of the Inner Sea. That does us small service."

Cale was glad to move the conversation away from Sephris's prophecies. He said, "We need to locate Riven before he takes ship."

"How?" Jak asked.

"Sakkors is somewhere off the coast of Selgaunt," Cale answered, thinking aloud. "Sephris said that Riven would take a ship."

Jak started to say something but stopped when realization dawned. "You don't think he'd take a ship out of *Selgaunt?*"

"It makes sense," Cale said. "Riven knows the city. So do the slaadi."

"It *is* one of the ports nearest to their destination," Magadon added.

Cale said, "And if we can find their ship. . . ."

"Then we can find them," Jak finished. "We can finish this before it ever starts. That's a lot of ships to check."

Cale nodded. Selgaunt was one of the busiest ports on the Inner Sea, and countless contraband runners docked in secret harbors along the coast outside of the city to avoid the harbormaster's taxes. Still, it was a place to start. He said, "Let's take a room down in the Dock District and put out some feelers."

After securing the services of *Dolphin's Coffer*, Azriim and Dolgan indulged in some spirits at a nearby pub. As dusk fell, they lurked in the shadows of an alley near the wharves and watched *Demon Binder*. From time to time, Dolgan had to dissuade a prostitute and her customer from coupling against the alley wall, but otherwise the slaadi encountered no one. They spied on the ship for hours in silence, learning what they needed.

Several members of the crew left the ship for the dock-side taverns, but the captain, first mate, and a sizeable contingent of the crew—hard looking seamen, all—remained aboard and armed at all times. Crewmen eyed passersby with suspicion. A simple system of whistles and hand signs alerted the captain or first mate any time the harbormaster, his undermasters, or any of the Scepters approached. Azriim took that behavior as confirmation that the ship had slaves in its hold.

After a time, the slaadi called upon their new abilities granted by their partial transformation into gray slaadi, and willed themselves invisible and airborne. Each could see the other, of course, since slaadi innately saw invisible objects, but they were completely invisible to all others. Azriim enjoyed the sensation of flying. He found that flight was effortless, and speed and direction answered to his mental urgings. He could even hover.

Unseen, they flew over the ship, watching, listening, telepathically exchanging the names of crewmen and the layout of the ship. Captain Kauzin ruled *Demon Binder*, and his first mate was called Greel, though the crew often called him by a nickname, Hack, no doubt earned in combat. Azriim studied the captain's appearance and mannerisms with care. The human tended to bark orders, laughed rarely but sharply, and walked with a stiff, gingerly step that bespoke an old back injury. Dolgan studied the first mate with the same intensity. They did not set foot on the deck, in the forecastle, or below decks, for fear of being noticed or triggering a magical alarm.

The slaadi patiently watched until the sky darkened and the stars shone down on the bay. Both Azriim and Dolgan could see well in the dark and continued to watch for a while longer. By the time a distant bell tower sounded the eighth hour, the slaadi knew *Demon Binder* and its crew well enough to maintain their planned charade.

I believe I have him now, projected Azriim. *They should be returning to their quarters soon.*

I am ready also, answered Dolgan, hovering in the air beside him.

They watched until the captain and mate disappeared into the forecastle, which held their quarters.

Azriim said, *Bring the bodies to the alley when it's done.*

Dolgan's unhappiness carried through the mental connection. *The alley? Why? Can I at least eat his head?*

Azriim smiled. *We will see.*

With that, Azriim drew his blade and his teleportation rod. Dolgan did the same and both of them turned the dials on the rods.

Do try not to get stuck in the floor this time, Azriim said.

Dolgan smiled in answer.

Azriim was jesting only by half. There was always a risk in teleporting to a location they had never visited, or at least seen. Still, he was nothing if not a risk taker. He called upon the magic of the rod to teleport him into the forecastle, to the captain's quarters. The magic would need to fill in the gaps.

He gave the rod a final twist, felt the familiar tingle in his flesh as his body moved instantaneously from the air above the ship to the captain's cabin.

He appeared in one corner of a small room. A neatly made bed hugged the far wall, with a sea chest at its foot. A small writing desk stood near the bed with a logbook, quill, and inkwell atop it. A covered clay lamp and some papers sat on a night table near the bed.

Disappointed to find the cabin unoccupied, Azriim sat at the captain's desk to wait. He leafed through the log, noting the repeated references to "sacks of cured meat," no doubt a euphemism for slaves. He looked over the papers on the night table: charcoal sketches, and well done—a pod of leaping porpoises, a three-masted schooner on the horizon, an island in the distance. The captain was an artist, a slaver with a sensitive spirit. Azriim liked him immediately. Too bad he had to kill him.

He did not have to wait long. Shortly, the door to the cabin opened and the captain strode in, huffing and mumbling under his breath. Azriim pulled one of his wands, pointed it at the captain, and said, "Stay."

The moment he said the word, he became visible.

The captain went wide-eyed. His hand went for his blade. He shouted aloud, an inarticulate cry of alarm.

Azriim cursed. The human had resisted the magic. He tried again. "Stay, you stubborn arse!"

That time the captain froze, his mouth open in a shout that would never escape his lips. Azriim grinned, but his smile vanished when a loud rapping sounded on the door.

"Captain?" a voice called. "Captain Kauzin?"

Azriim quickly changed his form to that of the captain—thick limbed, full belly, sallow skin, bad teeth, beard, and short, black hair—and walked to the door. He had the wrong clothes and had kept his natural mismatched eye color, but he figured the seaman would not notice.

He crossed the room and opened the door part way, using his body and the door to block visibility into the room.

"What is it?" he growled, and was pleased to hear the captain's voice exit his throat.

A thin crewman with a pointed chin and a thin moustache and beard stared at him in surprise.

"Er, sorry, Captain. I thought I heard something amiss."

Azriim smiled. He knew the real captain could hear the exchange and he could imagine the human's frustration at not being able to move or say anything.

"You did hear something," Azriim said. "I tripped on my chest and gave my back another twinge."

The sailor nodded knowingly. No doubt all the crewmen knew of their captain's troublesome back.

"Ah. Sorry for the interruption."

Azriim grunted acknowledgement and shut the door. He waited a moment with his ear to the door to ensure that the crewman was gone.

He circled around to the still-paralyzed captain and stared into his face. The man was sweating profusely, even through the spell. He knew what was coming.

"I will make it painless," Azriim said, "But only because I do not want to ruin your clothes with blood." He smiled into the human's face. "And because you are an artist, which I respect." He tapped a finger on his chin. "But after you are dead and I've taken your corpse from the ship, I may eat your brain. Done?"

The captain only sweated.

"Done, then," Azriim said. He smiled, took the captain's head in his hands, stared into his fearful eyes, and snapped his neck.

Afterward, he stripped the captain of his clothes, donned them, and used his rod to teleport himself and the corpse back to the alley. He found Dolgan already there, in the form of the first mate, waiting with the body of the real mate. Dolgan had not been as elegant in disposing of his target. The mate's throat was torn out and his shirt stained crimson. His hair was slicked too, not with blood, but saliva. Dolgan must have been gumming his skull.

"I have been waiting a quarter hour," hissed Dolgan, his voice that of the human.

"I ran into a complication," Azriim said. "But all is well. Is there blood in the mate's quarters?"

Dolgan grinned and licked his lips. "Not anymore."

Azriim could only shake his head and wonder how he and Dolgan had been born to the same brood.

"May I feed?" Dolgan asked, holding the slack body of the mate by his head.

Azriim nodded indulgently. "Take him farther into the alley. And be quick."

Dolgan grinned, retreated into the alley with his meal, and changed to his natural form. A crack announced the opening of the mate's skull and slobbering sounds bespoke the emptying of the brainpan. Dolgan returned to human form and dragged the corpse along, wiping his mouth. Atypically, Azriim felt no desire to feed when he glanced at the human's hollowed-out skull. The partial transformation to gray had perhaps changed his tastes.

Clucking his tongue, Azriim piled the corpses together, looked out on the waters, and picked a suitable point off the coast. He touched his teleportation rod to the bodies and sent them out into the waters of the bay, near a pier. They would be found and identified soon enough. No doubt the opened brainpan of the first mate would set tongues wagging.

Exactly as Azriim planned.

If the priest of Mask and his allies *were* following them, Azriim wanted to ensure they followed along the path he marked.

Back to the ship now, he projected to Dolgan. *Our assassin should be arriving soon. And we are setting sail tonight.*

CHAPTER 6

FISHING

Cale procured a single room for the three of
them in a dockside, two-story inn called The
Murky Depths. The inn served wealthy itin-
erant merchants who did not want to spend
their evenings aboard ship while they were in
port. Well-dressed men and women filled the
common room, chatting and laughing. Several
subdued games of draughts, *sava*, and scales
and blades went on at various tables. Business
negotiations went on at others. Dice were not
in evidence.

The sweet smell of quality pipeleaf filled the
room and bluish smoke circled the roof joists.
A large kettle of fish stew simmered over the
larger of the taproom's two hearths. The Depths
had only a few windows, all tightly shuttered.

Dim glowglobes in the corners shed cerulean light of varying intensity, giving the taproom a deep-sea feel. Permanent illusions of small sharks, dolphins, jellyfish, marlins, and other exotic fish "swam" through the air between tables, between the roof rafters. An auditory illusion kept up a soothing chorus of distant whalesong. Permanent visual illusions made the floor appear to be transparent with a sea floor far below. Kelp, giant clams, and anemones dotted the sandy bottom, and schools of fish swam lazily under the feet of the patrons.

Cale could imagine the expense the proprietor must have spent on hired illusionists.

The three comrades sat in a shadowed corner of the taproom at a sturdy round table edged with an inset shell border. Ceramic tankards filled with quality house ale sat before them.

"Hardly our kind of place," Jak said, eyeing the clientele. He reached out to touch a bright red illusory fish coasting past their table. It darted away from his touch and into the depths below the floorboards.

Cale agreed. Other than dinner knives and a couple of obviously ceremonial cutlasses that hung from the hips of two overweight merchants, the three comrades wore the only weapons in the room. The Depths was a place to which Cale might have accompanied Thamalon to close a trade deal.

Cale said, "I wanted us to have—"

The patrons scattered as an illusory shark burst out of the floor chasing a large silver fish. Prey and predator swam a frenetic course over three tables before knifing neatly back into the floorboards' depths. Eventually the fish found shelter in a cave on the sea floor and the shark went hungry. Laughter and clapping followed.

Cale, Jak, and Magadon shared a look. All three had pushed back their chairs, half stood, and put hands to hilts. Cale had Weaveshear halfway from its scabbard.

Sheepishly, they released their blades and settled back

at their table. Some of the nearby patrons eyed them and whispered behind their hands.

Cale ignored them and took a sip of ale. "As I was saying, I wanted us to have a peaceful place from which to operate. One with few distractions." He thought of the tavern back in Skullport, when he and Riven had fought off some mercenaries. That would have been a pointless distraction too, had it not led to him meeting Varra. He put thoughts of her from his mind. "I also figured it might as well be a nice place. We could use a reprieve, even if temporary."

Jak tilted his head and raised his glass in a salute. A trio of golden fish swam near their table and Jak snapped out his free hand to grab at one. The little man proved faster than the illusion and all three illusory fish vanished at his touch. They reappeared, swimming peacefully, near the ceiling across the room.

"Got you," Jak said to them, smiling, and took a long, congratulatory draw on his ale.

Magadon returned them to their task. "Sakkors is underwater. We know that. Hopefully, we can catch the slaadi and Riven aboard ship, but if not. . . ."

"Then we go under," Jak said, and looked down through the floorboards.

Magadon nodded. "And that adds to our enemies—the ocean is cold, dark, airless, and the weight of the water increases with depth. My mental abilities are of no help. What of your spells?"

"Within limits," Cale said, and Jak nodded agreement.

"The slaadi can shapechange," Magadon said. "They will take the form of something native to the depths. We will be at a disadvantage if it comes to that."

"Then let's not let it come to that," Cale said. He looked to Jak and said, "Call in any markers you have, even your old Harper contacts."

Magadon raised his eyebrows at that; the guide had not known that Jak once was a Harper. Cale went on.

"I will do the same. We angle for anything suspicious. A sailor, passenger, or merchant with mismatched eyes. Anyone asking after Sakkors or the Eldritch Temple. A ship unexpectedly departing. Anything at all. Drop as much coin as you need. We start tonight."

"I will be of little use in this," Magadon said, his lips pursed.

"You have been of great use in everything else, Mags," Cale said. "Leave this to Jak and me. This is what we do."

Jak drained his ale, wiped his mouth, and stood. "I'll get started tonight."

Cale nodded.

"I will try scrying," he said. "If that does not work, I'll join you on the wharves."

Dressed in the tailored black doublet, trousers, high boots, and fur-trimmed cloak of a middle-aged, wealthy, potbellied merchant, Riven walked the pier toward *Demon Binder*. To maintain appearances, he had hired a laborer to bear his chest of traveling goods— in reality, his weapons, armor, clothing, and a few other useless gewgaws he had purchased to add weight.

As he neared the gangplank, two crewmen hurried down to the pier to assist the laborer with his burden. Both sailors wore cutlasses and hard looks. Riven threw a silver to the laborer and sent him on his way.

"The captain said you was comin'," the first said, a thin, tattooed sailor missing two fingers on his right hand.

"We'll bear that for you, now," said the other, a burly crewman with burn-scarred hands. His sour breath stank of distilled spirits.

Riven wiped fictional sweat from his brow, made as though he was catching his breath. He adopted a Chondathan accent and offered his thanks.

"Cap'n's holdin' a cabin for you," said the thin one. "Leavin' with the moonrise, he said. Where'll we be headin'?"

Captain Azriim must not have told the crew the destination. Riven could not have told them if he'd wanted.

"I will leave it to the captain to tell," Riven said, and boarded.

"Must be something special, to divert our course as we are though, eh?" the thin sailor said. He worked with the other crewman to carry the chest.

The bigger took a half-hearted swing with his free hand at the smaller's head. "Shut yer hole, Nom. We'll know when the Captain wants us to know. He's never sailed us wrong, has he?"

Nom grumbled agreement and the two led Riven to his cabin—little more than a closet with a flea-ridden bed and small dressing table—and left him alone with his chest. Riven wandered onto deck later, where he found Azriim and Dolgan walking the ship, supervising the preparations to set sail. Riven grudgingly conceded that the slaadi were at least as good as he at playing their roles. He noticed that Azriim surreptitiously held one wand or another against his forearm as he moved over the deck.

"Welcome aboard, Mendeth," Azriim said. The slaad looked exactly like the captain except that he had retained his mismatched eyes. Riven was not surprised that none of the crew had noticed, but a professional would. Cale would.

Dolgan, in his guise as the first mate, grunted a greeting.

Riven pretended to make insignificant conversation, but caught Azriim's gaze and indicated the wands the slaad rotated in and out of his hands.

Warding the ship, Azriim explained.

Above them, the crew was at work in the rigging, unfurling sails.

"We sail at moonrise," Azriim said, confirming what

the crewman had said to Riven. He continued to walk the deck, with Dolgan at his side.

Riven tired of the slaadi's company in short order. With nothing to do but wait for the ship to set sail, Riven returned to his quarters and brooded. The thump of activity went on for several hours, then shouts were heard, and the ship began to move away from the pier.

As *Demon Binder* sailed out of the harbor and out into the open sea, Riven emerged onto the deck, up the stern-castle to the aft railing. He felt the eyes of the crew on him, saw the questions in their expressions, but ignored them and offered no information. He leaned on the rail and watched Selgaunt and its torches and lamps vanish into the distance. For a moment, he wondered what his girls were doing, if they would miss him. He wondered, too, if Cale was in the city, looking for him.

He suspected so.

For the hundredth time, he wondered if he was doing the right thing.

From their room in the Murky Depths, Cale tried to scry Riven or the slaadi but met with no success. He was not surprised. No doubt the Sojourner had bolstered the ability of the slaadi to avoid detection. He tried, too, to scry Sakkors, focusing the spell's magic using only the city's name. That failed as well. He and Jak would need to use more mundane methods.

For a night and two days Jak and Cale frequented the taverns and eateries of the Dock District, carousing among the watermen. It felt good to Cale. The atmosphere reminded him of his early professional life in Westgate, when things had seemed less complicated and earning coin had been his only concern.

He and Jak sprinkled fivestars and drink among sailors, courtesans, merchants, ferrymen, serving girls, bartenders, dockworkers, and anyone else who might have had an ear to recent events. Cale used his ability to stand invisibly in the shadows to move unseen among the crowds.

As always, the dockside establishments were awash in rumors and schemes—dragon attacks in the north seemed a popular bit of nonsense—but none of them fit what Cale knew of Riven and the slaadi. Cale watched dozens of ships come and go from the harbor, wondering with each if he was watching the slaadi escape. After a time he began to suspect that Riven and the slaadi had not returned to Selgaunt after all, or that they had secured passage on a smuggler's ship outside the harbor.

The second night, after another fruitless day, he and Jak walked back toward the Murky Depths.

"You ever think about doing something like that?" Jak said, and nodded at a group of glory-seekers walking along the docks: two warriors in mail hauberks, both armed with swords and bows, what looked like a paunchy wizard, to judge from his robes and the esoterica hanging from his belt, and an armored priest of Lathander, with a yellow sun enameled on his breastplate and a mace at his waist. The four adventurers joked among themselves as they walked the waterfront, laughing about some jest made at the wizard's expense.

"An itchie?" Cale asked, incredulous. "Are you jesting?"

Jak shook his head. "I don't mean an adventurer, Cale, at least not exactly. I mean . . . you know, someone who does big things." He cleared his throat. "A hero, is what I'm saying."

Cale would have chuckled if not for the earnestness in Jak's voice. He said, "Adventurers are coin grubbers and tomb robbers, Jak. They're not heroes, if there even are such people."

Jak stopped and faced him, brow furrowed. "What do you mean, 'if there are such people?' You do not think there are any? What about Tchazzar? The Seven Sisters?

Khelben Arunsun? Even King Azoun of Cormyr, before he fell."

Cale shook his head and said, "Those people have done big things, great things maybe, but to call them heroes? I don't know, Jak. The word . . . reduces a man, makes him more myth than real."

"What does that mean?" Jak asked.

"It means. . . ." Cale fumbled for words. "Do you think that what we know about the men and women you named amounts to even a fraction of who they were or what they did? They slew a dragon, defeated an army, faced a demon. All well and good. But how did they treat their friends? Their family? I'll wager they experienced more failures than successes. Should that not factor into the evaluation? We take one aspect of who they were or what they did, grab onto it because we like it or think it admirable, and call them heroes. Hells, Jak, you and I have faced demons, even a dragon. No one knows, no one will remember but us, and I would wager a fortune that no one will call us heroes. Will they?"

Jak surprised him by saying softly, "I don't know. Maybe they will."

Cale laughed to hide his shock. "You waxing philosophical as you age?"

"No," the little man said, and they started walking again. "I just think that doing something good and being remembered for it—even if for nothing else—is worthwhile. And whether the histories call you a hero or not doesn't change the *fact* of the heroism."

Cale thought about that, then said, "Maybe you have some truth there. But aren't we already doing good things, little man? Big things?"

Jak looked past the ships, out to the bay. "Most of the time I think so. Still, if we get a chance. . . ."

"What?"

Still looking out to sea, Jak said, "If we get the chance, let's be heroes." He looked back at Cale. "All right?"

Cale could think of nothing to say. He was not sure that he was made of the stuff of heroes, the stuff of Storm Silverhand and Khelben; he was not sure that a priest of Mask could be a hero. But to satisfy Jak he managed, "All right, Jak. If we get a chance."

"Is that an oath?" Jak asked.

"That's an oath," Cale answered. "What's animating this, little man?"

"Nothing," Jak answered. "Just thinking aloud."

Cale let it rest there, and with that, the two friends walked back to the inn.

The next day they caught a lead. The docks buzzed with news of two bodies found floating in the bay. Most of the stories suggested that both corpses had been muti-lated. Most also suggested that the bodies were those of two sailors, both from the same ship. Cale and Jak took hold of the tale, its various incarnations, and followed it to its end to find the truth of it. Sprinkling coin among the laborers on the docks and finally bribing one of the harbormaster's undermasters, they learned that only one of the bodies had been mutilated—his skull had been opened and emptied—and the sailors had been the captain and first mate of a Thayan ship, *Demon Binder*, that had set to two nights earlier. Cale learned too that *Demon Binder* transported slaves. The rumors spoke of a mutiny. Cale knew better.

"That's our ship," Cale said as the three of them sat around a table in the Depth's taproom. Cale figured that the slaadi had taken the form of the slain captain and mate and brought Riven aboard, probably in disguise.

Jak frowned. "They put to sea two days ago. We don't know where they're headed. Even if we can find a faster ship, how can we catch them?"

Cale already had an idea. "The Sojourner may have warded the slaadi and Riven against scrying, but he did not ward the ship. We know its name and there's power in that. A divination can find it. And if I can see it, I can move us there during the night."

Jak and Magadon looked at him, and both grinned.

The three finished their meal then retired to their opulent room. Sitting on the end of one of the three down-stuffed beds, Magadon checked and rechecked his arrows, oiled his bow, meditated in silence. Jak inventoried his pouches, his tobacco, sharpened his blades. The *schk schk* of steel on whetstone kept the time.

Cale sat at an oak desk, on which rested a basin of clear water. He held Weaveshear across his knees and waited, silently imploring Mask to ensure the success of the scrying. Streaks of shadow moved from his hands into the blade, from the blade back into his hands. Sunlight spilled through the western window and painted the floor. The light crept across the slats as sunset approached. The shadows in the room grew longer, darker.

Even without looking out the window, Cale knew the very moment the sun sank below the horizon. He thought of casting then, but decided against it.

"What are we waiting for?" Magadon asked.

"Midnight," Cale answered. Midnight was the hour sacred to Mask. Cale would wait for it. "Have some food brought up," he said to Magadon. "Eat. Keep up your strength."

Magadon and Jak did just that. Cale did not eat. He focused. He knew intuitively when midnight arrived. Moonbeams strained through the shutters. The shadows were at their deepest; Cale's connection to his god was at its most profound.

"Now," Cale said, and his comrades rose to stand beside him.

Cale leaned forward over the basin, studied its still water. Running his thumb along Weaveshear's edge, he slit his skin and drew blood. His flesh regenerated the wound almost immediately but he had what he needed. He let a few drops of blood fall into the basin. He swirled shadows around his fingertips until they grew tangible and he let them, too, fall into the water. He breathed on the basin and stirred the mixture with his fingertips.

Calling upon Mask to show him *Demon Binder,* he cast the divination. With nothing more than the ship's name to drive the spell, the casting faltered. Cale compensated with his will, forcing the magic to reveal what he needed to know.

Within moments, the water in the basin solidified into a surface as smooth, black, and shining as polished basalt. A wavering image took shape in the blackness—a two-masted cog with great, square sails full of wind, sailing on the smooth sea. The perspective showed the vessel from a distance, as though Cale were seeing through a bird's eye above it.

"There it is," breathed Jak, standing on his tiptoes to see into the basin.

The ship had two crow's nests, one on the mainmast, one on the mizzenmast. A two-story forecastle squatted on the decks to fore, and a sterncastle to the rear. Lanterns hung from the stern, the gunnels, the post over the helmsman. Cale saw no sailors moving on deck, though one of the crow's nests contained a watchman. The crew slept on deck or in quarters. The ship was on nightwatch but had not set its anchor or furled its sails. It was sailing through the night, by the light of a waxing Selûne and her tears. Cale knew that to be unusual. Azriim must have been in a hurry.

"The crew will fight," Magadon said, "unless they can be shown the slaadi's true form."

Cale nodded. He figured the cog's crew numbered perhaps a score.

"We'll go in fast and quiet," he said. "We find the slaadi, put them down, and get out. But if the crew gets in the way . . . " He looked his friends in the eyes. "They are Thayans and slavers. Remember that.

Neither Magadon nor Jak protested.

"Riven?" Jak asked.

Cale shook his head. He did not know what to expect from Drasek Riven. "If necessary, we put him down too."

The little man pulled out his holy symbol and prayed to Brandobaris. When he completed the casting, a soft glow covered him, Cale, and Magadon. The glow faded but left a warm feeling in its wake.

Jak explained, "A prayer to Brandobaris. We may need the help."

"A good thought," Cale said.

He felt a tickling under his scalp.

We are linked, Magadon said.

Cale nodded. They were as prepared as they could be.

He pulled the shadows around them, found the link in the darkness between their room in the Murky Depths and the aft deck of *Demon Binder*.

In a moment, they were on the open sea, aboard a Thayan slave ship.

Riven awoke, certain that he had heard Cale whispering something to him. He sat up with a start, hand on one of his sabers, and looked about his quarters. He saw no one.

He had been dreaming, and the dream had been a vision sent to him by the Shadowlord. He had seen a tower in ruins but rebuilt before his eyes, a priestess of Cyric screaming in rage. The shadows had laughed at the priestess's ire. He had seen himself and the slaadi together in the tower as darkness fell.

His skin went gooseflesh at the memory. His heart was racing. He could not shake the feeling that something was wrong, that someone was watching him. Long ago he had learned not to ignore those feelings.

He rose, donned his weapons and an overcloak, and padded out of his room.

❧ ❧ ❧ ❧ ❧

A gentle chiming in Azriim's head awoke him from sleep. One of his alarm spells had been triggered. Erevis Cale was aboard. He climbed out of bed and as he donned his clothing and weapon belt, reached his mental fingers out for Dolgan, who slept in the mate's quarters nearby.

The priest of Mask is aboard.

Dolgan answered back, his consciousness noticeably groggy. *He is?*

Azriim rolled his eyes as he buckled his belt. No matter the situation, Dolgan could always find a way to ask a stupid question.

Find the assassin and meet me outside the forecastle, Azriim projected.

Should I alert the crew to intruders? Dolgan asked.

Not yet, Azriim answered. *Let us see what events bring.*

He stayed in Captain Kauzin's form but willed himself invisible. He exited his quarters, walked a short corridor, and exited the forecastle. There, he waited for Dolgan.

His broodmate's mental voice sounded in his mind: *The assassin is not in his quarters.*

No? Azriim asked. *How interesting.*

He reached out with his mental perception and tried to contact Riven.

CHAPTER 7

DEMON BINDER

The darkness dissipated and Cale, Magadon, and Jak found themselves near the aft railing on the sterncastle of *Demon Binder*. A short, bearded crewman, perhaps thirty winters old, stood a few paces from them, looking out over the sea. Cale had not seen him in the scrying lens.

The crewman noticed them at the same moment they noticed him.

Surprise widened the man's dumbfounded eyes and temporarily stole his shout.

Cale did what he must. In the space of two heartbeats, he lunged forward and impaled the man through the heart with Weaveshear. The man groaned, bled, sagged toward Cale. Cale caught him up before he fell and heaved him over the rail. The crewman never uttered a scream but the splash of his corpse hitting the sea sounded loud to Cale's ears. He, Jak, and Magadon shared a tense look while they waited for a cry of alarm.

It never came. No one had heard. All three visibly exhaled.

Cale wiped a bloody hand on his cloak. He noticed the way his friends looked at the blood and projected a reminder: *These are slavers, not spice merchants. They do not deserve your pity.*

Magadon and Jak looked over the railing, back at Cale, and nodded.

The ship was quiet, the deck barely moving on the calm sea. A brisk wind from the south stirred their cloaks, snapped the sails above them. Masts creaked. The sea lapped against the hull as it cut its way through the water.

Selûne, gibbous and waxing, hung low in the sky, trailed by her glowing train of silver tears. Along the deck of *Demon Binder,* a few covered oil lanterns hung here and there from the railings. Otherwise, the ship was dark.

Soft steps, Cale projected, and pointed at the deck of the sterncastle below his boots. He figured some of the crew—the masters who ranked below the first mate— were sleeping in quarters below them. The cabins of the captain and mate, where Cale expected they would find Azriim and Dolgan, would be at the bow of the ship in the forecastle.

Soundlessly, the three slid forward to the edge of the sterncastle until they could look down on the maindeck below. A score or so crewmen lay sprawled about, sleeping. Some hung in canvas hammocks strung between posts. Others slept in the large, cloth-lined leather bags Cale had once heard a sailor call a "deckbag." Cutlasses, knives, and belaying pins lay within ready reach of all of them. Slavers kept their weapons ready at hand.

The night helmsman stood at the tiller in the steering pocket almost directly below them, presumably guiding the ship by the stars. Across the ship, Cale saw two sailors standing on the forecastle to either side of the bowsprit, looking out at the sea ahead.

Cale's heartbeat accelerated. Hopeful that he had found the slaadi, he whispered the words to the spell that allowed him to see magic.

Nothing lit up on the two sailors, but Cale did detect a diffuse magical aura glowing before the door that led to the interior of the forecastle. The slaadi must have warded it. He would examine it more closely when he got there.

A man in the forward crow's nest, Magadon said, peering up the masts. *I see no one in the rear nest.*

Could you cover the deck from the forward nest? Cale asked.

Magadon eyed the nest, the deck, judged lines of sight.

The sails will create some blind spots, the guide answered, *but otherwise, yes.*

Cale nodded. He looked down at the top of the helmsman's head. The man was unsuspecting, vulnerable, alone. Cale could see no way that they could move across the ship unseen without first putting down the helmsman.

First the helmsman, he said. *Then the lookout in the nest.*

He started to move but Jak's hand closed on his shoulder.

A spell first, the little man projected. *If it does not work, we put him down.*

Cale looked into Jak's eyes. He did not see weakness there, but neither did he see bloodthirst.

They're slavers, Jak. Remember Skullport?

Jak nodded. *I know what they are, Cale. But that doesn't mean that I want to kill everyone aboard, at least not if we do not have to. We're here for the slaadi. Well enough?*

For a moment, Cale imagined himself through Jak's eyes. He must have looked a bit too ready to shed blood. Perhaps he *was* a bit too ready to shed blood. He did not want to become so much a shade that he forgot how to be a man.

Well enough, he said. *I'll get in position. Then you cast. If your spell doesn't work. . . .*

Jak nodded.

Cale sheathed Weaveshear and merged with the darkness, becoming invisible even to his friends. He circled the sterncastle, silently padded down one of the two ladders that led to the maindeck, and took station directly behind the helmsman. He drew a dagger.

The helmsman wore a sweat-stained tunic and wool breeches. His beard and hair were ill kept, his arms gnarled and scarred. He stood in a large opening, almost a box, that sank below the level of the deck—the steering pocket. The tiller shaft stuck out of the rear of the box. An elaborate metal device, no doubt for charting course, and a waterskin sat on a small table within arm's reach. The helmsman hummed to himself while he held the tiller, probably to help stay awake.

Now, Cale projected to Jak.

Cale did not hear Jak cast his spell but he knew when the spell was completed because the helmsman's humming ceased. The man stood rigid and silent, tiller in his frozen hand.

It worked, Cale projected to Jak. *How long will it last?*

Hard to say, Jak answered.

Cale did not like the uncertainty but decided that he would accept it for Jak's sake.

The one in the crow's nest? he asked Jak.

After a moment's hesitation, the little man answered, *Too far.*

Cale had expected as much. *He is mine, then. Give me a ten count.*

Magadon said, *I will meet you there.*

Jak projected, *I'll go invisible and seal the door out of the sterncastle with a glyph. I'll meet you at the bottom of the mainmast.*

Good, Cale said. He looked up to the crow's nest and felt the darkness there. He stepped in one stride from his place behind the helmsman to the rear of the crow's nest. The crewman occupying the nest made no sign that he heard Cale appear. The sailor, who could not have seen many more than twenty winters, leaned on his elbows over the front of the crow's nest, staring out over the sea.

Cale hesitated, torn. He could have used a spell like Jak's. There was no guarantee that it would work, but he could have tried. But then he reminded himself that the crew made a living selling other human beings into bondage. When he remembered Skullport, the despair he had seen in the eyes of the slaves there, he needed no further justification. The sailor had chosen this occupation. There were consequences to that choice.

Cale stepped behind the man, jerked his head back to expose his throat, and slit his jugular. Cale became visible the moment he attacked but the man never saw him. The sailor's scream was nothing more than a wheezing gurgle through the new opening in his throat. He flailed for a moment in Cale's grasp but his strength left him as quickly as his blood. Cale lowered him to the bottom of the nest as he died. It was soon over. Cale peeked over the edge of the nest to the deck below and saw no sign that anyone had heard.

Mags?

On my way, the guide answered.

Cale turned around to see Magadon sprinting silently across open air, as though an invisible ramp connected the sterncastle to the crow's nest. In the space of three breaths, the guide was climbing into the nest. Again, no sign of alarm from the sleeping crew below. The two men standing atop the forecastle continued to stare out to sea.

"Mind your footing," Cale said softly. "It's slick."

Magadon looked down at the slain sailor, the pool of blood, and said nothing. He picked his spot in the nest.

He removed his quiver of arrows, set it beside him, and unshouldered his bow.

Jak? Cale projected.

The door on the sterncastle is warded, the little man answered. *I'm on the maindeck now, near the hold door.* He paused, then said, *I can see what's down there.*

Cale and Magadon shared a glance.

And? Cale asked.

Jak answered, *Cages. Maybe a score or so slaves. All men.* He hesitated before saying, *We should free them, Cale.*

Jak's words did not surprise Cale but he was not certain how to respond. He knew that freeing the slaves would complicate matters, might mean putting down the entire crew. There was one ship's boat rigged to the side. Perhaps they could force most of the crew off the ship and into the boat.

Perhaps.

Cale stared into Magadon's pale eyes. The guide said nothing, merely waited.

Cale? Jak prompted.

All right, Cale said. *We'll free them. It will mean a lot of blood, little man.*

I know. But now that I've seen them, I can't walk away. We did that in Skullport. Not again. Not here.

Cale nodded. He understood. Jak was not a killer by nature, but for the right reasons the little man could be as savage as any assassin Cale had ever known.

First the slaadi, he said.

First the slaadi, Jak acknowledged.

I'm coming down, Cale said.

"Luck," Magadon whispered, and drew an arrow.

Cale nodded and looked down from the nest. He picked a patch of darkness at the base of the mast and stepped to it.

The moment he felt the deck under his feet he pulled the shadows more closely around him and drew Weaveshear.

Jak? He projected.

An invisible hand closed on his elbow.

Here, the little man said.

Out of habit, Cale turned to look at the little man but of course saw nothing. Cale weaved darkness and shadow around him to make himself invisible too. He and Jak would not be able to see each other, but they could stay in ready contact through the mindlink. Besides, they had worked together so often that they virtually knew the other's thoughts.

While Cale knew that the slaadi could see through invisibility spells, he figured the glamers would at least keep wakeful crewmen from spotting them as they moved across the ship. Cale remembered too that the slaadi made frequent use of invisibility themselves. He decided to take a moment to counter that.

Hold a moment, little man.

Holding his mask, he softly intoned the words to a prayer he had never before used. When he finished the spell, his perception changed. His skin and the hairs on his arms became finely attuned to the slightest differences in the pressure of the air against his body, the subtlest movement of the wind, the nuance of temperature. The spell enabled his mind to process tactile information and convert it into something perceptually akin to vision. Cale could not distinguish colors, but at a distance of fifteen paces he could "see" with his eyes closed better than he could with them open.

Beside him, Jak was visible through his new sense. The little man eyed the forecastle, blades in hand.

The slaadi will be in the forecastle, Cale said to Jak and Magadon. *Mags, we are both invisible.*

Keep me apprised of where you are, Magadon answered. *I don't want an errant shot to hit you accidentally.*

Cale sent an acknowledgement and he and Jak silently crept among the sleeping crew toward the forecastle. They updated Magadon as to their location every five or so paces. Cale checked the faces of the sleeping crewmen closely, in case a disguised Riven was among them. He was not. Cale figured Riven to be with the slaadi.

Together, the two made their way invisibly over the deck.

It took Azriim a moment to spy the priest and his halfling companion. He spotted them on the maindeck, near the mast. He watched them creep across the deck toward the forecastle, as silent as specters. Their invisibility spells did not shield them from Azriim's vision, but he had almost missed them—despite their invisibility, they both kept to the shadows, seemingly out of professional habit. Azriim pointed them out for Dolgan. Azriim did not see Riven, and the human had not responded to Azriim's mental call. He decided to try again.

Answer me, assassin, he sent.

Be silent, Riven finally responded. *Their mindmage may detect the communication. Maintain the connection and I will contact you when I'm ready.*

Azriim had not seen the mindmage. He scanned the ship but still did not see him.

We are on the maindeck behind the forecastle, Azriim said. *The priest and the halfling are moving right toward us. Where are you? Where is their mindmage?*

The assassin did not respond and Azriim sighed with perturbation.

Cale and the halfling drew closer, checking the crew as they approached.

Beside Azriim, Dolgan grew eager for bloodshed. He shifted from foot to foot and grunted softly.

Silence, Azriim commanded him.

The big slaad bit down on his lip until it bled and asked, *What are we going to do?*

Azriim could have simply fled *Demon Binder* for

Dolphin's Coffer. That had been his plan, after all. He had put *Demon Binder* on a course far from *Dolphin's Coffer* and the vicinity of sunken Sakkors. And he could see to it that Cale and his companions would have difficulty following him after they left the ship.

But that would not have been fun at all. Better to just kill them, he thought.

He grinned at his broodmate and said, *Let's shoot a lightning bolt down their gullets and burn the ship out from under them.*

Dolgan chuckled and pointed his finger at the halfling. Azriim slapped his hand down.

Not yet. When they get close. I want to see his face when it happens.

A dagger toss from the forecastle, Cale saw the slaadi with his magical sense. They were in human form, standing invisibly under the eave of the forecastle's deck. The captain—Azriim, Cale presumed—held a wand in one hand. The mate—Dolgan, no doubt—shifted from foot to foot, licking his lips.

Cale managed not to give a start, though he wondered how they had learned that he was aboard. An alarm spell of some kind, he supposed.

Thinking quickly, he feigned examination of a crewman sleeping in a deckbag near him.

Little man, look at this. He nodded at the sleeping sailor, a grizzled slaver of no interest whatsoever. The man smacked his lips and turned over in his deckbag.

Jak turned and came to Cale's side. Before he could speak, Cale said,

The slaadi are standing to either side of the forecastle door. They see us. I don't think they know that I can see them.

Jak stiffened, but only just. Cale hoped the slaadi had

not noticed. He knew he had only a few moments before the creatures would get suspicious.

Can you make them visible? he asked Jak.

Jak nodded, as if at something Cale was saying about the crewman. Cale gestured at another crewman, as though they were making conversation about something.

Just as you're about to finish the spell, you signal me, Cale said. *I will close on them. Mags, you shoot at Dolgan the moment he is visible to you. He's to your right of the forecastle door. I will tell you if he moves.*

Understood, Magadon answered.

Cale and Jak both nodded, pretending to be in accord about something. They turned and started back toward the forecastle, continuing to move as slowly as before.

Jak palmed his holy symbol and began to incant.

From his vantage in the crow's nest, Magadon looked down at the forecastle. He imagined the slaad's location and drew an arrow to his ear. He found his mental focus, summoned his energy, and caused it to manifest physically on his arrow. The tip's edges glinted dim red, charged with power.

He judged the wind and the distance, and readied himself. The moment Jak rendered the slaadi visible, he would let fly.

His heart nearly stopped when the cold edge of a sharp blade settled against his throat, and the sharp point of another settled against his spine. Magadon had heard nothing.

"Goodeve, Mags," said a voice.

Drasek Riven's voice.

Magadon went cold.

Jak whispered the final word to his spell even as his mental voice said to Cale and Magadon, *Now!*

Cale stepped from the shadows around him and into the shadows beside Azriim. He materialized at the same moment that the magical pulse from Jak's spell reached the slaadi. The pulse hit Cale and the slaadi and stripped all three of their invisibility.

Cale drove Weaveshear into Azriim's side, through his ribs, through his lungs, and into his heart. The slaad gasped with pain and sank to his knees, his mismatched eyes wide with surprise. Blood poured from his open mouth.

Cale expected a mentally-charged arrow to come streaking out of the crow's nest but it never did. He had his back to Dolgan but his augmented magical sense saw the slaad as he pointed his hand at Cale.

Cale jerked Weaveshear free of Azriim and tried to intercept whatever was coming but he was too slow. A white-hot lightning bolt issued from the slaad's palm, slammed into Cale's side, burned a hole into his flesh, and sent him skidding across the deck. For an alarming moment, his pain-wracked body would not respond to his commands. The air smelled acrid, with an undertone of burning flesh and cloth. But as his shade flesh regenerated the injuries, the pain subsided and his body answered.

Mags! Cale projected to Magadon, climbing to all fours and turning around. *Shoot!*

Jak became visible as he chanted the words to another spell and fired a bolt of white energy into Dolgan. The divine force hit the slaad in the side. He grunted and took a backward step. Jak charged at him, blades bare.

Meanwhile, Azriim had found his feet. Like Cale, the slaad's flesh was already regenerating. He leered at Cale as he stood, still bleeding from a hole in his side, and spat a gob of blood to the deck.

Cale rose on wobbly legs and brandished Weaveshear.

The noise of the battle was waking the slavers. On the maindeck, sailors rose, assessed the situation, shouted, and grabbed for weapons. A call went up: "Invaders at the forecastle! They're at the captain and Hack. Arms! Arms!"

Cale had only moments. He advanced on Azriim but Magadon's mental voice sounded in his brain. *Erevis, stop! Riven . . . has me.*

It took a moment for the words to register. When they did, Cale stopped cold and cursed. Jak, too, stopped his charge.

"Now, now," said Azriim, favoring his side but still smiling. "Mind the cursing or I'll have Riven gut your mindmage."

Cale gritted his teeth. Magadon's mental projection must have reached the slaadi. Azriim took out his bronze teleportation rod and began turning its dials, slowly, just to gloat. In his other hand, he held a wand of blackened iron capped with an orange jewel.

"Thank you for the amusing diversion," the slaad said. "Regrettably, I cannot linger. I had hoped to kill you myself, but alas, we often do not get what we wish."

Before Cale could reply, Azriim projected to Riven, *Kill the mindmage, Riven. Then we travel. . . .* The connection was cut and Cale did not sense whatever last bit of information Azriim sent to Riven.

Magadon's mental scream caused Cale to clutch his head. A sympathetic stab of pain traveled through the psychic connection and doubled Cale over. He felt Magadon die and the mindlink terminated.

Smiling even as his body began to transform again, Azriim turned the dial on his teleportation rod with his thumb while pointing the iron wand at the forecastle.

"Farewell, priest," Azriim said.

Cale and Jak both dived for cover.

A tiny ball of fire shot from the wand, hit the forecastle, and blossomed into a globe of flames. The sheath of shadows around Cale kept the flames and heat from his flesh. When he looked up, he did not see the slaadi. They were gone. Jak's cloak was smoking but otherwise the little man appeared to have avoided the flames.

The forecastle was ablaze. The entire ship would soon be afire.

The crew stood stunned for a moment, clutching weapons, wearing snarls, watching their ship burn.

"They've burned the captain alive!" shouted a bald, tattooed giant of a man. "At 'em, lads!"

Cale and Jak stood and went shoulder to shoulder. The crew advanced warily. Cale could see their courage building. They would soon charge.

"We could return to the Plane of Shadow," Cale said out of the side of his mouth, though he figured he knew Jak's answer.

Jak shook his head. "We cannot leave the slaves, Cale. Let's finish this. I can take care of the fire."

Cale nodded, brandished Weaveshear, and awaited the advancing crew. Meanwhile, the little man hurriedly incanted a prayer. When he finished, the ship listed to one side, as though struck by a powerful wave. Cale barely kept his feet.

The crew exclaimed, several fell to the deck, and all looked around in alarm.

Cale looked out to sea, which appeared calm. What could—

A wave surged upward from the sea and crashed over the railing. To Cale's astonishment, and to the open-mouthed shock of the crew, it did not soak the deck but instead held the form of a churning pillar, about the size of an ogre. It moved rapidly over the deck with an awkward undulation until it stood before Jak and Cale. Sound emerged from it, like the crashing of surf, or the swirl of a whirlpool. The cadence suggested that the sounds were speech.

The crew froze in their boots.

Cale realized that he was looking at living water, an elemental. He had heard of priests summoning such creatures, but he had never known Jak to do so. The little man continued to surprise him.

"A servant of the sea-bitch!" one of the crew shouted.

"Quench the flames and begone," Jak ordered the elemental.

The elemental responded in its incomprehensible tongue, thinned, elongated, and stretched forth for the forecastle. Its body soaked the flames, steaming and sizzling and smoking. In three heartbeats the fire was quenched.

The living wave instantly dissipated, drenching Jak's and Cale's boots and those of the crew. The elemental had returned to its place of origin, leaving a watery trail behind.

"Nicely done," Cale said.

"We're at sea," Jak said. "I thought I should be prepared."

Unfortunately, the angry crew did not seem as impressed. With the fire extinguished, they charged full on, weapons bare.

    ⚜ ⚜ ⚜ ⚜ ⚜

Azriim, Dolgan, and Riven appeared on the maindeck of *Dolphin's Coffer*. Azriim had retaken the form he had used when he first set foot on *Dolphin's Coffer* back in Selgaunt.

Spherical glowglobes lit the deck. Crewmen lay sleeping in leather bags, hammocks, and among coils of rope. The ship was anchored, with sails furled, just off the coast of an island that was little more than an enormous mountain jutting from the sea—Traitor's Isle. A single spire sat on the rocky island, the tower in which a treacherous wizard long ago had been sealed.

Azriim smiled. *Dolphin's Coffer* was exactly where it was supposed to be.

The crewmen on nightwatch noticed their sudden appearance and shouted in alarm. The rest of the crew awakened, scrambled out of their deck beds, and grabbed for blades. Three of the crew who had been on watch near the side railing rushed forward with steel and teeth bare.

Azriim held up his hands—he still held his wand and teleportation rod—and called out, "We are expected by Captain Sertan."

The captain must have prepared his crew, or perhaps the sailors recognized Azriim from his previous visit—Captain Sertan had given him a tour of the ship a few days ago—for the three sailors halted their advance, though they continued to stare at Azriim and his cohorts menacingly. Riven answered with a sneer and a stare.

The seamen did not hold the assassin's gaze.

Azriim liked Riven more and more.

A call went out and Captain Sertan quickly appeared at the forecastle rail. Azriim attuned his vision to see dweomers and saw that his charm on the captain remained in effect.

"All is well, seajacks," the captain shouted to his crew. "These are the friends I spoke of."

The crewmen lowered their blades. Those who had been sleeping grumbled at their fellows for disturbing their slumber and curled back into their deckbags and hammocks. At least a few muttered about the ill fortune that accompanied having mages aboard.

The captain left off the railing, slid ably down the forecastle ladder to the maindeck, and walked toward Azriim. Azriim used his arm to hide the bloodstains on his shirt caused by the wound Cale had given him. His flesh continued to regenerate.

The captain wore a wool jacket, dark trousers, and high boots. A thick-bladed cutlass hung casually from his hip. The bags under his eyes were more pronounced than when Azriim had first met him. He probably had slept little.

When he reached them, Captain Sertan said, "Welcome aboard, goodsirs. I am pleased to see you. I was beginning to doubt that you would show."

Azriim gave him a courtly bow. As he did, he pocketed his wand and rod, at the same time drawing forth the wand with which he had previously enchanted the captain.

"I am a man of my word, Captain," he said.

"So I see. An honorable man who pays well is welcome on the *Coffer*. My ship is in your service, as we agreed. Where to?"

Azriim smiled and shook the hand on which he wore the magical glove. The movement and Azriim's will summoned the Sojourner's magical compass from its extra-dimensional space and it appeared in his hand.

The captain marveled, wide eyed.

The needle within the gold-chased, transparent sphere bobbed for a moment before pointing steadily in one direction: west, out to sea.

"The helmsman should follow the indicator on this compass until it points straight down," Azriim said. "That's when we'll be disembarking."

The captain looked at the compass, then in the direction of the indicator. "Nothing lies in that direction but open sea for twenty leagues. There's nowhere to disembark."

Azriim put a friendly hand on the captain's shoulder. As he did, he surreptitiously touched the small wand in his hand to the captain's arm and thereby renewed the charm.

"That will be our problem, Captain Sertan. Your problem is simply to get us there."

The captain pursed his lips but Azriim's spell turned it quickly into a smile. "Well enough. But I'll ask you for the second half of our payment now."

Azriim could not help but smile. Sembians remained Sembians, even when enspelled.

"Of course, Captain. We're all friends here, after all."

Azriim withdrew three large rubies from a pouch at his belt and handed them to Sertan. The human eyed them, eyes glittering, and put them into his sash belt.

"I have quarters reserved for you in the sterncastle," he said, and turned to leave.

"One more thing, Captain," Azriim said, and Sertan turned back to face him. Azriim pulled an enchanted emerald from his pouch. He held it up for Sertan to see, then placed it on the deck and spoke a word of power. The emerald shattered, leaving in its wake a soft green glow that quickly spread to the entirety of the ship.

To prevent another unwanted appearance of the priest of Mask, Azriim projected to Dolgan and Riven.

In truth, he figured Erevis Cale to be dead or at least incapable of following them. *Demon Binder* was leagues and leagues away. And with this dimensional lock in place, the priest could not teleport through the shadows to *Dolphin's Coffer,* even if he could somehow find them.

The crew grumbled about the glow and shared hard looks. Before the captain could protest, Azriim said,

"I know it is awkward, Captain, but it is a necessary precaution."

"We are like a beacon out here," one of the crew shouted to the captain.

"Wizards be damned," growled another.

"What are we into, Cap'n?" asked another.

"Take this," Azriim said, loudly enough to be heard by the crew nearby. He produced another ruby, his last, from his belt pouch. "To compensate for the inconvenience. The magic will harm neither crew nor ship. In fact, it will protect us all."

The captain looked at Azriim, at the ruby, and took it.

"Be about your rest or your duties, jacks," the captain said to the crew. "We can trust these mates."

The captain's firm reassurance quieted the crew.

Captain Sertan ran a professional ship and his men obviously respected his word.

"I appreciate your trust, my friend," Azriim lied.

The captain nodded, took the compass from Azriim's hand.

"I'll get this to Nimil at the helm."

"I would like to set to immediately," Azriim said. "Time is of the essence."

The captain hesitated, nodded, and walked away. As he did, he called out to the crew, "On your feet, lads. Selûne is bright and her tears are shining. Let's set to now. The sooner we get the lubbers to where they are going, the sooner we get to spend the coin they have paid. You'll all be in whores, grub, and drink for two tendays."

A round of tired cheers greeted the captain's words. The crew rose from deckbags and started to prepare the ship for sail. She'd be underway soon enough.

Azriim smiled at Dolgan and Riven. The wounds Cale had given were fully healed, though his shirt was ruined.

"An eventful evening, not so?" he said, still smiling. He looked down at his clothing and frowned. "I need a new shirt."

❧ ❧ ❧ ❧ ❧

A score or more slavers swarmed the deck toward Cale and Jak. The seamen brandished steel in their fists and scowls on their faces. Across the ship, the door to the sterncastle suddenly splintered, forced open from inside. It triggered Jak's ward.

A blast of ice shards and cold exploded from the door jambs. The four ship's masters who had tried to exit screamed, grabbed at flesh torn apart by blades of ice and wood, and fell to the deck.

"I tried to stop you by jamming the lock, you dolts!" Jak shouted.

Many of the advancing crew heard the commotion from behind, saw the dead or dying masters, and slowed their charge.

Cale clutched his mask and incanted a prayer to the Shadowlord. The spell summoned a magical blade of force that answered to Cale's mental command. The blade materialized in the air beside him and at his mental urging, streaked at the big slaver who had ordered the charge. The man tried to parry with his overlarge cutlass, but the blade's darting attacks drove him back.

Two of the slavers tried to assist their comrade, while the rest continued to advance. Several hurled daggers or knives. Cale and Jak hunched, and most flew wide or short, but a few struck home. The shadows that surrounded Cale prevented the two daggers that hit him from doing any more than bruising his skin, but one knife slit a furrow in Jak's cheek, and another dagger stuck in his shoulder. He jerked it out with a grunt—it had penetrated only slightly—glared at the crew, and incanted a prayer to his god.

When the little man finished his spell, he pointed his holy symbol at the slavers. Three went wide-eyed, turned, and fled in terror as if chased by a prince of Hell; two others turned with a snarl and began punching their comrades; three more stopped where they stood, let their blades fall from their hands, and babbled nonsensically in their native tongues.

"It will not last long," Jak said.

"There's only two, jacks!" shouted one of the crew, to bolster his comrades.

The rest nodded, brandished their blades.

With a mental command, Cale formed the shadows around him into a confusing, constantly shifting jumble of illusory images. When he was done, there were not two but seven.

Still the crew advanced, wary but determined. Fifteen paces. Ten.

From nowhere, two slavers landed in a crouch beside Jak and Cale. Cale had only a moment to curse himself for forgetting the two men he had seen atop the forecastle. They must have avoided the blast from Azriim's ball of fire.

The approaching sailors cheered at the appearance of their comrades and rushed forward as one.

"Ware!" Jak shouted, and dodged back from the slash of the smaller of the two, a hard-eyed Thayan. The larger, his three gold earrings glinting in the moonlight, seemed confused by the shifting array of shadow duplicates that surrounded the actual Cale. He hacked wildly with his cutlass at the nearest and the touch of his blade dispelled the image. Cale answered with a slash across the man's chest and finished him with a stab through his throat. He whirled around to see Jak driving his shortsword into the gut of the little slaver, who fell to the deck, screaming and bleeding.

They turned to face the rest of the charging crew and watched with surprise as one of them fell face first to the deck, an arrow sprouting from his back. The slavers around the fallen man shouted, stopped their charge, looked around the deck. Cale, too, tried to pinpoint the source of the fire as another arrow took a second slaver in the throat. Another hit a third in the arm and sent him spinning to the deck, screaming with pain.

The shots were coming from the crow's nest.

I'll explain, Magadon's voice said in their heads.

Cale gave a shout, stepped through the shadows and into the midst of the crew, slashing with Weaveshear. The blade opened the throat of one surprised slaver, pierced the chest of a second. One of those whose mind was clouded by Jak's spell took an awkward cut at Cale, slipped on the deck, and fell at Cale's feet. Cale stabbed him through the chest. He died clutching Weaveshear's edges.

A cutlass slashed across Cale's back, a blow that would have felled him but for the protection granted by the shadows. Instead, the weapon merely opened a painful gash that his skin soon closed. Cale spun around with a reverse slash from Weaveshear but the slaver parried the blow, snarled, and bounded back. Cale followed up, at the same time mentally commanding his summoned blade to attack the slaver. It streaked in from the side and opened a gash in the man's shoulder. While he screamed, Cale decapitated him with a crosscut from Weaveshear.

From the forecastle, Jak shouted the words to a spell and a white beam of energy streaked into a slaver near Cale. The energy seared the man's skin and drove him to the deck, where he lay prone and unmoving.

"This ship is ours!" Magadon shouted down from the crow's nest. "Flee on the ship's boat or you all die!"

An arrow thumped into the deck, vibrating, near a slaver's feet. Another arrow went through the chest of a second slaver.

With an effort of will, Cale caused a cloud of impenetrable shadows to surround him. Cale could see through the blackness perfectly, but he knew the slavers would be able to see nothing. He took up Magadon's call.

"Run, you whoresons!" he shouted, and advanced on the slavers. "This ship is ours!"

Those who were not still enspelled turned and fled for the ship's boat. Cale slammed his pommel into the heads of those still under the mind-muddling effect of Jak's spell. They fell to the deck, dead or unconscious.

Let them go, Cale projected to Magadon, as perhaps six slavers worked to lower the ship's boat from its rigging. They had it lowered within a few breaths and all of them leaped over the side and scrambled into it. They cursed their conquerors as they rowed away. They would die or not on the sea. Cale did not care.

The ship was quiet.

Cale and Jak stood on a deck littered with corpses, a handful of unconscious slavers, and the still-enspelled helmsman. Jak called on the Trickster and healed himself with a prayer. Cale let his flesh repair the wounds he had suffered.

They watched with disbelieving smiles as Magadon descended from the crow's nest. Just to be certain that Magadon was Magadon, Cale spoke the prayer that empowered him to see magical auras. Magadon showed no aura, though his bow and several of his arrows glowed in Cale's sight. The guide was himself.

Cale and Jak met him at the bottom of the mast, full of questions.

"I felt you die," Jak said.

Cale took the guide by the shoulders and shook him. "As did I. Or so I thought."

"A play," the guide said and smiled. "Riven wanted the slaadi to believe he killed me, so I projected a false sensation to you two and to them."

The guide let the words register with Cale and Jak.

"Riven?" Jak said. "A play?"

"Why?" Cale asked. "If he's with us, why not just help us kill the slaadi here and now? We could have done it had he not interfered."

Magadon looked at Cale and answered, "I asked him the same thing. He said Mask wanted it this way, that Mask wanted the slaadi to escape. This time. He said you would understand."

Cale considered that, finally gave a slow nod. He did understand. The Shadowlord had an agenda that he had not yet seen fit to share with either his First or his Second. Riven was just doing what he thought Mask wanted. Cale had been on that path once.

"The Zhent's playing us," Jak said, and could not keep the hostility from his tone.

Cale knew that it was not Riven but Mask who was making the play.

Magadon shook his head. "I do not think so. I have a latent visual leech on him. He suggested it, so that we could follow. He said he would stay with the slaadi until the time was right. I believe him, Erevis. He's with us."

"Agreed," Cale said softly.

Jak shook his head and muttered, "That Zhent has more angles than a prism. I hope we know what we're doing."

Of course, Cale did not know what they were doing. Mask had directed Riven to help the slaadi escape *Demon Binder*. Cale could not imagine why.

CHAPTER 8

AGENDAS

Vhostym prepared to leave his pocket plane. He knew that he would not return. He would send for the Weave Tap when the time arrived.

He felt no nostalgia over his departure. The place had served him well as an isolated location from which to put his plan into place, but its utility was at an end. And Vhostym retained nothing that did not have utility.

The binding spells with which he had confined the demons, devils, and celestials he used in his research would degrade over the coming centuries. Eventually, the creatures would be free to slaughter one another or to return to their home planes. Or not. Vhostym did not care what became of them. Their utility too was at an end.

In his mind, he cataloged the threescore spells

he had spent the last few hours preparing. He inventoried components for the spells, checked the magical paraphernalia that adorned his person. He reached into a belt pouch and counted the twenty magical emeralds he had personally crafted to prepare for this night. They were all there, with the exception of the one he had provided to Azriim.

He was ready.

His ragged breath sounded loud and wet in his ears. He felt increasingly tired. The pain in his limbs, in his muscles, his bones, wracked him. He reached into his mind and diminished his brain's capacity to register painful sensations. The agony decreased but did not end. He endured it. His illness was advancing quickly, inexorably. He needed events to move just as quickly. He had only a little time remaining, and therefore none to waste.

From the extradimensional storage space within his robe pocket, he withdrew a fillet of jade. Rather than lift his arms to place it on his head—the motion would have caused him added pain—he instead took hold of it with his mind and floated it atop his brow. He then incanted the words to one of his most powerful transmutations, a spell that would allow him to take an incorporeal form. All of his items and components would accompany him into incorporeality, and would remain as solid to him as the real world would seem insubstantial.

When the magic took effect, his flesh tingled, its malleability palpable. He regretted that he would have to once more spend time in a form other than his natural body, but he was not yet prepared to set foot on the surface in his own flesh.

His body dissolved relative to the material world. His flesh, clothing, and spell components turned gray and insubstantial. The world around him lost color. A channel opened between his being and the Negative Material Plane—a necessary element of the spell—and a preternatural cold suffused him. He willed his body to stand on the chamber floor, though he could have floated through it had he wished.

The transformation did nothing to end his pain, which, like his equipment, had followed him into his ghostly form. But the new form did not have the sensitivity to light that was the congenital curse of Vhostym's material flesh.

He incanted another spell and turned invisible. Afterward, he cast again and teleported from his pocket plane to the surface of Faerûn, to a mountainous region on the frontier of the realm of Amn.

He materialized where he intended, in a thicket of century-old ash trees, near the bottom of a tree-dotted, steep-sided mountain vale. Darkness shrouded the valley. Mountains walled him in, dark and ominous. A brook wound its way through the vale's trees.

Vhostym's form allowed him to see well even in darkness, allowed him to sense the lifeforces of the animals around him. The creatures perceived the negative energy of his form and cowered in their dens, instinctively terrified of him.

They were wise to be frightened, for he had death on his mind.

Neither Sclûne nor her tears were visible above the mountains, but a window of stars shone down from a cloudless sky. The wind stirred the ash leaves, but his form felt nothing but the pain of his illness. He longed to smell the air, feel the breeze.

Soon, he reminded himself.

Vhostym knew that a single, twisting pass behind him was the only nonmagical means of entering or exiting the vale. He knew too that mages and priests in service to Cyric kept the pass hidden with illusions and spell traps to protect the vale's secret—a tower hidden within the ash trees. Vhostym could mark the tower from where he stood only because he knew where to look.

The windowless, square spire of gray stone stood in the

center of the vale, near the brook, barely visible through the trees. The crenellated top, silhouetted in the starlight, looked like a mouthful of broken teeth. Four soldiers armed with glaives and armored in mail stood watch on the ground before the temple. They were all human, so Vhostym assumed they must have some magical device that allowed them to see in the dark.

A raised drawbridge lay flat against the tower's face. The drawbridge did not rest at ground level, but about a troll's height up the wall. Vhostym knew that the double doors behind the drawbridge opened onto the second floor of the tower.

Vhostym floated forward through the trees, toward the tower, an invisible harbinger of doom. Nothing visible on the tower's exterior bespoke its dark purpose but Vhostym knew it to be a temple of Cyric the Dark Sun, one of two towers built in hidden vales in the Small Teeth, a mountain range that made up the southern border of Amn. Though a distance of a few leagues separated the two temples, a secret underground tunnel wormed under the mountains to link them.

The Towers of the Eternal Eclipse, the worshipers called them. Vhostym found the name ironic and appropriate.

Decades ago Vhostym had scoured Faerûn for the material he would need, along with the Weave Tap, to complete his greatest spell—a peculiar type of stone that fell from the heavens. The stone had a latent property—the ability to amplify arcane power cast through it.

One of Vhostym's divinations had at last located a large deposit of the stone in the Small Teeth, in the form of Cyric's temple. Further magical inquiries had determined the origin of the stone. Millennia before, a small rock with this special property had blazed a path of fire across the sky and smashed into the mountains, exposing a seam of granite. The impact pulverized the otherworldly rock and left a crater in the mountains, but the heat and pressure of the impact had transferred the stone's properties into the local granite. Later, a sect of Banites—the original builders of the temple—had quarried the stone to build their towers. The temple was later taken over after the Time of Troubles by the Cyricists. Neither the Banites nor the Cyricists ever learned of the amplifying properties of the stone.

For months after learning the nature and history of the towers, Vhostym scried them repeatedly. He had memorized their interiors, their defenses. He knew the locations of the warding glyphs and spell traps that guarded some of the towers' interior doors. He knew the number and nature of those who garrisoned each spire: roughly fivescore soldiers, a dozen priests, and a handful of mages. The High Priest of Cyric who reigned over the towers, one Blackwill Akhmelere, occupied the eastern tower this night, so he would be spared.

No one in the western tower would live more than another hour.

Vhostym cast a long series of protective spells. When he finished, an array of invisible magical wards sheathed his person. Unless they could be dispelled—and no one within the tower had the power to counter Vhostym's dweomers—he was virtually invulnerable to harm from either weapons or spells.

The most powerful of the defensive wards would not last long, however, so speed would be his ally. He removed a root from his pouch, chewed it, swallowed, and recited another spell. When he finished, his spectral body felt energized, faster.

He was ready to begin. Vhostym started forward.

A sudden call went up from the guards before the tower and he stopped his advance. The guards scrambled aside as the sound of a winch mechanism carried through the valley and the drawbridge started to lower. In moments, the drawbridge's edge was flat on the ground, forming a ramp from ground level to the elevated double doors. The twin iron slabs of the temple doors swung open, torch-light poured out, and a group of twenty sword-armed and mail-armored soldiers trooped down the drawbridge.

All of them wore the hard looks of experienced fighters. Each bore a longbow and stuffed field pack over his shoulders. A short-haired, dark-eyed priest in plate armor led them, trailed by a boy who steered a mule loaded with field gear. The priest bore a black staff capped with an opal. The opal radiated a soft, red light that allowed the humans to see, but would not itself be easy to see from a distance. The red light highlighted the priest's breast-plate to reveal an enameled image: a white, jawless skull, the symbol of Cyric the Mad. The gate guards bowed their heads as the priest stalked down the drawbridge and passed them. Waving his staff, the priest offered them Cyric's blessing.

A raiding party, Vhostym guessed.

He knew the Cyricists often raided the merchant caravans that braved the mountain paths between Amn and Tethyr. Sometimes they raided for food and supplies, other times they raided only to murder or take captives for later sacrifice.

The double doors closed behind the raiding party and the drawbridge clicked its way back up.

The ringing of the raiders' mail and the stomp of their boots sounded loudly in the night as they picked their way through the trees. The priest gazed about alertly as he walked but his eyes passed over Vhostym without hesitation. The party walked along the path near Vhostym and marched on toward the pass. Within moments, the night swallowed them and their red light.

Vhostym stared after them, pondering the capricious-ness of the multiverse. Had the patrol been scheduled to move out only a quarter hour later, it never would have left at all. Vhostym was reminded again of the utter randomness, the absolute meaninglessness of the multiverse. He might have wished that existence had a greater purpose but he knew better and refused to deceive himself. It simply *was*. Of course, an existence without external purpose was also an existence without boundaries, at least for one of Vhostym's power. The reminder spurred him to action.

He turned back to the tower and spoke aloud a word of power.

Time stopped, at least subjectively. The world froze, except for Vhostym.

The spell would last only a short while, but he could cast it again if necessary.

Taking his pouch of enchanted emeralds in hand, he spoke a stanza of arcane words and teleported into the first floor entry hall of the tower. Torchlight lit the room but the brightness did not trouble Vhostym's incorporeal form. Two soldiers and one of the temple's wizards stood within, frozen between breaths. The drawbridge winches stood in alcoves to either side. Two closed wooden doors awaited in the opposite wall.

Without hesitating, Vhostym dropped one of the emeralds on the floor—the gem took corporeal form when he released it—and spoke a command word. At his utterance, the jewel shattered into a rain of shards and left in its wake a green glow that encompassed the entirety of the entry hall and extended through the wooden doors. The abjuration embodied in the glow restricted any form of extradimensional magical travel, including teleportation, into it or out of it.

Vhostym's hastening spell augmented the already-rapid flight granted him by his spectral form and he passed rapidly through the wooden doors. A wide stairway led down. Murals depicting the Dark Sun stained the walls. The corridor linked with several rooms as well as the watch stations set in each corner of the tower. Vhostym dropped a gem, and another, until a green glow covered the entire first floor. He noted the location of those within as he moved—the guards armed with long bows at the watch stations; the servants asleep in their beds.

He floated downward through the floor and did the same on the ground floor, where most of the guards were quartered, and in the dungeon, where a few guards kept watch over prisoners. Then he floated up through the floor and did the same on the third floor, which featured a large central room around which lay the chambers of underpriests and lesser mages. In moments, that entire floor too was cloaked in green. He moved up to the next floor and repeated the process, this time painting in green the rooms of the senior priests and wizards.

A sudden rush and blur of sound told him that time had resumed. He was in the uninhabited, large central room on the fourth floor. Other than an endless series of wall murals depicting the Dark Sun reading the Cyrinishad, the room featured nothing other than several doors, four pillars, and two stairways, one leading up and one down.

He imagined the surprise the inhabitants of the tower must have felt—between blinks, the rooms they occupied had lit up with a green glow. From below, he heard alarmed shouts. No doubt someone was rushing for one of the tower's many alarm bells.

A door to his left flew open and a priest in his night clothes, but with a blade clutched in his hand, burst out. He looked through and past Vhostym and padded toward the stairway.

Vhostym put the priest out of his mind, repeated the word of power, and again stopped time. The priest froze in mid stride. Vhostym floated up through the floor to the fifth story. There, he found almost the entire level to be a single, open chamber dedicated to the wretched rites of Cyric the Dark Sun. Inlaid tiles formed a sunburst in the center of the chamber, on which sat a pedestal of white stone shaped like a jawless skull. Vhostym could feel the magic in the room as a tingle on the nape of his neck. Wrought-iron braziers with skull motifs stood in each corner. A score or so of skeletons in plate armor lined the walls. Vhostym ignored it all and placed his abjuration gems.

He floated to the only room off the ceremonial chamber—the bedchamber of Olma Kulenvov, the highest-ranking cleric in the tower. The embers from a dying fire lit the chamber, and Olma slept comfortably in her opulent, carved ash bed. Vhostym dropped a binding gem, activated it, and exited through the roof.

Each corner of the tower's roof featured an external observation ledge. Vhostym cast a holding ward on the doors that led to each of the posts. Three guardsmen stood on each ledge, immobile between moments. Vhostym rapidly cast a series of spells that conjured a cloud of noxious green fumes over each post. The clouds of gas appeared over and around the guards. The men were dead but did not yet know it. They existed between the last two breaths of their lives. When time resumed, the men would inhale the choking fumes and die painfully.

Vhostym flew down to the ground and cast a spell at the feet of the guards on the exterior of the tower. The evocation summoned a small, spinning ball of potential energy that would explode after a delay, the length of which Vhostym chose as he cast: a fifteen count. Then he cast another holding ward on the drawbridge and double doors.

No one would be allowed to escape the tower.

He sank below the surface of the vale, blind while he traveled through solid rock, until he reached the beginning of the broad, earthen tunnel that linked the western tower with the eastern. Timbers set at even intervals supported the ceiling. A simple incantation twisted the wood of the score or so timbers near Vhostym. They shattered, shooting splinters and chunks of jagged wood in all directions. Several passed through Vhostym's form.

The sudden loss of support caused the roof of the tunnel to sag, crumble, finally to collapse. There would be no escape through it either. Vhostym returned to the surface and examined his handiwork.

He had turned the temple into a tomb. Those outside it would be dead when time restarted, and those within could not escape.

He waited, eager to begin.

After less than a ten count, the blurry rush of sound and motion told him that time had resumed. It was time to kill.

❧ ❧ ❧ ❧ ❧

Cale, Jak, and Magadon stood on the maindeck of *Demon Binder*, looking at one another.

They had a ship, still cutting through the sea, but had no one to man it.

"What now?" Jak asked.

Cale thought about it and made his decision.

"We take a moment to free the slaves, then find the slaadi and kill them. Right now." To Magadon, he said, "You have a link with Riven?"

Magadon nodded. "Erevis, are you certain? Riven said he would signal us when the time was right."

"Mags," Cale said, "Mask wanted the slaadi to escape and they escaped. That's all I am going to give Riven and that's all I'm going to give Mask. We want the slaadi dead for our own reasons. Mask's are . . . incidental to those."

Jak's eyebrows raised but he held his tongue.

Magadon blanched and shook his head. "I should have such nerve when it comes to speaking of my own father."

Cale knew that Magadon was born of Mephistopheles, an archdevil. The guide did not even care to speak his father's name.

"Mask isn't my father," Cale said.

"No," Magadon agreed, though the word sounded more like a question than a statement.

To Jak, Cale said, "Go release the slaves, little man.

See if any of them can sail this ship to take the rest back to land. We are leaving as soon as they're out."

Jak nodded. "I saw keys for the cages on one of the corpses." He turned and sped off.

"Show me, Mags," Cale said.

Magadon furrowed his brow in concentration and a rosy glow haloed his head. He held out his hand to Cale. Cale took it, felt his mind meet Magadon's, and saw what the guide saw through Riven's eyes. . . .

They were on a ship sailing its way through the night and the dark water. A soft, inexplicable green glow shrouded the entire vessel. Cale had no notion what it was. The ship sported three masts to *Demon Binder*'s two, and its sails were triangular rather than square.

Riven stood on the maindeck and looked out over the sea. An enormous peak exploded up from the sea behind the ship. Sheer sides rose from the waters and extended toward starry skies. A single tower on a high promontory was backlit by the starlight.

Cale knew the name of the island, though he had never seen it before. Everyone who lived near the waters of the Inner Sea had heard of Traitor's Isle. Sailors used the island and its magical tower as a distance marker. Cale let the mental image of the ship sink into his mind. He extended his senses to feel the shadows aboard and. . . .

Felt nothing.

He tried again but still could not feel the shadows aboard the other ship. Something was blocking him.

The green glow. It was somehow blocking his ability to transport himself aboard. He clenched his fists in frustration. He considered trying to transport them into the water near the ship, but dismissed the idea. Even a small mistake in the transport could leave them alone on the open sea. Besides, even if he could put them next to the ship's hull, how then would they get aboard?

"What is it?" Magadon said.

"A problem," Cale answered, and left it at that. He

released his hold on Magadon and considered.

He looked toward the hold. Jak had hung a rope ladder from the top of the hatch. One by one, the freed slaves climbed up it and stood on deck. They wore only ragged tunics and trousers. All were bootless. All had a tenday's growth of beard on their faces. Many coughed or swayed on their feet.

Their gazes went to the dead and unconscious Thayans, still scattered about the deck, to Cale, to Magadon. Most gave hard smiles and nods.

They stood about near the hatch, obviously unsure what to do. Other than the coughing, they looked to be in decent health, nothing like the slaves Cale had seen in Skullport.

Cale and Magadon walked over to the slaves as more continued to climb the ladder. Before Cale could speak, one of the former slaves, a short, thickset man of about thirty winters, stepped forth and said, "Seems we owe you thanks, lubber, for freeing us and giving these Thayan flesh peddlers what they deserved." He grinned—his front teeth were gone—and extended his hand. "So, thanks to you."

Cale took the man's hand in his own. Nods around. Murmured gratitude.

The man had called Cale "lubber." Cale's hopes rose.

"You are a sailor, then?"

"Aye," said the man.

"As are we all," said another bass voice, from just inside the hold. A thicket of black hair appeared in the hatchway, followed by a head the size of a bucket, and a body as large as a great orc. A black beard, shot through with gray, hid his mouth, but the man's dark eyes carried a hardness Cale had seen only in his own reflection and Riven's single eye. An overlarge, misshapen nose jutted from his face like a weathered crag.

"Captain on deck," said the man with whom Cale had been conversing, and the rest of the former slaves stood at attention.

"Ease, men," the captain said, and lifted himself fully out of the hatch. The men relaxed and the captain's gaze swept the ship, the sea.

"This whore is still underway. Jeg, Hessim, Veer, Pellak, get the mainsail furled. Nom, get her anchor down until we know what's what. Ashin, get on the helm."

Without hesitation, the men snapped to their duties. Cale considered protesting, thought better of it, and got out of their way.

"Runnin' hard at night," the captain said to Cale. "Thayans are fool sailors. You're not seamen, are you?"

"No," Cale answered.

"But you two and the little fellow would be the men who freed us."

Cale nodded, as did Magadon.

"Then you have my gratitude and that of my crew." He extended his hand. "Captain Evrel Kes, out of Marsember. These are my men."

Cale took his hand. Despite the captain's age and the fact that his large body had gone somewhat fat, there was strength in his grip.

"Erevis Cale," Cale answered.

"Magadon, out of Starmantle."

"Jak Fleet," said the little man's voice as his red head popped out of the hold and he climbed onto deck. To Cale, Jak said, "That's everyone. Still some stores down there. Grain and spices, I think."

Cale realized the captain had come up from the hold last, only after all his men had been freed and sent above. Cale liked him already.

Above and around them, Cale and his comrades watched as the captain's men scaled the mast and began drawing up the mainsail. They hollered down to Nom to drop anchor.

"I can see, you fish turds," Nom shot back from the bow, and released the anchor.

Evrel smiled at his men's banter.

From the helmsman's perch, Ashin called, "This one's still alive, Captain."

"As are a few of these," called another crewman, sticking his foot into one of the Thayans Cale had left unconscious on the deck.

Evrel looked at Cale and said, "The punishment at sea for slavery is execution."

Cale saw no bloodlust in the captain's eyes, no need for vengeance. Evrel was simply proposing to do what he saw as his duty.

"You are captain of this ship, now," Cale answered, and not even Jak protested.

Evrel nodded. "You know the law of the sea, Ashin. They go over. All of them."

Ashin nodded, heaved the still immobilized slaver over his shoulder, carried him to the side, and cast him over. Three other crewmen threw the unconscious Thayans over the rail.

"The corpses go after them," said Evrel to the crew. "Step to it, lads. This ship stinks badly enough."

The crew gathered the remaining dead and pitched them over, but not before stripping them of weapons and valuables. The captain watched it all, then turned back to Cale.

"I left my manners in the hold," he said, and smiled. "Well met, Erevis, Magadon, and Jak. Now, if you were sailors, I'd wonder at a mutiny. As it is, I wonder how you got aboard. I do not see another ship."

"Spell," Cale said, and left it at that.

Evrel frowned. Cale knew that sailors were notoriously suspicious of magic, and captains more than most.

"You're hunting Thayans, then?" Evrel asked. "Or slavers maybe? Or did this crew in particular do something to run afoul of you three?"

Cale shook his head. "None of those. What we are hunting escaped us. The slavers just got in our way."

The captain stared at him a moment.

"Reason enough," Evrel said. "And fortunate for me and my men. I'll remember to stay out of your way."

The dropped anchor noticeably slowed the ship. The rest of Evrel's crew, having cleared the decks of bodies, set about familiarizing themselves with the vessel's operation and layout. The heavyset man Cale had spoke with earlier issued frequent orders. Cale assumed him to be Evrel's first mate. He soon walked over to confer with his captain.

"My first mate," Evrel explained. "Gorse Olis."

Gorse nodded a greeting. Cale, Jak, and Magadon reciprocated.

Jak asked, "How did you and your crew end up here, like this?"

The captain's lips curled and Gorse gave a harsh laugh.

Evrel said, "I commanded *Sea Reaver*, a carrack out of Marsember. We were taken on the open sea by a three-ship pirate fleet out of the Pirate Isles. These bastards," he made a gesture to indicate the Thayans, "bought us from the slave blocks there. I don't know what they had in mind for us."

"Nothing good," Gorse said.

"That's certain," answered the captain.

Cale had given the captain and crew time to get their hands around the ship, so he cut to his question. He had no other options. They would have to pursue the slaadi using ordinary methods of transport.

"We need your services, captain. Can you sail this ship? The . . . men we are pursuing are aboard another ship and we have to catch them."

Evrel and Gorse shared a look and Gorse nodded.

Evrel looked back to Cale and said, "She's an ugly Thayan bitch, but we can sail her, Erevis Cale. Where is the other ship you're after? Be difficult to track her by night."

Cale said, "Near Traitor's Isle is the last we knew of her."

Evrel nodded and called over his shoulder to the helmsman's post. "Ashin, where in Umberlee's realm are we? And how far from Traitor's Isle?"

Ashin plucked the mechanical device from the table near him and climbed out of the steering pocket. He held the device to his eyes, looked skyward, and manipulated the mechanism.

Evrel said, "As long as he can see the sky, Ashin can locate us on the Inner Sea better than any helmsman I have ever seen. He can make a decent estimate even without the astrolabe."

Gorse added, "The men think his father was a water elemental with a bent for studying the stars. He knows sea and sky as well as any."

Cale smiled. He liked the new crew of *Demon Binder*.

In short order, Ashin pulled the device from his eye and shouted, "We're far west of that, Captain. Nearest port is Procampur. More than eighty leagues from Traitor's Isle."

Gorse whistled and shook his head.

The captain turned back to Cale, brow furrowed. "You're sure you marked this ship near Traitor's Isle?"

Cale nodded.

"More sorcery," Gorse muttered.

Evrel said, "There's no catching it, Erevis. We are two days from that island sailing day and night and assuming favorable winds. So unless you can lift this ship out of the water and fly it there, your hunt is over."

The moment Cale heard Evrel's words, he understood why Mask had arranged for the slaadi to escape, or at least understood one reason. The Shadowlord wanted to test Cale, to see how far he could push his abilities, and he wanted Cale to sink deeper into the shadows.

Jak must have seen something in his expression. "What is it, Cale?"

"An idea, little man." Cale put a hand on Jak's shoulder and said to Evrel, "Captain, I am going to do exactly that, if you and your crew are willing."

At first Evrel smiled, as though Cale were making a joke, but a frown quickly swallowed the smile. An even deeper frown formed on Gorse's lips.

"You are not jesting?" the captain asked.

"I am not."

"You're not?" Jak asked.

The captain studied Cale's face, looked to Jak, to Magadon.

In Chondathan, Gorse said, "*Captain, we hardly know these men. They could be pirates, Zhents, evil men who just need a crew. We should be careful.*"

Before Evrel could respond, Cale said, "Gorse, I speak and read nine languages. You will need to use something more obscure than Chondathan to communicate secretly in my presence. And you're right. You do not know us. So know this: I once killed for coin. Now I serve Mask the Shadowlord as a priest. And I am as much shadow as man."

He held up his hand and let shadowstuff leak from his fingertips. Both captain and mate went wide-eyed.

"Umberlee's teats," Gorse cursed.

"I am a mindmage and woodsman born of an archdevil," Magadon said, doffing his cap and showing the stubs of his horns.

His words did nothing to set the seamen at ease.

Jak grinned and said, "I am the ordinary one, it seems. A one-time Harper and priest of Brandobaris the Trickster."

Cale looked the two sailors in the eyes and said, "That is all you are going to get. But now you know us as well as most. Well enough?"

Gorse cursed, but to his credit, also smiled.

"I'm just a fisherman's son out of Arabel," the mate said.

The captain, too, grinned through his beard.

"Talos take me, Erevis Cale, but if you can make this ship fly, I swear that you will always have a welcome berth on any vessel I command."

Cale wondered if the captain would feel the same after he learned what Cale intended. Cale would not make the ship fly. He would surround it in darkness and move it and the whole crew from where they were to the shadow of the cliffs of Traitor's Isle.

CHAPTER 9

SAILING THE NIGHT

Get your men ready," Cale said to Evrel.

In no time, word went from the mate and captain to the crew. So, too, did the description of who and what Cale, Magadon, and Jak were, or once were. Few of the crew made eye contact after that. All muttered, but all obeyed the captain's orders. They seemed both fascinated and fearful.

Cale took a position in the bow, standing just over the leering wooden demon's face that decorated *Demon Binder*'s prow. Jak and Magadon stood beside him. Behind them on the deck and above them in the rigging, the crew waited in pensive silence. The calm sea, as black as jet under the starlight, seemed also to be waiting.

Cale imagined in his mind's eye the towering

cliffsides of Traitor's Isle, the long shadow cast over the water by its tower, even by starlight. He started to draw the night around him, around Magadon, around Jak. He spread it out to the rest of the ship like a dire fog. A rustle went through the crew but they held their ground.

Cale waited until pitch cloaked the entire vessel. He alone could see within the darkness. He reached out with his mind, found the correspondence between the darkness that shrouded him and the darkness near Traitor's Isle. He tried to take the entire ship in his mental grasp. It defied an easy grip. He struggled, sweating, praying, asking Mask for aid. Finally he mastered the darkness and took it.

Somewhere, he knew, Mask was pleased.

Cale felt the flutter in his gut that bespoke instantaneous transport. He let the darkness subside. It flowed off the ship's decks like mist to reveal . . . water the color of pitch, a sky as dark as a demon's heart. A sourceless ochre light backlit clouds shaped like the faces of screaming men. Green lightning ripped the sky to pieces.

The Plane of Shadow.

"Trickster's toes," Jak muttered.

The crew echoed Jak's sentiment. A chorus of oaths ran from bow to stern, a fearful chorus.

"Erevis. . . ." Magadon began.

The feat had left Cale drained, wrung out. His body felt worn; his breath came hard. He sagged, leaned on Magadon for support.

Magadon took his weight. The guide stared at him, studied him.

"You look different, Erevis," Magadon said. "The shadows around you . . . they're darker."

Cale nodded. He had taxed himself, sunk deeper into the shadows, and even still he had not quite accomplished what he wished. He saw Mask's hand in it.

Evrel climbed the forecastle, eyes hard, brow furrowed. When he saw Cale, he stopped in his tracks.

"Talos, man! Your eyes."

Cale looked away. He knew his eyes glowed yellow on the Plane of Shadow.

"What do you want, Evrel?" Magadon asked, his voice stern.

"What do I—? Look around. Where are we? This is no sea that I know."

The crew nearby murmured agreement.

Magadon started to speak but Cale held up a hand to cut him off.

"We are on the Plane of Shadow, Evrel," Cale said, his voice heavy with fatigue. "Do not be concerned. I'll be taking us back to Faerûn soon. This is just a waystop."

"Soon?" Evrel asked, and rubbed his chin.

"Soon," Cale answered. The shadows nourished him and his strength already was returning. He patted Magadon on the shoulder and stood on his own feet.

A cry from up the mast drew their eyes.

"There, look there!" called a crewman, and pointed to the sky.

High above them, a swirling mass of black forms like a flock of giant bats detached from a cloud and wheeled downward.

Thunder boomed in the distance.

The forms circled and wheeled, finally headed for the ship. They became distinguishable as they got closer. Pinpoints of red light dotted the mass.

"Shadows," Jak said, and pulled out his jeweled pendant holy symbol. "Trickster's hairy toes."

Hundreds of undead shadows were streaking for the ship.

"Arms, men," Evrel ordered, and the crew started snapping up weapons. Those in the rigging and nests rapidly descended toward the deck to stand with their fellows.

Cale saw Mask's purpose then, understood why the Shadowlord had brought him back to the Plane of Shadow. He put his hand on Evrel's shoulder and shook his head.

"Unnecessary, captain. They will not harm you. They're coming for me."

"What in the twelve seas does that mean?" Evrel asked.

"Cale?" Jak asked.

Cale stared into the sky, watching the horde approach. The Shadowlord had put a weapon in his hand. He had only to use it.

"Put away your symbol, little man," Cale said, and donned his mask.

"Stay your hands!" Evrel ordered his crew.

The sailors looked at each other nervously but let their weapons hang loosely at their sides.

The shadows circled downward until they swarmed the air near the masts. Several creatures broke off and wheeled over the deck. They were humanoid in shape, but amorphous, trailing streamers of shadow as they flew.

Cale waited. Several descended to the deck, floated in front of him, and stared into his face. He let shadows leak from his flesh. Red eyes flared in response and the creatures flew back up to join the black mass over the mast. From there, hundreds of pairs of red eyes fixed on Cale, watched him, measured him. The sky was blanketed with a cloud of the unliving. The creatures radiated cold and the entire crew shivered under their gaze. Not Cale.

The shadows hovered there, waiting. Cale knew they were his to command. He held up his hands and let Mask's power run through him and reach into the sky. The cloud of shadows swirled in answer, excited, eager. Cale gave them only a single command, and his voice carried clearly into the sky. "Come when I call."

The shadows churned around the masts, around the sails, and their red eyes flared. Cale took it as an acknowledgement. With that, the cloud dispersed and the shadows vanished into the darkness of the plane.

The crew stood silent. Cale felt Jak and Magadon's eyes

on him. He thought of Sephris's words to him: *The darkness has soaked you. But there is more to come.*

Cale knew it to be true. Mask had only some of what he wanted. The Shadowlord always wanted more.

But so did Cale. And while serving Mask had its price, it also brought power. The darkness answered to Cale more than it did to anyone. And now it had given him the means to catch and kill the slaadi.

Lightning lined the sky. Thunder boomed its approval.

"What in the Trickster's name just happened?" Jak asked.

"Nothing," Cale said. "It's time to return to Faerûn."

Magadon said, "Are you . . . able?"

Cale nodded. The energies of the Plane of Shadow had restored his energy quickly.

"Not nearly soon enough," Evrel said, and did not make eye contact with Cale.

"Ready your crew," Cale said to him.

In moments, Cale drew the darkness around the ship once more. When the pitch engulfed *Demon Binder,* Cale again pictured Traitor's Isle, seized the ship in his grasp, and moved it through the planes. The effort did not tire him this time; his power had grown.

He let the darkness fade away to reveal the sheer, rocky sides of Traitor's Isle. *Demon Binder* floated in the waters a bowshot away from the island's cliffs.

A satisfied murmur sounded from the crew. Even Jak and Magadon sighed with relief.

"Look there," one of the sailors said, and pointed toward the sky.

Above the midmast whirled a black maelstrom, a portal that Cale had left open between the Prime Plane and the Plane of Shadow. It hung in the air above the mast, an empty hole in the sky. Red dots began to appear within it.

The shadows were gathering.

Cale could feel their anticipation. He had but to call them forth.

"What are you doing, Cale?" Jak asked, and Cale heard the alarm in his voice.

"I am using the weapons at hand," Cale said. "I'm sending the entire swarm of shadows after the slaadi."

He knew the creatures would catch the slaadi's ship. They flew as quickly as arrows.

"What? What are you saying? The crew, Cale," Jak said.

Cale whirled on Jak. "What about them, Jak? They're in league with the slaadi, aren't they?" Jak did not quail before Cale's anger. "Maybe, but maybe not. They might just be a hired ship. And no one deserves to die like that, Cale." Jak pointed up at the gathering shadows.

"Dead is dead, little man," Cale said, and held up his arms to call forth the shadows.

Jak's hand closed on his cloak. "No, Cale. It's not. Listen to me. You don't see it, but I do. This is how he's trying to bring you in all the way. He sets you up to seek revenge and gives you a method, *his* method, to achieve it. But that doesn't have to be your method. I've said it to you before." He shook Cale's cloak. "Cale, I've said it to you before—keep yourself. *Keep yourself.*"

Jak's words tweaked Cale's conscience. He stared up at the shadows, looked at his hands, at the eyes of the crew, the eyes of his friends. The horror on their faces brought him back to himself.

What was he thinking?

"Take off the mask, Cale," Jak said. "Take it off."

Cale nodded and removed his mask. He saw it then, saw it the way Jak saw it. Mask kept feeding him power a little at a time, just when he needed it so much that he would use it. That was how Mask hoped to win his soul, control him.

Cale would not allow it. He shook his head.

"No," he murmured to the shadows.

He knelt down, turned, and looked Jak in the eye. "I hear your words, Jak. We do it our way. With *our* methods."

Jak smiled, thumped him on the shoulder.

Cale stood and with an effort of will caused the portal to the shadow plane to close. The shadows wailed as the portal squeezed shut. The moment it did, a wave of fatigue nearly brought Cale to his knees. He leaned on Jak, who grunted under his weight but kept him upright.

"Are you all right, Erevis?" Magadon asked, helping Jak bear him.

Cale nodded. He took a deep breath and stood on his own feet.

"Mags, look through Riven's eyes, try to determine which way they're heading." He hurried to the back of the forecastle and shouted down to Evrel, "Captain, get this ship ready to move as fast as it can."

The captain overcame whatever wonder he felt at Cale's feat, nodded, and started barking orders. Within moments, *Demon Binder* raised anchor and lowered her sails. Evrel's crew even raised the topsails.

"Mags?" Cale asked.

The rosy halo around Magadon's head faded and he opened his eyes.

"Due west," he said to Cale.

"Due west," Cale shouted down to Evrel, who relayed it to Ashin.

Demon Binder was soon underway.

An hour later, Jak and Cale stood at the prow, staring ahead at empty sea. There was no sign of the slaadi's ship. Cale turned and looked behind them. Traitor's Isle was lost to the darkness.

"Not fast enough," he muttered.

"Let's remedy that," Jak said. The little man removed his holy symbol from his belt pouch and spoke the words to a spell. Cale recognized it as the spell with which the little man previously had summoned the water elemental.

When he spoke the final word, Jak leaned out over the prow and waited. In moments, two watery pillars as tall as Cale rose from the sea, keeping perfect pace with the speed of the ship.

Jak ordered them, "Help speed the ship and your service will be short."

The elementals swayed in response, offered susurrous replies, and vanished below the waves.

Moments later, the ship noticeably gained speed.

"Well done," Cale said.

Jak nodded, cast the spell again, and again. By the time he was done, half a dozen water elementals had hold of *Demon Binder*'s hull and were driving her through the sea.

Evrel and the crew could not stop grinning.

"We could catch a gull on the wing at this pace," the captain shouted to Cale and Jak.

Cale did not smile. He wanted only to catch two slaadi and an assassin, and he wanted to catch them *his* way.

Vhostym listened with satisfaction as shouts of alarm sounded from atop the tower. Clouds of toxic green fumes capped the crenellations. Men screamed and died. Two of the roof guards jumped to their deaths rather than endure the painful death spasms brought on by the gas.

Before the doors, the ball of potential energy that Vhostym had left spinning at the feet of the guards exploded. A spider web of lightning shot out in all directions. Bolts knifed into the guards, blew them from their feet, burned their flesh, stopped their hearts. All of them died quickly, with arcs of lightning dancing over their still-jerking corpses.

Alarm bells rang from within the tower.

Still invisible—for Vhostym's invisibility did not end when he attacked, as most such illusions did—he spoke the command word to bypass his own wards and flew through the drawbridge and double door into the entry foyer.

Ten bewildered soldiers stood crowded within, weapons bare. Two tried to lower the drawbridge and open the double doors to the outside but Vhostym's spell held the portals closed.

"Sealed," one of them shouted back to a bearded sergeant.

The sergeant cursed.

"Get the priests," he said to another.

Before the soldier could leave the foyer, Vhostym seized the far doors with his mind and slammed them shut. He waved his staff and placed a seal on the door that would keep it closed.

The soldiers, their fearful faces highlighted in the green glow of the dimensional lock, whirled around.

"Something is in here," one of them said.

"Here? What do you mean *here*?" asked another, a young soldier with a thin beard.

Panic was setting in.

"Hold your ground in the Dark Sun's name," the sergeant said, but Vhostym could hear the fear in his voice too. "Lis, try the door again."

Vhostym floated into a corner of the room and softly incanted a spell. A wave of invisible energy went forth from his outstretched hands. The magic hit the soldiers, one, then another, another, until all of them went rigid, immobilized by the power of the magic.

They were nothing more than statues of flesh waiting to die.

Shouts sounded from the other side of the closed double doors. Something slammed fruitlessly against the sealed door. Vhostym heard an invocation—one of the priests attempting to counter his locking spell. The attempt failed, of course.

A sudden wave of pain wracked Vhostym's body, sent a charge through his bones. Not an enemy's spell, but his disease. He hissed with pain.

Not now, he thought, and waited what seemed like an

eternity for it to pass. When it did, he put it out of his mind and withdrew a small leather bag and a wax candle from his component pouch. He lit the candle with a mental command, tossed the bag to the floor amidst the immobilized soldiers, and cast a powerful summoning. The candle flame turned black as he spoke the words. He completed the summoning by pronouncing the name of the gelugon devil he was calling. "Emerge, Kostikus."

The candle flared out in his hand and the leather bag squirmed, expanded, opened like the mouth of a beast. The bag's opening became a gate, a portal to the Hells. Screams emerged from it, the agonized wails of tortured souls.

"What is happening in there?!" shouted a voice from behind the door.

The bag's mouth grew until it was as large as one of the tower's doors. A silhouette filled the opening.

Kostikus stepped forth.

At his appearance, ice crystallized on the floor and walls of the room. Warded and incorporeal, Vhostym did not feel the cold radiated by the fiend.

The ice devil towered so high he had to duck to step out of the gate. His head nearly touched the ceiling of the room. Skin the color of old parchment wrapped a hairless head that looked like an exposed skull. Bow legs and overlong arms jutted from a thin, humanoid frame. The devil was naked. In one hand it held a spear as long as Vhostym was tall.

Vhostym knew that devils could see invisible creatures. Kostikus looked around the room until his gaze settled on Vhostym. The black holes of the creature's eyes flashed recognition. And fear. Vhostym could have annihilated the powerful devil within moments and Kostikus knew it.

"How may I serve?" Kostikus asked, nodding his head in a bow. The devil's voice sounded brittle and his respiration formed clouds in the air.

Vhostym indicated the immobilized soldiers and projected, *Kill all of these where they stand and return to your Hell.*

Vhostym did not want to waste time killing each of the soldiers himself. Besides, he took no pleasure in killing. For him, murder was a purely utilitarian exercise. He needed the tower empty and he wanted no survivors with loose tongues spreading the tale of its destruction.

The devil seemed surprised at the simplicity of the request but asked no further questions. Presently the towering fiend set to his work. His spear pierced the flesh and organs of one of the soldiers, then another. The devil laughed as he killed—a high pitched sound like the squeal of a delighted child.

More shouts from behind the door, then silence.

Vhostym turned his back to the gleeful fiend and cast another spell, summoning to his side a sphere of nothingness an arm's span in diameter. The void sphere would disintegrate whatever it touched. Another spell summoned a magical eye that, like Vhostym's incorporeal body, could travel through solid objects and project his vision whither it went.

Vhostym sent the eye, invisible to all but him, through the sealed door and into the room beyond. He transferred his vision to the sensor and saw the stairway and main corridor on the other side of the doors crowded with defenders. Few were fully armed or armored, and many still wore nightclothes. They must have poured out of their bedrooms at the sound of the alarm. Perhaps two score soldiers, three of the temple's priests, and two wizards waited there. All of them stood ready, the priests in front with their silver holy symbols in one hand and their blades in the other. Magical wards, visible as distortions in the air, shielded both of the wizards, who flanked the priests. Both held wands at the ready.

They were hoping to ambush Vhostym the moment he walked through the door.

Vhostym turned his sight from the sensor back to his body. With the devil still impaling soldiers behind him, he spoke the words to a powerful evocation, infusing some of his mental strength into the spell to maximize its effect. Just before he pronounced the final phrase, he mentally commanded the void sphere to touch the door. It did and the wooden slab disintegrated instantly into dust.

Vhostym completed his spell at the same moment the wizards beyond fired their wands through the door.

Energy streamed forth from Vhostym's hands, saturating the room beyond, and the tower's defenders began to scream. But not before a ball of flame, a bolt of lightning, and a wave of negative energy streaked through the door.

The flames, lightning, and life-draining energy passed through Vhostym's incorporeal form without harm or dissipated into nothingness on his wards. Only the flames from the ball of fire reached Kostikus, and the devil, immune to fire and heat by virtue of his fiendish flesh, stood in the midst of the inferno and laughed.

In the room beyond, the high-pitched, agonized screams of the defenders rose to a crescendo and ceased. A wet gurgle sounded for a moment, then nothing.

Vhostym floated through the doorway and into the room beyond.

From behind, the now euphoric fiend shouted, "Roasted manflesh!" and impaled a partially immolated soldier on his spear. The smoke from burning flesh chased Vhostym through the doors.

Every living creature within the room lay dead. Many were scattered over the stairs, but most lay in a heap on the floor of the main corridor. Vhostym's spell had left the corpses thin, pruned, desiccated. Night clothes and piecemeal armor hung from the dead as if they were skeletons. A layer of cloudy, pinkish water soaked the stairs and the floor. Vhostym's magic had sucked the water from all his victims' bodies, drawn it through their eyes, ears, their very flesh, and left little more than husks.

Vhostym started to float upward but remembered that he needed to kill the prisoners the Cyricists kept in cells below the tower. Leaving behind for the moment his magical sensor and his void orb, he floated down through the now-empty first floor to the dungeon level, blind for a moment until he reached the open space of one of the dungeon's hallways. Numerous cells and several torture chambers filled the level. Moans and whimpering sounded from down the hall.

Vhostym would put them out of their misery.

He took a small black pearl from his component pouch, weakened it with his mind, and crumbled it between his fingers. As he cast the fine powder before him, he recited the words to a necromancy spell whose power snuffed out all life forces but his own within thirty paces in any direction.

One of the prisoners must have heard him pronouncing the spell.

"Help us," the man cried, his voice plaintive and broken.

Vhostym finished the spell. The moment it took effect, the dungeon fell silent. Vhostym glided down the hallway, looking from side to side, and saw naught but corpses, all of them of prisoners. They had died instantly and painlessly, better than their captors. He floated up through the ceiling.

Nothing moved on the second floor. Vhostym was alone with the dried corpses. Kostikus was gone, as were the bodies of the soldiers Vhostym had immobilized. Vhostym had as yet seen only a few mages and priests. He assumed the temple's remaining forces had realized that they were trapped within the tower and were organizing a stand on one of the upper floors. Probably they had assembled around Olma, the highest ranking priestess in residence, perhaps in the sanctum itself. Vhostym would get to them soon enough.

Methodically, he moved through the rooms of each floor one by one. He easily countered the defensive wards cast on the doorways of important chambers. He found a few guardsmen and a wizard seeking to hide, and two guards trying and failing to squeeze out of an arrow slit. He touched them all with his void orb, reducing them to dust. He also used the void orb to disintegrate the various religious icons and statuary that he encountered. Slowly but inexorably, he was effacing Cyric from his own temple.

When that work was done, he floated through the ceiling and found the next floor abandoned. As he had surmised, the survivors had gathered on the fifth floor, in the sanctum of Cyric. Again, he took time to destroy the Cyricist iconography and ensured no one was trying to hide from him. He found no one.

Only a single stairway led up to the fifth floor, into a foyer with double doors that led into the sanctum. Vhostym hovered near the base of the stairs. He could hear chanting leaking down from above. He studied the stairs, activating a permanent dweomer on his eyes that allowed him to detect and analyze magical dweomers.

The surviving priests and mages had been busy. Several glyphs warded the stairs, as did a firetrap. Should anyone ascend, they would cause an explosion of fire, lightning, acid, and cold, and trigger an unholy symbol that would wrack the body with agony. Of course, Vhostym did not have to ascend the stairs. He could simply float through the floors. The tower's defenders had not anticipated that.

The wizard concentrated for a moment, took control of the arcane sensor he had created, and sent it up through the floor.

Though the eye, he saw that the armored skeletons he had seen in the room earlier now stood assembled around the top of the stairs, just before the sanctum's double doors. They were designed to slow him, nothing more. Behind them, just within the sanctum, stood nearly a dozen priests and mages, including Olma Kulenvov in a hurriedly donned breastplate and vambraces, and fully two score guardsmen. The priests and mages held wands and staffs pointed at the stairs, and the warriors held bare axes and swords. One of the mages turned to silence a warrior with a glare and his gaze fell upon Vhostym's sensor. His eyes widened and he gave a shout. Clearly, the wizard had magic that allowed him to see invisible objects.

Olma whirled around, brandished her platinum holy symbol, the jawless skull, and cast a spell that attempted to counter Vhostym's sensor. The priestess's magic met Vhostym's and was overpowered. Her lips peeled back in a snarl and she shared a look with the other priests and the wizards. All of them visibly tensed. They had an inkling of the power of their foe and it visibly frightened them.

Vhostym decided to give them another inkling.

Still standing near the bottom of the stairs, he summoned arcane power, pictured Olma in his head, and softly whispered a single word of power. "Die."

In the room above, Vhostym watched through his sensor as the priestess grabbed her chest and paled. The other priests scrambled about, looking for the source of the attack. Vhostym expected Olma to fall over dead, but the attack passed and she grinned fiercely. She must have protected herself with a deathward.

Prudent, Vhostym thought.

A shout of challenge rang out from the assembled troops.

"For Cyric!" they called, and "Come up, wizardling!"

Vhostym supposed he would need to use blunter tools. He softly intoned the words to a sophisticated glamer and crafted a highly detailed illusion of himself. He structured it around his annihilating orb, masking it. He sent orb and illusion up the stairs and into the foyer. For good measure, he caused the illusionary Vhostym to incant a spell as he ascended.

The entire stairway vibrated with the impact of spells and wand fire as the defenders let fly with wands, staffs, and evocations. Smoke, flames, and green energy poured down the stairwell. A scream suggested that at least one of the defenders tried to touch the illusion, encountered the orb instead, and was reduced to nothingness. Vhostym floated away from the stairs, estimated the position of the middle of the Sanctum, and floated up into the room.

The illusionary Vhostym advanced up the stairs and through the foyer, seemingly unharmed by the storm of arcane and divine power. The illusion continued to incant a spell that would never be cast. A soldier lunged at him, blade extended. When the blade hit the orb, man and weapon turned to dust. Two skeletons, mindless automatons, did the same and also turned to dust.

The defenders fell back before the illusionary juggernaut.

Behind the defenders, the real Vhostym began to cast one of the most destructive spells he knew.

"A ruse," Olma shouted, finally recognizing the illusion for what it was. She ordered the skeletons to cease destroying themselves on the illusion and turned around. Her vision must have been magically augmented, for she saw the real Vhostym.

"There!" she shouted, and pointed at Vhostym.

The wizards whirled, ignoring the illusion, leveled wands, and fired. Lightning and a green beam ripped paths toward Vhostym. His wards absorbed both as though they had never been.

"It's a ghost!" shouted one of the priests.

"An invisible wizard in ghostform," corrected a mage. She attempted a spell to counter Vhostym's incorporeality. It failed.

As one, the guardsmen rushed in Vhostym's direction, blades bare, snarls on their faces. Unlike the mages, they could not see him. Still they charged.

Vhostym finished his spell, adding a final vocalization

that allowed him to sculpt the spell's effect around his person. When he pronounced the final syllable and held forth his hand, four fist-sized spheres of superheated, glowing rock flew forth. Two he directed past the charging soldiers at Olma, and one each he directed at the two wizards who had fired their wands at him.

The spheres slammed into their targets, knocked them from their feet, and exploded into an inferno of red flames that blanketed the entire sanctum in fire. The explosions overlapped, intensifying the heat. Soldiers, priests, and mages burned in the conflagration. Their screams lasted only moments.

As Vhostym had intended when he sculpted his spell, the explosions spared the space in which he floated. Clouds of flame circled around him but he stood untouched in the eye of the inferno. Burning men staggered through the island he had created, fell over, and died. Black smoke poured from their corpses.

Then it was over.

Vhostym surveyed the smoky room.

The soldiers' bodies were so consumed by the flames that they were barely recognizable as men. They lay curled on the floor before him, lips burned away to reveal blackened teeth. The skeletons looked like little more than piles of charred sticks. The protective spells on the wizards and priests had shielded them from some of the damage but the inferno had been so intense that it had overcome even their defensive wards. Almost all of them lay prone, motionless. Only the chest of Olma rose and fell, and her breathing sounded as labored as Vhostym's.

The pedestal, tiles, and murals depicting Cyric or his iconography had been burned away or reduced to shapeless chunks. The temple was Cyric's no more. It was Vhostym's.

He floated over to Olma, looked down on her blackened face, the charred, tangled mass of her hair. One of the priestess's eyes was little more than a seared hole, but the other stared out from the charred ruin of its socket. It focused on Vhostym, saw him.

"What are you?" the priestess whispered. "Why have you done this?"

Vhostym frowned. Humans, more than any race he had encountered in his travels, always sought to know why things occurred.

He answered, *There is no reason that you would understand. And I am what I am.*

The priestess's lips peeled back in a snarl. "I go to death with the Dark Sun's praises on my lips."

Thank him for providing me with what I needed, Vhostym answered.

He dispelled the illusion around the void orb and summoned the black sphere to his side. Olma's eye twitched when she saw it.

Vhostym caused it to touch her. A green outline flared around her and she turned to dust. She went to her death not with praises on her lips but with fear in her eyes.

Vhostym floated back through the temple and caused the void orb to touch all of the corpses, sparing only their magical trinkets. He collected the magical paraphernalia of the tower's defenders and piled it in one of the side bedchambers. He did not know what he would do with it, but it seemed a waste to destroy it.

After a short time, nothing remained of the former occupants of the temple but dust. There would be no bodies for Blackwill to resurrect and question. In fact, there would be no temple at all.

CHAPTER 10

PREPARATIONS

The intensity of the sensations and images issuing from the Source lessened. Ssessimyth's tentacles spasmed slightly in perturbation. The ruins in which he nested shifted. Stone grated against stone. The whole vibrated above him. His startled minions communicated their pleasure and terror to one another.

Ssessimyth sensed the Source awakening from its long sleep. Something on the surface had drawn its interest. It was trying to climb out of its torpor.

Ssessimyth linked his mind to the Source's external perception and sent his consciousness surfaceward. The projection did not allow him to see images or hear sounds so much as it empowered him directly to perceive facts.

He sensed a calm sea, and in the distance, a ship. Some of the surface dwellers aboard had sensitivity to the Source's emanations, though they had not yet sensed them. The Source, even in sleep, must have perceived the sensitivity. The presence of other creatures with mental powers was drawing it up from sleep, drawing its attention from Ssessimyth.

Anger surged in Ssessimyth, ire that a creature other than him might dare draw on the bliss of the Source. It was his, and his alone.

He tried to lull the Source back into its sleep, failed, then struggled to force the Source to turn its attention fully to him. The Source resisted. Ssessimyth still perceived the images and sensations that he wished, but the experience paled in intensity from that to which he had become accustomed. He was left as little more than an observer, when he long ago had grown addicted to being a participant.

His tentacles spasmed again, shaking loose a rain of unstable stone and particles. The call went out among his minions for one of the priests to come forth and interpret Ssessimyth's movements.

Ssessimyth controlled his anger. Still drinking the mind of the Source, he called upon a power innate to those of his kind, something he had not done in decades.

A pulse of power went forth from him, powered by his will, and raced for the surface. Even if he could not fully control the Source, he could at least destroy those who were trying to share it with him. Then the Source would again be his alone and he could sleep at the bottom of the sea and dream lives and worlds.

Far above him, he knew that his magical power was darkening the sky, summoning the wind. Probably the sea already was beginning to surge. He used the Source's power to send a mental projection to the priests of his minions, ordering them to take to the surface and kill the interlopers. If the storm did not force the ship back or sink it, his minions would kill everyone aboard.

Within moments he sensed the urgent, excited preparations of his minions as they organized their warbands. He returned his attention to the Source and tried to lose himself in the pale images it showed him.

Demon Binder cut through the sea. With her smaller topsails unfurled over the mainsails and the elementals pulling her through the water, she fairly skipped over the waves. Hours passed. The day dawned and moved toward welcome night and still those on board had seen no sign of the slaadi's ship.

Magadon used the visual leech from time to time to ensure that the slaadi were still sailing west. They were. The slaadi's ship had only the wind to propel it. Cale knew *Demon Binder* had to be gaining.

As dusk fell, darkness gathered in the sky ahead. Cale saw it for what it was: a thunderhead as black as a demon's soul. It looked as though a titan had charred the clouds. Lightning split the cloudbanks. The light from the setting sun caught the moisture in the air before the storm and created an arc of color that reached across the sky. The crew of *Demon Binder* seemed to regard it as an ill omen. Under the thunderhead, the air was hazy with rain.

The crew stopped for a moment in their work and all eyes looked westward, to the gathering storm. Nervous mutters sounded across the deck.

Captain Evrel said, "A colored arc at sea is the bridge between us and the Stormlord's realm. And that looks to be enough of a storm that Talos would take a father's pride in it."

Magadon, standing near the captain on the forecastle and eyeing the clouds, said, "I do not think it is natural. It gathers too fast."

"The slaadi?" Jak asked, speaking his thoughts aloud.

Evrel had the sense to pretend he had not heard, or at least had the sense to ask no questions.

Magadon shrugged. "No way to know."

"Doubtful," Cale said. He shaded his eyes with his hand against the light of the setting sun. "They do not know we are after them."

Evrel said, "And they would be fools if they brought that storm down themselves. They'll be caught in it, same as us." He paused, looked a question at Cale, and said, "That is, *if* we're sailing into it."

Cale looked into Evrel's face. "Captain, it is important that we catch those we're after. I cannot tell you why it's important, but it is."

He offered no more than that, and in truth, could not offer more. He did not know what the slaadi or the Sojourner planned. He knew only that it would not be good.

Evrel stared into Cale's face for a moment, chewed his moustache, and finally nodded. Over his shoulder, he said to Ashin, who stood at the helm, "Steer a course right into it, Ashin."

"Aye, Captain," answered Ashin without blanching.

Evrel summoned Gorse and ordered, "Batten down every hatch on this tub. Not a drop gets into the hold or she'll founder for certain. All spare rope below decks is made into lifelines. Turn the decks into a web and remind the men to take extra care. If anyone goes over in that storm, there'll be no gettin' him back."

Gorse nodded, eyed Cale, Magadon, and Jak, and turned to his duty.

"Gorse," Evrel called to his back, and the mate spun. "Find something suitable and round up Rix. Have him make an offering to Talos."

Gorse nodded and hopped to his work, barking orders at everyone within earshot. The crew answered his commands immediately and set to their appointed tasks. They knew their business well.

"An offering to Talos?" Jak asked Evrel.

"Ship's custom," Evrel explained. "You encounter a storm at sea, you throw a sacrifice to the Stormlord over the bow and ask him to spare the ship. Rix is no priest, but he takes the duty seriously enough that Talos might hear him, or at least won't be offended by him trying."

Jak nodded, looked thoughtfully ahead to the gathering storm, and back to the captain. He reached into a cloak pocket and pulled out a large garnet.

"Give him this to sacrifice, too," the little man said.

The captain laughed aloud and took the gem.

"A storm at sea makes a man feel small, doesn't it?"

Jak only smiled sheepishly.

"This also," Magadon said. The guide withdrew from his pocket an almost perfectly round, polished river stone that featured bands of gray and red.

"It's not worth much, but it took my fancy. I've had it for years. Kept it for luck. I took it from the bed of the Cedar River, deep in the Gulthmere. Who knows, it may please the god of storms."

The captain took the stone, added it to Jak's gem, and left the three of them alone on the deck.

"Can't hurt, I figure," Jak explained to Cale and Magadon.

"I thought the same," Magadon offered.

Cale stared at the black, lightning-torn sky ahead and wondered if he shouldn't have offered Talos something himself.

Azriim watched the storm clouds gather. The crew watched them too and muttered nervously. Lightning veined the clouds. Thunder boomed overhead. The wind picked up, carried to them the smell of rain. Sails snapped in the rising breeze. The swells started to grow. The ship began to noticeably rise and fall in the waves.

"That ain't no natural storm!" A sailor perched in the crow's nest atop the mainmast called his observation down to the captain.

Murmurs of agreement sounded from the rest of the crew. Eyes looked accusingly at Azriim, Dolgan, and Riven, the "wizards" who had brought them trouble.

"It's as natural as the rock your mother struck against your head at birth," shouted another crewman, and the joke elicited some nervous smiles from the crew.

Beside Azriim, Dolgan projected, *We may have a mutiny if we force them to sail into that.*

Riven snickered and answered, *We kill a few and the rest will fall into line. I've seen it before.*

Azriim smiled at that. *None of that should be necessary.*

His spell still held Captain Sertan enchanted, and from everything Azriim had seen, the crew would follow their captain down the River of Blood if he commanded it. They would grumble, but they would obey.

"Come," Azriim said. "Let us go see Sertan."

The three of them walked over the maindeck to the captain, who stood beside his helmsman near the sterncastle. Azriim smiled a greeting while he eyed the Sojourner's compass, sitting on a stool beside the helm. The needle pointed directly into the storm and—if Azriim was not imagining it—it also pointed ever so slightly downward.

Sertan, one hand holding a line above him, nodded at the sky and said, "My friend, we should turn back. I've seen ships vanish in storms that made less dire promises than that one."

"She's a black heart," the helmsman agreed.

Azriim made a show of looking at the cloudbank and nodding. He turned to Sertan and said, "My friend, we need to continue onward. I can double your pay, if need be. It's important that we proceed. In the name of our friendship, don't fail me now."

Riven masked a laugh with a cough. Even Azriim had to admit that he was laying it on pretty heavily.

"More coin does drowned men no good," Sertan answered, though the sly look in his eye belied his words. "And I no more want you to drown than me."

I will eat him, Dolgan projected. *And you take his form.*

Shut up, Azriim answered his broodmate.

Dolgan crossed his arms and huffed.

"Come now, you are no ordinary seaman," Azriim said. "And this is no ordinary crew. *Dolphin's Coffer* can cut a path through that, I have no doubt. Triple the pay when we return to a Sembian port."

Sertan frowned, but licked his lips greedily.

"I thought you were disembarking? You will be returning to the ship then?"

"Of course," Azriim lied, smiling. "We will disembark for a time, descend below the waves, and return. How else would we get back to land?"

Sertan chewed his moustache.

"Come, my friend," Azriim chided. "Nothing dared, nothing won. Isn't that right? I'm offering all I have. It's that important to me."

Sertan's Sembian greed and Azriim's enchantment made the outcome a foregone conclusion. After only a few moments, Sertan nodded and said, "Done. And we'll get you through."

To the crew, Sertan shouted, "String some lines, lads, and reinforce the sail rigging! Get the boys out of the nests! No one on the masts! We're sailing down that storm's gullet and out its arse."

Azriim allowed himself a smile. He had won the only battle with Sertan that he would have to fight. Once the storm had a grip on *Dolphin's Coffer*, there would be no turning back.

Outside the former temple of Cyric, Vhostym prepared to cast one of the most powerful spells known to any caster on any world. The magic defied categorization. In the end, it brought into being what Vhostym willed—but within limits.

The casting required for its power a small tithe of the wizard's own being. Vhostym, of course, had only so much to give, or would have had only so much to give, if it had been his being that would power the spell. But it would not. Instead, he would draw on the stored power contained in the Weave Tap. The artifact would power the spell, sparing Vhostym the necessity of sacrificing some of his already dwindling lifespan.

Unfortunately, the spell brought with it certain peculiarities. The magic could have only limited effects on sentient beings. Perhaps that suggested something about the power inherent in a self-aware creature, but Vhostym chose to ignore the implication. Too, the spell could be capricious. The magic required that the caster articulate his will. Sometimes the spell answered the caster's intent, and sometimes—when the caster tried to do too much—the spell answered a strict interpretation of the caster's words, which often led to a perversion of the caster's intent.

Still, Vhostym had no choice but to use the spell. No other magic could accomplish what he wished. He readied himself and began.

In his mind's eye, he pictured the uninhabited island that he had chosen to be the site of his triumph and his death. He pictured it as though seeing it from far above, as he had often done in his scrying lens—a sheer-sided, mountainous chunk of land that rose high from the sea. Human sailors called it the Wayrock. Vhostym called it his.

He looked upon the temple before him—empty, dark, also his. He sensed the latent amplification properties present in the stone. Properly awakened, that power would turn the temple into the largest magical focus ever made or conceived. And Vhostym would need it. For the spell he was about to cast was feeble compared to the spell he planned to cast after all the pieces of his plan were in place. With it, he would create and control a Crown of Flame.

He focused, and opened the connection between his mind and the primitive sentience of the Weave Tap. The artifact reached across Mystra's web and drew power from the mantle of Skullport, where its seed had been planted. It channeled that power to Vhostym.

Arcane energy rushed into him until he was nearly aglow with it. Holding his hands out before him, ignoring the pain of his failing body, he spoke the short stanza of his spell.

Power continued to gather in him as he spoke, enough to obliterate an army. He controlled it, concentrated it, projected it outward to the temple.

The magic took hold and the temple vibrated under the magical onslaught. The stone shimmered silver. Vhostym gave voice to his will. "Let this tower and all of its current contents be removed at once to the Wayrock. Let a suitable foundation be prepared there upon which the tower can safely stand as it does before me now, and let the tower so stand."

Vhostym's hands shook, glowed white with the power they channeled. The tower shook, flared brightly, then . . . disappeared.

The magic departed Vhostym. He sagged and disconnected himself from the Weave Tap.

He allowed a smile to split his thin lips. He was close now. Very close.

Only a jagged hole in the soil indicated that the western Tower of the Eternal Eclipse had ever stood in the vale. Vhostym had erased it.

He took a moment to let his strength return, then spoke the words to a spell that would transport him to the Wayrock.

He wanted to prepare his new spell focus for his next casting.

CHAPTER 11

THE GATHERING STORM

The wind rose as the sun sank below the horizon. The storm swallowed the stars and the sea grew increasingly rough. *Demon Binder* sailed headlong into the storm's teeth. The rain started slowly, thick dollops that felt like sling bullets, but soon fell in wind-driven sheets. Immense swells alternately lifted the ship up to touch the sky or sent it careening down to nearly bury the bow in the waves. Foam sprayed. The decks were awash. Through it all, Cale held station in the bow, leaning out over the prow, trying to increase the ship's speed through sheer force of will. His stomach fluttered every time they descended a swell, but he refused to give ground to the storm. Jak stood beside him, clutching the rail with white knuckles and groaning with every roll of the ship.

The rain hit Cale's face so hard it felt like hail. His soaked cloak felt as though it were filled with stones. He looked ahead, blinking in the rain, the spray, the foam. They had to be gaining on the slaadi. They had to be.

There!

Atop a distant swell he spotted a green glow. He strained to see. He was not certain that his eyes had not deceived him.

Lightning ripped through the sky, silhouetting a dark shape atop a mountainous swell—a ship, the slaadi's ship! Like *Demon Binder*, it had all of its sails unfurled and was riding straight into the waves.

"There!" Cale shouted above the storm, in his excitement using his voice rather than the mindlink.

"I see it," Jak hollered in answer. The little man slipped and nearly fell as *Demon Binder* slid down a trough. The slaadi's ship was lost to their sight.

Did you see it? Cale asked Magadon. *We are closing.*

I saw it, Magadon answered. *So did Evrel. He's concerned for the ship, Erevis. And his crew.*

Cale knew. He was concerned for them too.

Above them, the billowing square sails strained to contain the fierce wind without shredding. Rigging frayed. The masts creaked, bending under the force of the wind. Thunder rolled. Cale did not know how much more the ship or its crew could endure.

Below them, the water elementals Jak had summoned pulled *Demon Binder* through the churning sea, keeping her prow square to the waves. Watery appendages stuck out of the rolling sea to clutch the hull. Cale caught snippets of their rushing voices above the storm. They, too, must have been shouting to one another.

Tell him to hold on, Mags, Cale projected. *We're getting close. We'll have them soon.*

Before Magadon could reply, Cale felt a pressure in his temples, an itching under his skull. He looked to Jak, whose expression told him that he was feeling much the same thing. At first Cale thought it was a side effect of the storm, but the pressure intensified, as did the itching. Both grew painful. Cale squinted, clutched his brow.

"You feel that?" he shouted to Jak.

Jak nodded, holding two fingers to his temple and wincing with pain.

Mags? Cale asked. *Do you—*

I feel it, Erevis, Magadon answered, and Cale heard the strain in his mental voice. *More intensely than you, I think. The whole crew feels it. I can see it in their faces.*

What is it? Cale asked, and felt the connection between him and Magadon waver.

I . . . not know, Magadon answered, his reply partially cut off. *Not an attack. . . .*

The pressure grew worse as they moved deeper into the storm. Cale's eyes ached. His head throbbed. He felt as though his eyes soon would pop. He looked back and saw that many members of the crew were balled up on the deck, writhing.

A wave of dizziness hit Cale and nearly sent him over the side but he managed to get both hands on the rail and his feet stable beneath him. He reached out and took a fistful of Jak's cloak to ensure his friend did not tumble into the water.

"What is this?" Jak screamed. He pulled at his hair.

Cale would have ordered Evrel to turn back if it were possible, but he knew it was not. Any change in course risked swamping the ship.

The pressure grew worse, caused his senses to deceive him. He imagined that he saw flashes of color dancing across the waves—not the green of the slaadi's ship, but will o'wisps of red and blue, flames of violet and orange, a sunset, a moonrise. Too, he thought he heard music and mumbling voices behind the roar of the storm. A huge shadow formed above him, a floating city. He cowered, then it was gone. He tasted ale in his mouth, beef, anise, onion.

Beside him, Jak shouted in a slurred voice, "What in the Nine Hells isth happening? I'm stheeing things. Hearing voices in the wind."

Cale could only shake his head and answer, "As am I. Hang on to the rail and do not let go, no matter what."

He was conscious of shadows gathering protectively around him.

Cale projected to Magadon, but the mindlink flickered in and out.

What is hap . . . Mags? Is there . . . you can do?

For a time, Magadon did not answer and Cale feared for his safety. He looked back but could see nothing through the storm and pain.

Wait, Magadon said, and Cale heard wonder in his tone. *Wait. . . .*

Without warning the pressure in Cale's head decreased, then ceased altogether. Cale gasped, sagged. Jak did the same. Cale's senses returned to normal. The storm still raged around them but Cale felt a peculiar, inexplicable calm.

Magadon's mental voice sounded in Cale's and Jak's minds, and the connection was clear, powerful.

There is a presence here, Erevis. An ancient presence.

Dolphin's Coffer rose and fell in the swells like so much flotsam. Lightning split the sky. Thunder rolled. Rain poured down, thumped hard against Azriim's adopted flesh. Above him, the sails billowed outward in the breeze, straining the masts.

Azriim, Dolgan, and Riven stood on the maindeck near Captain Sertan, just in front of the helmsman's station. Lifelines were strung across the deck to form a web of rope over the entire ship. The crew clutched the lines tightly as they moved. Azriim and Dolgan, too, kept their grip on a line. Only Riven and the captain seemed able to hold their balance unassisted on the listing ship and slippery deck.

"Keep us square to the wind, Nimil!" Sertan shouted to his helmsman.

Veins stood out on Nimil's temples, his forearms. He held the tiller so tightly that Azriim figured he had left an imprint of his hands in the wood.

"Aye, Captain," grunted Nimil, his thin hair pasted by rain against his head. "This gets much worse, we'll lose the rudder."

"She'll hold," Sertan answered. He stared out at the storm and the sea, evaluated his sails and masts, eyed his crew.

"Sharp about your business, lads!" he shouted to every crewman within earshot. "Sharp about your business and the *Coffer* will carry us through. This blow cannot last much longer."

Sertan looked at Azriim, squinted through the rain. "If we get sideways to this, Umberlee will claim us all this day. How close are we?"

Azriim clutched the Sojourner's compass in his hand. He had taken it from the table beside Nimil the moment the storm had hit. He did his best to hold it flat in his palm and examine the needle. The movement of the ship made it difficult. Finally, he took a satisfactory reading: the needle in the center of the sphere pointed westward and slightly downward.

"Very close!" Azriim shouted, and added for effect, "Hang on, my friend."

The enspelled Sertan put a comradely hand on Azriim's shoulder and grinned.

"We will make it!" Sertan said. "And the first round of drinks is on your coin!"

Azriim only smiled in answer.

Not more than a quarter hour, Azriim projected to Riven and Dolgan, as the *Coffer* rose up another swell, then plummeted back down. *Then—*

He cocked his head, sensing mental contact. At first

he thought it might have been the Sojourner, but realized quickly that the sensation was too severe for his father. He looked at Dolgan and saw that the big slaad was wincing.

Do you feel that? asked his broodmate.

Azriim nodded. Riven and the rest of the crew looked around, rubbed their temples. The pain intensified until slaadi and men clutched their heads in pain. Two seamen lost their grip on the lifelines and went over the side. The storm's wail swallowed their shouts. No one else witnessed their fate and Azriim did not care.

What is this? Riven projected, his mental voice tight. He had a hand on his blade and the other on his brow.

"What sorcery is this?" shouted Sertan, holding his massive head in his hands.

Azriim was not certain. The mental contact was incredibly powerful but also primitive, as though born of a consciousness only half-formed. He had never encountered anything like it before.

He tried to answer the contact with an innocuous mental touch but felt no connection. The mental abilities with which the Sojourner had gifted Azriim and Dolgan were quite limited and the consciousness did not seem to sense him. . . .

Azriim looked at his compass, at the sea, and a realization hit him. It was the only explanation for this strange mental contact. No wonder the Sojourner had been unable to scry Sakkors.

The mantle was sentient, or nearly so.

We are closer than I realized, he projected to Dolgan and Riven, and smiled through his discomfort.

They nodded and tried to keep their feet on the slippery, rolling deck.

Riven and the rest of the crew still clutched their heads, grimacing at the pressure building in their skulls. Even Nimil released the tiller to hold his head. The ship started to turn.

Dolgan shoved the helmsman aside, took the tiller in his own hands, and wrenched it back into position. Azriim feared his broodmate's strength would break the rudder but it did not, and the ship straightened.

"I am seeing things!" Riven shouted, and finally took hold of a lifeline. "What in the Abyss is happening?"

The ship rolled up another swell, crashed down. A wave took another crewman over the side. Another.

The captain cursed through his haze.

Above, the rigging holding a sail on the mizzenmast finally snapped and the canvas flapped free in the wind. The sudden loss of the rigging sent a boom whirling a half-circle around the mast. It hit a sailor in the mid-section and knocked him overboard.

Azriim feared that *Dolphin's Coffer* soon would not have enough crew to sail her.

Then, the mental torture ended as abruptly as it had started. The crew looked up and around, dazed, but hurriedly set to retaking their ship from the storm. Crippled but unbroken, *Dolphin's Coffer* sailed on.

Still shaking his head, Riven asked, "What was that?"

Azriim smiled. "Not what. Who."

The assassin and Dolgan both looked a question at him but Azriim offered no further explanation.

"The storm is breaking," said a crewman huddled on the forecastle. He pointed ahead, to a break in the clouds through which stars were visible.

Almost as soon as the crewman said it the rain slowed, then ended. The wind fell off entirely. The ship sails went slack and the vessel gradually coasted to a stop. A thankful rustle wound its way through the men, followed by a hoarse cheer.

"Well done, lads," the captain said to his crew. "Well done. Didn't I say she'd hold together?"

Azriim was not sure what to make of the calm. He found it portentous. Beside him, Riven must have felt much the same thing. The assassin eyed the sky, the black, rolling expanse of the sea, and said, *I do not like this.*

Azriim smiled. *Not to worry, assassin. We are not remaining aboard.*

Azriim held up the Sojourner's spherical compass on his palm. The needle within pointed straight down.

Vhostym appeared inside the sanctum of his tower, now safely removed to the top of the Wayrock. Still incorporeal, he floated into the outer wall of the tower and down to the root of the structure. There, he examined the bonds between the native stone and the transplanted tower. His spell had done its work well. The tower looked as though it had been built atop the Wayrock rather than moved from a secret mountain vale in the south of Faerûn. He would need it to be well rooted when he began the spell.

He was pleased. Things had unfolded exactly as he had hoped.

He glanced skyward, to the stars, to Selûne, to her tears. He already knew which of them he would use. He picked it out of the glowing field of silver points that trailed after their mistress. He imagined his spell taking effect, imagined how it would feel.

The time was drawing near. He needed only the power of Sakkors's mantle and he could begin.

Extending his consciousness across the Inner Sea, he reached out for Azriim's mind but could not make contact. He assumed that meant that his sons were in proximity to Sakkors. The ruined city's mantle had rebuffed Vhostym's attempts to scry it, so it surprised him only a little that it also interfered with mental contact.

A sudden, sharp pain ran the length of Vhostym's spine. He gritted his teeth and waited for it to pass but the pain lingered longer than usual. He bore it, hissing, and it passed at last.

He needed to complete his work soon.

He flew back up to the top of the tower, floated through a wall, and entered the former sanctum of Cyric. He dismissed the spell that made him incorporeal and his flesh solidified instantly. The sudden weight on his weak muscles and bones caused him to stumble. He fell to the floor, on all fours, and the impact sent knifing stabs of pain into his kneecaps and wrists. He screamed from the pain—the first time that he had ever given voice to his agony with more than a hiss—certain that the fall had cracked several bones.

Physically and mentally tired, he remained in the undignified posture for some time. He had taxed himself by using so many spells to claim Cyric's temple. It had been decades since he had done so much in so little time.

And there was more yet to do.

His breath came rapid and wet. He prepared himself to stand. He could have used a spell or mental power to assist himself but refused out of pride. He would stand under his own power; he had to.

He moved one leg, then another, gingerly asked them to bear his body. The memory of the pain still lingered in his knees, but he straightened them and made them bear him up. When they did, he allowed himself a moment's satisfaction, but only a moment.

Despite his fatigue, he had to prepare the tower.

He first whispered the words to a spell that summoned the Weave Tap from the pocket dimension in which he had left it. He pronounced the final couplet, energy flared, and the dendritic artifact appeared before him. It stood about as tall as a dwarf maple. Dim light pulsed along the silvery bark of its bole. Golden leaves dripping stored arcane power hung from its limbs.

Vhostym felt the Tap's distress at being removed from its nursery in the pocket plane. The twisting mass of its roots and the tips of its gilded limbs squirmed for a moment in agitation, seeking purchase in the Weave and Shadow Weave. Roots dug into the stone of the floor, found a home in the Shadow Weave and went still. Limbs reached upward for the ceiling but the tips disappeared into the net of the Weave before reaching the roof. They, too, went still.

Vhostym felt the Tap's agitation change to contentment.

Rest easy, he projected to it, though he did not think it could understand him. Or perhaps he could not understand it. The Tap had been born in shadow to serve the priesthood of the goddess of the night. Like Vhostym, it was vulnerable to the sun, but unlike Vhostym, it felt no loss from its vulnerability, no need to conquer its weakness.

The Tap simply existed, and in that existence found contentment.

Vhostym stared at the living artifact. He suspected that the Tap felt contentment only because its sentience was limited. Aware of little beyond itself, the Tap did not crave, need, or covet. Not in the way Vhostym did, not in the way all sentient creatures did.

The curse of sentience, Vhostym knew, was that it bred desire, ambition. And those birthed discontent. Vhostym exemplified the point. In the course of satisfying his own desires, he had razed worlds, killed millions.

He felt no guilt over his deeds, of course. Guilt required for its existence the failure to meet some moral absolute. Vhostym had learned better thousands of years ago. Mathematics was the only absolute in the multiverse— two and two were always four. Morality, on the other hand, was merely a convention with which men mutually agreed to delude themselves. There were no moral facts, just preferences, and one was no better than any other.

"Take solace in your simplicity," he said to the Tap.

He used a spell to lift his feet from the floor and floated out of the sanctum. He closed the doors behind him and warded them with a series of spells, a precaution born more of habit than necessity. No one knew of his refuge on the Wayrock. No one knew what he intended to do there, not even his slaadi, and by the time anyone did, it would all be over.

He floated through the halls of the tower until he reached the central room two floors below the sanctum, a chamber more or less at the midpoint of the tower.

Slowly, painfully, he lowered himself to the floor. Lying on his back on the bare stone, he placed his arms out wide and spread his legs apart. The floor felt cool through his robes. Attuning himself to the energy of the stone, he closed his eyes and started to hum. As he did, power gathered in him. He channeled it through his body and into the stone of the tower. When he felt the stone vibrate slightly in answer, he changed from humming to chanting. His voice, carrying power in its cadence and tone, rang out through the large chamber, reverberated against the walls, ceiling, and floor. The stone absorbed the power he offered and its vibrations increased to a mild shaking. He felt the floor softening under his body, as though it would embrace him. He ceased his inarticulate chant and recited words of power. They fell from his lips and hit the shaking stone. With the words he coaxed the power of the rock to the surface. He felt as if he were resurrecting the dead. He knew he had succeeded when the floor beneath him grew as warm as living flesh.

The power was awakened.

He nearly ended the ritual there but decided to do something more, something he had not contemplated initially, something for his sons—a final gift from their adoptive father. They had earned it.

Vhostym knew that slaadi spent most of their lives striving to metamorphose from their current form—whatever that might be—into the next, higher form. Azriim and Dolgan thought they would find content-ment with their full transformation into gray slaadi, but Vhostym knew better. The change to gray would itself birth in them another drive, a need to transform yet again into another, higher species of slaad. That form was the most powerful his sons could attain, and only in that form could they find the contentment that Vhostym hoped to find when he brought forth the Crown of Flame.

He decided that he would spare them the lengthy search for the means of that transformation. Instead, *he* would transform them, and that would be his legacy.

He changed the cadence of his incantation and laced into the words a second spell, one that would take effect when his sons appeared within the tower. After only a short time within the tower, they would be transformed from gray slaadi into death slaadi.

Vhostym imagined the pleasure his sons would feel, and the thought made him smile.

When he finished the spell, he sat up, dizzy and light-headed. He took a few breaths to recover, then attuned his vision to see dweomers. He immediately saw not active magic but a complex matrix of magical lines that criss-crossed the tower's walls, ceilings, floor.

The entire tower was now a focus that Vhostym could use to amplify the power he soon would draw from the Weave Tap.

He rose cautiously to his feet. Behind him, he saw that he had left a silhouette of his body pressed into the stone. He stared for a time at the image of his body. He had not realized how frail he had become.

It does not matter anymore, he thought, and looked away. His work was nearly done. All was prepared. He had only to wait for his sons to plant the second seed of the Weave Tap in Sakkors's mantle.

Then he would summon the Crown of Flame.

A second ship had joined the first. Ssessimyth sensed the tiny vessels floating on the sea far above him—floating on *his* sea, drawing the attention of the Source. The storm he had sent had not dissuaded the crews. They had sailed into its teeth and survived. He knew the ships had come to take the Source from him. What else could be their purpose?

He had ended the storm as his minions neared the surface. They would find it easier to attack a becalmed ship than a moving one. He used the dreaming Source's power to fill his minions with rage, hunger for manflesh.

Feast, my children, he sent to them. *Feast.*

Frustratingly, the Source continued to feed him only half-measures, realities that Ssessimyth felt but did not *live*. His anger swelled. He tried and failed again to pull the attention of the Source back to himself alone, to share its dreams with only him. It resisted and Ssessimyth's body jerked in agitation. He became conscious for the first time in a long while of the throbbing pain in his head, of the ruins around him, the coldness of the water, the darkness of the deep. His waking dream—more beautiful than reality ever had been—was ending. At least temporarily. As it did, he felt something he had not felt in centuries: rage. He would not let his universe slip away easily.

If his servants did not kill those who dared try to share the Source with him, he would kill them himself. He knew that at least one creature aboard the ships was in contact with the Source, stealing its visions from Ssessimyth. He would not tolerate it much longer.

CHAPTER 12

OUT OF THE DEPTHS

Cale and Jak shared a look

What kind of presence? Cale asked Magadon. *Under the sea? Is that what the slaadi are after?*

I am not sure, the guide answered, and curiosity colored his tone. *There's a consciousness here, Erevis. It's primitive, almost childlike, but very powerful. It's also torpid, as if sleeping. It does not communicate in a way that I can make sense of, but it makes itself . . . available.*

What does that mean? Cale asked.

Magadon answered, *I am not certain yet. I need some time.*

Cale did not think they had time to spare.

"It is breaking!" shouted a sailor from the forecastle. "There, look!"

Cale followed the man's gesture and saw a

hole in the clouds ahead. Stars peeked through.

As if in answer to the sailor's words, the rain slowed, stopped. The wind, too, died. Cale put a hand on Jak's shoulder and smiled. *Demon Binder* had made it through.

From the maindeck behind them, Cale heard Evrel ordering a headcount.

Do what you must, Cale projected to Magadon. *But do not lose track of the slaadi.*

I won't, the guide answered.

Cale turned and looked out on the calming sea, where the swells already were settling.

That was when he saw it.

The slaadi's ship floated not more than three bow-shots away, glowing green on the black waves. And *Demon Binder* was closing fast. Despite the lack of wind, Jak's elementals propelled the vessel rapidly over the sea.

The light from the slaadi's ship was growing larger, brighter.

"Tell the elementals to stop us, Jak," Cale ordered. "Right now." To Magadon, he projected, *Mags, tell the captain to snuff all lights aboard ship and to keep the crew quiet. Now.*

Cale knew that light and sound traveled far across a calm sea. As though to make his point, a cheer carried across the water from the slaadi's ship.

Cale unhooked the lanterns from the prow and let them fall into the sea. Within moments, the crew had snuffed all other lights aboard *Demon Binder*. The ship's forward progress stopped. Jak must have dismissed his spell and released the elementals from their service. *Demon Binder* bobbed in silence on a calm sea, within eyeshot of the slaadi.

Cale and Jak doffed their cloaks and wrung them out, checked their gear. Cale eyed the sea suspiciously as he did so.

"Like it's waiting," Jak said, reading Cale's expression.

Cale nodded. *What is Riven doing, Mags?* he asked.

Before Magadon answered, Cale felt a thump against the ship's timbers. Another.

"That's from below the waterline," Jak said.

Another thump.

Confused shouts sounded from the maindeck. Cale cursed, fearing the slaadi would hear.

Splashing sounded from below, the crack of splintering wood. Bestial grunts carried up from the sea and caused Cale's heart to accelerate.

Something was coming out of the water.

Cale and Jak leaned out over the side as far as they could and looked along the hull of the ship.

A dozen or more dripping, green-skinned creatures were scaling the hull. Thin, overlong arms and legs ridged with muscle and sinew ended in long claws that dug furrows in the ship's side as the creatures climbed. Long, straggly hair the color of seaweed sprouted from their round heads. Their fang-filled mouths could take off a head at one bite.

"Scrags," Jak said. "Dark!"

From the maindeck, shouts of alarm from the crew echoed Jak's words.

"Sea trolls! Scrags!"

From below the waterline, the thumping against the hull continued, as did the grating sounds. No doubt some of the scrags were trying to tear a hole in *Demon Binder*'s bottom. Cale had seen their claws and had little doubt they could do it, given enough time.

Chanting sounded from down in the water. Cale recognized the cadence of a spell.

"They've got a shaman," he said.

He pulled Weaveshear free of its scabbard, and he and Jak raced over the forecastle to the maindeck.

Azriim watched the huge heads and fang-filled mouths appear over the sides of the ship. Straggly green hair hung from the trolls' oversized heads.

"Scrags!" screamed several members of the crew, and grabbed for weapons. "Trolls on the deck!"

Riven started to draw his blades but Azriim stopped him with a hand on his wrist. He showed the assassin and Dolgan the compass. The needle pointed directly down.

"Here is where we disembark," Azriim said.

Several of the trolls already had scrambled over the rail. They shook the water from their long, stringy hair, roared, and charged the nearest crewmen. Sertan shouted orders, men fought with whatever weapons were at hand, screamed, and bled. Trolls answered with growls and grunts. The chant of a spellcaster sounded from somewhere and a bubble of darkness formed over the melee. Within the blackness, sailors screamed in pain.

Azriim knew the trolls had olfactory senses sharper than even his. They could hunt and kill the blinded sailors by scent alone. *Dolphin's Coffer* was lost; its crew, dead.

Azriim looked out over the gunwales and selected a point in the water a short distance from the ship.

"There," he said, and projected the location into the minds of Riven and Dolgan.

The assassin grabbed his arm. "I do not swim well."

"You soon will," Azriim answered.

Not ten paces from where they stood, another three trolls gained the deck. A sailor lost his footing at the edge of the darkness. The trolls swarmed him. They tore gobbets of flesh from his body as he screamed, bled, and died.

Riven started to remove his gear.

"I'd be quick," Azriim advised.

Azriim had little to leave behind. He wore only his clothes, his wands, and his blade. Dolgan secured his axe on his back. Riven stripped off his pack, his boots, his leather armor, everything but his weapons.

From behind them, Sertan shouted, "Use your wizardry, friend! Spells, man! And quickly!" The captain pointed at the trolls.

Another sailor died under troll claw. In their panic and desperation, two or three of the crew dived over the side. Azriim had no idea where they thought they would go. A troll dived after them, roaring with bloodlust.

Azriim smiled innocently at the captain, withdrew his teleportation rod, and teleported into the sea. He knew the salt water would ruin his clothes but nothing could save them now.

He found himself floating in the calm water a spearcast from the ship. Kicking to keep his head above water, he looked back on the slaughter.

Six or seven trolls had gained the deck, and another four were climbing up its sides.

"Farewell, Sertan," he said.

Dolgan appeared in the water beside him.

"Damned trolls get to eat the sailors and I got to eat none," the big slaad said.

Azriim cuffed him once across the face, hard, splitting his lip. "No cursing," he said.

Dolgan smiled and licked the blood from his lip.

Riven appeared. Azriim guessed that the assassin would find the water cold. The human foundered, but managed to keep himself afloat. Riven took a fistful of Azriim's shirt, and a sharp prick in Azriim's back indicated that the assassin had a blade at his kidney.

"I trust you have something in mind," Riven said. "Because I'll bleed you out before I drown here."

Azriim could not contain a grin. The assassin reminded him more and more of Serrin.

"Of course I have something in mind."

With obvious reluctance, the assassin removed the blade from Azriim's back.

Azriim removed from his thigh quiver the thin ivory wand with which he had turned a human into a cave shrimp back in Skullport. The wand allowed him to trans-mogrify a target into whatever shape Azriim desired. He held the wand up out of the water to confirm he had the right one. He did.

He touched it to Riven and said, "Aquatic elf."

The magic flared and the human began to change. Riven's one good eye went wide as gill slits opened in his throat, his body thinned, and his skin turned pale blue. His ears elongated into points, and his eye sockets broadened. The assassin held up a hand to discover flaps of flesh between his fingers.

"There now," Azriim said. "Well enough?"

The assassin grunted acquiescence, dived underwater, and emerged a short time later. He took a deep gulp of air. The new form allowed him to breathe both air and water. His mouth did not smile, but his good eye did.

"Well enough," the human said. "How long will it last?"

"Long enough," Azriim answered.

Azriim did not intend to remain underwater long. The mantle obviously had guardians—scrags at least. Azriim would descend to the provenance of Sakkors's mantle, plant the Weave Tap seed, and use the teleportation rod to exit. He expected it to take no longer than half an hour.

He tried to send a mental message to the Sojourner, to inform him of their progress, but the interference caused by the sentient mantle prevented him from making contact.

"And how will you two travel?" Riven asked.

"Something similar," Azriim answered.

He and Dolgan called upon their innate ability to change shape and converted their human forms into green-scaled, muscular bipedal forms, each with clawed, webbed hands and a mouthful of shark teeth—creatures known as sahuagin.

"I like to keep my fangs," Azriim said to Riven, and smiled a mouthful of razors.

With that, the three turned their faces to the dark deep and began to descend.

Demon Binder's crew, armed with cutlasses, met the trolls as the lumbering creatures tried to scramble over the sides.

Cutlasses hacked into troll flesh and black blood wet the decks. The trolls clutched the ship's rails with one hand and lashed out with claws from their other. Men screamed in pain, shouted in rage. Red blood joined the black. The trolls roared, deep and bestial. Cale did not see the shaman.

Two of the towering creatures clambered over the side and gained the deck. Sailors swarmed the pair, but troll claws tore into two seamen and kept the rest at bay. One sailor's chop with his cutlass brought him too close and one of the trolls caught him up in both of its clawed hands. The crewmen hacked at the creature but the second troll forced them back with a reckless charge, claws flailing. The pinned man screamed and kicked while the troll tore out his throat with his fangs and gulped down the gore. It roared victory to the sky, leaking red blood from its mouth, clutching the crewman's corpse in its arms.

From the other side of the ship, more trolls appeared over the sides.

"The other side too, lads!" shouted Evrel, and charged across the deck. A troll cut off the two sailors who would have joined their captain. Cale and Jak leaped down from the forecastle and joined the captain's charge.

Two trolls climbed over the side and onto the deck just as Cale, Jak, and Evrel arrived. The larger of the two lashed out with a claw that opened Evrel's shoulder, spinning him to the deck, bleeding and cursing. Cale lunged in front of the creature and stabbed it through its gut. It grunted with pain and struck out with its other claw at

Cale's face. Cale dodged backward, but too slowly. The tips of the creature's claws tore gashes in his cheek and nearly took out his eye. Blood flowed but his regenerative flesh closed the wound quickly.

Cale twisted Weaveshear, still embedded in the troll's viscera, and the creature roared and bled. Unlike the trolls Cale had encountered on land, the scrags did not appear to be regenerating their wounds. Perhaps they needed to be in the water to do so.

The troll tore a gash in Cale's shoulder, and Cale ducked another rake that would have torn his face from his skull.

Grunting with pain and exertion, Cale jerked Weaveshear free of the troll's gut and bounded back. He spared a glance to his left to see that Evrel had regained his feet. The captain and the little man were fighting the other troll. Jak looked tiny standing before the towering creature, but its futile attempts to grab hold of the halfling, who was much faster, led it to growl with anger. Evrel chopped at its arms, shoulders, and chest at every opportunity.

Cale's troll, still bleeding from the hole in its gut, produced a necklace of shells and stones in its palm and chanted something in its guttural tongue. A globe of darkness formed around Cale, but his shade eyes saw through it perfectly. Darkness was Cale's element.

Thinking him blinded, the troll sniffed at the air and charged.

Cale braced himself and sidestepped the charge at the last moment. He caught a claw rake across his chest, but managed to put a foot under the troll and send it sprawling to the deck. He leaped atop it, driving a knee into its back. The creature bucked, trying to throw him off, but Cale drove Weaveshear into its ribs until he felt the blade dig into the wood of the deck. The troll roared. Cale jerked the blade free and drove another strike into the flailing creature's neck. It lay still, blood pooling around it.

Mags! Where are you? Cale projected as he rose. He had neither seen Magadon nor heard the thump of arrows from the guide's bow.

Cale looked to Jak and Evrel to see the troll knock Evrel flat and loom over the prone captain, fanged mouth wide. Jak darted in, drove his dagger into the troll's chest, and sank his short sword to the hilt into its side. The creature emitted a squeal of agony and struck out with a backhand strike at Jak. The blow hit Jak in his stomach and sent blood spraying, but the little man held his ground. He pulled his short sword free and drove it home again. The troll gave a final squeal and collapsed atop Evrel. The captain, covered in black blood, rolled the corpse off and stood.

"Cale?" Jak shouted, staring at the globe of darkness.

"Here, little man," Cale said, and emerged from the pitch.

Jak grinned, wincing a bit at the pain in his stomach.

Erevis, Magadon finally answered. *It calls itself the Source. I think I can take what it's offering and use it to help us.*

Cale looked across the deck and saw a troll bodily lift a sailor to its mouth and snap off his head with a single bite. The neck stump sprayed blood onto the creature's face, and the troll eagerly slobbered it up. Two more crewmen lay dismembered on the deck. Cale did not see that any trolls had been felled other than the two he and Jak had put down.

Do it, Mags. They're being slaughtered.

A hesitation. Then, *I will pay a price, Erevis.*

That gave Cale pause. He scanned the deck for Magadon and finally spotted him standing alone in the darkness near the mainmast. The guide's white eyes were wide, distant. Cale could see the sweat on his face.

What price, Magadon? he asked, his mouth forming the words his mind asked.

Another crewman screamed. The trolls roared, charged

the survivors. The sailors fell back, slipping on the blood-washed decks. Three of the trolls looked across the deck and caught sight of Cale, Jak, and Evrel. They charged and their clawed feet tore divots in the deck boards as they loped across the ship.

Jak and Evrel stepped to Cale's side, blades bare.

"Come on, you ugly bastards," Evrel muttered.

It's mine to pay and I'm willing, Magadon said.

Before Cale could respond, white light flared around Magadon's head. The trolls charging toward Cale aborted their charge, clutched their heads, and screamed in agony. Blood erupted from their noses, their eye sockets, their ears. They fell to the deck, writhing, bleeding, dying. Their lives were over in five heartbeats.

"Trickster's hairy toes," Jak breathed, eyeing Magadon.

Cale could only agree. He saw the strain in Magadon's face. The veins in his brow were as pronounced as those in the trolls' arms. A trickle of blood dripped from Magadon's nose.

Stop, Mags! Cale ordered. "Stop now!"

Magadon shook his head and white light flared again around him. The trolls on the other side of the ship began to die. Blood poured from the creatures' faces. They fell to the deck, squirming in agony. Their heads were softening; brains and blood leaked from their noses. The surviving sailors jumped on those who fell and hacked them to pieces.

Erevis, Magadon said, and Cale felt the pain in his mental voice. *Riven and the slaadi have changed form and have gone underwater. The ship is safe. Go after them. It's the Source they want. It's on the bottom, Erevis.*

Cale hesitated. *What about you?*

I will be all right, Magadon answered, but Cale thought he heard the lie in it. *I will keep the mindlink open.*

Cale stood unmoving, torn.

Go now, Magadon said, and Cale nodded.

"Little man, let's go," he said to Jak.

Both of them hurriedly stripped off cloaks and armor, keeping only trousers, shirts, weapons, belt pouches, and holy symbols. Jak used a spell of healing to close the wound in his stomach. The wounds in Cale's flesh caused by the troll had already healed.

"Where are you going?" Evrel asked.

"Under," Cale said.

The captain was too dumbfounded to speak.

"We will return," Cale said.

Evrel only nodded.

"I've got the pressure and swimming," Jak said.

"And I have warmth and breathing," Cale answered.

Both cast simultaneously—one spell, then another, then another, each including the other in the effect of their spells. In moments, both were insulated against cold, free to move easily even in water, able to breathe both water and air, and safeguarded against the pressure of the depths.

"And one more so I can see," Jak muttered, and he made a last plea to the Trickster.

When he finished, Cale asked, "Ready?"

Jak grinned, actually *grinned*. "As ready as I can get. I hate the sea. Give me a calm lake every time."

"Follow me," Cale said, and he sprinted toward the bow.

Magadon had said that Riven and the slaadi had changed forms. No doubt they had transformed into aquatic creatures that could swim fast. Even with the assistance of spells, Cale and Jak would not catch them unless. . . .

In the bow sat one of the four anchor lines aboard *Demon Binder*. Cale used Weaveshear to cut the thick rope. He took hold of the anchor. Even with his shadow enhanced strength, he found it hard to bear.

"Take hold of me, little man," he said, and Jak did.

Cale pulled the darkness around them, eyed the waters near the slaadi's ship, and made the shadows move them there.

They materialized in the open sea perhaps a bowshot from the slaadi's ship. Cale had only a moment—he thought he saw trolls aboard, it, too, and they were also clutching their heads and dying—before the anchor pulled them under.

Sound fell away. Light disappeared. The sea enshrouded Cale and he took comfort in the darkness. They sank like a stone into the deep.

CHAPTER 13

THE SOURCE

The water swallowed them. The surface fell away. Cale held his breath out of instinct and it took a conscious effort of will to inhale water. When he did, the fluid stung his nose as it rushed into his lungs. He could not control a reflexive fit of coughing. It passed soon enough, and after only a few deep breaths, inhaling water felt as natural to him as breathing air, save that his chest felt heavier.

Strange sensation, he said to Jak, and the little man nodded as they fell.

Pulled by the weight of the anchor, they descended rapidly. The darkness grew profound. Only the lightlessness of the Plane of Shadow compared with the pitch of the depths. Cale's transformed eyes allowed him to see but only to about the distance of a long dagger toss. Shadowy forms moved in and out of his field of vision, all of them finned, and some of them large. They fell through a school of orange fish as big as Cale's forearm. He kept his eyes open for scrags, but saw none. Cale suspected that Magadon had left no survivors.

They descended deeper. Cale looked down and saw only a black abyss. He glanced up and saw only a trail of bubbles left in their wake, spiraling away into the dark. The surface was lost to them. They were alone, sinking into the soundless depths.

Cale had no idea how they would find the slaadi down there.

Trickster's toes, Jak projected. *I am at a thirty count and no end in sight. My ears are popping.*

Cale nodded. His ears were popping too, and he had deliberately not kept a count. He did not want to know how far down they had gone.

The bottom finally came into view. Cale saw a wasteland of broken rock, hillocks, and rolling dunes of dirt that stretched as far as he could see in every direction. It looked as desolate as a desert.

Cale let go of the anchor before it took them all the way down. He and Jak kicked to end their downward momentum. With their lungs full of water, they hung at equilibrium ten paces above the sea floor. The anchor continued its descent, hit the sand, and in silence sent up a cloud of mud.

They glanced about, looking for any sign of the slaadi. Cale saw nothing. Other than the disturbance caused by the anchor's impact, the sea bottom was as still as a painting—no movement, no life. Cale found the bottom so alien it might as well have been another plane of existence. He was very conscious of the fact that he and Jak were intruders, bringing life and motion to the still death of the bottom.

Eerie down here, Jak projected. An understatement.

Both held their blades in hand. As an experiment, Cale made a stabbing motion with Weaveshear. The water did not interfere with his movement. Jak's spell allowed them to move as easily in the water as they could in air.

Large chunks of broken rock lay embedded in the sea floor below them, scattered across the mud like the gravestones of giants. Several were as large as towers, some as small as a man. Worked stone, too, jutted from the sand: pillars, the limbs and heads of ancient statuary, pedestals, columns.

He remembered Sephris's words and realized that they were looking upon the ruins of a city that had been old when Sembia had been nothing more than a collection of farming hamlets. The sea had kept Sakkors in stasis for centuries.

Cale could see only twenty or so paces in any direction, but he had the sense that the rubble field extended over a vast swath of the bottom. Sakkors must have been a large city, as large as Selgaunt.

What is that? Jak asked, and pointed behind Cale.

Cale turned and saw a diffuse red glow, dimmer than moonlight. He thought it odd that they had not seen it on the way down. Though distance was hard to gauge in the depths, Cale figured the radiance to be a long bowshot away, maybe farther.

Shadows leaked from Weaveshear and flowed lazily in the direction of the light.

Mags, we're on the bottom, heading for a light, Cale projected.

Magadon made no response. Cale and Jak shared a look. The halfling shrugged.

Let's go, Cale said, and they set off, following the rope of shadows that bled from Weaveshear.

Cale saw that they were swimming above a wide furrow torn in the bottom of the sea by the floating city that had crashed into the ocean and rolled along the floor. He did not allow himself to imagine the terror the inhabitants must have felt as they hit the water.

Dark, Jak said. *This was no small town. Look at the damage. Imagine the number of people.*

Cale nodded. Sakkors was a graveyard for tens of thousands.

The bottom sloped upward as they swam, slightly at first, then more steeply. The light grew brighter with each stroke. They came to a ridge and . . . the sea floor fell away beneath them.

They stood at the top of a cliff so steep and smooth it looked like the sea floor had been sheared with a vorpal blade. At the bottom of the cliff, easily five hundred paces down, a mass of ruins spread beneath them. Broken buildings lay piled haphazardly on more broken buildings, one after another, until they formed a mountain of ruin. The heap reached a third of the way up the cliff face. Only underwater could such an unstable mass not collapse. The red glow emerged from somewhere within the pile of ruins, near the bottom.

Looking down the cliff face, Cale understood the geography. The smooth cliff must have once faced the sky, part of a massive chunk of mountain that had borne Sakkors through the sky. When the city crashed into the sea, the slab of earth upon which it had been built had come to a stop on its side and much of the city had poured off and slid downward to form a pile at its base.

For a few moments, neither Cale nor Jak said anything. The destruction was too big for comment. The red glow bathed the ruins, cast them in blood. Shadows poured from Cale's blade toward the bottom of the mountain of ruins, toward the red glow.

Jak swam out over the cliff, turned, and looked down.

There are caves carved into the cliff face, he said. *Above the ruins.*

The scrags' lair, Cale guessed.

Jak gave a start, peered downward.

Cale followed his gaze and saw what had drawn the little man's attention.

Far below them, perhaps a third of the way down the cliff face, three silhouettes knifed through the water. Cale could not see them clearly but the figures were too small for scrags. They swam rapidly, with the speed and undulating movement of something native to the depths.

Is that them? Jak asked.

It has to be, Cale said, but cursed himself for not casting a spell ahead of time that would have allowed him to see dweomers. He might have confirmed for himself that the three humanoids were the shapechanged slaadi and Riven. Now he could cast nothing because he could not give voice to his prayers.

But the darkness would still answer him. Controlling the shadows did not require him to speak. He needed only his will.

Ready yourself, he said to Jak. *I'll move us there.*

Jak nodded and Cale called upon the shadows. He first molded the darkness of the depths into simulacrums of himself that mirrored his motions. The images flickered about him, continuously changing positions around the real Cale.

Jak tried to follow their motions, failed, shook his head.

Focus on Azriim, Cale said. *He will have the Weave Tap seed.*

How will we know which is him? Jak asked.

Cale had no answer for that. They would not be able to mark the slaad's unusual eyes underwater.

We will have to improvise, little man.

Jak hefted his blades, nodded.

Cale looked down the cliff, picked his spot, and drew the darkness around them. With an effort of will, he moved them instantly from atop the cliff to the water beside the three forms.

The moment they materialized, the three forms recoiled and shouted a bubble trail. Cale marked Riven as the one-eyed aquatic elf, and the slaadi as the scaled, fanged, and clawed sea devils.

Riven, in the flesh of the aquatic elf, darted backward from the combat and jerked a pair of daggers from his belt. The assassin caught Cale's eye and shook his head as if to say, *Not yet*!

Cale ignored him, noted a thigh sheath of wands on one of the sahuagin, and knew that was Azriim. He lunged forward and stabbed Weaveshear at the slaad's chest. The surprised slaad responded quickly, darting out of the way of the stab and answering with a claw slash across Cale's exposed forearm. Trailing blood, Cale swung Weaveshear in a reverse slash that bit deeply into the slaad's side. Azriim screamed, bled, kicked, and swam backward away from Cale.

Dolgan gave a roar, audible even underwater, and tried to wrap his arms around Cale. Instead, he grappled a shadow image and it winked out of existence. The big slaad lashed out with a claw rake that struck another image, destroying it.

Jak appeared behind the big slaad and drove dagger and short sword into Dolgan's side. The slaad roared with pain, whirled around, and caught the little man with a backhand slash across the face. Blood poured from Dolgan's wound, trickled from Jak's cheek and lip.

Cale swam toward Azriim.

The slaad held his ground and glared at him around a forced, fang-filled smile.

You truly are proving to be inconvenient, Azriim said, and fired what should have been a bolt of energy from his hand. The water diffused the lightning into a globe that charged the water in a sphere all around the slaad. White light flared and the water sizzled. The discharge popped Cale's eardrums, caused his heart nearly to stop, and left him momentarily stunned. It appeared to have no effect on Azriim, and Riven had backed clear of its effect. A cloud of smoky bubbles raced surfaceward.

Before Cale could recover, Azriim pulled another wand from his thigh sheath and fired it at Cale. Cale could not get Weaveshear into place in time and a thin green beam struck him. Instantly a green glow formed around his body. Cale recognized it as the same type of glow he had seen on the slaadi's ship, the magic that had prevented him from shadow stepping through patches of darkness.

Cursing, Cale swam for the slaad, Weaveshear held high. Azriim swam backward, his form much more adept in the water than Cale's. The slaad easily kept the distance between them as he pulled his teleportation rod and worked its dials.

Enjoy the scrags, priest, Azriim said, and vanished.

Cale cursed aloud, and it came out as merely an inarticulate shout and a stream of bubbles. He turned back to Jak and saw the little man swimming a few strokes away. Riven and Dolgan were also gone.

I'm fine, Jak said, in answer to Cale's look. The halfling appeared to have suffered no wounds other than the scratch to his face. Jak, too, must have been clear of the effect of Azriim's spell. *Strong whoreson, that slaad. What about you?*

Fine, Cale answered. His ears tickled as the drums regenerated. *But that is the last time we let those bastards escape us. Done?*

Done, Jak answered. The little man looked past Cale toward the cliff face and his eyes went wide.

Cale whirled and saw a dozen scrags swimming out of the caves toward them. They probably smelled blood in the water.

Cale cursed. Glowing green with the effect of Azriim's wand, he knew he must look like a beacon to the trolls. He could not use the shadows to move them from place to place while Azriim's spell still enshrouded him. And neither he nor Jak could attempt to dispel the effect until they reached the surface. He touched Weaveshear's blade to the glow, hoping it would absorb the spell. It had no effect.

Move! Cale said.

They turned their backs to the trolls and swam as fast as they could downward, toward the ruins and the source of the red glow. Despite the spells that aided them underwater, Cale still felt that he was moving too slowly. He spared a glance back.

The trolls' powerful bodies undulated and the creatures cut through the water. Their fangs—many as long as a finger—jutted from their open mouths and promised Cale and Jak a painful, bloody end. Their thick-lidded, yellow eyes focused on Cale and Jak with the intensity that all predators regarded their prey.

Move, Jak! Move! Cale said.

But the trolls were gaining.

The awakening Source, perhaps out of instinct, blocked Ssessimyth's parasitic use of its mental powers. Ssessimyth's expanded consciousness ceased functioning. He could no longer sense the ships above him; he could no longer sense his minions in the caves near him, in the waters above. It was as if someone else were drinking the mind of the Source, stealing it from Ssessimyth.

He shifted his tentacles and pressed his head farther into the Source, trying to hold onto whatever it had left to give him.

His dream was ending. He was no longer content.

Azriim, Dolgan, and Riven materialized where Azriim had intended—near the base of the mountain of ruins. Slabs of stone, columns, statues, broken rock, and millennia of detritus lay piled against the cliff face in a towering heap. The whole reminded Azriim of a monstrous hive.

As they swam in place, framed in the red light leaking from the pile, much of the heap unexpectedly shifted and rumbled, as if shook by a small earthquake. Stones cracked, rock grated against rock. A few large slabs of stone slid from the top of the pile and crashed to lower positions. A cloud of dirt rose up and befouled the water.

The pile resettled, and the tremor did not recur.

What was that? Riven asked.

Azriim only shrugged.

The ruins lay in a messy jumble and the pile featured innumerable openings, crevices, and tunnels. Red light leaked from several of the cracks near the bottom, casting red beams into the surrounding water. The largest of the tunnels opened at the very base of the ruins. The light was brightest there. That was their route in. Somewhere within that tunnel, they would find the heart of Sakkors's mantle.

Not far from the tunnel lay a haphazard stack of immense bones, picked entirely clean. Spines as long as ships rested alongside jawbones that could have contained a dozen men.

Whale bones, Riven observed.

Azriim nodded. The scrags must have been voracious eaters. The bones of at least a dozen dead whales littered the sea floor.

I wonder what a whale's brain tastes like, Dolgan said, eyeing a skull curiously.

Azriim ignored his broodmate and looked upward, through the swirling dirt. High above them he saw Cale, glowing green beside the halfling, swimming downward. A dozen or more scrags trailed them. The trolls were gaining with every stroke.

Follow me, Azriim said, and he swam for the large tunnel. He would have teleported directly to the mantle's origin but saw no need to risk a blind transport in such close quarters. They could swim to it. It would not be far.

Cale and Jak swam through the cloud of mud and dirt that floated up from the bottom. Whatever had caused the tremor had destabilized the mountain of ruins. Jak and Cale swam clear of it as they descended, to avoid falling stones or shifting rock.

What in the Hells caused that? Jak asked.

Cale shook his head and kept swimming. He spared another glance back and saw through the hazy water that the trolls had closed the distance. Their long arms threw water behind them with alarming efficiency.

Cale looked ahead and down, toward the red glow emitted from the bottom of the ruins. He thought he caught a glimpse of three figures entering a tunnel at the base of the ruins but could not be certain. He was certain that he and Jak would not make it. The trolls would catch them first.

As always, Jak knew what he was thinking.

Go, said the little man. He pulled up and started to turn around. *Stop the slaadi. I'll hold the trolls here.*

Cale did not slow. He grabbed Jak by the shirt and pulled him along.

Not a chance, Cale said. *We pick a spot and make our stand together.*

We have to stop the slaadi, Jak answered.

Cale nodded. *We will.*

But—

Save it, Jak, Cale snapped. *Neither of us is dying today.*

Like Jak, Cale wanted to stop the slaadi. He had said himself that something large was at stake. But he would not sacrifice a friend to do it.

There, Cale said, and pointed down to a pocket formed in the ruins. A pile of pillars and statues created a shallow tunnel. If they could reach it, the trolls would be able to attack them from only one direction.

Jak nodded and they angled toward it.

Behind them, the trolls roared. And continued to close.

❦ ❦ ❦ ❦ ❦

The slaadi and Riven swam abreast through the broad passage. Slabs of broken stone lined the tunnel walls and braced the ceiling. Statues, their features long ago worn away, jutted from the ruins like specters rising from the grave. The movement of the threesome through the tunnel disturbed the fine sediment of the sea floor. They left a fog of dirt in their wake.

Between the sea water, the slash from Cale's blade, and the ubiquitous dirt, Azriim despaired for his clothes. Then he realized he was becoming giddy and took control of his emotions.

The red light grew brighter and drew them in. The tunnel angled slightly downward. Azriim wondered why the trolls—if the trolls were responsible—had cleared the passage. Perhaps they worshiped at the mantle's source. They were simpletons, after all.

Ahead, an opening beckoned, as wide as the mouth of a dragon. Light poured from it. Azriim picked up his pace, swam through the portal, and found himself at the end of a large hemispherical pocket, at the very root of the ruins. Dolgan and Riven followed.

Across the chamber was the provenance of the mantle—a red shard of glowing crystal as large around as the trunk of a mature oak. One end of it jutted out of a strange mound that made up the far wall of the chamber, and the other end disappeared into the rock of the sea floor. Only part of the shard's middle section was visible. Its length must have been three or four times Azriim's height.

Invisible magical energy soaked the chamber. Azriim's body tingled in the concentrated power. Swirls and eddies of crimson and orange flowed deep within the crystal's exposed facets. Azriim found the movement hypnotic.

The wall from which the crystal extended must have been transmogrified in some way by long exposure to the magic of the source crystal. Azriim thought it some kind of unusual coral mound, for it had literally grown around the crystal. Where crystal and coral met, the coral's edge was thin and ragged, and tendrils grew out of the mound and onto the surface of the crystal. From afar, the surface of the coral looked almost like leather. Azriim had never seen anything like it.

Riven, as though reading the slaad's mind, said, *That's not stone, is it?*

Azriim did not bother to answer. He shook the clawed hand upon which he wore his fingerless magical glove. The movement and Azriim's mental command summoned the silver, black-veined seed of the Weave Tap. He closed his fist over it. It vibrated slightly in his hand, perhaps in response to the mantle's energy.

Beside him, Dolgan stabbed the claws of one hand into the palm of the other. Blood leaked into the water.

Do it, his broodmate projected, his excitement palpable.

Azriim nodded and swam forward. Before he had gotten halfway across the chamber, a faint shudder shook the mound out of which the shard jutted, a pulse that sent a ripple along the rock. The shard flared crimson at the movement.

That shudder looked like something an animal might do.

Understanding dawned, and Azriim stopped cold in the center of the chamber. He looked hard at the tendrils and saw them for what they really were—veins. The implications settled on him.

The wall mound was not coral; it was flesh, the flesh of an enormous animal that had melded with the crystal. Perhaps the mantle was not sentient at all. Perhaps the creature used the magic of the mantle to project its consciousness surfaceward.

But then why had it taken no notice of Azriim and his companions?

What was that? Riven projected.

Azriim shook his head. He was not certain what it was.

He stared at the wall of flesh, astounded despite himself at the size of the creature that must be buried beneath the ruins. It was so large that its size had become a disguise. It was like looking at a speck of soil and trying to infer a farm.

Azriim understood now the source of the tremors. He also realized what had eaten the whales. Probably the scrags brought the creature food, perhaps as an offering. Azriim was pleased that the source crystal did not share whatever chamber afforded access to the creature's mouth.

What are you waiting for? Dolgan asked.

Azriim swam forward. The aura of magical energy emitted by the source crystal grew more intense as he neared it. So too did the pressure in his brain. He blocked it out as best he could. Azriim felt as if he were swimming against a current. His eyes ached; his vision grew cloudy. One stroke, another.

A second ripple ran through the flesh of the beast and somewhere, deep within a hidden part of the ruins, the rest of the creature's body began to stir. The entire pile of rock shook. Debris and chunks of stone rained from the ceiling. Azriim feared the entire mountain would collapse atop him. He, Riven, and Dolgan darted out of the way of several blocks of falling stone and covered their heads.

The tremor passed. The chamber remained intact.

Do what you came to do, Riven said.

Have your teleportation rods in hand, Azriim answered. *The moment I plant the seed, we return to. . . .*

He remembered that the Sojourner had told him not to return to the pocket plane. The slaadi's father was to provide them with a new location for their return. Unfortunately, Azriim had been unable to contact his father.

. . . Selgaunt. We return to Selgaunt's wharves. We will contact the Sojourner there.

Azriim withdrew his own teleportation rod and turned

the dials until he had only a single half-turn remaining to activate it.

Ready to retreat, he eyed the crystal, thought of what it would mean when he planted the seed: full transformation to gray, freedom from the Sojourner. The fact that the mantle was sentient, or that tapping it might kill the huge creature, bothered Azriim not at all.

Here we go, he said, and reached out his hand toward the crystal.

He touched the silvery seed to an exposed facet and the source crystal exploded in blinding red light. Beams of crimson fired in all directions. In an instant, the current of magical energy became a maelstrom and Azriim had to kick frantically to hold his position. He watched through squinted, aching eyes as the Weave Tap seed merged with the crystal, spread its black veins throughout the facets, entwined around and strangled the veins of the creature that had melded with the crystal.

The creature gave a lurch that shook the entirety of the ruins. The sudden movement tore the beast's flesh where it had grown over and into the crystal. Red blood poured from the wound and clouded the water, mixed with the maddening red light. The mountain of ruins quaked, shook, began to collapse.

The creature was waking.

Azriim turned the dial on his teleportation rod, felt the familiar quiver in his stomach, and was gone from that place in an instant.

The Source's consciousness moved groggily toward wakefulness and as it did, the power of its nearly conscious dreams sent mental energy pouring up from the sea bottom. The energy soaked Magadon, filled him, saturated him. He opened his mind and drank it in. He felt the Source's power weaken as the Weave Tap seed took hold, but even then its consciousness was more powerful than any Magadon had ever encountered.

Ages of history and knowledge passed through his memory in little more than a flash. He understood the nature of the Source. It was a sentient Netherese mythallar, unique in Faerûn's history. Its mental and magical energy could be diffused over an entire city—enough to keep a metropolis afloat, or render nonmagical items mildly magical. Or, unlike an ordinary mythallar, its power could be concentrated in a single item or person. Its sentience allowed it to answer the wants of its creator. But in its dreaming state, it did not recognize its creator, and sent its energy forth for any to use.

Magadon seized all the energy he could, and as he absorbed more, he became able to contain and control still more power, and more. He felt as though his mind had expanded to the size of the multiverse. He shouted, not with pain, but with the ecstasy of revelation. The power in his voice shredded *Demon Binder*'s sails. Around him, the ship's crew fell to the deck screaming, bleeding from their ears.

"What are you doing, man?" Evrel shouted.

Magadon did not respond. Instead, he drank in more power, and more.

Cale and Jak reached the cave, turned, and went shoulder to shoulder. The trolls were right behind them. Cale still had a few shadow images flitting about him, but they would be of little use in such close quarters. The pocket was little more than a cul-de-sac, with shards of stone and pillars jutting from the walls. The trolls would be able to attack them only through the cave mouth, and only two or three at a time. The glow from the magical effect on Cale cast the cave in green.

Cale held Weaveshear before him. Shadows poured from

the blade. Jak brandished his dagger and shortsword.

The trolls appeared in moments. Two charged the opening, claws extended, fanged mouths wide. Cale and Jak, their movement magically free of water resistance, easily dodged under the scrags' claws and answered with shouts and steel. Cale severed an arm from one of the trolls and Jak drove both of his blades into the chest of the other. The creatures snapped and thrashed, destroying two of Cale's images and opening a gash in Jak's chest. Their bulk pushed Cale and Jak backward. The small cave became filled with bubbles, floating sediment, a cloud of troll and human blood. Cale stabbed blindly with Weaveshear, felt it bite into troll flesh. Beside him, Jak shouted, stabbed with his dagger.

Unexpectedly the trolls darted backward out of the cave and swam away, trailing streams of blood. Their wounds closed as they swam away and Cale understood their strategy. Able to regenerate underwater, the scrags would continually attack and withdraw, until Cale and Jak were too tired or too wounded to defend themselves.

Regenerating, Jak said. *Dark and empty! We've boxed ourselves in.*

Cale nodded, thinking fast. He came up with little.

We'll have to charge them, he said to Jak. *Cut our way through and make a dash for the surface.*

Jak looked at him and nodded, but Cale could see in his face that the little man understood how unlikely they were to make it. The trolls were faster swimmers and stronger combatants, albeit less skilled.

Still, both of them understood that they had no choice. If they stayed in the cave, the trolls would eventually kill them.

The scrags—Cale counted fourteen of the hulking creatures—swarmed the waters about ten paces from the cave mouth. They looked to be squabbling over which of them would attack next. Bestial eyes glared at Cale and Jak. Fangs jutted from cavernous mouths.

Without warning, the red glow from the base of the mountain flared, turning the sea to blood. Cale and Jak shared a look, unsure of what to make of it. The trolls, too, gave a start and went wide-eyed. They gestured toward the base of the ruins and grunted frantically to each other in their bubbly, guttural tongue. Two of them started downward and swam out of sight.

Cale was just about to call for a dash when a tremor, more powerful than the last, wracked the entire mountain of ruins. The ceiling of the cave shifted, and two huge chunks of stone fell. A block clipped Jak's shoulder and the little man screamed a stream of bubbles. A large slab struck Cale squarely in the back and drove him face-first to the cave floor. The shadows surrounding him saved his ribs from breaking, and his shadow-enhanced strength allowed him to shake the slab loose. He rose to all fours.

The shaking intensified.

What in the Hells is that? Jak asked, eyes wide.

Cale had no idea, but he did know that they had to get out of the cave. He found his feet.

Outside the cave, the scrags' wide eyes showed fear and surprise. Their attention was turned from Jak and Cale toward the base of the ruins. They were as vulnerable as they could be.

The trolls, Jak! Cale said. *Right now!*

Side by side, Jak and Cale darted out of the cave and charged the dozen remaining trolls.

Cale stabbed one through the chest, jerked his blade free, and unleashed a cross cut that severed the troll's head. Black blood poured from the stump and the body began to sink. Jak plunged his blades into the throat and ribs of another troll. It roared, arched its back, tried to swim clear of Jak.

The attack disconcerted the already fearful trolls. As one, they growled and fled in the direction of their caves. Cale and Jak floated in the cloud of troll blood, stunned. Cale could not believe their luck.

The Lady is smiling on us, Cale, Jak said. *Let's get the Hells out of—*

Below them, above them, around them, the entire mountain of rubble shook, lurched as if the earth were trying to dislodge from the ruins. Rock and finished stone rained down from the heights. A cloud of dirt went up from the base of the mountain, dimming the red light, obscuring the bottom, mixing with the troll blood. Cale watched the headless corpse of the troll he had killed spiral into the depths.

Stones crashed against each other, splintered, grated on each other with a deafening roar. The entire mountain seemed ready to be uprooted.

The underwater landslide continued for several moments, then silence.

Cale had seen enough. He would find the slaadi on the surface. He grabbed Jak's shirt and pulled him upward.

By the gods, Jak said, and Cale heard awe in his voice.

Cale turned, followed Jak's gaze downward. What he saw froze him. His numb hand fell from Jak's shirt. No wonder the scrags had fled.

A virtual mountain of flesh was squirming itself loose from the rubble. Cale had never seen a creature so large. He recalled the size of the shadow dragon they had encountered on the Plane of Shadow. This creature was easily several times that size.

Kraken, Jak said, and the word turned Cale's body cold.

The ruins that made up the base of the mountain had been blown outward by a lurch of the creature's immense body, exposing its form. Eight tentacles, each as big around as a tree trunk, sprouted from the bottom of a cylindrical body topped with a sleek, arrow-shaped head. The body alone stretched the distance of several bowshots, and the two longest of its eight tentacles—the outer two—could have reached halfway across Selgaunt.

The source of the red glow, too, was exposed—a huge shard of glowing red crystal, partially embedded in the sea floor and partially embedded in the top of the kraken's head. The open gash in which the crystal rested reminded Cale of a dragon's maw. The crystal itself called to mind the orange crystal that had been the source of Skullport's mantle.

Cale knew that the slaadi had come to tap this crystal the same way the other had been tapped. He knew, too, that they must have succeeded, and in so doing, had awakened a monster.

Tentacles squirmed amidst the ruins, casually brushed aside blocks of stone that a team of oxen could not have moved. The kraken emitted a high-pitched shriek so loud, so full of rage that it made Cale wince.

The creature levered itself against the sea floor with its inner tentacles and gave a powerful lurch, either to detach its head from the crystal or to detach the crystal from the sea floor.

We have to go, Jak said, and pulled at Cale's shirt. Cale nodded and started to swim surfaceward. But he could not take his eyes from the kraken.

The flesh of the creature's head gave way before the rock of the sea floor. Skin tore partially away from the crystal. Blood poured from the gash. The kraken emitted another shriek and contorted itself to reach around its head with its two outer tentacles. They twined themselves around the crystal. The creature was going to pull it from the sea bed.

And after that, it would be free to move.

The image of the kraken swimming free in the same sea as Cale and Jak brought Cale back to himself.

Move, Jak, he said, tearing his eyes from the kraken. *Now. Move!*

They turned their feet to the ruins and swam. They threw water behind them as fast as they could.

Too slow, Cale's mind kept repeating. Too slow.

Another screech from the kraken filled the sea. The ruins rumbled as the movement of the creature's body shook the pile. A sharp crack sounded and the kraken uttered another shriek, this one in exultation. Cale knew what it signified—it had torn the crystal free of the sea bed.

Faster, Cale! Jak said, his voice filled with panic.

But both of them knew they already were swimming as fast as they could.

Magadon, Cale projected to the surface, but received no response. *Mags! If you can hear me, get the ship out of here. Right now. Something is coming, something . . . big.*

The Source is awakening, Erevis, replied Magadon, and his mental voice boomed inside of Cale's head. *I understand its language now, its purpose, its powers. I can use it—*

Mags, forget all of that, Cale said. *Just get the ship out of there. Right now. Make for Selgaunt. We'll meet you.*

Cale said that last though he did not expect to survive. Bubbles streamed from his mouth; shadows leaked from his skin. He kicked, threw his arms out and down. Already his limbs felt like lead. His muscles were burning. How long had they been swimming upward? Where in the Hells was the surface?

He glanced downward just as the kraken squirmed its body entirely free from the ruins. The pile started to collapse, the roar of falling stone loud enough to hurt Cale's ears. Sakkors was lost in a cloud of silt.

The kraken, with one powerful undulation of its enormous body and tentacles, wiggled free of the destruction. It swam backwards, leading with its head, and the glowing red crystal stuck out of the gash in its head like a unicorn's horn. The two outer tentacles ended in diamond-shaped pads covered in suckers the size of kite shields. The creature swam an arc around the ruins, as if testing out a body long atrophied through lack of use. It angled upward and its eyes—as large as wagons—seemed to fix on Cale and Jak.

Keep going! screamed Jak.

They swam with an energy born of terror.

Another shriek of rage filled the deep. Cale looked down to see the kraken undulate its body and swim after them. Its huge form cut through the water as cleanly as a razor. It matched a bowshot with each undulation. Its eyes never left them.

Cale looked up and saw nothing to indicate that they were nearing the surface. No light, no anything. Terror birthed panic.

The kraken was closing, eating up the distance. Cale could feel it.

They were dead, he knew it.

Still, he kept kicking. It was not in him to surrender. He kicked, swung his arms, swam for all he was worth. His heart must surely burst.

He looked back and saw nothing but the kraken's eyes, the pupils as big across as he was tall.

They breached the surface. Air. Starlight.

Gasping, spent, Cale did not allow his astonishment to cloud his thinking.

"Dispel it, Jak!" he shouted. "Hurry!"

Jak pulled his holy symbol and began to cast. Both of them knew that if Jak's spell failed to overcome the magic of the slaad's wand, they would die right there.

As Jak mouthed the words to his spell between gasps, Cale tried to look out over the water, to spot *Demon Binder*. He did not see it. He hoped Magadon and Evrel had gotten the ship clear of the area.

Selgaunt, Mags, he projected again, and received no response.

He did not bother to look down. He knew what was underneath them. He knew too what would happen if it reached them. The water was blood red and growing brighter. The kraken, with its horn of glowing crystal, was closing. Cale could feel it coming within his bones, the same way he could feel a storm on the winds.

He drew the darkness around himself and Jak. If Jak's spell succeeded, he would take them into the shadows instantly. If Jak's spell did not succeed, then he would die cloaked in the darkness that had become his constant companion.

Jak shouted the last word to his spell and pointed his holy symbol at Cale.

The green glow that tethered Cale to the Material Plane winked out.

Cale felt the waters rising under them. The kraken was right below them. A scream from the creature rose up from the water and burst into the night air.

Cale hoped never again to hear such a sound.

The shadows around them deepened, swallowed them, and took them away.

Magadon felt it when Jak and Erevis traveled the darkness and vanished. If only *Demon Binder* could have done the same. There was no wind. The ship had no way to go anywhere.

And the creature that long had held the Source's mind captive was surfacing. Magadon sensed its anger. He saw it in his mind's eye—a body as large as a town, tentacles lined with suckers like shields, a savage, curved beak that could rend a ship in two with a single bite.

Kraken.

And it was bringing the Source with it. Magadon's expanded consciousness sensed that the Source jutted like a narwhal's horn from an open wound in the kraken's head. The Source was awakened and surfacing.

Magadon was terrified at the implications.

A crewman called out from the starboard side of *Demon Binder* and the rest of the crew pelted past Magadon and across the ship to look over the side. Magadon knew what they saw: The glow of the Source had turned the sea blood red between *Demon Binder* and the slaadi's ship. Magadon heard the alarmed voices of the crew, sensed their growing fear.

The Source, nearly awake now, was still feeding him. He drank all he could, despite the harm it did to his body. He had never felt anything like it. Knowledge poured into him. His head pounded and he felt blood leaking from his ears, his nose. He hoped the warm fluid running out of his eyes was clear and not red. He groaned with the pain, exulted in the power.

Selgaunt, Mags, Cale had projected.

The crew began to point, shout. The glow was growing brighter. The water off the starboard side roiled. Foam sprayed into the air as tentacles as thick around as kegs burst from the sea. The kraken's glistening body followed, displacing so much water that it sent waves into *Demon Binder* strong enough to cause it to list. The kraken's huge eyes, half-exposed above the waterline, looked first on *Demon Binder,* then on the slaadi's ship.

It turned and headed for the other ship.

The panicked screams of the survivors aboard the slaadi's ship carried over the sea. The kraken cut through the water like a blade. It closed the distance to the slaadi's ship rapidly. Its body dwarfed the vessel. The screams of the ship's crew grew louder. Tentacles thicker than the mainmast squirmed over the deck, crushed men to pulp, wrapped the ship from maindeck to keel. Wood splintered, shattered. The masts toppled. The ship buckled. The creature pulled all of it underwater and fed on what it wished.

The slaughter had taken less than a five count. There was no sign of the slaadi's ship. The kraken swam a tight circle and started for *Demon Binder.*

The crew shouted in alarm, and alarm quickly turned to panic. Evrel shouted orders but no one heeded. Some stared at the onrushing mountain, some screamed, some milled about, looking for something, *anything,* that might allow them to be spared.

Magadon stared not at the kraken but at the Source, sticking out of the creature's head. It was still pouring mental energy into him. Magadon knew what he had to do. He knew it might kill him.

The kraken was closing. Several of the crew screamed defiance at the sea, shook their fists at the beast; others wrapped their arms around their bodies, fell to the deck, and awaited death.

Awaken, Magadon said, and used the power granted him by the dreaming Source as a prod to spur the sentience of the crystal awake.

The kraken was two bowshots distant. One.

Awaken!

The Source stirred to wakefulness. The crystal in the kraken's head flared blazing red, a pulse of power and light so bright it seemed for a moment as though a crimson sun had dawned over the sea.

Magadon screamed; the kraken shrieked; the crew wailed.

The awakened Source sent a call into the sky, along the Weave, so powerful that Magadon knew it could be sensed across Faerûn. It spoke only a short phrase, in a language—ancient Netherese—that Magadon had learned only moments before.

I am here, it projected. *Help me.*

Magadon did not know to whom it was speaking—perhaps it had called to no one—and he had no time to consider the implications.

The surge of power emitted from the awakened, fully-conscious Source knocked Magadon to his knees. He lowered his mental defenses and took into his mind everything the Source offered. New mental pathways opened; understanding dawned; realizations struck him, revelations. He grabbed his head and held it, fearful it would fly apart. Sounds were coming from his mouth—gibberish—but he could not stop them. In those few moments he learned more of the Invisible Art, more of himself, than he had learned from a lifetime of study.

But he needed more.

Give it all to me, he projected to the Source, and was astounded at the power contained in his mental voice.

The Source answered.

The power that filled Magadon doubled that which he previously had received. His mind felt aflame. He felt his veins straining. Dagger stabs of pain wracked his skull. Blood gushed from his nose, his ears. His vision went blurry. He forced himself to hold onto consciousness. Despite the pain, he let the power come until the Source had given him everything it had.

The Source dimmed while Magadon glowed with the power contained in his mind. He was soaked in blood, snot, saliva. He did not care. He roared and his voice boomed over the water. The crew turned from the kraken to face him. Their wide eyes showed fear, wonder. Evrel shouted but Magadon could not hear him. He heard only a keening in his ears, punctuated by the drumbeat of his heart. In that instant, he knew that his mental abilities exceeded even those of the Sojourner.

Behind the crew, he saw the mountain of flesh closing on *Demon Binder,* saw the glowing facets of the Source coming closer.

Magadon looked inward and found his mental focus. It brought him calm. He reached out with his mind in a way he had never before done. As his consciousness expanded, he saw the fluidity of reality, the uncertainty of outcomes, the interconnections not between events but between possible events. He knew he could affect those possibilities; he knew he could make the improbable—even the highly improbable—reality.

At his command, reality conformed to his will. At the bow of *Demon Binder,* a glowing, golden vertical line appeared. It expanded rapidly in width and height until it formed an oval larger than the ship. The glow wavered, steadied, and an image appeared—a shoreline, the lantern light from a city, a thicket of masts and ships.

Selgaunt Bay. The crew stirred, ran for the bow as if to jump off the ship and into the bay.

Magadon exerted his will and pulled the portal toward *Demon Binder*.

A golden glow suffused ship and crew as they entered the portal. The kraken's shriek of rage chased them through. A tentacle struck the ship just before the magic took hold and sent it careening forward. The crew fell to the deck, shouting in alarm.

In a blink, *Demon Binder* floated peacefully on the still waters of Selgaunt Bay. Magadon, wobbly, sealed the portal behind them.

Cut off from the Source, he felt bereft. Knowledge and power flowed out of him, as ephemeral as the memory of dreams. He held on to what he could, but it was disappointingly little.

The crew rose to their feet and looked around with dazed expressions. One cheered, another, another. Soon the whole crew was shouting, singing, thumping each other on the back.

Smiling faces turned to Magadon and lost their mirth. Magadon touched a hand to his face. It came away bloody. His vision blurred and he fell.

CHAPTER 14

THE SPELL

The surge of power from the planted Weave Tap seed caused the tower to shake under Vhostym's feet. His sons had done it! They had planted the second seed of the Weave Tap in Sakkors's mantle.

A charge went through Vhostym's frail body, a wave of exultation that would have caused him to leap for joy had his body not been so broken. He controlled his emotions only with difficulty.

Soon he would have the Crown of Flame.

Vhostym had been young when he and his father first had walked in the shadow of the Crown. Vhostym had been stronger then, not as sensitive to light. He still remembered the smell of the wind off the water, the feel of the air on his skin, the sounds of the surface heard through his own ears. He recalled the moments with fondness. The light had burned his skin but he had endured; his father had made him endure. Father had intended to harden Vhostym to pain, and to excite his ambition by showing him the possibility of a life on the surface, under the sun.

Father had taught the lesson well.

Vhostym had come to believe that nothing was unattainable, not for him, and he was about to prove it. He could track the course of his life back to those moments shared with his father under the Crown of Flame. In a sense, he had been born that day on the surface. He could trace all the accomplishments of his life back to that single event.

It was fitting, then, that he would end his life with the same event. He would create a Crown of Flame, tame it not only for a few moments but for an entire day, and walk in its shadow before he died.

He thought of his sons and reached out his mental consciousness for them. He linked with Azriim and Dolgan immediately. He saw through their eyes a dark city street. They were in Selgaunt, and both were restless.

He allowed Azriim to sense the contact.

Sojourner, his son said. *We wish what we were promised.*

Soon, Vhostym answered. *It would be dangerous for you to return here now. Wait where you are. I will contact you after I have completed my task. All of this will be finished soon.*

He sensed Azriim's perturbation, Dolgan's disappointment, the human's . . . ambivalence.

He reassured his sons. *You will have what you were promised. I will keep my word. I will leave here what you require for your transformations.*

Leave it for us? Azriim asked. *You will not be there?*

Vhostym heard no concern in Azriim's mental voice, merely curiosity. He had taught his sons well. Sentimentality was a shackle with which the weak yoked the strong.

Yes, leave it for you, Vhostym affirmed. *We will not see each other again.*

His sons fell silent. The words surprised them.

I will contact you not long after dawn, Vhostym said. *Remember that what you see this day is my doing.*

He cut off the connection before they could trouble him with further questions. He had preparations to make.

"What now?" Dolgan asked. Sea water soaked the street at the big slaad's feet.

Azriim and Dolgan had assumed their preferred half-drow and human forms, and Riven had returned to his natural form. The three stood on a narrow street in Selgaunt. All were soaking wet and the human's lips were blue. No doubt he was cold from the night's chill.

Dawn was still an hour or two away and only dung-sweepers populated the otherwise deserted streets.

"We wait," Azriim said. He looked down at his filthy, torn, water-stained clothing. "And as soon as the shops open, I buy some new attire."

Cale and Jak materialized in the darkness of one of Selgaunt's countless alleys. Cale recognized the location—not far from Temple Avenue. Their sudden appearance startled several cats and the felines screeched and fled. The sound reminded Cale of the kraken's shriek. He put it out of his mind. They were safe now.

For a time, they simply caught their breath. Water dripped from their clothes and bodies. Jak bore a scratch on his face from Dolgan, as well as several deep gashes from troll claws on his midsection. Cale's flesh had healed his wounds. The little man took out his holy symbol, called on Brandobaris, and spoke a spell of healing. His wounds closed entirely.

"What about Magadon?" Jak asked, as he wrung out his shirt. They had left their cloaks and almost all of their other clothing on *Demon Binder.*

Cale shook his head, removed his own shirt, and wrung it out. The night air would have chilled him had his warming spell not still been in effect.

"I think he got *Demon Binder* clear," Cale said to Jak, hoping that by saying it he might make it true. "I did not see the ship when we surfaced. Did you?" "No time to look. But . . . wouldn't Mags contact us if he could?"

Cale had been thinking the same thing but did not say so to Jak. Instead, he said, "He has only so much mental strength, little man. Could be that. I can scry for the ship, see if they're all right."

Jak brightened at that. "Right now? Here?"

"No. Midnight next."

The scrying spell took preparation and Cale could not be ready until then.

Jak deflated a bit but nodded. He mumbled to himself, fished in one of his three belt pouches until he found his pipe.

"Did it stay dry?" Cale asked.

"Dry enough," Jak murmured, and searched another pouch for his pipeweed. "I have never seen anything as big as that kraken, Cale. Never."

"Me either," Cale said softly.

Jak removed a small leather pouch tied with a drawstring and pried it open. Cale caught the aroma of the weed.

Jak pulled out a pinch and held it up. "Dry as a fallen leaf. Now that's a pouch worth its price."

Cale saw that Jak's hands were shaking, and not from the chill. Cale pretended not to notice. It *had* been a close call with the kraken, and Cale had been close to panic himself.

The little man managed his emotion by humming

while he pressed the pinch of pipeweed into the bowl of his pipe. He searched his pouches for a tindertwig and found several—all of them ruined by sea water. The humming stopped.

"Where am I going to get tindertwigs two hours before dawn?"

"You're not," Cale said.

"No, I'm not," Jak said, and Cale saw tears in his eyes. Exhaustion and emotion were taking their toll.

Again, Cale pretended not to notice.

Jak recovered himself with a deep breath. He popped the pipe in his mouth and chewed its end.

"What do we do now?" the little man asked.

"We wait," Cale answered gently. "And relax while we can."

"That sounds about right. The Murky Depths, maybe?"

Cale grinned and shook his head. "I've seen enough of the depths to last a good while, little man. We'll find something else dockside."

Jak nodded and they set off.

Cale put his hand on Jak's shoulder as they walked the quiet, predawn streets of the city in which they had met, just as they had done countless times before, and just as they would countless times after.

"This is almost over, little man," Cale said.

Jak looked at him sidelong, nodded, and said nothing.

Cale did not tell Jak that he thought this reprieve to be the deep breath before the plunge. They still had to find the slaadi and the Sojourner and kill them all.

They could not find an inn that would open its doors, so they wandered onto Temple Avenue. It was deserted, except for the cranks who slept on the benches. The starlings nesting in the Hulorn's statuary rustled at their passing. The wind stirred the leaves of the dwarf maples.

"Let's sit down a minute, eh?" Jak suggested.

Cale agreed and they sat on two unoccupied benches

overlooking a still pool, across from the shrine of Tymora. Cale smiled, thinking that they must have looked a bit like cranks themselves. Sighing, he stretched out on the bench. Jak did the same on the other.

Through the maple leaves, Cale saw the stars shining down. He kept his gaze away from the Sanctum of the Scroll, though he felt it lurking there in the darkness, whispering Sephris's dire prophecies at him. He did his best to put them from his mind.

Exhaustion settled on both of them quickly. They did not speak and both lay looking up at the sky, alone with their thoughts. Within moments, Cale heard Jak snoring. He smiled and drifted off to sleep himself.

He dreamed of Magadon and tentacles and a foaming sea.

Vhostym spoke the words that allowed him to pass through the warded doors that led into the sanctum. He opened the doors with his mind and floated through. They closed behind him.

He felt calm, and his self control pleased him.

The Weave Tap stood in the center of the room, its golden leaves charged with the stored power of two Netherese mantles, possibly more magical power than ever had been assembled in a single place.

It would be enough, he thought. He would poke a hole in the sun and take a day, a single day, and make it his.

He floated forward, under the sparking canopy of the Weave Tap, and touched its silvery bark with his hand. It was warm, almost hot with the power it contained. He looked at the walls, the ceiling, the floor. Lines of arcane power veined the stone.

Everything was ready.

He found a suitable spot between the Tap's exposed roots and lowered himself to the floor. He crossed his legs, ignoring the pain the movement caused him, and closed his eyes.

Formulae moved through his mind, numbers, equations, variables, all of them designed to anticipate the movements of the bodies in the heavens. He moved through each one methodically, checking and rechecking the calculations. They were critical to his spell. Throughout the day, the magic would have to adjust continually to account for the movement of Toril, to keep the Crown of Flame intact over his island.

He was prepared.

With a slight mental exertion, he opened a channel between his body and the Weave Tap. Arcane energy flowed into him, powered him, the feeling more delightful than even the pleasures of the flesh he had enjoyed in his youth. He let the power gather in him. It built slowly but inexorably. As he drew from the artifact, the Weave Tap continued to draw power from the mantles of Skullport and Sakkors, replenishing the power that Vhostym took.

Vhostym inhaled and began his spell. Magical syllables fell from his lips in a complex incantation. His hands traced a precise, intricate path through the air before him. His fingers left a silver glow in their wake. He wove the mathematical formulae into the incantation. Vhostym accounted for the speed of Toril's spin, its precession on its axis, the speed of its revolution about the sun, the size of Selûne's tear, the necessary distance that he needed to move it, the power he would need to hold it there, a host of other factors. The equations grew increasingly complex.

Vhostym kept focused and worked the equations into his spell. His fingers and hands became a blur. For a time, a short blissful time, he was lost in the casting and felt no pain in his body.

He worked for over an hour, all of it preparatory to the spell's finale. His voice grew hoarse and still he recited the arcane words. Sweat dripped from his body.

When he finished the preparatory casting, he found

himself sitting in the middle of a cyclone of magical energy. The formulae he had spoken were a storm of glowing, silver characters whirling about his person. They wanted only their purpose.

Vhostym gave it to them.

He drew everything from the Weave Tap that it could give. His body glowed with contained power. The numbers and equations whirled around him so fast they formed a silver wall.

He put his palms flat on the floor of the tower and let the magic flow through him and into the stone. The silver wall of numbers swirled through the tops of his hands and into the tower.

The entire structure shuddered. A glow in the stone started at his palms and rapidly spread to the rest of the sanctum, to the rest of the tower. The structure amplified the magical power Vhostym channeled into it until the spire itself radiated with power. Numbers and equations raced along the walls, glowing silver.

Vhostym pictured in his mind the largest of Selûne's tears, a perfect sphere of rock roughly fifty leagues in diameter, almost exactly a twentieth of Selûne. Vhostym needed to bring the tear closer, such that its distance from Toril was a twentieth that of Selûne's distance. He would have preferred using Selûne itself, but not even his empowered magic could control a celestial body that large.

He spoke the words to the spell that would pull the tear to the place Vhostym needed it. There it would remain, awaiting dawn, when it would put a hole in the sun and cast its shadow on the Wayrock. The magic would continually adjust the position of the sphere against the sun, so its shadow would not race across the surface as Toril continued to spin. Instead, his magic would move the tear with the sun—the shadow would remain stationary on the Wayrock throughout the day.

Speaking the final phrase of power, Vhostym channeled

all his energy into the tower, sent it soaring in a beam from the top of the spire and into the Sea of Night. Vhostym felt the beam's magic take hold of the tear and pull it toward Toril. He could not contain a shout of joy.

It would be in position before dawn. Once he pulled it from its orbit, the spell would move the tear so that its surface would not reflect the light of the sun, as did Selûne. It would move through the night sky in darkness, but Faerûn would wake to the sight of a new satellite in its sky.

When Vhostym released his hold on the spell, exhaustion settled in and he sagged. Fortunately, nothing more remained for him to do. The tower still vibrated, still glowed, and Vhostym knew that a beam of magical energy reached from its top and into the night sky, where it pulled a ball of rock the size of a city toward Toril. The spell would remain in effect until the mantles of Skullport and Sakkors were utterly drained—about a day, perhaps two, Vhostym had calculated.

Despite his mental fatigue, despite the pain of the disease that wracked his bones, he smiled.

He had now only to recover his strength and wait for the dawn. Then he would exit the tower and walk under the Crown of Flame in his own skin, as he had done in his youth.

After that, he would die content.

Magadon opened his eyes. His blurry vision cleared and he found himself staring up at the grinning face of Captain Evrel. A faint breeze stirred a sail. The sky behind the captain was brightening with the rising sun.

Magadon was lying flat on his back on the deck of *Demon Binder*. His head felt as if it had been beaten by a war hammer. Each thump of his heart caused his temples to throb.

The last thing he remembered was . . . moving the ship to Selgaunt. He recalled the power the Source had given him, its taste, its feel. He felt empty at its absence. He longed for another taste.

"There you are," the captain said. "Welcome back."

A relieved rustle arose from around the deck. The crew, Magadon presumed.

A gray-haired man in nightclothes and an overcloak stood beside Evrel, looking down on Magadon with a soft expression. The man held in his hand a thin chain from which hung a bronze symbol—a shield-shaped pendant engraved with the image of a cloud and three lightning bolts. Magadon did not recognize the symbol but he assumed the man to be a priest.

"He is fine now," the gray-haired man said to Evrel. He smiled down at Magadon. "You will be well."

Magadon tried to thank him but his mouth was too dry to speak.

The priest said, "No need to speak, goodsir. Rest, now. Evrel is a very old comrade of mine and it was my pleasure to do him this service." He eyed the captain sidelong. "But he must think highly of you to have roused me from my sleep."

"He saved the ship," Evrel said. "And all of us besides. I tend to think highly of such men."

Beyond Magadon's sight, several members of the crew voiced agreement.

The priest nodded, straightened his cloak, and said to Evrel, "Be well, my friend. It's back to the sheets for me. Valkur keep you and your crew."

"My thanks, Rillon. A drink soon."

"Soon," Rillon agreed.

The two clasped arms and the priest walked away.

Evrel extended a hand to Magadon and pulled him to a sitting position.

"I was afraid to move you until I had a priest at my side," the captain explained.

Magadon nodded in understanding. Crusted blood caked his face, his neck, his ears. He rubbed it off as best he could.

Several crewmen approached and offered Magadon thanks or a comradely thump on the shoulder. The guide nodded in response.

"You've allies here, now," Evrel said. "Me included. I've never seen anythin' like that. Talos take me, but I hope never to see it again."

Magadon did not know if the captain meant the kraken or Magadon's movement of the ship or both. He swallowed to moisten his throat and croaked, "My comrades? Erevis and Jak?"

Evrel's expression fell. "They never came up from the bottom."

"Yes, they did," Magadon said, and allowed the captain to pull him to his feet. His consciousness, while expanded by the Source, had felt Jak and Cale reach the surface and escape the kraken into the shadows. Cale's last words to him had been: *Selgaunt, Mags.*

Magadon's mental strength was limited. He still had a latent connection to Riven but otherwise had little left with which to work.

"You look . . . different," Evrel said, but Magadon ignored him. Still leaning on Evrel, he summoned a mental reserve and reached out for his friends: *Erevis. Jak. Do you hear me?*

Cale thought he heard Magadon's voice. He snapped awake and sat up. It did not repeat.

Had he dreamed it?

Mags?

Yes, Magadon answered. *Yes. Erevis, I'm glad to know you're all right. Jak?*

Cale grinned and reached out to shake Jak.

"Little man," he said.

Jak sat up, grinning. "I hear him."

We're glad to know that you are all right too, my friend, Cale answered. *Where are you now?*

Selgaunt's docks, aboard Demon Binder.

Cale and Jak shared a look of surprise.

How in the Hells did that happen? Jak asked.

Magadon hesitated, and when he replied, his mental voice sounded grim. *That is a story for later. For now—*

Cale answered, *We're on our way.*

Cale and Jak rose and sprinted through the streets toward the dock district. They stopped only long enough to throw a few fivestars at a shopkeeper in exchange for new boots and new cloaks. The sky was lightening above them. Dawn began to swallow the stars. They had slept only a few hours. Behind them, the Tower of Song rang the hour and the Sanctum of the Scroll promised doom.

Cale and Jak located *Demon Binder* at one of Selgaunt's piers. Gouges from troll claws marred the hull and the sails were shredded. Magadon met them at the gangplank, leaning on Captain Evrel. The guide looked drawn, as haggard as Cale had ever seen him. He was not wearing his hat and Cale saw that the small stubs of his horns had grown half a finger's length overnight.

Magadon and the Captain hailed them, smiling, as did several members of the crew.

Cale returned their greetings and he and Jak embraced Magadon, clasped Evrel's forearm in turn.

"We thought you two were dead," Evrel said.

"Damned close," Jak said.

Evrel nodded. "Damned close for all of us. The whole ship would have been lost if not for this one." He indicated Magadon.

Magadon smiled with embarrassment.

"You look different," Cale said to Magadon, as delicately as he could manage.

"The horns," Magadon said, nodding. "There have been . . . other changes too," he added, but left it at that. "I don't know what it means."

"I'm certain it's fine," Cale said, but was not sure it was.

Magadon shook his head and waved dismissively. "Forget all that. Listen to me. When the Source awakened fully, it called out to someone or something, called out across Faerûn. I am concerned, Erevis. The Source is an item—a consciousness—of great power."

Cale and Jak shared a look. Evrel pretended not to hear.

"To whom did it call?" Cale asked.

Evrel cleared his throat. "I'll be leaving you to your business, then." He nodded to them and strolled up the gangplank.

"I don't know," Magadon said. "It called out in . . . Netherese."

"Netherese?" Not even Cale spoke that ancient tongue.

Magadon nodded.

Jak looked from Magadon to Cale and said, "Do you remember what Sephris said? That we would summon the storm?"

Cale nodded. He remembered the loremaster's parting words to him—*Sakkors is only the beginning.* His skin went gooseflesh. He tried to put it out of his mind.

"I remember. And I hear your words," he said to Magadon. "But first things first. We stop the slaadi, we stop the Sojourner, and we deal with what comes after when it comes. Agreed?"

Magadon looked him in the eye, nodded. Jak too.

Cale said, "Do you still have the link with Riven?"

"I do," Magadon answered. "A latent link. But no strength to activate it, and no strength to project the image into your mind. Took almost all I had to contact you two."

"How long before you are ready?" Cale asked.

"An hour," Magadon answered. "Maybe two. I can recover some strength by then."

Cale nodded. They would wait aboard *Demon Binder*. They had no choice.

"Let's go aboard," he said. "Get you some food and rest."

Together, the three comrades climbed the gangplank and boarded *Demon Binder*.

Jak said, "And someone on this tub damned well better have a tindertwig."

CHAPTER 15

WAYROCK

Riven, Azriim, and Dolgan aimlessly walked Selgaunt's streets as the false dawn lightened the sky. By accident, they had ventured near Riven's garret. He found himself scanning the streets and alleys for any sign of his girls, at the same time hoping and not hoping that he would catch a glimpse of them.

"What are you looking for?" Dolgan asked.

Riven chided himself for his carelessness. "Nothing. Mind your own affairs, slaad."

Dolgan grunted, Azriim grinned, and the three walked on. The street traffic was beginning to build as dawn approached. Shop doors and shutters opened. Farmers and their wagons entered the city and made their way to market. Sellers of sweetmeats and stale bread took their favored spots on the street. Riven gave a fat, already sweating sweetmeat seller his first sale of the day, purchasing two candied pears. He ate both without offering any to the slaadi.

"Where are all the clothiers?" Azriim said. "I am dressed like a pauper."

Riven knew several booths that sold clothing but did not mention any to the slaad.

Dawn broke and they walked on, awaiting word from the Sojourner.

Within a quarter hour, Riven noticed concern among the pedestrians. Eyes were wide; brows furrowed; strides were a step too fast. The rustle turned to an alarmed murmur.

"What is going on?" he said, more to himself than to the slaadi.

"What?" Dolgan asked.

A young laborer pelted down the street in their direction.

"Did you see it?" he shouted. "Did you see it?"

He looked like a madman.

Riven stepped in front of him and grabbed him by his cloak.

"Have you seen it?" the young man said, his breath coming in heaves. Riven saw real fear in his eyes.

"Seen what?" Riven asked.

"The sun," the boy said.

Riven gave him a shake. "What are you talking about?"

The daylight noticeably dimmed, then grew darker.

Riven released the boy and looked up to the east. The sun was too close to the horizon for him to see; buildings blocked his view. He jogged up the street until he reached an open square. The slaadi followed. So too did a gathering crowd of Selgauntans.

A small crowd had already assembled there, strangely hushed. All of them gazed to the east. Riven followed their looks and could hardly believe what he saw.

Overnight, another moon had appeared in the sky. A pitted sphere of dark rock hung in the sky just above the horizon line. It appeared as large as Selûne. Its edge blocked part of the rising sun. The sphere did not move as the sun rose; it just hung there, foreboding, waiting. As the sun continued its ascent, the sphere ate more and more of its face.

Riven was too astonished to speak. Those in the crowd around him muttered in ominous tones. Others moved closer to each other, as though for comfort. Horses neighed.

"Has Selûne abandoned us?" a woman cried.

A man said, "What in the Seven Heavens is it?"

"Where did it come from?" asked another.

"The gods keep us," said an old woman. "It is Alaundo's prophecies!"

Riven remembered the Sojourner's words and knew that the orb had nothing to do with the gods or prophets: *Remember that what you see this day is my doing.*

The Sojourner had summoned or created another moon. He was causing an eclipse. Riven marveled at the power represented in the sky.

In a flash, Riven understood the meaning of the Crown of Flame. But he could not understand why the Sojourner wanted to create it.

Beside him, Azriim chuckled, then laughed full out. Several people in the crowd looked at him as if he were mad.

Dolgan smiled tentatively and looked from Riven to Azriim.

"What is funny?" the big slaad asked.

Azriim laughed the louder.

A tingle in Riven's head announced the presence of the Sojourner.

It is finished, the creature said. *This day is to be my last day, and I will spend it alone. Your service to me is over. Return to this place and claim what you've earned.*

An image of a tower fixed itself in Riven's mind, a stone spire atop a mountain island in the Inner Sea. Riven recognized the island. Everyone who lived in a port on the Inner Sea had heard of the Wayrock. Sailors used it to aid navigation. But no mention of the Wayrock ever spoke of a tower on its top. The Sojourner must have raised it there, or moved it from elsewhere, just as he had done with the moon.

Dolgan and Azriim shared a glance, and Riven saw the eagerness in their expressions.

Playing to the end the part Mask had assigned him, Riven asked, *And for me?*

Name it, said the Sojourner, and the offer nearly caused Riven to renege on his plans. But he thought of his god, his girls, his . . . friends, and held fast.

Let me consider.

There is only a short time, the Sojourner responded.

"We will come now," Azriim said, speaking aloud in his eagerness. "The human can choose his payment later."

The slaadi withdrew their teleportation rods and Riven did the same. Just before Riven made the final turn, he sent his thoughts to Magadon and spoke a single word: *Wayrock.*

The rod transported him across Faerûn in a breath and he appeared with the slaadi in a door-lined chamber, presumably within the tower the Sojourner had showed them. The walls, ceiling, and floor glowed faintly silver, casting enough light for Riven to see by.

"The air feels strange," Dolgan said.

Azriim nodded.

Both transformed into their natural bodies—mottled gray skin, sinew, claws, fangs—and sniffed the air.

Riven felt nothing peculiar. He looked around the large chamber. Several doors led out to adjacent rooms and halls. The stylized door handles caught his eye. He stared at them, trying to discern their shape. When he did, the realization made his heart race.

All of the hardware featured a similar motif: a jawless skull in a sunburst.

The hairs on the nape of his neck rose. He understood in that moment what the Shadowlord had intended all along, why he had required Riven to escape with the slaadi from *Demon Binder,* why he had wanted Riven to play his part through to the end.

The tower was once a temple to Cyric, Mask's enemy. The Sojourner had taken the entire structure, and presumably murdered its priests. The god of shadows and thieves had manipulated all of them—*all* of them—to orchestrate the grandest theft of all. He'd arranged to steal an entire temple of the mad god.

Riven marveled at the scheme. It had been a bold play, as bold as he had ever seen. And he had been the Shadowlord's hand in the play. Or at least one of Mask's hands.

He could not help but smile, and the smile turned into a chuckle.

"You are amused?" Azriim said. The slaad held out his hand and examined his fingers, and his brow furrowed.

"What is happening?" Dolgan asked. He too stared at his body as if it were a foreign thing.

"Not amused," Riven answered, still chuckling. "Free."

"Free from the Sojourner," Azriim said, and nodded. His voice had grown deeper. His claws were longer. "What is happening to me?"

"No," Riven said. "Not from the Sojourner. From you two. From this charade."

Riven knew that Mask wanted him for one more thing.

"What do you mean?" Azriim asked. The slaad's gray skin bubbled and stretched, as if something were moving just under it.

"Allies and enemies, slaad," Riven said, and sneered. Riven's feigned allegiance to the slaadi was over. He was allies only with Cale, his brother in faith.

Azriim caught his tone and backed up a step. Dolgan began to growl.

"Enemies, I take it?" Azriim asked.

"Enemies it is," Riven answered. He drew his blades. He knew that the Sojourner was not in the tower. It was just him and the slaadi.

"You're standing in my temple," he said.

Azriim's gaze narrowed. "Your temp—"

The word turned into a bestial scream that Dolgan echoed. The slaadi raised their hands to the ceiling and roared. Veins, muscle, and sinew lined their flesh.

Riven stepped backward, unsure of what was happening.

The slaadi began to change. As before, when Riven had watched the Sojourner transform them from green slaadi to gray, now they were transforming before his eyes into something even greater. A chaotic flash of colors sheathed the slaadi. Both went rigid; both roared at the ceiling. Their claws extended; tufts of skin sprouted from under their chins; they grew slightly in stature; fangs darkened; green-gray skin lost its mottling, became like dark slate.

Then it was over. The slaadi eyed him with hunger in their eyes.

Riven pulled his holy symbol from under tunic and let it dangle openly. He knew the slaadi had just become more dangerous but he held his ground. Mask had put the temple under his feet, and he was a Chosen of Mask. He would not abandon it.

Cale and Jak stood on the deck of *Demon Binder,* surrounded by crewmen, all of them staring up at the dawn.

"Gods," Jak whispered.

Cale watched the rocky sphere slowly swallow the sun. He knew it was the Sojourner's doing. It had to be. Whatever the creature was planning, it was about to happen. Cale had seen enough eclipses on Faerûn to know that a partial eclipse in one region might be a full eclipse in another. He knew that wherever the Sojourner was, the eclipse was total. The water rose, causing the ship to bob.

The darkness lengthened, stretched a shadowed hand over the bay. He thought of the Fane of Shadows, of Shar, the goddess of night, of Mask, of the Sojourner, of his own transformation, of the Weave Tap. He saw the thread that connected them all. He knew what he had to do.

"Go get Mags," he said to Jak.

Magadon was meditating alone in a cabin in the forecastle.

"Tell him we have to go now, Jak. We're going to kill the Weave Tap."

Jak stared at him for a moment, uncomprehending.

"We're going to act like heroes, Jak. Go."

The little man grinned, nodded, and sped off.

Cale stared up at the heavens. He and his companions might not be able to defeat the Sojourner, but they could destroy his tool, stop whatever it was that he intended. Cale thought he knew how to do it—like him, the Weave Tap was a creature of darkness, created by the priesthood of the goddess of the night. Like him, it was vulnerable to the sun.

Jak returned shortly with Magadon. The guide stared up at the sky, pale eyes wide.

"Activate the leech on Riven, Mags. We have to move. Jak, cast every protective spell you can. Quickly, now. And the moment we arrive, divine the location of the Weave Tap. This time the Tap comes first. The slaadi are secondary."

Jak nodded and began to cast. Magadon concentrated and a soft red light haloed his head.

"I've got him," he said.

"Show me," Cale said, and took Magadon's hand.

❧ ❧ ❧ ❧ ❧

The slaadi parted to either side of Riven, crouched low. The creatures' transformation had changed their outward appearance little, but Riven did not fail to notice the coiled grace with which they moved. Dolgan flexed his claws and growled. Azriim showed his fangs and hissed.

Riven remembered that the slaadi's transformation from green to gray had granted them new magical powers. He assumed their new transformation had granted them still more such powers. He decided not to wait for a demonstration.

He showed his back to Dolgan and feigned a charge at Azriim, who leaped backward. As Riven had expected, Dolgan lunged at his exposed back.

Riven spun a half-circle and slashed a crosscut at Dolgan's throat with his right saber. The move surprised the slaad, who could do nothing but sacrifice his arm to save his neck. The saber cut hard into the slaad's bicep. The blow should have sunk halfway through the muscle, but instead cut only a deep gash into the slaad's flesh.

Grunting with pain and dripping black blood, the slaad swung wildly at Riven with the claws of his other hand. Riven had expected the attack and tried to ride the momentum of his slash into a full spin out of arm's reach, but he was too slow. The slaad's transformation had made him faster, and his claws caught Riven's back and tore through cloak and flesh to cause a painful slash. Riven grimaced and chopped with his left saber at Dolgan's head, but the slaad used the momentum of his own swing and bounded a few steps away from Riven.

He snarled as the wound in his arm began to close.

Riven caught motion out of the corner of his eye—Azriim. He doubled up his sabers in his right hand, jerked a dagger from his belt, and flung it at the slaad. The short blade flew true and hit Azriim in his chest, but deflected off his hide as if it were a breastplate. The slaad pointed a clawed finger at Riven. A sickly green beam issued from the digit and hit Riven in the stomach.

Riven's heart stopped. He gasped, clutched his chest, and fell to all fours. He tried to pull in a breath, to force air into his lungs.

A breath came. Another. He closed his hands around the hilts of his sabers and tried to rise. Before he could regain his feet, Dolgan's huge hands closed over his shoulders, pinning his arms. The slaad lifted him bodily toward his fanged, open mouth. Riven stared into the tooth-lined opening.

Thinking quickly, he brought his knees to his chest, kicked out, and drove his feet into the slaad's throat. The blow would have crushed a human's windpipe but only caused Dolgan to gag, cough, and drop Riven.

Riven hit the floor in a crouch and slashed the slaad's gut with both sabers. The blades opened two gashes in the creature's midsection. Dolgan hissed with pain and lurched backward. His regenerative flesh was already closing the wounds.

Riven whirled a half-circle to face Azriim. The slaad bounded forward and let fly with a flurry of claw strikes. Parrying wildly, Riven gave ground, countering where he could. The slaad pressed, caught Riven in the chest with a claw, then a shoulder, and nicked his throat. Riven finally managed a more aggressive counterattack. He ducked beneath a claw strike and drove his saber half its length into Azriim's chest.

The slaad expectorated a spray of blood. Before Riven could finish him, Azriim bounded backward, hissing with pain as the saber withdrew from his flesh. Riven pursued but Azriim leaped upward and the leap never ended. The slaad went airborne, hovering near the ceiling, spattering the floor with his blood. Riven's slash hit only air.

Like Dolgan, Azriim's wounds, too, were closing before Riven's eyes.

Riven knew his situation was dire. The slaadi were

faster than before, stronger, and they regenerated wounds that should have killed them. Riven was breathing hard and bleeding from a handful of painful wounds.

"You see it now, don't you?" Azriim taunted. "This isn't your temple. You're in your tomb."

Riven donned his sneer and answered, "What I see is you and your boy unable to close the deal." He put his fingers to the gashes on his face and they came away bloody. He looked at them, spat on the floor. "And if this is the best you have, neither of you are walking out of this room."

Azriim grinned. "I always liked you. It's unfortunate that I have to kill you."

Dolgan roared a challenge.

Riven resolved to take at least one of the bastards with him before he died. He readied himself. . . .

The darkness on the far end of the room behind Azriim deepened and Riven could not contain a grin.

"It's about godsdamned time," he said.

Cale had finally arrived.

Answering Dolgan's roar with a shout of his own, Riven charged the slaad.

Cale, Magadon, and Jak materialized in a large chamber in the tower they had seen through the leech, near a stairway leading upward. Doors dotted the walls of the chamber, and the whole room glowed a soft silver. Even through his boots, Cale could feel the magical power moving through the structure.

Azriim floated in the air in the center of the chamber with his back to the newcomers. Riven and Dolgan fought across the chamber. The assassin's blades whirled, darted, slashed. The big slaad held his ground and answered, lashing out with his claws.

Magadon drew an arrow to his ear, caused its tip to glow red with mental energy, and let it fly at Azriim.

The shaft sank to the fletching in the slaad's back. Azriim screamed, clutched at the tip protruding from his chest, and turned around. The scream distracted Dolgan and the big slaad also turned. Riven made him pay for his inattention.

The assassin drove a saber into the big slaad's throat, pulled the blade free, and swung a decapitating strike with his other saber. Somehow the big slaad kept his feet and ducked under Riven's slash. Blood poured from the hole in his throat. He held up one clawed hand and a small glowing ball appeared in his palm. Without a moment's hesitation, he threw it to the ground at his feet and it exploded into a ball of fire. Slaad and assassin flew backward from the point of the blast.

Cale, Magadon, and Jak raised their arms to shield themselves from the heat.

"The Tap," Cale reminded Jak, then drew Weaveshear and ran to Riven.

"You again, priest," Azriim said from near the ceiling. "My, but you are stubborn."

Cale risked a look up and saw the slaad pull Magadon's mentally-enhanced arrow through his body and let it fall to the floor. Magadon fired several ordinary arrows but they deflected off the slaad's hide.

"Enough of that," Azriim said, and launched a fireball from his palm at Magadon and Jak. The ball exploded in their midst, engulfing both of them in flames. When the flames dissipated, neither showed so much as a scorch mark on their clothes. Jak's wards had shielded them both from incineration.

Cale reached Riven's side and pulled him to his feet. Burns covered the assassin's face and hands. His good eye was seared shut.

"They've transformed," Riven said through his burned lips. "More powerful now."

Cale nodded and hurriedly incanted his most powerful spell of healing. Mask's power flowed through him to

Riven and the assassin's burns vanished entirely.

Riven smiled his thanks, hefted his blades.

Ten paces away, Dolgan laughed. "That hurts," he said, and lifted himself to all fours.

Cale ignored him.

"I'm here for the Tap," he said to Riven. "We kill it first, then we kill them. Where's the Sojourner?"

Riven shook his head. "He said he would not see the slaadi again. He's not in the tower."

Cale nodded, relieved despite himself. Still, he thought he knew where he would find the Sojourner when the time came.

Behind them, Dolgan found his feet, still laughing. His flesh was healing the burns even as he stood.

"I've got it, Cale," Jak shouted to his back. "It's here. In an upper floor."

Cale and Riven sprinted across the room. Above them, Azriim incanted a series of arcane words and a pulse of black energy spread from the slaad in a visible ring across the entire room. It could not be avoided.

When it hit Cale, he felt a preternatural cold seize him, but a ward that Jak had cast flared and chimed. Cale recognized it as a death ward. The spell might have killed him but for Jak's protective spell.

The slaadi had indeed transformed into something more powerful.

Similar chimes and flares sounded from the wards on Magadon and Jak. Unprotected, Riven gasped and stumbled. Cale shrouded him in shadows and kept him moving.

"Are you all right?" he asked Riven.

Riven waved and nodded. They reached Jak and Magadon near the stairs.

"Up," he ordered. "Keep the divination active, little man. The Sojourner is not here so we move fast."

He turned around to look at the slaadi. Azriim's spell appeared to have done no harm to Dolgan. Azriim floated down to the floor to stand beside the bigger slaad.

"Come back," Azriim taunted. "Things are only now getting interesting."

Cale ignored the taunt and ushered his friends up the stairs. He delayed a moment behind them and incanted a spell that summoned a wall of stone at the base of the stairs. The magic of the spell caused the edges of the wall to meld with the stone of the tower, blocking access.

It would only delay the slaadi, he knew.

"We should stand and fight," Riven said, seemingly recovered from the death spell.

"We will," Cale said. "But the Tap is first. The only way to stop the Sojourner is to kill it. This is bigger than our personal grudges."

"That's right," Jak said.

"Nothing is bigger than the personal, Cale," Riven said, but did not argue further.

Cale stared at him a moment, turned to Jak. "Which way, little man?"

"Follow me," Jak said.

The slaadi appeared behind them at the bottom of the stairs, bronze rods in hand. They had teleported through the wall.

"Go," Cale said to them.

Azriim and Dolgan rushed up the stairs, taking three steps at a stride. They raised their hands as they raced upward and balls of energy streaked out of them.

Cale stood in the path of the fireballs, held Weaveshear before him, and intercepted both before they exploded. Shadows poured from the weapon.

"Move," Cale called again over his shoulder, and his friends went. Cale pointed Weaveshear down the stairs and released the pent-up energy directly into the slaadi. The magic slammed into the creatures' chests, knocked both of them back down the stairs, and engulfed them in fire.

Both roared, leaped to their feet, and bounded back up

the stairs. Their clothing was aflame and smoke poured from both of them.

Cale turned and sprinted after his friends. With his shadow-enhanced speed, he caught up with them quickly. They crossed another broad, bare chamber and found themselves at the foot of another set of stairs.

"Up again," Jak said. "We're close."

"Here they come," Magadon said, looking behind them. He turned, dropped to one knee, and drew an arrow to his ear.

Across the large chamber, the slaadi appeared. Other than some slight charring, their bodies showed no wounds from the fireballs. Both roared.

"Trickster's toes," Jak oathed.

"Keep your concentration on the Tap," Cale ordered him. He did not want Jak trying to cast a spell against the slaadi and losing the thread of his divination.

Magadon spent more of the little mental energy he still had, charged his arrow, and let fly. The missile hit Dolgan in the hip, sank deeply into his body, and sent him spinning to the floor. Azriim leaped over him and continued his charge.

Holding his mask around Weaveshear's hilt, Cale incanted a spell. When he spoke the last word, he called into being a magical wall that spanned the width of the room. Composed of shadows and veined with viridian lines, it audibly sizzled, radiating magical energy from only one side—that facing the slaadi. Cale could barely see through it.

Azriim halted his charge and hissed, skin smoking in the presence of the magic. Behind him, Dolgan climbed to his feet, his skin also smoking. The big slaad jerked Magadon's arrow from his hip. Azriim withdrew a wand from his thigh sheath.

"Up," Cale said. "Go."

Like the wall of stone, he knew the magical wall would slow the slaadi for only a few breaths.

The four comrades raced up the stairs. They found themselves in a wide foyer. A pair of large wooden double doors bound in brass stood on the other side of the foyer.

"In there," Jak said. "That's it."

Below them, the sizzling sound from Cale's wall of energy went silent. Azriim must have countered it somehow.

The slaadi were coming.

"How are you going to kill it?" Riven asked.

"I'm not," Cale answered. "The sun is."

As they charged down the hall, Cale whispered the words to a spell that allowed him to see dweomers. The double doors glowed in his sight, the wards evident to his magic-sensing vision. The Sojourner had warded the doors well. Cale did not hesitate. Blade in hand, he threw his shoulder against them and knocked them open.

Glyphs flared and magical energy blazed out of the jambs. Weaveshear drank it all and Cale suffered no harm. Power rushed into the blade's steel and it emitted a cloud of shadows. The weapon vibrated in Cale's grasp, pregnant with the Sojourner's power. Cale whirled around, pointed the tip at the head of the stairs, and waited.

The moment the slaadi appeared, he discharged the energy.

A beam of viridian light streaked from Weaveshear's tip—the recoil drove Cale back a step—and hit Azriim in the stomach. The slaad bared his fangs and grimaced but the energy seemed to have no effect. Even Azriim looked surprised. He looked up and grinned a mouthful of sharp teeth.

"Go," Jak said to Cale. "We'll hold them off. Get the Weave Tap. Kill it."

Cale hesitated as the slaadi advanced.

"Go," Magadon said over his shoulder.

Cale nodded, turned, and ran into the room. Judging from its size and the defaced murals painted on the walls, the room once was a religious sanctum of some kind. Scorch marks marred much of the floor, as if a magical battle had been fought there.

In the center of the chamber stood the Weave Tap, grown to ten times the size of the sapling Cale had seen the slaadi remove from the Fane of Shadows. Silver limbs formed a canopy for golden leaves sparkling with arcane power. A silver pulse periodically raced up the bole, like the beat of a heart. The energy in the room stood the hairs of Cale's arms on end.

The Tap's roots stood exposed, the ends melded with the floor of the chamber. The entire ceiling of the room glowed silver. Cale visualized the tower shooting a beam of magical energy from its top into the sky. If he killed the Tap, he would kill the beam, kill the eclipse, stop the Sojourner.

He stepped through the space between shadows and covered in one stride the distance between the doorway and the Weave Tap. He materialized amidst its roots, near the bole.

Behind him, he could hear his comrades fighting for their lives with the slaadi. The combat had leaked through the doors into the sanctum. Cale turned to see Azriim unleashing a flurry of claw strikes against Riven. The assassin held off the attack with a whirling counter of his sabers, but barely. The slaad forced Riven backward through the doorway and fired a bolt of energy from his palm at Magadon, who was fighting alongside Jak to finish off Dolgan. The energy struck the guide squarely and drove him into the wall—hard.

Dolgan took the opportunity to tear into Jak. A claw strike sent the little man careening backward, bleeding from his chest. He answered with a stab of his shortsword and a shouted spell. White fire flew from his hand and struck the slaad in the chest. It scorched Dolgan's skin, but the slaad only grinned.

Jak looked over his shoulder and caught Cale watching.

"Kill it, godsdammit!" the little man shouted. He turned and charged Dolgan. Magadon climbed to his feet and joined him. Blades and claws met.

Cale turned, sheathed Weaveshear, and wrapped his arms around the Tap's bole. The wood felt warm, like skin, and the moment he touched it, he knew the Tap possessed sentience.

He gritted his teeth as the Tap's awareness reached for his mind. He did not resist it. The mental touch was not hostile, merely unfocused, flailing. Still, it indicated a living, self-aware creature.

Cale sensed its nature through the mindlink—born of the Weave and the Shadow Weave, of light and darkness, forever existing in the gray area between the poles of its being.

Just like Cale.

And Cale was going to kill it. He had no choice.

I'm sorry, he thought, and hoped it understood.

For a breath, but only a breath, he almost reconsidered. But the sounds of combat from behind brought him back to himself. Jak screamed. Magadon shouted. Another spell sizzled into the stone.

Pulses of silver light throbbed between Cale's arms as regular as a heartbeat. Cale pictured the first place in Selgaunt that came to his mind and called upon the darkness to move both himself and the Weave Tap there.

The darkness answered. Pitch surrounded him and the Tap. He felt the familiar sensation of being stretched parchment-thin, and in the next heartbeat found himself blinking in the half-light of Temple Avenue. He had brought the Weave Tap with him. It stood beside him, towering and unstable on its exposed roots.

Shouts of surprise greeted his appearance. The street was crowded.

"Look! Look there!"

The street traffic stopped. Horses started, snorted at his sudden appearance. Heads poked out of coaches, out of temple windows. A hundred faces, formerly upturned to watch the partial eclipse, turned to regard him. The pilgrims near him backed away quickly, warily. Children regarded him with wide eyes. A walkway philosopher pointed his finger at Cale and berated him as an agent of devilry.

"Is that a tree?" someone shouted. "Look at it!"

Exposed to the partial sunlight, the Weave Tap began to writhe and smoke beside Cale. The silver pulses came faster, faster, the frantic beat of terror.

Cale backed off, eyes wide. People poured out of the temples to watch.

The Tap's branches and roots twisted, curling with agony, blackening in the partial sunlight. Formerly glowing leaves of pure arcane power fell from smoking limbs, showering the street and disintegrating in small explosions of sparks. The Tap's consciousness still had a vague hold on Cale's mind and he distantly sensed its pain and fear.

Bark peeled; the tree's trunk split. Cale imagined the equivalent happening to a man—bones shattering, skin burning, peeling away. It was too much.

The Tap started to topple over.

"Get out of the way," Cale shouted to no one in particular, and the assembled crowd retreated.

The Tap caught for a moment on one of the Hulorn's statues, then crashed fully to the street. Limbs shattered. Magical energy sprayed out in all directions.

"I'm sorry," Cale said to it again.

The Tap's death throes became increasingly violent as it burned in the sun. The crowd shouted, oohed. The Tap's thrashing limbs and roots threw off intense flashes of power. Where they landed, unpredictable magical effects occurred: cobblestones sprouted legs and scurried into the crowd; flowers rained from the sky; a horse was transmogrified into a mouse; one of the bestial statues that lined the street—a manticore—sprang to life and flew roaring into the sky.

The crowd of pilgrims turned and ran, panicked. From afar, Cale heard the telltale clarion of a trumpet. A squad of Selgaunt's watch, the Scepters, was coming.

Cale wanted to wait, to ensure that the Tap died and that the geyser of magic accompanying its death would cause no real harm. But his friends needed him. He stood for a moment, torn. The Tap's silver heartbeat slowed. He felt it dying.

Erevis! Magadon projected into his brain, his voice urgent. *We need you!*

Magadon's tone sent alarm through Cale.

The Scepters rounded the corner at a run, blades bare. They were a dagger toss from Cale. The watch sergeant looked first at Cale, then the burning, dying Weave Tap, and slowed his advance. He pointed the tip of his weapon at Cale.

"Hold there, goodsir," he said.

Beside Cale, the Weave Tap burst into flames. Gray-green smoke poured into the sky. Cale glanced into the faces around him and saw. . . .

Sephris.

The loremaster was staring at him out of the crowd. He shook his head and mouthed some words. "Two and two are four."

Erevis! Magadon called again, and the despair in the guide's voice made Cale's mouth go dry.

Ignoring the Scepters and the loremaster, Cale stepped into the shadow of a nearby statue and imagined in his mind the chamber in which he had found the Weave Tap. He drew Weaveshear.

"I said do not move," the watch sergeant commanded again.

The darkness gathered around Cale.

The Scepters rushed him.

The last thing he saw before he moved across Faerûn to the tower was Sephris, calculating.

CHAPTER 16

GOOD-BYES

Cale materialized in the shadows of the sanctum, an eerie void with the Weave Tap gone. What he saw near the doorway froze him.

Magadon, prone, bleeding, and laboring to breathe, cradled Jak in his lap. He had a hand on the little man's brow. Jak lay across the guide's legs, covered in blood, unmoving.

Unmoving.

Riven stood near them, watching, blades held slackly at his sides. His expression was impossible to decipher—it could have been controlled grief, contained rage, or indifference.

"Jak?"

The word came out of Cale's mouth before he could stop it. He tried to move but his body would not respond.

"Jak?" he said again, his voice louder.

He knew his friend would not answer.

A ragged gash opened Jak's throat. The little man's blades lay on the ground near him. He was not breathing.

Neither was Cale.

"I tried to save him. . . ." Magadon choked as he looked up. Tears glistened in his colorless eyes.

Cale swallowed. His vision was blurry. His body went weak, numb. He managed a step forward, another. He could not take his eyes from the body of his friend, his best friend.

"I thought you were going to miss the festivities," said a voice, Azriim's voice. "I am glad to see you return."

For the first time, Cale noticed the slaadi. They stood on the other side of the sanctum's double doors, denied entry by a barrier of force. Magadon must have raised it. The barrier distorted the air like a lens of imperfect glass. The slaadi's forms looked twisted and distended through it, but Cale could still see Azriim's smirk. Both held their teleportation rods in their hands.

Cale ignored the creatures, sheathed his blade, and moved to Magadon's side. He knelt and pulled Jak's limp body from the guide. Jak felt so . . . light. The little man's eyes were open but unseeing. Cale could not quite believe how small his friend looked, how fragile. Had he always been that small?

Jak's shirt was twisted around his torso and for some absurd reason Cale found himself straightening it. He tried to ignore the sticky fluid that clung to his fingers. He noticed that the little man's left fist was clenched around something. Cale gently peeled back the fingers— he had never noticed how tiny were Jak's hands—to reveal the jeweled pendant that served as Jak's holy symbol. Jak must have taken it in hand before the end. Cale's eyes welled and he closed his friend's hand over the symbol.

He stood, cradling his friend, and carried him a few

steps away from the doors. It seemed right to him that they be apart from everyone else.

"Look at him," Dolgan said from behind the barrier, and Cale heard the mockery in the slaad's tone. "I think he might weep."

Cale kept his back to the slaadi and looked down into the little man's green eyes. A thousand memories rushed through his mind. In all of them, Jak was smiling, laughing, smoking. Cale could not remember laughing except when he had been in Jak's company. What would he do without him?

The tears pooling in his eyes fell down his cheeks, welled in his eyes, splashed on the little man's face. He wiped them away. A sob wracked him.

His mind was empty. He wanted to say something, anything, but no words would come. Instead, an inarticulate animal sound emerged from his throat, a primal expression of the inexpressible.

They had been through so much. Survived so much. Only to end like this?

His mind kept repeating: How can this be? How can this be?

Jak's body was cooling in his hands. His best friend was growing cold. Cale was distantly conscious of his rage beginning to build. It welled up from the core of his soul, soaked him, caused his body to shake. Shadows swirled around him, little flames of darkness.

The rage gave him a focus, something to hold onto, a purpose.

His tears stopped. His sobs stopped. The world restarted.

He turned, met Riven's gaze, held it. Neither of them said anything. Cale saw something in the assassin's eye, something he had never seen. Riven's breath came fast; he bled from half a dozen small cuts. Magadon still lay on the floor, propped on his elbow, trying to staunch the gashes in his chest and abdomen. From the grotesque angle from which the guide's leg jutted from his hip, Cale could see it was broken or out of joint. The guide's face was nearly as white as his eyes. His eyes were glassy but focused.

Cale had healing spells at his command but he could not use them on Magadon, not then. At the moment, Cale's grief was the whetstone that sharpened his rage, that honed his hate. He had no healing in him. He had only anger. He could do only harm.

He knelt down on one knee and set Jak on the floor, against the wall. He brushed his hand over the little man's face and closed his eyes, gently. It was the last gentle thing he would do for a time.

"He *is* crying," Azriim said. Dolgan chuckled.

Cale thought back to the docks in Selgaunt when Jak had told him they should be heroes if they had the chance. He would honor his promise to the little man. But not yet. Before he could be a hero, he first had to be a killer.

He rose, looked over at Magadon, and said, "Which one?"

Magadon stared at him uncomprehending. He was going into wound shock.

"Which one did this?" Cale snapped. His tone was harsh; he had not meant it to be. Shadows boiled from his skin. His fists were clenched.

"The big one," Magadon stammered, his words slurred.

Cale nodded. He looked through the barrier at Dolgan—the big one. The distorted air magnified the slaad's claws. Blood coated those claws. Jak's blood.

Cale's hands opened and closed, opened and closed. The pounding of his heart filled his ears. With effort, he took control of his anger, channeled it.

"I think you've made him angry, Dolgan," Azriim jibed.

Dolgan fixed Cale with a hard glare and bared his fangs. "Good," the slaad said.

Moving with deliberateness, Cale took out his black mask and donned it. Behind its opaque curtain, he let the killer in him take hold. Jak was dead. For the moment, so was Cale's conscience. He was going to make the slaad suffer.

Never taking his gaze from the big slaad, he whispered a series of prayers, casting spells that gave him added strength, speed. The darkness in the sanctum deepened, mirroring his mood.

"Oh, he is definitely angry," Azriim said.

The slaadi paced along the edge of the psionic barrier, their movements predatory. Azriim removed first one wand, then another from his thigh sheath, touching himself and Dolgan in turn, no doubt augmenting their own abilities.

Cale watched the slaadi work and called upon Mask again, invoking a spell that infused him with a shard of the divine. A small part of Mask's power rushed into him, filled him, focused his rage, increased his spite. His body grew half again as large as normal. His strength increased still more. He stood as tall as Dolgan. His strength matched a giant's.

He was ready.

He turned from the slaadi to look back at Magadon.

The guide looked . . . drained. Cale could not help him, not until he had killed something.

"Hang on," Cale said to him, and his voice was deeper than usual, more commanding. "This will be over soon."

Magadon nodded, gritting his teeth against the pain.

"Lower the barrier, Mags," Cale told him, and turned back to face the slaadi. "Raise it behind us after we're through."

The slaadi stopped pacing.

"Don't trouble yourself," Azriim said, and held up his teleportation rod. "We'll come to you."

Cale stared holes into the slaadi.

Azriim lowered the rod.

"Have it your way, then," he said.

The slaadi backed off and spread to opposite sides of the wide corridor.

"Erevis. . . ." Magadon began.

"The big one is mine," Cale said to Riven.

The assassin nodded, stood at Cale's left shoulder. He spun his blades and pointed their tips at Azriim's chest.

"That's unfortunate. I have wanted to kill the stupid one for a long while. But I'll settle for the chatty one."

Azriim smiled, and the smile gave way to a hiss. Dolgan drew his axe from the sheath on his back, held it in his hands, and roared. Veins and sinew rose from the muscles of his arms, chest, and neck.

Cale put his hand to Weaveshear, started to draw it, but stopped.

Riven looked at him sidelong. "What are you doing?"

"Close work," Cale said, the words a threat and promise for Dolgan. He could not control the shadows pouring from his flesh.

Riven absorbed that. "I think I'll go with my steel, just the same."

"Lower it, Mags," Cale commanded again.

Dolgan dropped his axe and waited, claws flexing. He and Cale would fight hand to claw.

"Remember that they are stronger," Riven said to Cale.

"No, they're not."

Riven stared, nodded, bounced on the balls of his feet. "Do it, Mags," he said.

The psionic barrier flared once and disappeared.

The moment it disappeared, Azriim spoke a word and discharged a bolt of black energy from his outstretched hand. Cale and Riven threw themselves against opposite walls and the black ray streaked past them.

Riven bounded forward at Azriim, blades whirling.

Cale charged Dolgan.

Memories of a past life—or was it only a dream?—slipped away from Jak, gossamer wraiths of recollection floating away into oblivion. He knew he remembered things, he just could not quite remember what things. The loss pained him distantly, but even that soon faded.

It did not matter. He was happy where he was.

He stood barefoot on a rolling moor. Swells of plush green grass stretched around him for as far as he could see. The grass felt soft under his feet, between his bare toes. Golden sunshine showered down to warm him. Stately, solitary elms dotted the moor, their canopies casting great swaths of grass in shadow.

Shadow.

A memory bubbled up from somewhere. He almost got his mind around it but it drifted away before he could pin it down. Still, whatever it was made him smile.

A soft breeze stirred the grass, caused the leaves of the elms to whisper among themselves. It also carried from somewhere in the distance the smell of food cooking—a heavy, stomach-warming smell. The aroma was familiar to Jak but he did not know why.

"Oh well," he said, unperturbed.

Following his nose, he started walking. A cerulean sky roofed the land, dotted with puffs of white. He had to have a smoke. It was too nice a day not to have a smoke. He reached for his pipe and discovered that it was not in his belt pouch.

Strange, he thought, but his disappointment faded quickly.

He whistled a tune and walked on. After only a short while, another smell attracted his attention and caused him temporarily to forget about the cooking aroma—the unmistakably wonderful stink of pipeweed. And good quality.

Someone else had decided that the day required a smoke. Surely they would share a spare pipe with a fellow traveler.

"Hello there," Jak called. "Who's there? Who's smoking?"

"Here," returned a voice from the other side of a nearby hill.

Jak legged his way up the hill. When he crested the rise he saw a well-dressed halfling with wavy, sandy hair seated under an elm, his back to the trunk, a wooden pipe stuck between his teeth. A broad-brimmed green hat with a purple feather lay on the ground beside him. The halfling smiled around the stem of his pipe. Jak found the smile infectious.

"Well met!"

Jak returned the smile and said, "Well met."

He was certain he had seen the halfling before, maybe in some dark place underground. He searched his memory but found nothing.

The halfling climbed to his feet, dusted off his red trousers, and said, "You sure took your time. Seems like I've been waiting for you a long while." He banged his feathered hat against his thigh and replanted it atop his head.

"You have?" Jak asked, confused.

"I have," responded the halfling with a wink. "Now come on."

Green cloak swooshing, the halfling walked up to Jak, placed a tindertwig and pipe—already tamped, no less—into his palm.

"You'll be wanting this, I assume. Now, follow me. I know where you're going."

"You do?" Jak asked, and followed along, taking a whiff of the unlit pipeweed. "How? I don't even know where we're going. Do we know each other?"

The halfling looked at him out of the corner of his eye, green eyes glinting.

"We know each other very well, Jak Fleet."

Jak flushed with embarrassment. It was quite rude not to remember an acquaintance.

"Uh . . . I'm afraid I don't remember your name."

"No?" the halfling asked with raised eyebrows. "Well, I imagine you will in time. Are you going to smoke that or keep holding it hostage under your nose?"

"Huh? Oh." Jak grinned, struck the tindertwig on the rough leather of his belt pouch, and lit. He took a deep draw. Exquisite.

"Very good," he said. "Where's the leaf from?"

"Around here," the halfling said.

Jak resolved to get some more as soon as possible. Meanwhile, he blew a series of smoke rings as he walked along. His comrade did the same and for a time they held an unspoken competition over who could produce the biggest ring.

Jak lost, but barely. He found that he liked the halfling; he could not help it. Something about the rascal seemed so familiar and yet Jak could not remember his name. He was sure he would in time, just as the halfling had said.

What a strange way to think, he thought.

"Nice around here, isn't it?" his friend asked.

Jak nodded. "Where are we, anyway? I don't know this moor."

"We're right where we are," the halfling answered.

"I know that," Jak replied. He was beginning to think that his comrade was a bit . . . simple. "I mean, what is this place called?"

The halfling smiled. "It's called 'my place'."

Jak was incredulous and could not keep it from his tone. "All of it? Seems like a lot for one halfling."

His comrade grinned. "Oh, it's not for just one."

"No?"

"No. Look." The halfling took his pipe from his mouth as they topped a rise. With it, he pointed down into the valley.

Jak followed his comrade's gesture and saw. . . .

A small cottage. A smoking chimney rose out of a mud-and-thatch roof. The clank of plates and the wonderful, familiar smell that had drawn Jak across the moor floated through the open shutters. So too did laughter. The voices sounded familiar to Jak.

His comrade took a deep breath. "Smells good, doesn't it? Homey, like."

"It does," Jak answered. He inhaled, drank in the smell, and it triggered a sharp memory from his childhood.

"That's my mother's potato soup!" he said.

The halfling grinned wide. He tapped the stem of his pipe on his temple.

"It is, Jak. She's waiting for you. She and your father. Your grandmother too. Even your younger brother Cob. Do you remember him?"

"Remember him? Of course!" Jak could hardly believe his ears. He had not seen any of those people for years, not since they all had . . .

Not since they all had died.

But that didn't seem right. How could that be right? And his mother shouldn't be there either, should she?

As though reading his mind, the halfling said, "A lot happened after you left Misteldale, Jak. Go on. The soup's going to get cold. This will all make sense soon."

Jak turned, stopped. "Wait. I feel like I'm leaving something behind, something . . . undone."

His friend shook his head and smiled gently. "No. You've done all you can. Memories haunt even better than ghosts. Go on, now."

Jak could not make sense of the halfling's words but that did not keep him from smiling. "Come with me. My mother loves guests. And the soup is wonderful."

The halfling in the green hat shook his head gently and replanted the pipe in his mouth.

"I can't, Jak. Not right now, at least. You go. Go and rest. I'll come back when I can and we'll talk then. Well enough?"

"Well enough," Jak said, and he could not contain a grin. His family! "This is a great place."

"I am glad you think so," replied his companion.

Smiling, Jak turned and sprinted down the rise toward the cottage.

From behind, he heard his companion exclaim, "Oh, drat!"

Jak stopped, turned, and looked back up the rise to see the halfling looking forlornly at his pipe. He held it up for Jak to see.

"It's gone out," he said, and frowned. "Trickster's hairy toes!"

For some reason, that oath made Jak smile.

"You like that?" the halfling called down to him.

Jak nodded.

The halfling tucked the pipe into his cloak. "I always liked it too. See you soon, Jak."

Jak gave his friend one more wave, turned, and hurried to the cottage.

CHAPTER 17

CLOSE WORK

Magadon did not have enough mental strength left to raise the barrier behind his friends. He was so weak that he did not even have the strength to stand. He could do nothing but lie there and watch, awed, as the two servants of Mask engaged their enemies.

He was not certain that they were human, not at that moment. Or perhaps his wounds had thickened his mind. Magadon and Cale seemed too fast, too big, too . . . *present* to be mere men.

But his mind was clear enough to understand his role. He was to bear witness.

He watched Cale charge into Dolgan with enough force to vibrate the floor. Man and slaad roared into the other's face. The slaad's greater weight drove Cale backward, toward Magadon.

The slaad tried to claw at Cale's sides and back but Cale caught Dolgan's arms by the wrists and held them away from him. The shadows circling Cale intensified, reflecting his anger.

The slaad snapped his jaws at Cale's head, missed, then leaped up and drove his legs into Cale's stomach, rending cloak and flesh. Blood and shadows leaked from Cale, but still he did not buckle.

Still gripping Dolgan by the wrists, Cale spun a half-circle and flung the slaad into the corridor wall with such force that Dolgan's breath flew from his lungs and his bones cracked. Cale allowed no respite. So many shadows boiled from his skin that he looked ablaze in black fire.

Dolgan barely ducked out of the way of a punch that would have dented a kite shield. Bones crunched when Cale struck the stone wall instead of the slaad, but other than a growl of frustration at the miss, he did not seem to care. The slaad countered with a claw rake at Cale's throat, but Cale parried it with his forearm and drove a punch with his shattered fist into the slaad's abdomen. Dolgan staggered backward, bent double, coughing. Cale shook his broken hand at his side and Magadon could see the bones twisting, knitting. After only a few heartbeats, Cale rushed the huge slaad and the two went careening backward, a tangle of fists, claws, shadows, scales, grunts, and shouts. Shadows sheathed them. They fought in a black mist.

Magadon felt that he was watching giants grapple.

The ambient silver light from the tower dimmed. Magadon felt dizzy and feared he was losing consciousness. The corridor fell away. He saw only darkness. A tingle raced through his body, the same feeling he experienced when Cale moved them between worlds.

The darkness partially lifted.

He was sitting on a rocky plane on a small, featureless island set in a black sea under an oppressive, starless sky—the Plane of Shadow. Ochre lightning tore across the sky. Thunder rolled in the distance.

Consciously or unconsciously, Cale had moved the battle to the Plane of Shadow and had inadvertently brought Magadon along.

Ten paces away, Cale and Dolgan continued to roll on the ground.

The sounds of the battle between Cale and Dolgan started out loud, grew faint, and abruptly stopped altogether. Riven spared a glance back at them and saw. . . .

Nothing. They were gone.

"Just us, then," Azriim said through a mouthful of fangs. "And the dead halfling, of course."

Riven snarled and rushed the slaad, his sabers wheeling. Azriim parried with his own blade and danced backward out of Riven's reach. Riven followed, and for a few moments they circled, blades spinning, stabbing, slashing. Riven could see that he was the faster of the two, but the slaad was the stronger. Azriim used his off-hand claw as a second weapon, slashing at Riven's exposed flesh when opportunity allowed.

The slaad abruptly broke out of the circling and lunged forward, stabbing low with his blade. Riven parried with one saber while slashing crosswise at the slaad's throat with the other. Azriim rode Riven's parry into a spin, ducked beneath the slash, and lashed out with a claw strike at Riven's chest. The claws tore only cloth as Riven bounded backward.

"Fun, isn't it?" Azriim asked, and lunged forward again.

Riven did not bother to reply. He would not waste his breath on unnecessary words. The slaad again lunged forward, exposing his lead leg. Riven slid to the side of Azriim's stab and slashed a blade into the slaad's thigh.

Azriim hissed and countered with a slash of his own that opened the back of Riven's hand. Pain flared and Riven cursed as his wounded hand lost its grip on his blade. The saber clattered to the floor.

Magadon was fading. He felt thick, saw dimly. He hung doggedly onto consciousness and watched Dolgan disentangle his claws from Cale's grasp. Flat on his back, the slaad nevertheless unleashed a flurry of claw strikes, opening gashes in Cale's chest, arms, and face. The slaad tore Cale's mask off, opening red furrows in his dusky flesh.

Cale parried as best he could with his arms and shoulders and answered with his own punches and elbow jabs to the slaad's head and throat. Both combatants were bleeding, gasping, shouting, striking. Shadows cloaked them both, swirled around the combat.

With a desperate heave, Dolgan flung Cale off of himself sideways and climbed to his feet. He pulled his teleportation rod and twisted the dials.

Cale rode the throw into a roll, found his own feet, and charged back at the slaad, roaring. He drove his shoulder into Dolgan's chest, knocked the rod to the ground, and wrapped his arms around the creature. Dolgan tore at the flesh of Cale's back and bit his shoulder.

Grunting, Cale picked up the slaad bodily. Magadon could not believe what he was seeing; the creature must have weighed a few hundred stones. Cale slammed him down onto the rock. They went down together in a pile of flailing limbs and swirling shadows.

Dolgan drew in his legs and tried to get them under Cale—presumably to disembowel him—but Cale clung tightly to the creature while his hands sought the slaad's soft spots. Dolgan tore at Cale's arms and chest. The flesh of Cale's arms was nearly in ribbons. The slaad chomped down on Cale's shoulder, near his neck, and blood sprayed. Cale gritted his teeth in pain but ignored the damage. He closed his hands around the slaad's throat and levered the creature's head and teeth away from his shoulder. Dolgan's jaws dripped with Cale's blood.

Dolgan squirmed in Cale's grasp, snarled, tried to twist his head enough to bite at Cale's wrists and hands. Black and red blood pooled around the two.

With his hands firmly around Dolgan's throat, Cale slammed the slaad's head into the rocky ground twice—rapidly. Dolgan groaned and his eyes rolled, but only for a moment. He recovered quickly and began again to claw and frenetically shake Cale loose. Cale hung on, his body bouncing atop the slaad, the veins in his arms and brow plainly visible. Cale slid his hands to either side of the slaad's head. His thumbs crept across the slaad's face, toward his eyes.

Dolgan's eyes widened—he sensed his peril. He railed and clawed at Cale with renewed energy, tore great gashes in Cale's flesh. Cale screamed with pain but refused to release the slaad, though his cloak was saturated with blood. He smacked Dolgan's head onto the ground twice more.

Dolgan went slack for a heartbeat and Cale's thumbs found his eye sockets.

Screaming with rage, Cale applied pressure.

Lightning ripped across the sky.

Azriim rushed Riven, trying to force him down the corridor, away from his dropped saber. Riven gave little ground. He gripped his single saber in both hands and parried Azriim's slash, spun, countered, and gave a slash of his own. The slaad answered and the dance continued. Riven opened several gashes in the slaad's hide and received a few of his own. Azriim kept up the press, preventing Riven from collecting his blade, but Riven offered enough blows to keep Azriim from kicking the blade farther away.

And Riven had other weapons he could use.

He allowed the slaad to draw in close for another exchange, parried a crosscut designed to open his throat, and maneuvered his face nearly nose to snout with Azriim. Before the slaad could snap at him with his fangs, Riven shouted directly into Azriim's face the Dark Speech that Mask had taught him.

The word hit the slaad with the force of a war hammer.

Azriim hissed, took a wild swing with his blade, and staggered backward while trying to cover his ears. Riven bounded after him, driving the slaad back a few more paces with a flurry of two-handed slashes. Abruptly, he broke off the attack and retreated to his lost saber. He wedged his boot toe under it and flipped it up to his hand.

He decided then to show the slaad another gift granted him by the Shadowlord. Holding both blades before him, he intoned a prayer to Mask, asking for divine power to fuel his blows. When he completed the prayer, both of his sabers hummed in his hands with unholy energy; both leaked shadow. He advanced on Azriim, who shook his head to clear it of the damage caused by the Dark Speech.

"I did not know we were exchanging repartee," the slaad said as he parried a series of Riven's slashes. "I've a word or two for you, also."

With that, the slaad pronounced a word of power and Riven's world went dark. Azriim's spell blinded him.

He cursed and backed off several steps, his blades held before him. He tried to picture the corridor in his mind; he thought it perhaps eight paces wide, the slaad four or five paces before him.

"Having trouble with that eye?" Azriim said, laughing, still at a distance.

❧ ❧ ❧ ❧ ❧

Dolgan writhed like a mad thing, clawed frantically at Cale's hands. Desperate, the slaad spoke an arcane word and a clashing rainbow of magic exploded around him and Cale, slamming into both of them, firing in all directions.

The chaotic play of colors made Magadon's head ache.

The shadows around Cale's body absorbed the beams that would have hit him, leaving the spell with no visible effect.

Cale gritted his teeth and strained. Veins rose on his arms. He leaned into his work. To Magadon's astonishment, the slaad's strength seemed to be no match for Cale.

Cale's thumbs sank deeper into the slaad's eye sockets.

"This . . . is . . . for . . . Jak!" Cale snarled.

Dolgan's eyelids gave way and he screamed as the orbs popped. Pink fluid poured from the sockets. The scream turned into a high-pitched wail of agony. He kicked, flailed.

Cale slammed the slaad's head against the ground as he drove his thumbs all the way into the creature's skull, deep into the brain.

Dolgan's screams became a slobbery gargle, then stopped. Cale rapped the slaad's bloody head into the stone twice more. The skull cracked and opened. Black blood pooled on the rock.

Cale sat atop the dead slaad, clutching Dolgan's skull in his bloody hands, breathing hard.

"For Jak," he said.

He pulled his gore-soaked thumbs from the eye sockets with a wet, sucking sound and stood over his kill. He looked at his bloody hands in surprise, as if they were not his own. Shadows covered him, swirled about him like a cloak in a gale.

Cale knelt and retrieved something from the ground—

his mask. He donned it, drew Weaveshear, decapitated the slaad, and held the severed head in his hands. Then he chanted a prayer over Dolgan's corpse. When he pronounced the final syllable, a column of flame whooshed into being over the slaad, consuming his body. The fire lasted only an instant, but it left nothing but ashes and the smell of burned flesh in its wake. The slaad would not be regenerating.

"Erevis," Magadon called. His voice was soft but Cale heard him and turned. His eyes glowed yellow through the black, featureless velvet of his mask. The eyes narrowed.

Cale brandished Weaveshear and advanced toward Magadon.

Riven had often fought in total darkness but he did not want the slaad to know that. He put his back to a wall to narrow the field of approach and focused on his hearing.

Trying to make Azriim incautious, he feigned a stumble, an unassertive wave of his charged blades. Azriim did not take the bait. Riven could not even hear the slaad's breath. He knew the creature was picking his spot. Riven kept his blades up, ready. He was sweating.

He heard a sizzling sound a fraction of a heartbeat before a bolt of lightning slammed into his chest, melted flesh, and drove him so hard against the wall that several ribs snapped. His breath went out of him and he sank to the floor.

The hallway fell silent. Riven figured the lightning had affected his hearing.

And we could have been such boon companions, Azriim sarcastically projected into his mind.

Riven could not pinpoint the slaad's location—Azriim's mental voice originated in Riven's mind, not from an external direction—so he did the only thing he could. He shouted the Black Speech, filling it with his anger.

To his astonishment, no sound emerged.

The language trick again? Azriim mocked. *How very unoriginal.*

The slaad must have created a sphere of silence around Riven.

Using his blades to assist himself, he clambered to his feet.

All at once the slaad was on him, grabbing each of Riven's wrists in a clawed hand and sinking a kick with a clawed foot into Riven's already shattered chest. Riven's ribs scraped against each other and his breath went out from him in a silent scream. His sabers fell to the floor soundlessly. His body followed.

Did that hurt? the slaad projected, glee clear in his mental voice. He ground his foot into Riven's chest, causing the ribs to pierce organs. Agony tore through Riven and he screamed and squirmed in futile silence.

No cursing, Azriim projected, genuine annoyance in his tone. *As punishment, I will eat your brain, though I suspect it to be rather bland fare.*

Riven struggled to free a hand but Azriim's grip was stronger. The slaad's weight on his chest prevented him from moving, nearly prevented him from breathing. Riven knew he was dead. He imagined the slaad's huge, fang-filled mouth coming for his head.

He cursed a string of expletives—knowing Azriim could read lips—and awaited the bite of fangs.

❧　❧　❧　❧　❧

Magadon saw his danger. Cale's eyes did not show recognition.

"Erevis!" he said, and held up his hands. "Erevis, it's me. You brought me here when you brought the slaad. Erevis, it's me, Magadon."

Cale showed no sign of hearing his friend.

Fueled by fear, Magadon dug deep in his mind for strength, found some, and projected into Cale's brain: *Erevis! It is me, Magadon! Erevis!*

Cale stopped. He shook his head. Weaveshear fell to his side.

"Magadon?" he said, his voice distant. "Mags?"

Magadon exhaled. He started to speak but the words came out slurred. His vision blurred, doubled.

Cale pulled off his mask, saw Magadon's condition, and rushed to his side. Magadon's last sight before losing consciousness was a double image of Cale's concerned face. For some reason, one of the images looked darker than the other.

He came back to consciousness with Cale kneeling over him. Cale held his mask in one hand. The energy from Cale's healing spell still warmed Magadon's flesh. The broken bone in his leg had reknit. Most of the other wounds in his flesh were also healed. He had his strength back.

Cale pulled him to his feet. His grip smeared slaad blood onto Magadon's hands.

"Are you . . . all right?" Magadon asked.

Cale nodded.

"We need to go back," Magadon said.

"Riven," Cale said.

Magadon nodded.

Cale picked up Dolgan's head, left on the ground near his feet, as shadows gathered around them. Magadon felt cold in that darkness, exposed. The darkness intensified, deepened, and Magadon felt the telltale tingle in his skin that accompanied movement between planes.

They materialized in the corridor of the Sojourner's tower to find Azriim standing with one foot on Riven's chest and both hands closed over the assassin's wrists. The air smelled acrid. Smoke leaked from Riven's clothes the same way shadows leaked from Cale's flesh. Riven's sabers lay on the ground beside him. He was struggling to breathe. The slaad opened his mouth wide and bent to snap off Riven's head.

"Riven!" Magadon shouted, but neither the assassin nor the slaad showed any sign of hearing him.

Something whizzed past Magadon's ear and struck Azriim squarely in the side of the head—Dolgan's eyeless head. Azriim turned to Cale and Magadon and visibly hissed, though no sound emerged.

Riven sagged back, eyes closed. He was dying, or already dead.

Azriim's mismatched eyes widened when they went to Dolgan's eyeless head, to Cale's bloody hands, but he recovered his aplomb quickly.

Back so soon? the slaad asked. *And just in time for supper.*

Mouth agape, fangs dripping, Azriim took hold of Riven's cloak and pulled his head toward his mouth.

Cale dropped Weaveshear and stepped from Magadon's side over to the slaad in a fraction of a breath. Still enlarged and empowered from his spells, he intercepted Azriim's attack on Riven by sticking his hands into the slaad's jaws—impaling his palms on the fangs and pulling the creature's head around toward him. Cale's blood filled the slaad's mouth. Azriim tried to bite down on Cale's hands but Cale not only held the slaad's jaws apart, he started to stretch them open further.

Azriim's neck corded with muscles and veins; Cale's arms, too, strained with the exertion. Both combatants were screaming, but the spell of silence devoured the sound.

Increasingly desperate, Azriim clawed at Cale's hands and forearms as his jaws stretched wider and wider. The attacks tore Cale's flesh but the man seemed beyond pain. He continued to pry Azriim's jaws apart, attempting to tear the slaad's face in twain.

Eyes fearful, Azriim left off savaging Cale's arms,

groped in his pouch, and found his teleportation rod. Cale tried to knock it from his hands with a series of awkward kicks but the slaad managed to work the dials.

Magadon drew his blade and charged down the hall, intent on not allowing the slaad to escape. He was five strides away, four. . . .

Azriim gave the dial a final twist and disappeared, leaving Cale and Magadon staring at each other over Riven's body.

Cale's breath was heavy and audible. The slaad's silencing spell must have been centered on Azriim's own person.

"Your hands," Magadon said.

Cale looked at his palms. Each had ragged punctures that went all the way through. Even as they watched, Cale's flesh started to regenerate the wounds. He ignored what must have been excruciating pain and kneeled at Riven's side.

"He is still alive," Cale said. He withdrew his mask, held it in his hand, and uttered a series of healing prayers.

Riven's breathing grew deeper. He would live.

Cale stood, still large, still dark, still . . . something more than a man.

Riven's eye opened. He started to rise. Cale moved to help him to his feet and to Magadon's surprise, Riven accepted the aid.

"I cannot see," the assassin said, unsteady on his feet. "The slaad used a spell to blind me."

Cale incanted another prayer. When he finished the spell, he waved his hand before Riven's eyes.

Riven blinked and his eye widened when he saw Cale. He offered a nod of thanks.

Cale said nothing. He walked down the hall, into the sanctum, to Jak's body. He studied it as if committing it to memory. He turned to them and said, "I'll return when it's done."

"What?" Magadon asked.

"The Sojourner," Riven answered for Cale, and Cale nodded.

"We'll stand with you," Magadon said.

"I know you will. But not this time. This time, I work alone. Stay with Jak. I'll return."

With that, he vanished into the shadows.

CHAPTER 18

ENDINGS

Vhostym smiled through his pain. He had teleported out of his tower and now stood, in his own flesh for the first time in centuries, on the surface of Toril.

The starlight, visible in the dark sky around the Crown of Flame, caused needle stabs of pain in his flesh but he did not care. The pain on his skin was paltry compared to the agony of his rapidly deliquescing organs and bones. He would be dead soon, but he had accomplished what he had planned for so long. He could die content.

His spell, his greatest spell, caused the umbra of the Crown of Flame to fall directly on his island, casting a perfect circle of shadow over it and the surrounding sea. As Toril continued its orbit around the sun, as Toril spun and wobbled on its axis, the magic of Vhostym's spell constantly adjusted to keep Selûne's tear before the fiery orb, poking a black hole in the sky, projecting a black spot onto Faerûn's surface, onto Vhostym's island. He had turned day into night and claimed that night for his own. He reveled in his final act of dominion over the multiverse.

Looking up through watery, stinging eyes, Vhostym admired the white flares of the corona that shot out in vaporous streams from the black hole of the sun—it was his father, millennia ago, who had called the corona the Crown of Flame. Vhostym had thought it beautiful then and he thought it more beautiful now than a rage of dragons in flight, more wondrous than the magma cascades of the Plane of Fire. He thought of his father's face, something he had not done in a long while—the long chin, deep set eyes, the thin-lipped mouth that so rarely smiled. He wondered if his father would have been proud of all Vhostym had done, all he had created and destroyed.

Vhostym had only a short time left, he knew. He had finished his work only just in time. He who had lived for millennia now had only hours remaining to him. Vhostym felt no melancholy about his impending death. He had lived well and accomplished all he wished.

He could have walked Faerûn during a natural eclipse, of course. Toril experienced many. But during a natural eclipse the umbra raced across Faerûn's surface as the celestial bodies continued in their orbits. He would have been able to spend only moments in its darkness.

He wanted more. He wanted to *create* the eclipse, to hold it in place, to spend a day on the surface. To control it, as he had controlled so much in his life. And he had done it.

Instead of his habitual flight, Vhostym walked on one of the Wayrock's rocky shorelines, shoeless. He stumbled often, but the feel of the stones under his feet, the sound of the surf in his ears, the smell of sea salt, all of it was more precious to him than all of the treasures he had accumulated. He savored each moment. He would pass into nothingness with the satisfaction of having spent a life accomplishing much.

Cale's grief and rage had given way to a simmering, inexhaustible need that could be met only in the Sojourner's death. Cale did not understand the Sojourner's purpose in blocking the sun and did not care. He wanted only one thing—*chororim*. Justice, vengeance. For Jak and for himself.

He walked the shadow space to the island outside.

Darkness reigned, as black as pitch. In Selgaunt, the eclipse had been partial. Here, as Cale had expected, it was total.

For now.

A ring of white fire surrounded the black hole in the sky. Dim stars were visible beyond the absent sun.

The tower loomed behind him but no magical energy rose from it to seize the rocky sphere in the sky. Cale had ended that when he killed the Weave Tap. The eclipse continued for now, but soon Toril would spin the Wayrock out from under its shadow. The Sojourner's spell was dead; he just didn't know it yet.

And so was the Sojourner.

Cale saw nothing around him except the tower and an unending series of rocky outcroppings and sandy beaches. Even the gulls, tricked by the eclipse into thinking it was night, had returned to their nests. The roar of the breaking surf was the only sound. He stepped through the darkness to a high promontory and scanned the ground below. He did not see the Sojourner. He would need to scour the island, and do it rapidly. If the Sojourner did not yet know that his spell had ended, he soon would.

With an act of will, Cale caused the darkness to make him invisible, visualized the dark spaces between visible space, and stepped across the island, covering a spearcast at a stride. He moved methodically across the terrain, from beach to promontory to hilltop.

He heard the Sojourner before he saw him. Cackling, grotesque laughter carried above the sound of the surf. Cale followed it to its source, blood on his mind.

On a sandy beach below him, ankle deep in the foamy water, a pale, sticklike figure moved feebly along the beach. With effort, the figure held his thin arms out, as if enjoying the fresh air. He stumbled often in the surf, nearly falling several times. He grabbed at his thin chest from time to time, his breath rattling. Gasps of pain escaped his lips but always gave way to another bout of laughter.

He was dying, Cale saw, and the realization made his pulse pound. The Sojourner was going to die in only one way—by Cale's hand.

Watching the small, pathetic creature wade in the surf, Cale realized that there was no grand plan. The Sojourner had not strived for power or immortality. He had schemed and risked the lives of thousands to walk the sand in the darkness he had created. Nothing more. Cale could hardly believe it. Cale thought the Sojourner worse than any power-mad mage he had ever heard of. Jak had died for nothing.

Cale's anger flared, burned hot, but he resisted the impulse to attack. He knew the Sojourner's power. He knew he could not simply cut the wizard down. His defenses would be powerful. Cale needed an opportunity.

He looked to the hole in the sky and knew it would come soon enough.

So he did what all assassins do—he watched and waited for his chance to kill. He pulled on his mask and whispered the words to a series of protective spells, ending with a spell that allowed him to see dweomers.

Unsurprisingly, the Sojourner glowed like the sun in his sight. Layer upon layer of spells cloaked him. Cale studied them for a few moments, trying to discern their purpose. Some he recognized as defensive wards, others he could not identify.

The island brightened. In the sky above, a fingernail of light peeked out from the edge of the eclipse. Toril was turning and the misplaced moon was not keeping pace. A flare of magical energy, some last vestige of the Sojourner's spell, engulfed the moon, caused it to glow silver. Cracks formed in its surface.

The returning light made Cale uncomfortable but it made the Sojourner's skin blister. Cale could not distinguish between the Sojourner's continuing laughter and his hisses of pain. The sun sneaked farther out from behind Selûne's tear. The cracks in the moon grew wider. The light grew. The Sojourner stumbled again, looked up. He rubbed his bare arms. Wisps of smoke rose from his skin. He was burning in the sun. Cale saw his lips peeled back in a grimace of pain.

Cale drew Weaveshear and waited.

The Sojourner looked up as if to the great deepstars overhead, then quickly turned away, hissing with pain. The light surely must have burned his eyes. He stumbled, nearly fell.

Cale struck.

He stepped from the shadows near him and into the Sojourner's own shadow. His proximity triggered the Sojourner's defensive wards. Lightning flared, a fan of flame, a cloud of negative energy. Cale held Weaveshear before him and the blade drank what it could. But the power of the spells was too much for the blade to consume and some of the energy reached Cale. His muscles violently contracted and lightning burned a hole in his stomach. He bit down involuntarily on his tongue, so hard he nearly severed the end. Blood filled his mouth. The last of the negative energy ward stole some of his soul and chilled him to the bone.

He endured it all, cast Weaveshear aside—this was

not a matter for the weapon of Mask, but for Cale's own hands—and wrapped his arms, still powered by the spells that augmented his size and strength, around the frail body of the Sojourner. The creature did not struggle against his hold, did not even seem surprised.

Cale clamped one huge hand over the Sojourner's mouth and his palm nearly covered the creature's entire face. He would not let the Sojourner utter a magical word, not a sound. He felt the Sojourner's wet respiration against his fingers. The Sojourner stank of medicines.

Cale spit a mouthful of blood and said though his pain, "This is over."

Cale felt a tingling behind his eyes, the Sojourner's mental fingers, and feared that his protective spell had not worked. The creature's voice sounded in his head: *You have protected yourself against attack but not communication.*

Cale held the Sojourner still and said in his ear, "You killed my friend."

Did I? I would do it again. I've killed many. I suspect you have too.

Cale wanted to kill him then, but he could not. He had to know.

"Why all this? Did you do it for nothing more than a stroll in the *godsdamned sand*?"

A shudder wracked the Sojourner's body. It took Cale a moment to realize it was laughter and not pain.

Men always ask why, as if there must be some overarching reason for events. Not this time, priest. There is no such reason. Thousands will die to satisfy my whim.

Cale thought of his words to Riven: *This is more than personal.* He had been wrong; Riven had been right. There was nothing bigger than the personal.

He gritted his teeth and started to squeeze. Calmly, the Sojourner projected: *What moments do you remember most fondly from your youth, priest?*

Cale did not answer but he hesitated. He remembered nothing from his youth with fondness.

When death comes for you, you will look back to those moments, long for them as you do for nothing else. All that I have done, I have done to satisfy that longing. To walk the surface in my own form, to feel the wind, to see the Crown of Flame, as I did in my youth. Yes. Is that enough of a why for you?

Cale was disgusted, but in a barely acknowledged corner of his mind, admiring. He hung onto the disgust. He looked up to the sky, to the moon, to the growing slice of the sun. He remembered telling Jak and Magadon that the Sojourner would not involve himself in something small. But he had. His methods had been large but his goal was no more ambitious than that of any man.

"You speak of killing as if it were a small thing."

And you speak as though I should be concerned with the deaths of others. What are all those hundreds, even thousands, to me? I have killed entire worlds for less.

Cale struggled for words, found none.

The Sojourner said, *I have seen and done what I willed. Nothing matters anymore. I will be dead by the end of the day.*

"It's already night," Cale said.

He lifted the Sojourner from his feet and squeezed.

The frail creature gasped as Cale brought his strength to bear on the thin body, the weak bones. A final protective ward on the Sojourner flared green and Cale felt a surge through his body.

The Sojourner's ribs snapped, folded in on themselves, his collarbone cracked. Cale echoed with his lips the mental screams of the creature that he heard in his brain, for the final ward on the Sojourner was some kind of reciprocity spell. Cale experienced the damage that he inflicted on the Sojourner—the shattered bones, the pain, the pierced organs. His shade flesh tried to repair the damage but the pain made him vomit down his shirt, down the back of the Sojourner's cloak.

Cale did not know whether pain prevented the

Sojourner from casting a spell, or whether he was even interested in trying. Cale did not care; he squeezed and the Sojourner screamed. Cale took satisfaction in his own agony because he knew it mirrored what was felt by the Sojourner. He smiled at the creature's screams, smiled at his own, feeling soiled but unable to stop himself. He pulled the Sojourner so tight against him that they might as well have been melded. Cale's bones ground against bones; his lungs filled with blood. He forced his shattered chest to draw another breath, another.

He was killing the Sojourner, and he was killing himself. He did not care. He thought of Jak and squeezed. The Sojourner's frail body broke to pieces in his grasp; his own body shattered. Soon the pain became unbearable; he could not see, he could not breathe. His ruined arms could not hold the creature. The Sojourner slipped from his grasp to the beach. Cale too collapsed. He could not tell if he was screaming alone or if the Sojourner's mental screams continued.

The last thing he saw before he passed out from the agony was the sun emerging fully from behind Selûne's tear.

Cale awoke. He lay on his back on the beach, broken, twisted, in agony. His chest felt heavy; blood was filling his lungs. His arms and shoulders were shattered, immovable. The pain nearly caused him to lose consciousness but he held on doggedly. The sun was directly overhead. No shadows lay anywhere near him. His shade flesh could not regenerate in the direct light of the sun. He would be dead soon, long before the sun set.

He listened to the surf, watched in amazed horror as the Sojourner's cracked moon grew larger in the sky. Without the spell to hold it in place, it was plummeting toward Toril. He could not imagine the destruction it would wreak. He thought of Tazi, of Varra. He hung on to the memory of their faces. He wondered if Tazi was watching the sky fall.

Beside him, the Sojourner's broken body smoked and burned until it was nothing more than ash. The surf washed the ashes into the sand, pulled at scraps of robes, trying to draw them out to sea.

The moon caught fire as it fell, grew a long tail of flame. Its size quickly doubled as it approached. Cale could hear it pelting through the sky, sizzling.

It would destroy kingdoms.

He thought of Jak, of Sephris, and closed his eyes.

He snapped them open when an explosion thundered across the sky.

Selûne's tear had separated into five large chunks, each cutting a flaming path through the sky. Even as he watched, those chunks broke apart into smaller pieces, and those into smaller. Soon, thousands of tiny pieces of the tear blazed their way through the heavens.

He smiled, laughed, choked on his own blood.

It was beautiful.

Consciousness started to slip from him again. He sank into an oblivion of pain, watching a swarm of fireflies dart across the sky.

He awoke an indeterminate time later to the sound of boots crunching against the sand. Someone stood over him, a dark form—Riven.

"We split up to find you," Riven said. The assassin stared down at him but did not move to help. Riven shaded his eyes and looked up at the sun. "Light's bothering you, eh?"

The assassin looked down at Cale, his expression hard. Cale saw Riven's internal debate writ clear in the hard set of his jaw, the hole of his eye. Riven could kill Cale; the Second could kill the First.

The surf beat against the sand. Cale and Riven stared at each other, saying nothing. The silence stretched.

Cale tried to speak but his dry throat could not form words. He managed only a defiant snarl before pain assailed him and his vision went black. He fought his way back to consciousness. He would look Riven in the eye when he died.

When he regained focus, he saw that Riven had drawn his blade. The assassin gave a hard smile and jabbed downward.

Not at Cale, at the remains of the Sojourner's robes.

"He didn't like the sun much either, I see."

Riven laughed harshly, kneeled, and retrieved a handful of items from the pile of ash and bones that had been the Sojourner. He pocketed them as he stood. Cale assumed they were the magical stones that had circled the Sojourner's head.

Riven stood over him again, blade bare. He cocked his head to the side, considering. Finally, he sighed and said, "Look where we are, Cale. Look what we've become." He stepped around Cale until his body shielded Cale from the sun.

The darkness energized Cale. Covered in Riven's shadow, Cale's flesh began to regenerate. Bones and organs slowly reknit. Agonizing jabs of pain coursed through his body. He could not contain a hiss of pain. Riven stood by and watched it all in silence, like a Sembian wallman—a bodyguard—of old. Riven was Cale's wallman, his right hand.

When Cale's wounds had healed enough to allow him to stand, he climbed to his feet. He and Riven stared at each other for a moment.

Cale nodded his thanks. Riven nodded in acknowledgement. They did not need to say anything more.

"Let's find Mags," Cale said, squinting uncomfortably in the sun. "There's one more thing left to do."

"Fleet," Riven said, nodding. Cale was surprised to see Riven's expression soften as he spoke Jak's name.

"Yes," Cale said.

"He won't do it," Riven said.

The assassin did not need to say whom he meant by "he," or what he meant by "it."

"He will," Cale said. "I'll make him."

Together, Cale, Riven, and Magadon entered the Sojourner's tower. As they walked the halls, Cale noticed for the first time the images on the defaced murals. He noticed too the jawless skull motif that appeared on some of the door handles.

"This was a temple to Cyric," he said. "Or at least part of a temple."

Riven nodded and rubbed the black disc he wore on a chain around his neck. "That was why he did it, Cale. He arranged all of this to spite Cyric. To steal one of the Dark Sun's temples for his own."

Cale did not credit Mask as being that skillful a schemer. He said, "Or maybe he just got lucky. Either way, he did not do it—we did. He owes us."

To that, Riven said nothing.

They made a pilgrimage to Jak through the curving corridor. Riven and Magadon had placed Jak's body on the floor in a small, unused chamber off the central corridor on the second floor. The room bore no sign of having been used in Cyric's rites.

A wool blanket covered Jak up to his chin. He looked as if he were sleeping. Seeing his friend's body reopened the scab of Cale's grief. He donned his mask to cover his tears.

He sat on the floor next to his friend but did not touch him. After a moment, he reached under the blanket and took Jak's hand in his. The little man's hand was cold, rigid. Emotion flooded Cale.

"You owe me this," he said to the vaulted ceiling, to Mask. He raised his voice. "You owe me this!"

The Shadowlord had asked him again and again to sacrifice, and again and again he had—his family, his blood, his humanity, and his best friend. It was too much. He wanted repayment.

"Do you hear me?" His voice rang off the ceiling. "You owe me. And now you are going to pay."

It was not midnight but Cale nevertheless bowed his head, closed his eyes, and began to pray. Not for multiple spells, as was typical, but for a single spell. A spell that would bring Jak back from the dead. He knew it was possible. He had heard tales.

He sent his thoughts, his need to save his friend, flying through the planes to Mask. He knew the god heard him. He had to have heard him.

No response.

Cale's anger grew. He demanded that Mask listen, demanded that he answer.

Nothing came. Jak lay beside him, limp and cold.

A hand on his shoulder—Magadon's.

"Erevis . . ." the guide began.

Cale shook the guide's hand free. "No. No, dammit, Mags. He's going to answer me." He looked up and shouted, "You will give me this or I walk away from you forever. And if I do that, I swear on the soul of my best friend that I will hunt down and kill every one of your priests that I can find. Every godsdamned one! And I'll be able to find a lot. You've given me too much. Trained me too well. No one will be able to stop me. No one." He looked back over his shoulder to Riven.

The assassin stared at him, nodded.

Cale turned back. "No one will stop *us*."

He waited.

Nothing.

He waited longer, growing increasingly angry.

"Have it your way," he said softly, and started to stand. He would start in Sembia, then Cormyr, then the rest of the Heartlands, then—

Knowledge filled his brain, knocked him back to his knees—the words to a prayer that performed the greatest of miracles. It could bring the dead back to life.

He felt a surge, could not contain a fierce grin.

"I can do it," he said to the room. "He's answered."

Cale put his palms on Jak's chest and recited the words to the prayer.

Jak sat at the table of his mother's cottage, listening to the chatter of his family, inhaling the warm smells of his mother's cooking. He could not stop smiling.

"You'll fill your bowl more than that, Jakert Fleet," said his mother, while she buttered a piece of flatbread. "Look at you. You're a bag of bones. Eat. Eat."

"Yes, mother," Jak said. He knew better than to dispute his mother at the table.

As usual, his father offered him a consoling smile but said nothing.

"Pass the honey," Jak said to his brother.

Cob made as though he would throw a dripping honeycomb down to Jak, but his mother said, "Cobdon Fleet, if that comb leaves so much as a drop on my new tablecloth, not even Yolanda Warmhearth will be able to spare you my wrath."

Cob froze in mid throw and said sheepishly, "I was just funning Jak, mother."

"Of course you were, dearheart," his mother said, and took a small bite of her buttered bread. "Now put that comb back on its plate and pass the plate to your brother."

Cob did exactly that and Jak grinned at his brother's discomfiture. Jak dribbled honey from the comb onto a piece of bread and took a bite. It was as sweet as he remembered. Probably his father—a beekeeper—had taken it from one of his hives that morning. When Jak had

been a boy, Mal Fleet's apiary and the honey it produced
had provided well for his family. Of course, it also had
resulted in more stings to the Fleet boys than Jak cared to
recall. Still, he had long missed his father's honey at table,
and his mother's soup. It was good to be home.

He set to his mother's potato soup, dunking his hon-
eyed bread in the bowl between spoonfuls. His mother sat
at the head of the table and looked on with approval.

"The soup is wonderful, moth—"

From outside, somewhere in the distance, he heard
someone call his name. He could not quite place the
voice—a friend's voice, he knew, but the name escaped
him.

"Did you hear that?" he asked his brother, his father.

All of them kept their heads down.

Cob spoke around a mouthful of soup. "I didn't hear
anything."

"Nor I," said his father, soaking his bread in honey.
His mother always said of his father that if his nature
had been as sweet as his sweet tooth, he could have mar-
ried better. "There is not better," had always been his
father's reply, and it had always earned him a smile from
his wife.

"Eat your food, Jak," said his mother.

The voice called him again.

Jak pushed back his chair and rose. "There it is
again."

Power filled Cale. He had never before cast a spell so
demanding. His entire body shook. Sweat poured from
him.

But it was working.

A rosy glow suffused Jak's body. The wound in his
throat closed to a pink scar, to unmarred skin; the bruises
on his arms and face healed. The spell remade his flesh,

providing a complete and whole vessel for the returning soul. The spell then created a conduit between Jak's body and whatever plane to which his soul had traveled, opening a door that otherwise always remained closed. Cale put himself in the door, held it open, and called Jak's name.

Cale's voice grew in volume until it boomed, reverberated through the room, carried from the Sojourner's tower into the planes. He called Jak's name, trying to pull his soul back from its rest to re-inhabit his body.

"Jak!"

An unwelcome memory surfaced—Sephris Dwendon, changed after his forced resurrection, filled with bitterness. The memory of Jak's words surged back to Cale. *When I'm dead, leave me that way.*

Cale's voice faltered.

Was he doing the right thing? Was he acting to help Jak or satisfy his own desire to have Jak back? He did not like what he thought was the answer. But Jak had told him that friends, not places, were home, and Cale needed him.

His doubt caused the spell to start to unravel.

He remembered Sephris's bitter words, his admission that he had returned only out of a sense of duty. Jak would do the same. Cale could not bear to think of an embittered Jak.

Tears of guilt flowed down his face. He controlled the sob that threatened to burst from his throat.

He realized that he could not ask Jak to return. He would not. Wherever Jak was, that was home now.

He ceased the invocation and the power went out of him. He put his hand on Jak's forehead.

"Goodbye, my friend."

He reached into one of Jak's pouches, took his ivory-bowled pipe, and put it in a pouch at his own belt. He would keep the smell of Jak's pipeweed near to him—always.

❧ ❧ ❧ ❧ ❧

Jak cocked his head and listened. The call did not repeat. For a reason he could not explain, profound sadness struck him. He had lost something, he knew. But he did not know what.

"Finish your soup, son," said his father. "You're free to stay now."

Jak did not know what that meant and his father did not explain. His father smiled and said, "Cob and I have taken care of the hives for the day. We can all go fishing at dusk, if you'd like. There's pond nearby, stuffed with longfin."

That sounded grand to Jak. The sadness diminished in the glow of his family's love. He sat back down at the table with his family and ate his mother's soup.

❧ ❧ ❧ ❧ ❧

Magadon, Cale, and Riven stood looking at one another in a central chamber of the tower.

"What now?" Magadon said at last.

"I will take Jak and you both back," Cale said. "I have some things I need to do."

Magadon nodded.

"I'm staying," Riven said.

"Why?" Magadon asked.

"There are things I need to do also," Riven answered.

Cale looked around the temple, once Cyric's, now Mask's, and understood.

"This has only just begun," Riven said to Cale. "You realize that?"

Cale thought of Sephris, of the Source's call across Faerûn. He nodded. He knew that Mask was not through with them yet. But for now, he had his own matters to address.

"You can leave Jak here," Riven said. "With me. You'll have a reason to come back."

Cale looked Riven in the eye. He thought again of Jak's words to him on the streets of Selgaunt—*friends are home*.

He nodded. "You'll see to him?"

Cale could not put Jak's body in the ground, could not be there when it happened.

"I will," Riven said.

Cale looked Riven in the face. Riven returned the stare.

The moment stretched. As one they stepped forward and embraced, briefly. A warriors' farewell.

Cale stepped back, pulled the shadows around him, and said, "Let's go, Mags."

EPILOGUE

The surf roared far below them. The foam dancing in the shoals was barely visible in the pre-dawn light. A cool breeze rustled Cale's cloak. The glow from a cluster of lights far up the coast could only be Urlamspyr, one of Sembia's largest cities. Cale had never seen it. Perhaps now he would. He had no reason to return to Selgaunt. He had no reason to do anything.

Varra looked around, unable to see much in the darkness but the fading stars. Cale had convinced her to let him temporarily take her from Skullport. He could not yet commit to a *we*—he agreed with Riven that Mask was not done with them—but he wanted to do something for her, and at least for the moment, he did not want to be alone.

"It's been a long while since I've seen the sky," she said, her voice soft.

"I know," Cale replied. He held Jak's pipe in his fist.

She must have heard the tightness in his voice, the barely controlled grief. He did not seem able to make it go away.

"What's wrong, Vasen?" she asked. She did not touch him.

For a moment, he could not speak. Finally, he said, "I lost my best friend recently."

He was not certain how long ago it had been. One day seemed to bleed into another.

She stared at him for a time before saying, "I'm so sorry."

Quiet lay between them. Only the surf spoke.

Cale looked straight ahead, out on the whitecaps of the Inner Sea. He felt Varra looking at him, staring at him. He wondered what she was thinking. Cale still did not know why he had returned to her rather than Tazi, rather than staying with Magadon in Starmantle. They had shared little; they had exchanged only a few sentences. Still, he felt . . . drawn to her. He supposed everyone needed someone to whom they could confess.

"Tell me something about yourself," she said, and he thought she had read his mind.

"Like what?"

She did not hesitate. "Tell me something you've never told anyone else."

Cale's heart thumped hard in his chest. He still did not look at her.

"You don't know what you're asking."

"Yes, I do. Tell me."

He swallowed and turned to look at her. Her expression contained no judgment. He held her gaze. She waited, saying nothing.

"I've killed men for no reason other than coin," he said, and once he started, he could not stop. "Lots of men. I've killed many others for what I thought were good reasons. I serve a god who lives in the dark and now I think the dark lives in me. I've spent almost the entirety of my adult life doing violence. I've had only two close friends." The admission pained him distantly, but it was true. "Both of them are dead now." His voice broke but he recovered and finished. "I've done many, many evil things in my life. And now I'm alone."

She stared at him in silence with such sympathy in her brown eyes that he could not hold back tears—tears for Jak, for Thamalon, for himself, for everything. He squeezed the ivory-bowled pipe and put it back into his vest pocket.

She reached up and touched his face. "Oh, Vasen. . . ."

He turned his face away from her and stared out at the sea. He gulped down the knot in his throat.

"Call me Erevis. Erevis Cale. Vasen Coriver died a long time ago."

To her credit, she did not ask any questions about his name. Instead, she leaned against him, slipped her hand into his, and said, "You are not alone."

To that, Cale said nothing. There was nothing to say. He allowed himself to take pleasure in the smell of her hair and the feel of her skin.

After a time he said, "Don't wait for me, Varra."

"What do you mean?" she asked.

"There are things I have yet to do. Hard things. This may be the closest we ever get."

She was quiet for a while then said, "It's for me to decide if I wait."

To that, Cale could say nothing.

Together, they sat atop the cliff, took comfort in the other's company, and waited in satisfying silence as the stars vanished and the sky lightened. Within an hour, the sun broke the horizon.

When it did both of them gasped, but for different reasons.

"It's so beautiful," Varra whispered.

"It is," Cale said, and his hand vanished in the sun. He watched the sun crest the horizon and thought of Jak, of their conversation as they walked along Selgaunt's docks. Cale had promised the little man that he would be a hero, if he got the chance.

"Today is a new day," he said, more to himself, more to Jak, than to Varra.

He decided that he would keep his promise to the little man.

Riven had paid a guild mage to identify the properties of the Sojourner's stones, sold the four that did not interest him, and retained the three that did. Weighted down with several thousand platinum suns, he walked Selgaunt's nighttime streets. It would be the last time he set foot in the city for some time.

The city still bustled with rumors of what had transpired in the sky and on Temple Avenue and what each portended. It was said that the Oghmanytes had begun to quietly desert the city. All wondered what they knew but would not share. Riven couldn't have cared less. He cared only about what Mask wanted of him.

As always, the Shadowlord had spoken to him in his dreams. Riven was to use the wealth to fit out the tower of the Sojourner as a temple, taking what had been Cyric's and turning it to the use of the Shadowlord. Riven would be its caretaker, along with his girls. Riven had found a chamber within the tower littered with magical gear—weapons, wands, staffs. He assumed it once belonged to the Cyricists. Now it belonged to him. He was not certain what he was to do with all of it. Others would come, he assumed. Cale, at least.

But first he had something else to do. An honor to make. Then he would leave the past behind.

He walked the streets, stopping at every tavern and eatery he could find, asking if they had what he sought. None did. Finally, he found himself at the corner where the Black Stag tavern had stood until a shadow adept had burned it to the ground in an effort to kill Cale and Riven. That was when everything had begun.

A new tavern had been built on the site—The Charred Ruin.

Riven would have grinned at the name had he been in the mood for grins. Instead, he donned his professional sneer and pushed open the door to the Ruin. The moment he did, the smell of the night's soup hit his nostrils and he knew he had found what he wanted. Strange, that he would have found it there, of all places.

Scanning the dark-eyed patrons, none of whom held his gaze, he found a table along the wall and sat. The middle-aged bar wench plodded over to his table and took his order.

"Soup," Riven said.

"That's it?" she asked

"And a tankard of something decent," Riven said. He flipped her a fivestar and she hurried away to fill his order.

Sitting in the Ruin, Riven waited and brooded. His life had changed and he wondered where it all would lead. Riven saw now that he and Cale were linked, Mask's First and Mask's Second, neither able to exist without the other, the right and left hands of their god.

After a short time, the bar wench returned with a tin tankard of ale and a steaming wooden bowl of soup— potato soup. She set it down and said, "There you are."

Riven said nothing, did not even look up. She harrumphed and stalked off.

Riven stared at the thick soup, thought of the time he had shared with his comrades another bowl of potato soup on the Plane of Shadow. He was not entirely certain how he felt about Fleet. Had he been a friend? Riven did not know. He did know, however, that he would miss him.

He raised his tankard in a toast and turned his attention to the soup. He ate it all without a pause and set down the spoon. Overcome for a moment, he stared down at the empty bowl.

Finally he said softly, "No doubt it's a poor imitation of your mother's . . . little man."

With that, he pushed his chair back, stood, and walked out of the tavern. He wanted to see his girls.